They were beautiful. His mouth was the sort that was meant to curl into a smile, with the kind of lips that were created for kissing. In that dreamy moment, Alys imagined what it would be like to kiss him; how it would feel to slowly press her lips to his and taste what lay beyond. As she closed her eyes, licking her now tingling lips, the carriage lurched to a violent stop.

So limp from her fantasy was she, that she was pitched forward out of her seat to land at Lucian's feet in a tangled heap of bombazine and wool. In the next instant, strong hands gripped her beneath her arms, and she felt herself being hauled up.

"Good God! Are you hurt?" Lucian exclaimed, setting her on the seat beside him. He cupped her chin in his palm and tipped her face into the light to study it. As her gaze touched his, she again felt an electrifying, inexplicable pull of attraction.

"Alys," he uttered softly, "did you hit your head?"

"Um . . . no. Why do you ask?"

"Because you are looking at me strangely. Rather like a cow in need of milking."

A cow in need of milking, indeed! Why, the thick-skulled . . . dolt! No wonder he was unable to find love on his own!

STRONGER THAN MAGIC

Heather Cullman

A TOPAZ BOOK

TOPAZ
Published by the Penguin Group
Penguin Books USA Inc., 375 Hudson Street,
New York, New York 10014, U.S.A.
Penguin Books Ltd, 27 Wrights Lane,
London W8 5TZ, England
Penguin Books Australia Ltd, Ringwood,
Victoria, Australia
Penguin Books Canada Ltd, 10 Alcorn Avenue,
Toronto, Ontario, Canada M4V 3B2
Penguin Books (N.Z.) Ltd, 182–190 Wairau Road,
Auckland 10, New Zealand

Penguin Books Ltd, Registered Offices:
Harmondsworth, Middlesex, England

First published by Topaz, an imprint of Dutton Signet,
a division of Penguin Books USA Inc.

First Printing, January, 1997
10 9 8 7 6 5 4 3 2 1

 REGISTERED TRADEMARK—MARCA REGISTRADA

Printed in the United States of America

Dedicated to the living and loving memory of

Richard Ottens,

Friend, educator, and gourmet extraordinaire.
We miss you.

*"All things considered, we would rather be dining
at The Arches . . . with you."*

The Legend of Thistlewood Castle

Excerpt from the *History of Thistlewood Castle*
by Randolph Warre, Fourth Marquess of
Thistlewood, 1693

No chronicle of Thistlewood Castle would be compleat without an account of the legend of its birth. Though I give no credence to the veracity of this tale, many in the village of Thistlewood Downs hold steadfast to its truth. 'Tis for this reason, and this reason only, that I feel it of enough import to include it in this record.

The legend begins at Lammastide, the year of our Lord, 1315. On the Lammastide of our legend, the faeries were journeying from a hill near Copthorn Common to the one beneath the chalk cliff just west of where Thistlewood now lies. Leading the procession that day was Prince Aengus. With hair the color of flame and eyes the cool blue-green of a calm ocean shallow, Aengus, the eldest of King Dagda's sons, was counted among the faeries as the most handsome of their princes.

'Twas late morn when they passed the place that is now Thistlewood Castle. In those days 'twas but a barren down sparsely blanketed with speedwell, harebell, agrimony, and a single cluster of wild thistle. 'Twas beside that lone knot of thistle that Aengus spied a slumbering mortal, a maiden of uncommon beauty. As ofttimes happens in tales such as this, he loved her at first glance. Thus smitten, he parted from his retinue, vowing to woo and win her.

Lest you think such conduct commonplace among faeries, I must hasten to note here that 'tis almost unknown for a faerie man to offer his love to a mortal woman. The reason 'tis so rare is because otherworld maids are unearthly fair, and few mortal women possess the beauty to tempt their men. Indeed, 'tis only once in every thousand years that such a woman is born.

This particular maiden, Rowena was her name, must have been a goddess of loveliness, for according to the legend she was the first and only mortal ever to catch the fancy of an otherworld prince. But catch it she did, and when she finally awoke 'twas to the sight of a dazzling youth, playing music of irresistible sweetness upon a golden harp.

Of course she loved him at first sight. How could she not? He was the faerie god of youth, beauty, and love, and not a woman lived who could resist his charms. When he saw her awake at last, he fell to his knees before her and pledged his eternal devotion.

Long they tarried there, sunshine silvering into twilight, twilight graying to dusk. And as dark spread across the land, 'twas beneath an infinite canopy of stars that they tenderly plighted their troth. When they at last parted company, sometime deep in the still of midnight, Rowena was a maid no longer.

Every day thereafter she returned to the thistle, always to find Aengus awaiting her. Always they made love, and when the leaves rusted in the autumn chill, she conceived a child.

As faeries are wont to know, Aengus knew the instant his seed took root. And as it ripened, he divined that not one but two babes, a boy and a girl, grew within her. Though he greatly yearned to dwell as man and wife with his beloved Rowena, he could not. For as a faerie, 'twas forbidden by God for him to live in her world, and for her to abide in his would mean the certain loss of her immortal soul.

Now to understand why 'tis so, you must first be acquainted with faerie nature. Faeries, you see, are fallen angels cursed by God. As such they have no immortal souls and are instead enlivened by a stuff called faerie essence. They are granted only enough of this essence to last a thousand years. When it fades, the faerie turns to dust and simply ceases to be. The same fate befalls the mortal who lives among them, be he willing or nay. Over time he loses his soul and becomes as they.

Aengus knew this, and because he desired Rowena and his children to have the chance at heaven that he was denied, he commanded his subjects to raise a mighty fortress from the thistles. The legend says that it took only one night for the faeries to do so. And as dawn broke upon the newly erected stronghold, he dubbed it Thistlewood Castle, in honor of the flora beside which their love was born. There lived Rowena, with Aengus dwelling in the nearby hollow hill.

Seasons passed, fall freezing into winter, winter thawing into spring. And just past midnight on Midsummer's night, Rowena gave birth. As foretold by Aengus, one babe was a girl, whom they named Elinore, the other a boy called Lucan. Both babes were blessed with their mother's glorious golden hair and their father's remark- able aquamarine eyes.

Thriving beneath the grace of the faeries, the children grew strong and beautiful. From a tender age, Elinore showed a rare gift for healing, while Lucan excelled at the knightly arts. So fine a warrior was he that he was knighted at the tender age of sixteen.

Now while merely staying in the mortal world was enough to ensure Rowena a chance at heaven, the same could not be said for her children. Because they were the offspring of a faerie and a mortal, they had only half an immortal soul, the other half of their being made up of faerie essence. And as everyone knows, you must have a compleat soul to enter heaven.

What is not as commonly known is that by finding love, true love, with a mortal, 'tis possible for a half faerie to grow his bisected soul into a whole one. 'Tis said that the love of a mortal will make it swell with all that is good and righteous until it smothers and takes the place of his more fragile faerie essence. He then becomes a full-fledged human. If he lives his life with benevolence, he too can ascend to heaven.

Elinore was but fifteen when she met and wed a gentle knight, Alain de Warre. Theirs was a union forged of true love, one blessed with nine children and enduring happiness.

But Lucan—ah! His love was the thrill of battle. No thought of wedlock had he, though many a maid sought to woo him from swordplay to marriage bed. And who could blame them? His was a beauty to quicken even the most passionless feminine heart. Ever charming though he was to his legion of admirers, his heart remained unstirred until the day he beheld Alys le Fayre.

Alys, 'tis said, was as comely and golden as Lucan, and half the knights of the realm were smitten with her beauty. 'Twas at a Michaelmas fair where he first spied her. He was there to partake in a joust; she, to buy ribbons to bind her hair. And as with his father and mother before him, he loved her at first glance.

So enamored was he that he fell to his knees before her, begging to carry her new ribbons as a token in the joust. Of course she gave them to him. How could she say nay? He was the most magnificent knight she had ever beheld. 'Twas those ribbons that planted the first seeds of jealousy among her other champions; seeds that she cultivated with her wicked games.

Alys, you see, was a vain, fickle creature, and nothing flattered her conceit more than to pit the knights against each other in quest for her favor. To this end she would trifle with each admirer's heart, flattering and tempting him until he declared himself. Then she would haughtily scorn his suit, inquiring why she should accept him when she could wed someone as brave and handsome as whomever it was she was setting him against. The name she always uttered after the Michaelmas joust was Lucan de Thistlewood. 'Twas this game that got him murdered.

It happened at the Midsummer's tournament at Thistlewood. 'Twas a grand affair with a rich purse, and knights came from near and far to compete. Among those who entered that day was Bryan Fitzsimmons, the most bitterly jealous of Alys's suitors. He came not to win the prize, but to slay his rival, Lucan.

Though Lucan was the superior knight, Bryan's hatred made him strong and cunning, and during the melee he pierced his rival's breastplate with his sword. Deep the blade plunged, goring Lucan just below the heart. Mortally wounded, he was carried to his chamber, where he lay through the day and into the night, writhing in unspeakable pain.

Alys, anguished at what her folly had wrought, remained by his side, praying, weeping, and giving him what meager comfort she could. You see, in her own way she loved him, though her selfishness had hindered it from deepening into the true love he needed to save his soul.

Why the faeries did not protect him that day, nobody knows. What is known is that once death marks a person he is doomed, and all the faerie magic in the world cannot save him. And Lucan died at the stroke of midnight, the hour heralding his nineteenth year, with Alys's name on his lips. As his life left him, Aengus appeared in the chamber.

Keening and weeping in a way that rose a fierce storm outside, he gathered his son's lifeless body in his arms and rocked him like a babe. Alys, recognizing him as a faerie and fearing his wrath, crept off into a dark corner to hide.

One by one Aengus's brothers appeared, all seven score of them. The last two to appear seized the terrified Alys and dragged her forward to stand judgment before Aengus. Still cradling Lucan in his arms, he rose and charged her with murdering his son. Though she wept and pleaded, he remained unmoved. What happened then, no one knows for certain, but 'twas the last anyone ever saw of the vainglorious Alys le Fayre. Lucan's body disappeared that night as well.

'Tis said that his father buried him in the mound beneath the cliffs, for 'twas on that night that the odd symbols appeared inscribed on the cliff face above it. Though many in the ensuing years sought to decipher those marks, all failed. Thus they remained an object of mystery and conjecture for the next two centuries.

'Twas in the year 1543 that an Irish tutor to the Warre sons recognized those symbols as the cipher of a long-dead Celtic tongue. As fortune would have it, or perhaps 'twas not fortune but a contrivance of the faeries, 'twas a language that had been kept alive through the generations of his scholarly family. After much labor, he transcribed the marks thus:

Smite by death untimely,
A man, half faerie, half mortal,
Shall live again, tho' only once,
Through God's hope that he find heaven.

So it shall be with Lucan de Thistlewood,
Son of Prince Aengus,
Otherworld god of youth, beauty, and love,
And of Rowena, his beloved mortal wife.

Whether these words be a rightful translation, one can only speculate. Yet, as with the legend, many in Thistlewood Downs believe it to be true. And so they wait, wondering with the birth of every Thistlewood son: Is he the one?

They still wait.

Chapter 1

Sussex, February 1816

"He's back," Allura, Otherworld Chancellor of Affairs of the Heart, announced, staring solemnly at the woman before her.

"He?" Alys echoed, though she knew without asking exactly who "he" was. She'd been waiting for him for almost five hundred years, eagerly anticipating his return and the chance for freedom that came with it.

The fairy frowned slightly at her obtuse query. "Lucan de Thistlewood, of course," she replied.

After all these centuries of hoping, wishing, and praying for this moment, Alys should have felt joy at the news, euphoria even. Oddly enough, she felt only a sick sort of dread. What if she wasn't equal to the task ahead of her? What if she failed?

No. She wouldn't fail . . . she couldn't afford to. Alys drew in a shuddering breath, battling to vanquish her suffocating anxiety. The air was damp and musty . . . underground air . . . *prison* air. That air served as a potent reminder of what she stood to lose should she fail in her task, increasing rather than diminishing her apprehension.

Exhaling in a hissing sigh, she asked, "When?"

Allura picked up the gossamer-thin sheet of parchment and peered at writing too whisper-fine for Alys's mortal eyes to discern. She frowned as she scanned the page, as if she were having difficulty finding what she sought. Then she crowed a victorious "A-ha!" and replied, "Aengus says here that he was reborn in 1783, the twenty-fifth of June to be exact."

"1783?" Alys raised her upturned palms in a gesture of helpless confusion. "What year is it now?" One of the first things she'd learned about the otherworld was that time passed at a different rate than it did in the mortal world. Sometimes it passed more quickly, with ten mortal years equaling one fairy day. Other times it worked just the opposite, with what seemed like ten years in fairy time turning out to be just one day in the world above. It was so confusing that she'd stopped trying to keep track long ago.

"It's the sixteenth of February, 1816," Allura replied, sliding a slim volume across the desk and thumping the date with her long, white index finger.

Alys's eyes widened in surprise as she stared down at the ornately etched calendar. The last time she'd been above ground was in 1753, when she'd been assigned to make a match between the high-and-mighty Countess of Mountbury and Frederick Coddington, a poor but pure-hearted cooper. Why, that meant that it had been over sixty years since she'd last been up in the mortal world.

That troubling thought furrowed her brow. When Prince, now King, Aengus had condemned her to otherworld captivity, he'd turned her over to Allura, commanding that she be set to matchmaking in the mortal world. Hopefully, he'd said, she would become skilled enough in the vocation to successfully assist Lucan in finding true love when he was reborn.

Always conscientious of the duties of her office, Allura had assigned Alys to a dozen or more matches a century, and after each she sent her to report to Aengus. Upon hearing her account, he always asked her the same question: And what has your experience taught you about love? To which she'd stare at him blankly, not quite certain what he meant. Though she'd never once failed to bring her designated couple to the altar, to her bewilderment Aengus would then sigh and shake his head, murmuring, "Ah, well. Perhaps you'll be successful next time."

When she'd asked Allura what he meant, she too had shaken her head and cryptically replied, "Listen to your heart. Only it knows the true answer."

As Alys stared unseeing at the calendar, a hideous thought crept into her mind. Had Aengus and Allura given up on her learning whatever it was she was supposed to have learned during her matchmaking junkets? Was that why she hadn't been sent to the mortal world for so long? Was it the reason she hadn't been called upon to help Lucan's reborn soul find true love?

Alys swallowed dryly. It was apparent that she had been passed over for the assignment, for the reborn Lucan was what . . . thirty-two years old? Long past the age when most mortal men sought love and marriage.

With panic crawling up her spine, she raised her gaze from the calendar to meet Allura's glittering green fairy one. If it was true, then she'd lost her chance to right the wrong she'd done him all those centuries ago . . . which meant that she would lose her immortal soul.

The panic shot the rest of the distance up her spine and grabbed at her throat. When Aengus had sentenced her to otherworld captivity, he had promised her that if she could find the reborn Lucan the love she'd robbed him of during his first life, thus making atonement to his mortal soul, then she would be released and restored to the mortal world with her physical being exactly as it was when she'd left. If she failed, she'd spend the rest of her existence locked in her underground prison, where she'd eventually become one with the fairies and lose her soul.

As if reading her mind, and indeed sometimes Alys suspected that the powerful fairy could do just that, Allura said, "I know it's been a goodly while since you've been to the mortal world, but Aengus had a vision that Lucan would be reborn near the end of the last century, and he ordered me to let you rest so you'd be equal to the task of finding him love when he reached manhood."

Alys sagged with relief. "Then I wasn't—"

"—passed over for the assignment?" Allura cut in and finished. She released a laugh like the tinkling of tiny bells. "No. Of course not. He couldn't have, even if he'd wanted to."

At Alys's querying look, she elaborated. "You see, Alys, every mortal, even a half mortal, is born with a certain preordained destiny . . . a chain of life events, if you will, which his soul is compelled to follow. When that chain is broken by himself or by someone else, it must be mended and then completed before the person can be considered for heaven. Now, when a person breaks it himself through willfulness or wicked deeds, then it is up to him to repair it. When someone else is responsible, such as was the case with Lucan, then the guilty person, you, must do the mending. So you see? Aengus has no choice but to trust you."

Alys's troubled brow didn't smooth, though she did nod her comprehension. Glancing back down at the calendar, she murmured, "While I understand the reason why I must find Lucan love, I don't see why Aengus had me wait so long to do so. I mean, wouldn't Luc—" She shot Allura a questioning look. "I don't know what to call Lucan now. Who is he?"

"Lucian James Warre, the seventh Marquess of Thistlewood," the fairy replied with a significant lift of her brow. At Alys's gasp, she nodded. "Yes. As most often happens with half souls, he has been reborn back into his own family."

Alys's spirits lifted a notch at that bit of news. She'd encountered several generations of Warres during her matchmaking missions. Back in 1547, she'd even had to discourage one, a Philip Warre, from wooing a maid meant for another. Turning the poor lovesick girl's head away from him and back to her intended had been her biggest challenge yet as a matchmaker. For the Warre males, without any exception that she'd seen, were a charming and handsome lot, each the sort of man any woman would be thrilled to call her own.

"You were about to ask a question, I believe?" Allura prompted, though she wore that all-knowing look again.

Alys shrugged, suddenly far less worried than she'd been only moments earlier. "I was just wondering why Aengus had waited until this Lucian Warre was thirty-two years old to find him love. Love comes so much more easily to the young."

"Perhaps. But true mortal love, the kind that Lucian

needs to complete his soul, must be purer and stronger than the kind usually bonding the young. It's harder to find, yes, and sometimes almost impossible to recognize when it comes, but those difficulties make it all the more precious and rare. It's the sort of love that lasts an eternity."

"And who is the paragon who's going to grace him with such a love?" Alys asked, doubtful that such a powerful form of the emotion existed.

Allura shook her head. "I'm afraid I can't help you with that. Finding his true love is a part of your atonement."

"But I haven't even met the man! How am I supposed to know what sort of a woman will suit him?" she protested, her anxiety rushing back with gut-quivering force.

"Surely after all your matchmaking experience, you recognize the signs of love when you see them?"

"Are you telling me that there's a woman who already fancies him, and that I have only to look for the signs?" Alys asked, praying that it was so.

"With his reputation and title, there are plenty of women who look upon him with favor. Not," the fairy quickly amended, "that most of those women have actually met him. He was out of the country until recently, fighting at General Wellington's right hand. The women's infatuation is due mostly to the much romanticized tales of his battlefield exploits printed in the newspapers. He's become somewhat of a hero to London society." Her eyes narrowed then and she shot Alys a querying look. "You do know about the war with France, don't you?"

Alys nodded. Fairies loved war almost as much as they did music and dancing. So much so that the males often assumed mortal guise and joined the soldiers on the battlefield during the bloodiest skirmishes. The fairy warriors had found the most recent war particularly stimulating, and had brought more stories back to the underground than she cared to remember.

"Good." Allura nodded back. "Undoubtedly the war and Lucian's exploits shall be a much discussed topic among society." She paused thoughtfully for a moment, then exhaled in a loud sigh. "Too bad Bryan Fitzsim-

mons isn't still alive. He could have given you the details
of Lucian's heroics, as well as some insight into the sort
of man he is."

"Bryan is dead?" Alys gasped, remembering the
darkly handsome knight who had slain Lucan. "How? I
thought he was enslaved in the Surrey kingdom."

"He was up until the war started. Then Aengus sent
him into battle with Lucian Warre with strict orders to
safeguard his life. That was his atonement for killing him
when he was Lucan." The fairy looked almost regretful.
"He died at Waterloo taking a bayonet that was meant
for Lucian."

"Was he . . . I mean . . . do you know if he was under
Aengus's enchantment when he died?" Alys asked, her
voice little more than a strangled whisper. Some said
that if a mortal died while under an otherworld spell,
then his enchanted soul would be unfit for heaven and
that he must walk the earth as a ghost until judgment
day. The thought of Bryan, whom she'd once liked and
now blamed herself for driving to murder, condemned
to such a fate was enough to make her eyes well up
with tears.

Alys looked up at the feel of a hand lightly squeezing
her shoulder, her vision blurred by sorrow. Though she
hadn't seen or heard the fairy move, she wasn't surprised
to see Allura standing at her side. Like all fairies, Allura
had the ability to move quicker than the human eye and
quieter than the human ear could discern.

She knelt next to Alys's chair, her sea-green skirts
pooling around her in a way that made her look like a
mermaid rising from the sea. Taking Alys's hand in hers,
she reassured her, "The enchantment was broken the
second Bryan made the unselfish decision to sacrifice
his life for Lucian's. I'm certain he's in heaven even as
we speak."

Nonetheless, Alys said a silent prayer on his behalf.

"Now back to your matchmaking problem." Allura
rose in one graceful motion and began to pace the length
of the room.

Decorated in Allura's favorite colors, purple, green,
and gold, the room could easily have been the office of
a mortal solicitor or banker. Not that that came as any

surprise to Alys. Everything in the otherworld imitated the human one above. The reason for this mimicry, she had discovered, was because the fairies envied the humans their immortal souls, and it soothed that envy somewhat to pretend to be one of them.

Still walking the floor in an agitated manner, Allura said, "Lucian has been back in England for three months, and in London for two of them. Yet, he hasn't bothered to attend a single affair where he might meet an eligible lady."

The fairy stopped abruptly and pivoted on her heels to face Alys, annoyance lying heavy on her features. "The problem is, he doesn't believe in love, nor is he interested in having anyone prove its existence to him. He's not going to willingly place himself in a position where he'll have to spend more than two minutes with a marriage-minded miss, who not only believes in love, but expects it from a man." She shook her head. "The only women he'll tolerate are the kind he can buy for a night . . . or a week, or a month, or for however long they keep him amused in bed."

Alys's spirits sank to a new low. "What do you expect me to do then? Tie him up and drag him to wherever the marriageable women assemble?"

A slow, enigmatic smile curved the fairy's lips. "Yes. Though the kind of tying I have in mind doesn't require rope, and he'll do the dragging himself."

"I doubt even Aengus has the power to make him do that if he's as unwilling as you say," Alys scoffed. "Besides, you said yourself that it's against the rules to use any sort of fairy glamour to influence matters of the mortal heart."

Allura slanted her a sly look. "There's no magic required for what I have in mind. Just you."

"Me?" Alys mouthed in surprise, pointing to her chest.

The fairy nodded. "Yes, you. Alys Faire, sister of Bevis Faire, Baron of Fairfax."

"Sister? Of Bevis Faire?" Alys repeated, thoroughly perplexed. She knew that her family name, le Fayre, had become anglicized to Faire over the centuries, and that a barony had been granted to a William Faire a hundred

years earlier. Yet this was the first mention she'd heard
of a Bevis Faire.

"When we sent Bryan back up to the mortal world,
we changed him with Bevis Faire, a descendant of your
brother, Edwin," Allura clarified. "He—"

"What did you do with the real Bevis," Alys cut in,
feeling it only proper to inquire, though what she'd seen
of her brother's descendants had done much to diminish
her family pride.

"Oh, don't worry about him. He was perfectly content
to be changed," Allura replied with a snort of disgust.
"At the time we kidnapped him, his father had just
bought him a commission in the cavalry and he was
looking for a way to escape his duty. The elder Faire, I
heard, was hoping that the experience would make a
man of him. Being the coward he is, Bevis was more
than happy to change places with Bryan and live in the
otherworld where it's safe. Indeed, he's requested to stay
down here, though he knows he'll lose his immortal
soul."

Her grimace perfectly expressed her opinion of the
man's foolishness. "Anyway, with the aid of a little glamour to alter his appearance, Bryan became Bevis Faire.
Too bad Bevis's father died shortly thereafter, he'd have
been proud of the name his son made on the
battlefield."

Alys shook her head. "I don't see what any of that
has to do with getting Lucian out into society."

"What we intended to do was to have Bevis, or Bryan
as you please, save Lucian's life in battle a few times.
When the war ended, Bevis was to write to Lucian begging his help in finding his sister, who was to be you, a
suitable husband. The mighty Marquess of Thistlewood
might not believe in love, but he's a man of honor, and
that honor would have forced him to grant such a favor
to the man who saved his life." She made a broad sweeping motion with her hand. "Voilà! Lucian would have
had no choice but to accompany Bevis and his sister into
society so he could make the appropriate introductions."

"You were going to change the Faire daughter as
well?" Alys asked, appalled at the unheard of notion of
changing two members of the same family.

"There is no daughter. We were going to create one."
Allura shrugged nonchalantly. "It's simple enough. We
send the wind fairies to whisper of the girl in the ears
of the Faire's friends and neighbors. By the time they're
finished, everyone is convinced that they've known the
Faire daughter since birth, and there is no question as
to her identity."

"That was a good plan," Alys admitted, impressed, as
usual, by the fairy's cunning. "Too bad we won't be able
to use it."

One of Allura's slanted eyebrows lifted. "Won't we?"

"I don't see how. Not with Bryan dead."

The fairy looked positively smug. "Instead of Bevis
sending a letter to Lucian, we sent one from his solicitor
informing him that Bevis Faire, Baron of Fairfax, has
left the wardship of his young sister to him. It also stated
that it was Bevis's wish that he find the girl a husband
as soon as possible." She released a peal of her tinkling
laughter. "As I've pointed out, Lucian Warre is a man
of honor. As much as he'll dislike squiring a young miss,
he won't shirk his duty."

Alys clapped her hands in a sudden burst of enthusiasm. "Oh, perfect! Then I have only to accompany him
into society, decide which woman loves him the most,
and see them to the altar." Things were beginning to
brighten considerably.

"You're forgetting an important part in all this," Allura reminded her quietly.

"Oh?"

"He has to love the woman in return. That's where
you're going to run into some difficulty."

The fairy resumed her pacing as she explained. "When
Lucan died, his half soul went to a place somewhere
between heaven and hell. While we're not certain what
this place is like, we suspect that it is much closer to
hell than heaven in character, for the half souls always
return from there shriveled and scarred. The longer
they're there, the worse the damage. Lucan's, or Lucian,
as I suppose we should get used to calling him, was there
for over four hundred years, the longest any of us can
remember. The sad result is that his soul has become so
withered that there's not enough of it left to feel much

emotion. The ones he does feel aren't new, but merely
echoes of the ones he once felt when he was Lucan."

"If Lucian Warre hasn't the ability to feel emotion,
how in the world do you expect me to make him fall
in love?" Alys inquired, feeling her own imperiled soul
slipping away at the impossibility of her task. "You
know as well as I that true love is the most difficult
emotion for a mortal to form."

"Yes. But with coaxing, his soul will heal and renew
itself. Then he can be taught how to feel."

"And I suppose it's my job to teach him?" Alys
muttered.

"The first few lessons shall be yours, yes. However,
once his soul experiences a few emotions, it will crave
more and prompt him to seek them out himself. When
he reaches that point, he'll be ready to receive love."

"But how do I teach him to feel?" Alys asked, a note
of hysteria rising in her voice.

Allura ceased her pacing to smile at her. "You'll teach
him by simply being yourself."

At Alys's skeptical frown, she elaborated, "Lucian
Warre has spent most of his life isolating himself from
other people, avoiding situations that might make him
feel unfamiliar emotions. You have to understand, Alys,
that feeling is a terrifying sensation for those not accustomed to it. That fear is the reason Lucian purchased a
commission in the cavalry the moment he finished Oxford. War, and all the emotions that go with it, is the
one thing he truly understands. Lucan's warrior instinct
was very strong when he died, and it is now the domi-
nate force in what's left of his soul."

She paused to nod at Alys. "Anyway, you, being a
miss who he's honor-bound to introduce into society,
shall show him the side of life he's managed to avoid
thus far. He can't help but to derive new feelings from
the experience. Pleasant or painful, each one of these
shall serve to revive and in turn expand his soul. Before
you know it, he'll be ready and able to love."

"But—" she began to argue.

"But," the fairy interjected, "Lucian's fairy essence
expires at midnight on Midsummer's night, so you
haven't much time to accomplish all this. As you know,

if he loses his essence without his soul being complete enough to fill its place, he'll die and be lost forever. So it's crucial that you find him his true love and make it whole before then."

"But you've always told me that fairy essence lasts a full thousand years," Alys protested, feeling more overwhelmed by the second. "And Lucan's . . . um . . . Lucian's being was created less than five hundred years ago."

"Four hundred ninety-nine years and two hundred and thirty-five days ago, to be exact. Which means that you have only one hundred and thirty days to accomplish your task."

Alys made a quick calculation. "But that adds up to only five hundred years! How can that be?"

Allura was back sitting behind her desk in a twinkling. "Lucian, as a half fairy, has only half the amount of essence as a full-fledged fairy. That's five hundred years worth. And his being turns five hundred years old as June twenty-fourth slips into the twenty-fifth, Lucian's thirty-third birthday . . . and Lucan's five hundredth one."

Alys's pulse drummed in her throat as she considered Allura's words. If she didn't find Lucian Warre true love in four months time, she'd be responsible not only for him losing his life twice, but his immortal soul as well. Her shoulders sagged. The burden was more than she could bear.

Obviously she looked as downhearted as she felt, for Allura reached out and gave her cheek a comforting pat. "There, there, now, Alys. Don't look so glum. You'll do just fine. Aengus and I have all the confidence in the world that you'll find Lucian's destined lady."

Instead of feeling better, the fairy's words made her feel worse. His *destined* lady? What if she found him love, but with the wrong woman?

That all-knowing look was back on Allura's face. "Don't worry about him loving the wrong woman," the fairy reassured her. "He can't. His heart won't let him."

That made Alys feel better, but only slightly.

As Allura opened her mouth to add something, a swirl of sparklike flashes materialized at her elbow. Slowly the lights flared and merged until they formed a male figure perhaps three inches high. It was a wind fairy, or whisperer as the otherworld minions called them, the messengers of the fairy world.

"Yes, Etain?" Allura queried as the whisperer sketched a courtly bow before her.

With one flutter of his iridescent wings, he was at her ear, whispering. Allura nodded at whatever he said, then dismissed him. He dissolved back into beads of light, which in turn melted into nothingness.

Allura sat in silence for several moments, studying Alys thoughtfully. "It seems that Lucian Warre has sent for you sooner than we expected," she finally said. "Etain told me that Bevis's solicitor received a message from him today saying that he's sending his coach to Fairfax tomorrow to take you to his London house. Fortunately for us, the whisperer had the foresight to induce the household to think that you, Alys Faire, heiress to the Fairfax estate, which I might add is exactly who you'll earn the right to be if you succeed in this task, are visiting a friend in Exeter and are due home this very evening. I'll arrange for you to arrive there sometime around eight o'clock."

Alys nodded once, her throat suddenly too tight to speak. Everything was happening too fast.

Apparently it was happening too quickly for Allura as well, for she murmured, "I'd hoped to have time to instruct you in the strange new ways of society." She sighed. "Ah, well. Hedley's been aboveground these last three months spying on Lucian for us. I'm certain he'll be able to guide you."

"Hedley?"

"Hedley Bragg."

"You're sending Hedley Bragg with me?" Alys choked out, disgusted by the mere mention of the filthy hob. When she was sent up to the mortal world to make a match, she was always given a fairy helper to assist her and to serve as her contact to the otherworld should the need arise. Surely Allura didn't intend to assign Hedley to the task?

Apparently she did, because she nodded.

"But why!" The words practically exploded from

Alys's lips. "I mean"—her hands made a fluttering motion—"he's a hob. What do hobs know about matchmaking?"

"Nothing, unfortunately," the fairy admitted. "And if I had my choice, I'd send someone with several centuries of matchmaking experience, like Elfwine or Hertha. However, Aengus insists on sending Hedley. It seems that he too owes a debt to Lucan's soul."

"I can't imagine what business a smelly hob like Hedley could have had with a magnificent knight like Lucan," Alys retorted scornfully.

"Don't be fooled by his unkempt appearance. He was once, and I daresay could be again if he wished, the otherworld's greatest warrior. When Lucan was"—the fairy waved her hand dismissively—"well, Lucan, it was Hedley's duty to follow him into battle and keep him safe. That responsibility included protecting him during tourneys and jousts and such. Unfortunately, he's a bit overfond of the mortal's wine, and he'd imbibed too freely of it the day Lucan was killed. He was lying drunk on the floor of the armory when it happened. Aengus blames him almost as much as you and Bryan for Lucan's death."

"That being the case, why didn't Aengus let him atone by guarding Lucian during the recent war?" Alys asked.

The fairy stared down at her quill-wiper as if suddenly fascinated. "He's grown rather unpredictable and . . . mmm . . . more irresponsible over the centuries, and Aengus was afraid to trust him with the task."

Alys gaped at Allura, too appalled by her words to speak. Oh, perfect! She had to find an emotionless man true love in four months time with only a harum-scarum hob to assist her.

She was doomed for certain.

Chapter 2

London

"Are you asleep, Luc?" the woman whispered, running her hand down the muscular back of the man lying beside her.

His eyelids lifted, revealing eyes as cold and gray as the stone walls of Newgate prison. He lay unmoving for several seconds staring at her in his odd, unreadable way, then released a soft snort and flopped over onto his back. "What the hell do you take me for, Reina? Some beef-witted cub who spills himself and then promptly falls asleep?"

"No! No! Of course not. As always your lordship's lovemaking was"—she made a fluttering motion with her hand as she scrambled for a fitting word—"magnificent!" And it was. For all that he was the most passionless man she'd ever met, Lucian Warre truly was a magnificent lover. Not for the first time in the month she'd been his mistress, she found herself wondering how that could be.

He emitted another snort at her compliment, this one liberally laced with scorn. "Even an impotent old roué is counted as splendid by his mistress if he's flush in the pockets."

Reina opened her mouth to indignantly contest his words, but something in his narrowed gaze changed her mind and she instead murmured, "You mentioned earlier that you must leave me at seven to be at home for the arrival of a guest. It must be someone very important indeed for you, the mighty Marquess of Thistlewood, to be at their beck and call like that."

"Not a guest," he corrected her coolly. "My new ward. A chit of nineteen or twenty, I believe."

"Ward? You?" she gasped, unable to hide her amazement. Why someone would leave a young miss in the care of a stern, somber bachelor like Lucian was beyond her scope of imagination.

"Ward. Me," he echoed, tossing aside the sheet and slipping from the bed. "She's the sister of an officer who died at Waterloo taking a bayonet for me." He paused a beat to stretch his spine. "That being the case, I could hardly say no when his solicitor approached me about the matter."

Reina let her appreciative gaze follow him as he sauntered across the room to retrieve his clothes. Powerful muscles flexed and rippled beneath skin as lustrous as tawny silk, emphasizing the athletic grace of his every move. Never in all her years as a demi-rep had she seen a man so devilishly perfect in both face and form. Indeed, if it wasn't for his chilly demeanor, he would have been the most devastatingly desirable man in England.

Raising herself up on her elbows, she watched as he bent over to draw up his trousers, thoroughly enjoying the view of his tight buttocks and long muscular legs. When he'd pulled them up, thus occluding the tantalizing sight, she murmured breathlessly, "So, my lord. What are your plans for your new ward?"

He picked up his snowy shirt and drew it over his sculpted chest. "I intend to find her a husband, and soon," he replied, tucking his shirttail into his trousers with military precision. "The last thing I need or want is the millstone of a milk-and-water miss hanging around my neck." A pained grimace crossed his face. "I just pray that she doesn't resemble her brother."

"That bad?"

"Blonde," he announced in much the same tone one used to discuss harelips and crossed eyes.

Reina laughed. "That's hardly what I'd call a ruinous fault." At his scowl, she argued, "Believe me, Luc, there

are plenty of men who prefer fair women, though, lucky
for me, you find them unappetizing."

He grunted his disbelief as he turned to the mirror to
tie his cravat. "Considering that her marriage portion
consists of an indebted estate and a mismanaged wool
mill, a man will have to find her bloody exquisite to
want to marry her."

Reina remained silent for several moments reflecting
on his problem, while Lucian tugged and cursed at his
wayward neckcloth. Finally he expelled a frustrated
snort and turned from the mirror, his usually immaculate
cravat crookedly knotted and crushed. As he shrugged
on his biscuit-colored waistcoat, she pointed out,
"You're a wealthy man. If your new ward proves to be
as ill-favored as you fear, you can always fatten her
dowry yourself and buy your freedom. Lord Dunhurst
did just that a few years back. He got stuck with a ward
who had a squint, a mustache, and next to no dowry.
Not a single man spared her so much as a glance until
his lordship flushed her portion by a few thousand
pounds. As soon as word of her newly increased settle-
ment got out, she received not one but four offers.
Granted, they were all from rakes in Dun territory, not
exactly the sort of men a father would hope for for his
daughter, but she did well enough considering her
shortcomings."

Lucian ran his hand through his hair as he weighed
her suggestion, his tanned flesh appearing almost pale
against the raven-wing darkness of his tousled locks. "It
might work at that," he mused, almost to himself. He
sighed then and dropped his hand back to his side. "Unlike Lord Dunhurst, however, I feel obligated to make
certain that the man she marries is the sort her brother
would approve of. I owe him at least that much for saving my life."

Reina shrugged as she rose from the bed and donned
a scarlet wool dressing gown. "In that case, you must
invest some blunt in improving her." She strolled over
to where he stood buttoning his chocolate-brown coat,
reciting, "A wardrobe by Madame Fanchon is a must,
as are a clever abigail and tutors in deportment and
dancing. If she turns out to be a goosecap, you'll need

to hire Monsieur Boucher to teach her the art of witty repartee."

Standing on her tiptoes, she wrapped her arms around his neck and concluded between kisses, "Add all that to her newly fattened dowry, and I don't doubt that half the gallants in London will be cutting a path to your door."

"Remind me on Friday, my dear," Lucian said, disengaging himself from her embrace, "to take you to Rundel & Bridge's and buy you that bracelet you've been trying to wheedle from me."

It was all Reina could do not to squeal her delight and throw her arms around him again. Knowing his distaste for such displays, however, she settled for smiling and murmuring, "You're most generous, my lord."

He shook his head. "Not generous. Merely conscious of rewarding those who render me service."

"Which you do quite handsomely," she rejoined softly. "By the by, cook baked one of those apricot tarts you so enjoy. Perhaps you'd care to join me for dinner before you leave?" A hopeful note crept into her voice.

"The last time I stayed for dinner we ended up back in bed, and I completely missed the reception my sister held in my honor." He made a wry face. "She still hasn't stopped scolding me on that account."

"What if I promise not to seduce you?" she purred, remembering the night in question with heated fondness.

His gaze met hers then, his eyes so frigid that she shivered. "Don't flatter yourself, my dear. There's not a woman alive with the power to rob me of my senses enough to seduce me."

"Told ye it was a bloody damn palace!" Hedley crowed, leaping from the seat as the footman opened the door. Without waiting for Alys to respond, the foottall hob jumped from the coach, ran between the footman's legs, and disappeared into the wintery darkness beyond.

Alys didn't miss the way the servant's nostrils flared as he passed. Like most humans he couldn't see Hedley, but he could certainly smell him. And by the way he

was eyeing her, it was apparent that he thought the
stench was emanating from her.

"Oh, perfect!" Alys muttered to herself as she gathered up her skirts and prepared to exit the coach. She
could just imagine how many invitations she'd receive if
it got about that the Marquess of Thistlewood's new
ward smelled like the gutters of St. Giles. And if she
didn't get invited to the upcoming season's routs, balls,
and assemblies, she had about as much chance of finding
Lucian Warre true love as a fairy had of entering
heaven. It was clear that she was going to have to find
a remedy for Hedley's body odor and fast.

She was considering luring the hob into a bucketful
of lavender water when she stepped from the coach and
got her first glance at the house that was to be her tem-
porary home. Instantly her dismay melted into awe.

Hedley was right. It was a palace.

Built of soft yellow brick with white stone dressings,
the mansion was four stories high and nine bays wide.
Baroque in style, its origins were apparent in the elegantly carved roof balustrade and in the ornate pedi-
ments that crowned each of the flanking wings and the
center entry porch. The windows, all thirty-six facing
ones at least, were ablaze with light, imparting a sense
of warmth that she found as comforting as a welcom-
ing hug.

As Alys stood gaping like a green girl on her first trip
to town, she was snapped out of her admiring stupor by
a discreet cough. Whether that cough was meant to draw
her attention or was due to the close proximity of Hedley, who was hopping around the servant on one foot
chanting something unintelligible, she didn't know.
Whatever the case, the red-faced footman motioned her
up the sweeping front steps to where a stooped, rather
storklike butler stood guard at the open door.

With a gleeful cackle, Hedley darted up ahead of her,
turning a series of cartwheels as he vanished inside. Relieved to be rid of the hob, at least for the moment, Alys
followed at a more sedate pace. Her relief, however, was
short-lived, for without the distraction of the little man,
as unpleasant as it was, her mind was left free to medi-
tate on her upcoming encounter with Lucian Warre.

During the long ride from Fairfax Castle, she'd attempted to coax Hedley into telling her what he'd learned of the man while spying on him. To her everlasting vexation, the nasty little hob had decided to be contrary and answered her questions with nonsensical riddles. With growing exasperation, she'd proceeded to try everything from bribery to threats to extract the information, all with equally fruitless results. At last she'd given up and had spent the remainder of the miserable trip with her head hanging out the window, breathing in the icy but mercifully hob-stench free air.

So what would Lucian Warre be like? she wondered as she followed the butler into an entry hall resplendent with Italian stucco walls and a sweeping staircase. Aside from the fact that his soul could fit into a thimble, she knew nothing about him. Her eyes narrowed with speculation. Would he bear any resemblance, physical or other, to the man he'd once been?

In her mind's eye, she pictured Lucan de Thistlewood as he'd looked the day she'd met him. With his shimmering mane of pale gold hair and eyes the hue of turquoise, he'd been the most magnificent man she'd ever seen. It had almost hurt to look at him, he was so beautiful, especially clad as he was in his golden armor. And when he'd smiled at her, his expression so sweet and full of tenderness . . .

Remorse caught in her throat, choking her like it always did when she remembered Lucan. If only she'd been less selfish, less vain. If only she'd cherished him as the treasure he was instead of viewing him as a pawn to be used in her cruel little games. He'd given her his greatest gift, his love, and in return he'd received nothing but pain and torment.

So engrossed was she in her self-flagellation that she plowed right into the back of the dour butler, who'd come to an abrupt stop at the foot of the stairs. Apparently her traveling pelisse had taken on Hedley's odor during their hours cooped up together in the coach, for the man put a distance between them with a speed she found astonishing for a person of his advanced years.

In the stiff-jawed manner she'd noticed had become fashionable, he announced, "His lordship directed me to present you to him immediately upon your arrival. Unless, of course, you care to—ahem—freshen up first?" From the disdainful way he was staring at her down his beaky nose, it was clear that he thought a liberal application of soap and water was in order before meeting the marquess.

For one brief instant, Alys was overwhelmed with the desire to accept his invitation, and to primp and fuss like she used to do when she knew she'd be seeing Lucan. Then she reminded herself that he was no longer Lucan de Thistlewood, the courtly knight, but Lucian Warre, a stranger . . . a stranger whom she had just four short months to find true love. It was remembering that fact that made her say, "I shall see his lordship now, if you please." The sooner she met the man, the sooner she could decide what sort of woman would suit him and how best to go about finding her.

By the way the butler's beetled gray brows rose almost to his sparse hairline, it was obvious that he didn't please. However, like any servant mindful of his position, he merely intoned, "As you wish, Miss Faire. If you'll follow me?"

Without further comment, he pivoted on his heels and marched down the long corridor at his right. Like the entry hall, its plaster walls were worked in deeply sculptured relief, these in medallions with exquisitely detailed portraits. Unlike the entry, however, whose floor was of cold white stone inlaid with diamonds of black marble, this one was carpeted in pale blue drugget bordered with a green and rose trellis design.

As appeared to be his habit, the butler didn't slow upon approach to their destination, but came to a sudden stop in front of it. Without sparing her a glance to assure himself that she was by his side, he scratched discreetly at the paneled door.

"Yes?" responded a masculine voice, one whose cool, deep timbre bore no resemblance to Lucan's warm, lilting one.

"Miss Faire has arrived, my lord."

There was a long pause, as if he were deciding whether or not to receive her, then, "Please show her in, Tidswell."

At his command the butler opened the door, then stepped back, motioning for her to enter. Alys swallowed hard and willed her feet to move. They remained firmly rooted to the spot. She tried again, but they refused to budge. She scowled down at the leather-clad offenders. What the devil was wrong with her?

Her pounding heart and trembling palms gave easy answer to that question. She was nervous . . . terrified if the truth were to be told. Whatever was she going to say to the man whose soul she was bound to save? Though she'd rehearsed the coming scene in her mind a hundred times, she suddenly wished that she'd accepted the butler's invitation to freshen up so she could have practiced it a hundred times more.

"Miss?" Tidswell urged.

She looked up at him, her panic growing by the second.

He widened his eyes at her as if to command her to stop behaving like a ninnyhammer, and again waved her into the room.

Returning her gaze to her feet, she concentrated on ungluing her soles from the carpet. To her relief, she somehow managed to shuffle over the threshold. Without looking up or stopping to consider whether it was appropriate to do so in this day and age, she executed a shaky curtsy.

A deep chuckle resonated from her left. "Nicely done, Miss Faire. I'm sure my great-great-grandfather is duly impressed."

Alys looked up swiftly to find herself staring at a huge black marble fireplace, above which hung the portrait of a gentleman dressed in the fashion popular a century earlier. Flushing what she was certain was the same shade of crimson as the full-skirted coat of the gentleman in the portrait, she stole a glance in the direction from which the voice had come. What she saw only added to her discomfiture.

There was absolutely nothing of Lucan de Thistlewood in Lucian Warre. At least nothing readily visible. Oh, Lucian Warre was handsome enough, there was no debating it, but in a dark, aggressively masculine way that she found more disturbing than pleasing. Apparently he was none too pleased with what he saw either, for he was eyeing her with an expression that could only be interpreted as distaste.

More deeply wounded than she had thought possible, Alys looked away. This was the first time since her captivity that she'd been allowed to appear in the mortal world in her true form, and she'd fully expected to be as much admired now as she had been five hundred years earlier.

When Aengus had turned her over to Allura to be trained as a matchmaker, he'd done so with strict instructions that she be transformed into either an overplump matron or a hatchet-faced spinster every time she was sent among humans. He said that she, with her overweening vanity, needed a lesson in humility, and that the only way for her to truly learn it was to deprive her of the masculine admiration she so adored.

Alys sighed. Obviously the requirements for feminine beauty had changed so much over the centuries that Aengus no longer thought it necessary to transform her.

"Miss Faire?" Lucian prodded.

Alys forced herself to look at him again.

He was now standing courteously behind his desk, gesturing toward a comfortable-looking chair in front of him, his expression blessedly impassive. "Please have a seat."

As she moved forward to do as he bid, the butler stopped her with, "Might I suggest, miss, that you remove your pelisse and bonnet first?"

With a nod, she did as he suggested. Holding her eau de Hob scented garments with two fingers at arm's length, the man quickly exited the room.

"Now, Miss Faire, or may I call you Alys?" Lucian said, waiting for her to settle in her chair before sitting back down behind the massive desk. Unlike most men, who had the courtesy to grace a lady with a deferential look when asking leave to address her by her first name, he was staring at her hair as if it were a coiffure of poisonous vipers.

Reaching up self-consciously to touch the neatly coiled hair at her nape, she murmured, "Alys will be fine, my lord."

"And you may call me Lucian in private, though I do expect you to use the proper forms of address when we're in public." His gaze had dropped and he was now scanning her length. "As your guardian, I shall expect you to show me deference at all times and in all matters. Understood?" By the scornful curl of his lips, it was apparent that her figure didn't meet with his approval any more than her face and hair did.

Hating herself for caring and him even more for making her, for she truly was trying to conquer her cursed vanity, she glanced down at herself. Granted, the black bombazine mourning gown Allura had pronounced appropriate didn't do much to flatter either her figure or coloring, but she hadn't thought that she looked all that dreadful.

"Pompous ass, ain't he?" It was Hedley, who had materialized on the corner of Lucian's desk where he now sat swinging his stubby legs. Apparently he'd been stealing pastries, for there were crumbs in his matted brown beard and if she didn't miss her guess, the red gob on the corner of his mouth was preserves.

"Do you understand, Miss Faire?" Lucian repeated, loudly this time as if he suspected that she was hard of hearing.

Alys nodded, more in agreement to the hob's observation than to his lordship's instructions. Even after only three minutes in his company, it was clear that the Marquess of Thistlewood was the stiffest-rumped aristocrat she'd ever had the misfortune to meet. A truly dismal fact in light of the task before her.

"Good," he more snapped than replied. "You follow all my directives so readily and we shall get on well enough."

"Follow my directives. Follow my directives," Hedley mimicked, making a noise reminiscent of flatulence. "Just like ye was his bloody damn dog."

Alys watched as Lucian picked up a letter and scanned the contents, obviously so used to everyone meekly obeying his orders that he fully expected her to let his last remark pass unchallenged. That bit of high-handedness gave her an almost irrepressible urge to do something to deflate his overinflated sense of self-importance.

His beady brown eyes gleaming with deviltry, Hedley baited, "Ye ought to shove a bur up Lord High-Horse's tight arse and ask him what he'll do if ye don't follow his frigging directives." He guffawed. "Bet having someone talk back'd be something new for him."

Alys transferred her gaze from the hob to Lucian, whose nostrils were quivering slightly as if he'd just caught a whiff of the little man's stink. Hedley was right. It probably would be a new experience for someone to question the mighty Marquess of Thistlewood's commands.

She ducked her head to hide her face, certain that her expression was every bit as mischievous as Hedley's. Allura had said that any new experience, pleasant or not, would make Lucian Warre feel the emotions he needed to increase his soul. And since it was her duty to foster these emotions . . .

"What if I disagree with your directives and don't choose to follow them?" she blurted out abruptly.

He continued to read for a moment, then slowly raised his gaze to meet hers. Though his face was impassive, his annoyance was apparent by the narrowing of his eyes. "It's not your place to disagree with me. You shall do what I say, when I say it."

Alys forced herself to smile sweetly, though it made her face ache to do so. "That doesn't answer my question, my lord."

"That's because it does not warrant an answer."

As she leaned forward to challenge his reply, Hedley skittered to the center of the desk where he stood waving his fists, shouting garbled fairy nonsense at Lucian. Lucian's nostrils flared violently and his slitted eyes widened almost to the point of popping as he expelled, "Good God, Miss Faire. When was the last time you bathed?"

She gave a noncommittal shrug, but refrained from response.

"When I ask you a question, I fully expect an answer," he bit out, retreating from the smell as far as his chair back would allow.

"I don't see that your question warrants an answer."

Apparently Hedley was correct about nobody naysay-

ing him, for he looked almost stunned by her rebellious
response. But only for a second. Quickly recovering his
composure, he said in a surprisingly reasonable tone, "I
can see that this situation is no more to your liking than
it is to mine. Unfortunately, there is nothing either of
us can do about it." He slid the paper he'd been reading
across the desk to her. "As you can see for yourself, my
dear Miss Faire, you are legally bound to my guardianship, just as I am bound by my honor to see to your
welfare."

Alys picked up the letter and made a show of perusing
it. After several moments she lowered it a fraction to
meet his gaze over the top. "Where does it say that I
must follow your directives?"

"In the same place it states that you're not to question
your elders. It's an unwritten law, one that I'd have
thought you'd have been taught while you were still in
your cradle." He sighed as he plucked the letter from
her hands. "I fear that finding you a husband is going
to be a more difficult task than I had hoped."

She sniffed. "I'm perfectly capable of finding my own
husband, thank you very much. However, I must warn
you that I'm in no hurry to marry. Perhaps I'll consider
the matter seriously in, oh"—she waved her hand dismissively—"five or six years."

Apparently Allura wasn't jesting about the discomfort
involved in an unfeeling soul learning new emotions, for
if he weren't so young and obviously fit, she'd have
thought by the color of his face that he was suffering a
fit of apoplexy.

"You will be married when I say and to whom," he
finally choked out from behind gritted teeth. "Your
brother charged me with finding you a suitable husband,
and I intend to do so as soon as possible."

Alys met Hedley's gleeful gaze as she said, "When
Bevis entrusted you with me and my happiness, he fully
expected you to behave like the honorable man he
thought he was dying for. I'm certain he never dreamed
that you would force me into a loveless marriage." She
couldn't resist the temptation to heave a quivering sigh.
"My poor, poor—*darling*—brother. We were so close. I
doubt he'll be able to rest in peace if I'm miserable."

Hedley cackled so hard, he almost fell off the stack of ledgers he was now perched on. "Shove that bur an inch higher, and it'll be coming out Lord Tight-Arse's mouth."

At that moment Lord Tight-Arse seemed hard-pressed to push anything past his lips. No doubt he'd planned to lock her in the attic and force her to subsist on moldy bread and brackish water until she agreed to marry whatever odious creature he selected. By bringing up Bevis's sacrifice and appealing to the speck of honor he possessed within what Alys had determined was his pinhead-sized soul, she'd effectively pulled the rug out from under him and left him at a loss. By the way he was looking at her, being at a loss was apparently another first for him.

As before, Lucian was surprisingly swift in recovering his senses. "Your brother realized that, as a woman, you are susceptible to romantic fancies and are therefore incapable of selecting a husband for yourself. He wanted you to marry for sensible reasons, like financial security and social position, not out of the absurd illusion you females call love. He left it up to me to make certain you do just that."

Alys emitted an incredulous snort. "I didn't see all that in the letter from Bevis's solicitor. Is that another of your unwritten laws?"

He shrugged. "No. Just common sense, something which, as an inexperienced young miss, I don't expect you to have much of."

It was Alys's turn to be struck speechless. By the ease with which he said the condescending words, it was shockingly clear that he truly believed them. She gripped the arms of her chair so hard in her fury that it hurt her palms. Of all the arrogant, pigheaded . . . tight-arsed! . . . autocrats she'd ever met, he was the worse. She might as well have Hedley summon Allura now and surrender her soul, for she couldn't imagine any woman liking, much less truly loving Lucian Warre.

"I promise, Alys," he continued in a clipped voice, "that I shall select you a husband worthy of the sister of the man who saved my life. Though you might not approve of my choice at first, over time you shall see the wisdom of my judgment and undoubtedly thank me."

He looked so damnably smug that her tongue snapped out before she could still it, "Oh? And what sort of man would you, in your bloody wisdom, consider worthy? Someone as humorless and overbearing as yourself, I suppose?"

Apparently humorless and overbearing were terms frequently applied to his lordship, for he merely made a tsking noise and chided her, "Ladies do not use the word bloody. I see that we shall have to work on improving your speech as well as your manners and"—his nostrils twitched meaningfully—"grooming."

"I am not the one who needs a lesson in manners, and there is nothing wrong with either my speech or my grooming," she flung back indignantly.

He made a clicking noise between his teeth. "Why must you challenge everything I say? Surely you see that you cannot win in our battle of wills?"

"I wouldn't be so certain of that if I were you."

"Mark my words, Alys, and mark them well: no matter how much you fight me, you shall do as I say. You will be betrothed before the end of the season and married by the end of the year." She could almost hear the sizzle in the air as his icy gray gaze met with her burning blue one. "You see, my dear, I never lose . . . in anything."

Alys's eyes narrowed at his cocksure reply, then a slow smile curved her lips. "Never say never, my lord," she warned him cryptically.

Lesson number two? Losing.

Chapter 3

Lucian muttered an expletive beneath his breath and slumped deeper in his chair, ignoring the curious glances from his fellow club members. He had never felt so odd in his life, so wretchedly . . . disturbed. And it was all the fault of that damn Alys Faire.

He gave his head a mental shake of astonishment. That she, an inexperienced miss, had put a crack in what he prided himself as being his invulnerable composure was beyond all comprehension. In truth, this lapse of control was so alien to his restrained nature that he was utterly at a loss at how to deal with it.

"Demme, Thistlewood. Can't say as I've ever seen you looking so blue-deviled."

Lucian glanced up from the glass of port he was contemplating to see his best friend, Stephen Randolph, Earl of Marchland, drop into the chair next to him. Unlike the other gentlemen at White's who were attired in proper evening dress, the horse-mad Stephen was decked out in riding clothes that looked as if they had endured a recent tour of Tattersall's stables. Lucian smiled in spite of his misery. Indeed, if he didn't miss his guess, that was straw protruding from Stephen's unruly auburn hair. Glad to see his unfailingly jolly friend, he admitted, "I am feeling rather out of sorts this evening."

Stephen cocked his head to one side, his warm brown eyes bright with curiosity. "Odd admission from you. Can't imagine what could put you in the dumps, un-

less"—he tilted his head to the other side—"you're having a problem with a woman or a horse." A sudden flush
of excitement rose to his lean cheeks. "Say, this doesn't
have anything to do with your new stallion, does it? Be
glad to take him off your hands, you know."

"It's a woman."

"Oh." Stephen didn't bother to mask his disappointment. "Ah, well. I warned you about Reina. Quick temper, sharp tongue. Spanish blood, you know."

"Not Reina. Alys," Lucian said, tossing down the entire contents of his glass. Just uttering her name was
enough to drive him to drink.

Stephen signaled for the attendant to bring Lucian a
refill. "Alys? New bit of muslin, eh?"

Lucian made a derisive noise. "I'm hardly the sort of
man to brood over an unsatisfactory mistress. No. Alys
is my new ward. And the most whey-faced, undisciplined
little hellion I've ever had the misfortune to meet."

"Like blazes, you don't say! A ward?" Stephen's expression was every bit as shocked as Reina's had been.
"Who was cracked enough to do something like that?
No offense, but"—he gestured toward Lucian—"you're
hardly the fatherly sort. I mean—"

"You mean that I loathe children." He released a humorless grate of laughter. "No offense taken, Stephen.
I'm not the sort of man I'd wish as a father for my own
children, if I had any. Too bad Lord Fairfax wasn't as
accurate a judge of character as you."

"Lord Fairfax, eh? Isn't he the fellow who took the
bayonet for you?" At Lucian's solemn nod, he let out a
long whistle. "That does put you in a pickle. You do
rather owe him the favor of seeing to his daughter."

"Sister," Lucian corrected.

"A young lady?" Stephen's interest sharpened visibly.
"I'd assumed we were discussing a child."

"She might as well be a child for all the figure she
has," Lucian muttered. "All straight lines and no bosom
to speak of. As if that's not bad enough, she's blonde."
He released a groan as despairing as if he had just been
sentenced to transportation to Australia. Indeed, the
hardship of Australia looked mighty tempting when
compared to life with Alys. "The worse tangle of this

coil," he added, "is that the man left me charged with the duty of finding her a husband. Given the choice, I'd have taken the bayonet myself."

"There, there, Luc," Stephen consoled, clapping his friend on the shoulder. "Plenty of fellows like blondes. Taken to a few myself."

"Yes. But at least your blondes had bosoms."

Stephen shrugged. "I'm not adverse to a slender figure. Less likely to look like a Christmas goose after squeezing out an heir."

"Thistlewood! Marchland!" greeted voices from behind them.

Lucian glanced over his shoulder. Lords Stanton and Bradwell. He almost groaned aloud. The pair were the biggest prattle-boxes in London. They had noses like truffle pigs when it came to sniffing out juicy morsels of gossip. By the way they were peering down at him, their eyes agleam with interest, it was apparent that they'd caught a whiff of scandal-broth brewing in his corner.

"Was just telling Bradwell here that you're looking deuced out of sorts tonight, Thistlewood," Stanton said, his squinty blue eyes narrowing on Lucian's face. "Said, 'See here, Bradwell. We ought to try to boost Thistlewood's spirits.' Didn't I say just that, Bradwell?"

Lord Bradwell bobbed his pie-faced head in agreement.

This time Lucian vocalized his groan. Even at his best he had little tolerance for the pair's chitchat. In his current mood, he had the uneasy suspicion that his patience might snap altogether, giving the men something truly scandalous to talk about. He was just opening his mouth to discourage them when Stephen piped in. "Please join us, gentlemen." At Lucian's wrathful glower, he shrugged. "Thought they might help us with your problem."

Lucian's glare grew more intense.

Unlike most people, who turned to pudding when faced with the Marquess of Thistlewood's displeasure, Stephen merely grinned. He'd known Lucian since their boyhood at Eaton and had learned long ago that his friend wasn't nearly as ferocious as he looked.

"See here, Luc," he said in a low voice as the men

seated themselves in the two facing chairs, "Bradwell and Stanton know more about the ton than the ton knows about itself. Stands to reason that they will know which men are searching for wives this season. Could even suggest a prospect or two for your new ward." He nodded. "At the very least they will let slip that you have a ward on the marriage market. When the news gets out, you'll both be invited to every affair this season. And the more places she's seen, the better your odds of finding her a husband."

Lucian considered his words for a moment, then nodded his grudging agreement. As much as he dreaded the thought of enduring Stanton's and Bradwell's company, Stephen was right.

After settling himself in his chair, Lord Stanton pursed his thin lips and leaned forward. Everything about the man, from the shape of his ferretlike face to his black kidskin-clad feet, was rather thin and narrow. As Lucian coolly returned his gaze, he was reminded, not for the first time, of one of those oddly elongated figures one saw carved atop medieval tombs.

"So, Thistlewood," he finally said, reaching over to thump him on the shoulder. "Need our assistance, hmm?"

"Perhaps," Lucian replied, his voice gruff with reluctance. So protective of his privacy was he, that just the thought of opening himself up, even to the slightest degree, made him feel all fluttery inside. He frowned at the foreign sensation. Is this what people meant when they complained about having butterflies in their stomachs? He pressed his palm to his midsection. Whatever it was, it was damned uncomfortable.

He was saved the further discomfort of having to explain his predicament by Stephen, who interjected, "Thistlewood has found himself saddled with a ward . . . a young lady. Her brother, Lord Fairfax, left her to him with the express wish that he find her a husband. Thought you gentlemen might suggest a likely candidate."

Bradwell visibly puffed up with importance at being asked to act as an adviser to the powerful Marquess of Thistlewood, while Stanton slowly rubbed his gloved hands together. "Might be able to help you at that," Bradwell said with a nod. "Provided, of course, that the gel is acceptable in looks, nature, and, a-hem, dowry." He looked at Lucian expectantly.

Lucian stared back, struggling to think of a way to portray Alys in a positive light without lying. Lying in any matter, even for the purpose of extracting one's self from a difficult situation such as this, was out of the question.

Stephen, however, had no such compunction. "Oh, she's a taking little thing," he fibbed. "Exceedingly satisfactory in all regards."

"Coloring?" Stanton interrogated.

Wincing, Lucian murmured, "Blonde."

"Like a golden angel," Stephen gushed.

"Figure?" This was from Bradwell, whose main preoccupation when not gossiping was leering down women's bodices.

"Mm—" At a loss for something complimentary to say, Lucian made a vague hand motion in the air.

"Slender," Stephen interpreted. "Rather resembles the Grecian nymph statues at Vauxhall Gardens. Flatters the latest fashions to perfection."

Damned if Bradwell and Stanton didn't look impressed. Lucian nodded as the attendant refilled his glass. Didn't Stephen realize that his glowing descriptions were merely going to make Alys seem all the more disappointing in contrast when the men finally met her? With a sigh, he lifted his glass to his lips.

"Good. Very good," Stanton was saying, rubbing his hands together so vigorously that Lucian expected a hole to appear in the fabric at any moment.

"Pink of the ton by the sound of her," Bradwell piped in.

Lucian choked on his port at that description.

Patting his back, Stephen wickedly added, "Met the chit myself just yesterday. Pronounced her passing fair with a nature to match. A paragon. Isn't that so, Thistlewood?"

All gazes were trained on him now, Bradwell's through his ever-present quizzing glass. Resisting the urge to spear Stephen with his glare, he forced a taut smile on his lips. Not only was Stephen dragging his own credibility through the mud, he was dragging his with it.

Taking his smile for an affirmative answer, Bradwell boomed, "If her marriage portion is as up to nines as her person, she'll doubtless take the ton by storm." By the way he was peering at him through his ridiculous glass, it was apparent that he was waiting for Lucian to disclose the specifics of Alys's dowry.

Stephen started to say something, but Lucian gave him a sharp yet surreptitious kick in the foot so that all that came out was a breathless "Oomph!"

Having saved himself the embarrassment of hearing Alys's dowry pumped up to no doubt include half of England and the lion's share of the crown jewels, he replied, "Her portion is respectable enough. As the only living member of the Faire family, her dowry will include Fairfax Castle, three hundred and fifty acres of surrounding farmland, and a woolen mill." Though he didn't bother to add that the castle was tumbling down, the farmland fallow, and the mill barely operative, he'd at least told the truth.

Bradwell and Stanton seemed satisfied with his response, for they nodded in unison, Bradwell letting his glass drop in the process.

"One thing I must add, gentlemen," Lucian said, deciding that since Stephen had put him in for a penny, he might as well go for the entire pound. "Unlike many guardians, I shall not marry my ward to a rake with his pockets to let just to get her off my hands." He shook his head. "No. I shall insist on a man solid in both character and finances."

"Considering your ward's abundance of fine attributes, I should think that finding her a quality match shall present no greater problem than deciding what sort of a man she might prefer," Stanton assured him.

Lucian snorted softly. "Her preferences have no bearing on the matter. She shall marry whomever I choose, and I believe that I have already stated my requirements."

"Yes. A solid man," Stanton acknowledged, while Bradwell flagged a passing attendant to request a pen, ink, and paper so they could make a list. He paused for a moment to consider, then nodded. "If you're not overly particular about age, you won't find a steadier man than Lord Haddon."

Lucian tried to place the man, but failed. "I'm not certain I've met Lord Haddon."

"Not surprising," Stanton replied. "It's been nigh on two decades since he's been to town. He much prefers his seat in"—he shot a querying glance to Bradwell—"Leicestershire?"

Bradwell nodded his confirmation, then expelled a satisfied "Ah!" as the attendant placed the requested writing supplies on the small table at his elbow.

"Leicester, yes," Stanton echoed, returning his gaze to Lucian. "Heard tell that the holdings bring him an annual income of twenty-five thousand pounds. At any rate, I saw him riding in the park last week and struck up a conversation. Told me he was in town for the season to find a bride. Seems his wife died without providing him an heir, and he's most eager to remedy the situation. He—"

"Exactly how old is this Lord Haddon?" Stephen interrupted.

"Fifty. Sixty." Stanton shrugged. "Somewhere thereabout."

Lucian rubbed his jaw thoughtfully. Lord Haddon's age presented no problem that he could see. In fact, it might prove an advantage. Being so much older, he might be inclined to overlook Alys's plainness. He was also likely to be better prepared to take her willfulness in hand. Nodding slowly, he inquired, "Did this Lord Haddon specify what sort of bride he desired?"

"He said that she must be young and chaste, and, of course, healthy enough to bear him an heir," Stanton replied.

Bradwell cleared his throat noisily, drawing the other men's attention. "In regards to Lord Haddon, I do feel it only fair to inform you that he's a Methodist. A strict one."

Lucian shrugged. "Then he'll no doubt be a nice, sobering influence on the girl."

Stanton's squinty eyes narrowed at his words. "I wasn't aware that your ward required any sobering."

Lucian could have bitten off his tongue. Glancing from Stanton to Bradwell, who was staring at him through his quizzing glass again, he explained, "She's young, and like all young women she's impressionable. I was merely indicating that Lord Haddon would set a fine example for her to follow." He almost smiled as Stanton signaled to Bradwell to write Haddon's name on the list. He'd put the pair's misgivings to rest without a hint of a falsehood. He glanced over to see if Stephen had duly taken note.

Stephen was staring at him, his face scrunched up in a mask of horror. "You can't be serious about Haddon, Luc," he exclaimed. "Would be frightfully cruel to shackle the poor chit to a pulpit-drubber thrice her age."

"A man needn't be young to be a good husband," Lucian informed him in a clipped tone. "And there's nothing wrong with being devout."

Stephen guffawed. "Ha! Wager you'd change your tune quick enough if you were the one being forced to bed some long-of-tooth sermonizer."

"Bedding is only a small part of marriage, one that demands nothing from a woman," Lucian pointed out. "Unlike a man, who must be attracted to his spouse in order to perform, it isn't necessary that a woman find her husband physically pleasing. All she need do is lay back and receive his passion." He gestured dismissively. "Women don't expect, nor are they capable of, deriving pleasure from lovemaking."

"Maybe your women don't find lovemaking pleasurable, but mine certainly do," Stephen quipped, arching one eyebrow meaningfully.

Lucian snorted his disdain. "Doxies all. And you know as well as I that members of the demi-rep aren't normal women. Their libidinous natures are rare aberrations, freakish in that they feel desire."

"If such natures are so rare, then why do so many wives cuckold their elderly husbands with virile lovers?" Stephen asked. His eyes brimming with deviltry, he shifted his gaze to Bradwell and Stanton. "How would you gentlemen explain the phenomenon?"

The two men exchanged uneasy glances, visibly discomfited by the subject.

"Ah—" Stanton stammered, his gaunt face mottling purple.

"Atwood. Um, yes," Bradwell cut in, smoothly saving them both from having to respond. "There is always Lord Atwood if the gel seems disturbed by Lord Haddon's age. He's only twenty-two. Heard his papa is ailing and wishes to see him settled before he dies. Says he wants to see his grandchildren."

"Atwood?" Lucian echoed, frowning. The name sounded familiar.

"You know. Claringbold's boy," Stephen reminded him. "Spindly shanks, spotty complexion. Stutters whenever he gets within a league of a female."

Lucian mentally placed the thin, timid young man. He was a bit unfinished at the present, true, but he had the makings of a fine man. He was also the heir to several holdings in Surrey, one of which bordered a small section of the Faire farmlands. That in itself might prove enticement enough for the boy's father to encourage him in the match. Smiling, he nodded to Bradwell. "Add his name to the list."

"Hope old Claringbold has a few years left on his calendar," Stephen intoned in a funereal voice. "He'll need them if he wants to see Atwood's children. As awkward as the boy is around women, I doubt he knows how to do his manly duty."

"Then they'll learn together," Lucian snapped.

Stephen grunted. "Can't imagine that the clumsy fumbling of an unlicked cub would be any more pleasant than the groping of an old fanatic."

"Might I suggest that you consider Lord Drake?" Stanton chimed in, obviously trying to pull the conversation away from the marriage bed. "He is a man of much, uh, experience."

Lucian frowned at that suggestion. In his opinion the handsome, dandified Drake had too much experience to make a good husband. Indeed, his sexual conquests provided regular basis for wagers in the club's betting book.

Stephen, however, was clearly not of like mind, for he leaned forward and asked, "Are you certain that Drake is looking to tie the nuptial knot?"

"Overheard him tell Lord Talbot so just yesterday," Stanton replied. "Said his father is threatening to cut him off if he doesn't present him with a wife by the end of the season."

Stephen nodded at Lucian. "Young. Handsome. Heir to an earldom. Seems a perfect choice to me."

"Perfect?" Lucian echoed, staring at his friend as if he'd lost his mind, which, indeed, he wondered if he had. "Drake is a profligate blood. He'd no doubt have one hand down the bridesmaid's bodice while putting the ring on Alys's finger with his other." He gave his head a firm shake. "No. He'll never do."

"A-hem. May I say something on Drake's behalf?" This was from Bradwell. At their nods, he proceeded. "While Drake might not have the steadiest nature where women are concerned, he is shrewd in business and has managed to increase his family fortune several times over. Since he's not given to deep-pocket gambling, whoever he weds shall never want for anything, except perhaps for his attentions. And I doubt she'll be too eager for those once the babies start coming."

"There you go, Luc. A good, solid provider," Stephen said. "Sounds to me as if he's just the man to round off your list."

Lucian hesitated a beat, then nodded his assent. Bradwell was right. What would it matter what company Drake kept as long as Alys and her children had security and comfort? Not that he held out much hope for that particular match. Drake was notoriously fond of pretty faces and rounded figures, neither of which Alys possessed.

"Of course, once the season is in full swing we'll undoubtedly turn up more prospects," Bradwell said, setting down his quill and sprinkling sand on the freshly inked name. "Wouldn't be a bit surprised if we ended up with a dozen or so names." He held out the list to Lucian.

Lucian sighed inwardly as he took the paper. He hoped so. For Alys, he was going to need a very long list indeed.

* * *

How dare she! The nerve of the chit! Lucian turned on his heels as he reached the marble hearth and resumed his agitated pacing in the opposite direction. She must be possessed. What else could explain her awful behavior?

"I came as soon as I received your message, Luc," a feminine voice cut into his brooding. "Whatever is so urgent that you would send for me at this ungodly hour of the morning?"

Lucian whipped around so quickly that his head spun. He'd been so deeply engrossed in his thoughts that he hadn't heard the door open. "Charlotte. Thank God," he expelled in a sigh, more glad to see his sister than he'd ever been to see anyone in his life.

"By the pressing nature of your note, I half expected to find you on your deathbed," she said, peeling off her lemon-yellow gloves. "The lines, 'Come posthaste. Regards matter of grave concern,' generally mean that someone has died, is dangerously ill, or at the very least is in jail."

"It's worse than that. Much worse."

"What could be worse than death?" she asked, looking up with a frown.

"My new ward." Lucian more groaned than spoke the words.

Charlotte watched in amazement as her eternally self-possessed brother ran his hand through his perfectly brushed hair, worrying it into a wild disarray. The chit must be beyond terrible, for this was the first time in her thirty-six years that she had ever seen Lucian perturbed.

Firmly grasping his arm, she led him across the drawing room to a blue brocade sofa, clucking, "Now, now. I'm certain things aren't as bad as all that. Why don't we sit here"—she sank down on the sofa, patting the cushion next to her—"and you can tell me all about the girl."

Instead of sitting, Lucian resumed his pacing directly in front of her. "She's awful," he ranted. "Her behavior is wretched beyond all tolerance. If I were a papist, I'd send for a priest to exorcise whatever is possessing her."

Charlotte leaned forward a fraction in her intrigue. "What exactly did the girl do that was so dreadful?" she held her breath as she awaited his reply, expecting a tale of heinous deeds and demonic behavior.

"She tore up the list!" The words were flung with as much outrage as if he were accusing her of burning down the house.

"List?" She frowned. "What list?"

"The list of prospective suitors I made up for her." His stride speeded to a jog. "I presented it to her at breakfast, along with the pertinent details of each man such as his title, land holdings, and annual income."

Charlotte's head bobbed from side to side as she watched him race to and fro. "What exactly did you expect her to do with the list?"

"Look it over and decide which man she thought might best suit her." He made a derisive noise. "Last time I listen to Stephen. It was his suggestion that I offer her a choice. Said it would make her more amenable to the idea of marriage." He flailed his arms in a broad gesture of chagrin. "Instead she tore it up without so much as a glance, saying that husbands aren't saddles of mutton to be ordered from a menu."

"For the love of God, Luc! Will you cease pacing and sit down?" Charlotte exclaimed, grabbing the flying tail of his coat as he passed. "I'm getting a headache watching you."

Scowling and muttering something that sounded suspiciously like "the damn brass-faced hellion," he heaved himself into the chair opposite the sofa.

Charlotte stifled a smile as she looked at his flushed face. It really was amusing when you thought about it: the unflappable Marquess of Thistlewood thrown into a pucker by a mere girl. Why, she'd seen him remain coolly unmoved in situations that would have made a saint resort to violence.

Returning her gaze with an expression of . . . could that be bewilderment? . . . he groaned, "You're a woman, Lottie. What do you make of such behavior?"

She sighed and shook her head. "You honestly don't see, do you?"

"See what?" Yes. That definitely was bewilderment on his face.

"How you upset that poor girl. She's been under your

roof less than a day, and you're already trying to rid yourself of her. You've made her feel as unwanted as the pox."

"I'll take the pox any day," he muttered darkly. "I'd at least have a prayer of getting rid of it."

"I'm certain you're exaggerating her faults. Surely she isn't so very awful?"

"Not if you happen to like stunted, pasty-faced termagants who smell like a parade of unwashed beggars."

"Dear me." She stared at him in shock. "Are you telling me that the girl actually smells?"

He nodded. "Her stench is the only thing that saved her from being turned over my knee and receiving a well-deserved spanking when she tore up that list."

Charlotte made a clucking noise. "Perhaps the poor thing was never taught the virtue of cleanliness and just needs to be taken in hand."

"Are you suggesting that I discuss the problem with her?" He couldn't have looked more flabbergasted if she'd suggested that he toss her in the tub and scrub her himself.

"Of course not," she retorted, staring at him in wonder. Lucian, flabbergasted? Unheard of!

He made a helpless gesture. Helpless? Odder and odder. "Then what do you suggest I do?"

"Hire a mature, experienced abigail to guide her. I'll ask around and see if I can't arrange to have a suitable woman sent over within the next day or so."

"Hopefully the woman will be clever enough to do something to improve her appearance as well, though"— Lucian grimaced—"I suspect that that's asking a bit much of a mere mortal."

"You might be surprised by what a clever lady's maid can accomplish. I have seen them work miracles with the aid of a fashionable wardrobe and a pot of rouge."

He grunted. "We're going to need a miracle. You can only improve on nature so much, and nature was shockingly stingy with Alys."

"Still, unless she is afflicted with some sort of deformity, which I assume she isn't . . ." She slanted him a querying look.

"If you don't count being blonde a deformity, then no."

She sniffed at his comment. "In case it has escaped your notice, I happen to be blonde. And nobody has ever seen that feature as being anything but an asset."

Lucian eyed her hair critically. "I never considered you a blonde. Your hair is too dark . . . more brown than yellow."

"Nonetheless, I'm judged a blonde."

He shrugged. "Then I stand corrected. It seems that not all blondes are drab, colorless creatures."

She sniffed again, not a bit placated. "Considering your prejudice against blondes, it might be best if I meet your ward and judge her potential for myself."

"As you wish." Lucian sauntered to the door and summoned the butler, who appeared almost instantly. After bidding him to bring the girl to the drawing room, he returned to his chair. As he settled, a maid entered bearing a tray of refreshments. All discussion of Alys ceased while Charlotte poured tea and doled out jam-filled Naples biscuits and slices of saffron cake. She was just complimenting Lucian on the excellent baking skills of his cook when there was a scratch at the door.

"Enter," Lucian commanded.

Charlotte turned in her seat to look toward the door, while Lucian set down his cup and rose to his feet as dictated by good manners.

"Miss Faire," Tidswell intoned, ushering a petite, black-clad figure into the room. Apparently the girl wasn't as ill bred as Lucian seemed to think, for she sketched a most genteel curtsy.

"Come in, Alys," Lucian more ordered than invited. "My sister has expressed a wish to meet you."

Charlotte smiled her encouragement. "Please, dear. Do take tea with us." Without thinking, she patted the cushion next to her, only to regret the gesture in the next instant. What if the chit smelled as foul as Lucian claimed?

With an obedience she hadn't expected from the hoyden described by her brother, the girl nodded and did as she was told. Charlotte didn't miss the grace with which she moved, nor was she blind to the elegance of her figure that was all but shrouded by her bombazine mourning gown. As she came to a stop by Lucian's chair, politely awaiting an introduction, Charlotte studied her serene face.

This was the dreadful ward? Why the child was lovely, beautiful in truth. No doubt many a glass would be raised in toast to her pale golden hair and wide azure eyes once the young bucks got a glimpse of her.

After being properly presented, Alys perched on the edge of the sofa next to Charlotte. Discreetly sniffing in her direction, Charlotte handed her a cup of tea. Lily of the Valley. Hardly a stench, unless her brother had a prejudice against Lily of the Valley equal to that against blondes. She shot him a quizzical look.

He made a face as if to say, "See, I told you she was awful," then focused his attention on his cake.

"But, Lucian, she's enchanting," she said, feeling the need to defend the poor child.

To his credit, he didn't snort or make any other derisive noise. Instead, he drawled, "I'm glad you approve. I was hoping to persuade you to help me ready her for the coming season."

Charlotte reached over and gave Alys's cheek a pat, noting with approval the fine texture of her skin. "It would be my pleasure, Luc. I'm certain Alys and I shall get on famously. Shan't we, my dear?"

"Yes. I believe we shall," Alys agreed, liking Charlotte immediately. It stunned her to believe that this gracious lady had sprung from the same loins as Lord Tight-Arse, as Hedley persisted in calling him. Smiling demurely as the woman outlined her plans for the season, she slanted Lucian an appraising look.

Would Lord Tight-Arse lose his chilly hauteur and become more like his warm sister as his soul grew? She sighed soundlessly. She certainly hoped so. If he was to develop a nature as handsome as his face and form, he would be very easy for a woman to love.

"My dear?"

Alys looked up to see Charlotte peering at her expectantly. Casting the woman an apologetic look, she murmured, "Excuse me. I was, um"—she glanced at the cup in her hand—"trying to determine what sort of tea this is."

"In the future, I shall expect you to be attentive to my sister's every word," Lucian snapped. "Understood?"

"Now, now, Luc. There is no need to scold the girl," Charlotte chided. "It speaks well of her housekeeping skills to take notice of an exotic blend of tea." After giving her brother what Alys thought was a rather intimidating glare, she turned to her saying, "It's Bohea tea, from China. Luc refuses to drink anything else."

Alys nodded. "I can see why. It's delicious."

"Well, at least her taste in teas is something in her favor," she thought she heard Lucian mutter. However, when she glanced over at him, he seemed totally absorbed in eating his cake.

"What I was asking you, Alys, was how long you've been in mourning," Charlotte said.

Oddly enough, Alys was enjoying watching Lucian eat. He truly was a handsome man, and a perfectly agreeable one when his mouth was occupied with something other than talking. With great reluctance she transferred her gaze to Charlotte's pretty face. "Since June," she replied. "My brother died at Waterloo."

"Of course. How bird-witted of me to forget. Luc told me all about your brother's noble sacrifice." A faint frown puckered her smooth brow as she set down her cup. "What I don't understand is why it took so long for Luc to be informed of his guardianship."

"None of us were aware that Bevis wished Lord Thistlewood to be my guardian," Alys explained, repeating the story Allura had given her. "Not until his solicitor returned from the continent last month and informed us of the recently added codicil."

"And glad we are that he added it," Charlotte exclaimed, clasping Alys's free hand between both of hers. "Lucian and I owe your brother a great debt, one too immense for us to ever fully repay. I do hope, however, that you shall permit us a small measure of satisfaction by allowing us to see to your welfare. I'm certain my brother intends to do everything in his power to see to your happiness, as do I. Isn't that so, Luc?"

Lucian grunted and took a sip from his cup.

Taking that grunt for an affirmative, Charlotte continued, "Our first bit of business must be to get you out of mourning. Since it ended last month, no one can accuse you of disrespect if you add a dash of color to your wardrobe." She eyed Alys thoughtfully. "With your delicate complexion, I would suggest soft hues like pale pink, celestial blue, and willow green. Maybe even white, though we shall have to try it to be certain."

Shifting her attention to Lucian, who looked supremely bored by the whole conversation, she directed, "You must send a note around to Madame Fanchon's shop immediately, Luc."

Lucian's dark brows drew together, his boredom vanishing like a wind fairy in the air. "Me send the note?"

"Yes, you," Charlotte confirmed adamantly. "Madame is all the rage, and engaging her services this close to the season is as difficult as gaining an audience with the King when he's having one of his spells. Why, I heard she turned away the Duchess of Lyndonbury and her two daughters just last week."

His bewilderment was back. "What makes you think she'll accept my request?"

"Your handsome face and dashing reputation."

To Alys's gleeful surprise, his jaw dropped visibly at his sister's blunt response. "Excuse me?"

"You heard me correctly," she said, giving Alys a mischievous wink. "Like half the women in London, Madame Fanchon read of your battlefield heroics in the newspaper and fancies herself quite in love with you. No doubt she will accept your request just so she can make your acquaintance."

He made an impatient sound at the back of his throat. "I have neither the time nor the inclination to sit around some dressmaker's shop playing abigail. If you can't get this Madame Fanchon's services without using me as bait, then find another modiste. I'm sure there are plenty in London."

"But none like Madame," Charlotte protested. "Nobody is as clever as she at making the most of a woman's figure."

Lucian's gaze swept Alys's length. As if deciding from

that glance that her figure needed the most made of it, he heaved a sigh and mumbled, "What exactly would be required of me?"

Charlotte cast Alys a triumphant look. "Not so very much. You have simply to pen a note, then drive us to the shop at the appointed time. After escorting us inside and greeting Madame, you may go about your business. Just the prospect of seeing you when you drive Alys and I to fittings should be enough to entice her to provide us with her services."

His expression as pained as if he'd just had a tooth extracted, he growled, "Oh, all right. You win."

Alys bowed her head over her tea to hide her smile. She could cross losing off the list of lessons to be learned.

Chapter 4

It was a dismal morning, blustery and gray, with nary a ray of sunlight to cheer the winter gloom. Furious gales hurtled against the bedroom window, frosting the panes with icy crystals of sleet.

Alys hugged herself and burrowed deeper beneath her blankets, loath to leave the cocooning warmth of her bed.

"Time to get up now, miss," her new abigail, Lettie Deakins, prompted, tugging the embroidered coverlet down to her waist.

Alys gasped as a shock of cold penetrated the thin muslin of her nightgown. Her teeth chattering, she grabbed the covers and gave them a counter-tug, yanking them back up over her shoulders. For all that there was a fire blazing in the enormous gold and white fireplace, the room was freezing.

Lettie shook her head, disapproval lying heavy on her pinched features. "His lordship said that I'm to have you ready to leave for the dressmaker's by eleven o'clock. And"—she jerked the blankets from Alys's hands and flung them all the way to the foot of the bed—"ready you shall be."

"His lordship said?" Alys muttered, returning the other woman's scowl with one of her own. "Barked is more like it." In the four days since she'd arrived at the house, she had yet to hear Lucian utter a word in what she would classify as a pleasant tone. He snapped at her, no matter what she said or did, he growled at the servants and was positively brusque with his sister.

Sighing, she rolled from the bed and stepped onto the thick, plush carpet. Apparently everyone else in his acquaintance was used to his wretched disposition, for she was the only one who appeared disturbed by it. Indeed, Charlotte seemed to find it positively amusing.

Well, at least I won't have to spend much time in his disagreeable company today, she silently consoled herself, threading her arm through the sleeves of the black wool dressing gown Lettie held.

True to Charlotte's prediction, Madame Fanchon's response to Lucian's note had been swift and positive. And if all went as planned, it shouldn't take above a half hour for Lucian to drive them to the shop, give his regards to Madame, and then be on his way to do whatever it was he did to occupy himself during the day. Once she was rid of his surly presence, she would be free to enjoy several hours of shopping with Charlotte. She would also have the opportunity to ask her if Lucian was interested in any particular lady. It would be truly excellent if Charlotte said yes.

Alys smiled as Lettie steered her to a Chinese fretwork chair by the fire, and handed her a cup of steaming chocolate. Though she'd only met Charlotte twice, she felt as though she'd known her forever. There was something about the older woman's friendly smile and cordial manner that had put her instantly at ease both times.

As she finished her chocolate and went about her morning ablutions, her enthusiasm for the day ahead grew.

A new wardrobe. Releasing a rapturous sigh, she stepped into the muslin-lined copper bathtub. It had been almost five hundred years since she had worn anything pretty and fashionable, and just the prospect of doing so was heavenly.

During her centuries of matchmaking, she'd been allowed only the plainest and most unflattering of gowns . . . as if her homely guise wasn't frightful enough! Not, she had to admit, that some of the styles—horned headdresses, farthingales, and towering white-powdered wigs—were anything to mourn missing. It was just that

despite her efforts to curb her vanity, she still craved
finery and the effect it had on those around her. She
missed seeing men gaze at her with adoration, missed
their infatuated whispers and fawning flattery.

Slowly she sank into the liquid warmth of her bath,
savoring the spring-kissed sweetness of the Lily of the
Valley scented steam as it curled around her shoulders
and face. It wasn't that she longed to resume her heartless games. Indeed, she was so deeply shamed every time
she remembered her cruelty that she wondered if Aengus's punishment was perhaps a trifle too merciful.

No. What she desired were the worshipful glances and
passionate declarations of one special man. She yearned
for what every couple entrusted to her matchmaking had
found: true love.

But, of course, she would never get the chance to win
that most treasured of all emotional prizes if she didn't
find Lucian the woman of his destiny.

Suddenly depressed, she rose from the water and signaled for Lettie to help her out of her sodden bathing
shift. Apparently she looked as despondent as she felt,
for the woman's normally stern expression softened at
the sight of her. With a cheerfulness unexpected from
one so somber, the maid began to prattle about the won-
ders of the London shops. So rhapsodic were her descriptions that by the time Alys was laced into her
underclothes and hooked into her gown, she could
barely contain her eagerness to see the delights for
herself.

With visions of rainbow-hued gowns and ribbon-
bedecked bonnets dancing in her head, she hurried down
the stairs, bursting to quiz Charlotte about the Burl-
ington Arcade. Down she rushed, her feet barely touching the steps in her haste. Breathless as much from
excitement as from her mad dash, she leaped down the
last two steps . . . smack into a brick wall. One hasty
glance instantly informed her that the brick wall was
none other than Lucian Warre.

Weak-kneed and staggering from the impact, Alys instinctively flung her arms around his rigid form to steady
herself. Too shaky to move, she remained in that position for several seconds, her body crushed against his

with her face pressed into the crisp linen frills at his breast. Those few seconds, brief as they were, provided ample time for her to note the muscular strength beneath his clothes. And the way he smelled . . .

Without thinking, she burrowed her nose deeper into his shirt. Closing her eyes, she inhaled. Ah. He smelled wonderful, exactly like a man should smell: masculine, yet clean, like shaving soap mixed with musk.

Thoroughly entranced, she clung to him until he grasped her upper arms and shoved her away. That ungracious move snapped her out of her calf-eyed stupor as quickly as if he'd slapped her.

Whatever on earth had possessed her, she wondered, that she would cling to him like a lovesick goose with an unwilling beau? She didn't even like the foul-tempered beast, for God's sake! Confused and embarrassed, she managed, with much effort, to stammer, "S-sorry."

"You should be," he snapped, his slashing black brows drawing together over eyes as wrathful as thunderclouds. "You're late. I've been waiting for you a full five minutes." As if to prove her tardiness, he reached for his watch. Apparently he'd been studying it when she'd crashed into him, for the case was open and it was dangling on its black ribbon fob down the front of his buff trousers . . . his very tight, very revealing trousers, she couldn't help noticing.

Alys flushed and looked away when she realized exactly where she was staring. He not only smelled manly, he obviously was manly. Impressively so. Her face burned with shame at her own unmaidenly observation. Uneasily wondering if he had noticed her wanton scrutiny, she ventured a glance at him from beneath her lashes.

His nose was in the air, as usual, and he was gazing at something across the room that was apparently more worthy of his regard than she. She relaxed a fraction. Perhaps there was some advantage to being beneath his notice after all.

Still focusing on . . . was it that hideous oriental vase? . . . he directed harshly, "In the future, you shall be scrupulously punctual. Understood?"

"Umm, yes," she murmured, still too flustered to take offense at his high-handed tone.

Evidently her obedient response pleased him, for he smiled. Well, if you could call that tight, upward twitch of the corners of his mouth a smile. As she watched, his lips flattened back into their usual taut line. On second thought, it could just be that his breakfast was disagreeing with him.

He seemed about to add something, when Tidswell shuffled into the entry hall carrying his employer's coat, hat, and gloves. "Your carriage awaits you, my lord," he announced without any discernible movement of his lower jaw.

Without deigning to grace the servant with so much as a glance, Lucian extended his arms. Apparently dressing his lordship for outside excursions was part of Tidswell's customary duties, for he immediately slipped the coat sleeves over his outstretched arms.

It was all Alys could do to stifle a giggle as she watched the butler wrestle the multicaped garment over his master's shoulders, and then scamper around to button the front.

Was being dressed by a servant simply another display of the marquess's tyranny? Or could it be that he was so pampered as a child that he'd never learned to do the task himself? The titter she was struggling to suppress escaped as she pictured a helpless and bemused Lucian being coaxed into his underdrawers by his snotty valet.

That noise, faint as it was, drew the attention of her mirth's object. "I take it that you find something amusing?" The severity of his tone perfectly conveyed his disdain for humor of any sort.

For one brief instant she considered lying, then discarded the idea. By his haughty expression, it was apparent that no one had ever had the gall to laugh at him before. At least, not within his earshot. A smile crept across her lips. That meant that he was long overdue for a lesson in one of life's more unpleasant emotions: the indignity of being the object of ridicule.

Gesturing toward Tidswell, who was now fussily tugging at one of the coat's shoulder capes, she confessed,

"I find the sight of a grown, obviously competent man being dressed as if he were an infant rather funny. You would too if you could see how ridiculous you look, standing there all stiff while Tidswell primps you like an about-to-be-presented fashion doll."

The butler froze in the act of straightening his master's collar, his normally immobile jaw dropping in horrified shock. Lucian merely stared at her, his face utterly void of expression.

Taking his lordship's lack of response as a sign that he needed further instruction, she added, "What made me laugh, however, isn't the sight of you and Tidswell, as droll as it is." She shook her head. "But the notion that you might possibly be ignorant of how to dress yourself and thus require such services not out of arrogance, but out of necessity."

Slowly, Lucian's face darkened to that interesting shade of purple it had turned when she'd torn up his list. And yes, he was starting to get that same pained expression he'd gotten when Charlotte had bested him in the matter of the dressmaker.

Alys viewed her handiwork with satisfaction. Ah. She truly was a marvelous teacher. And as such, it was her duty to see to it that his soul got the utmost emotional growth from the lesson. With that end in mind, she goaded, "Well? Can you?"

"Can I what?" he spat from between clenched teeth.

"Dress yourself."

Shoving aside Tidswell, who had regained his dignity and was now adjusting his master's cuff, Lucian stalked toward Alys.

One look at his wrathful face was enough to send her previously soaring confidence crashing back to earth. This time she'd clearly gone too far.

Uneasily catching her lower lip between her teeth, she took a step backward. He looked furious enough to make good his thrice-delivered threat to turn her over his knee and give her a sound spanking. The thought of such humiliation was enough to send her into a stumbling retreat . . . a retreat that was thwarted when she tripped over the shallow bottom stair. Clawing frantically at air, she fought to regain her balance, then tumbled backward to land on the steps with derriere-bruising force.

Like a vulture spying a fresh kill, Lucian was on her in an instant. Emitting a noise that sounded alarmingly like a snarl, he grasped her arm and hauled her back to her feet. "Where the hell were you raised, Alys? In a stable?" he hissed, jerking her nearer until his anger-contorted face was almost pressed to hers.

Unwilling yet strangely compelled, she met his gaze with hers. The glow of the banking fury burning in his eyes was truly terrifying to behold. Thoroughly alarmed, she tried to look away, but he shoved his face yet nearer, completely filling her line of vision.

"You will look at me, just as you will listen to and heed my words," he growled, giving her a shake that rattled her teeth. "I have suffered your insolence thus far because I realize that you have lacked proper discipline, and therefore know no better. My tolerance, however, as endless as it might seem, does not extend to you mocking me. So be warned, Miss Faire: though you might not choose to like me, you damn well will show me respect." He gave her another shake. "Understood?"

Alys nodded as best she could with his face so close to hers. For the first time since they had met, she wasn't the slightest bit tempted to argue with him.

"Good." He released her so abruptly that she almost fell to the stairs again. "If you value the skin on your backside, you'll remember your agreement in the future." Without sparing her another glance, he turned on his heels and marched back to Tidswell.

The butler, ever mindful of his duty, held out his tall black hat and leather gloves. Snatching his hat from the servant's hand, Lucian jammed it on his head, then yanked on his gloves. Turning at profile, he snapped, "Unless you wish to anger the exalted Madame Fanchon and thus forfeit her services, I'd suggest that we leave now."

Alys started to obey, then stopped short, noting Charlotte's absence for the first time. "Shouldn't we wait for your sister?"

"She's not coming with us."

"What?" she gasped, dismayed at the notion of being alone in his company. So much for a pleasant day.

"I said that she shall not be accompanying us," he repeated, enunciating each syllable so that his words were unmistakable. "She sent a note around earlier informing me that she's feeling unwell. She implored me to take you to the dressmaker's myself, which I am doing only because I went to so much trouble to secure you an appointment."

"Look at me, Alys!" piped a voice from the top of the stairs.

Alys glanced sideways in time to see Hedley slide down the winding black and gold wrought-iron handrail. When he reached the spiraling finial, he let out a raucous whoop and in one froglike leap vaulted to the floor at her feet. Instantly she was engulfed in his nauseating odor.

Oblivious to, or more likely just ignoring, her faint gagging sounds, he cheerfully chimed, "Off to the dressmaker's are we?"

Trying to inhale as little as possible, Alys stole a glance over to where Lucian was selecting an umbrella from the somber-hued assortment now being presented by Tidswell. Since neither man was paying her the least bit of notice, she deemed it safe to hiss, "*I'm* going to the dressmaker's. *You're* staying here."

Apparently her hiss wasn't soft enough, for both men looked at her in query.

"Did you say something?" Lucian quizzed.

"Um—I—I said that I hoped your sister isn't seriously ill," she improvised, though once the words were out she was glad she'd uttered them. If Hedley hadn't distracted her, she'd have asked after Charlotte's health sooner.

He shook his head and returned his gaze to the umbrellas. "She shall be fine. She's just exhausted from passing a restless night. She said that she woke up this morning feeling as if she'd been pinched black and blue."

Alys slanted Hedley a suspicious look, recalling that bedevilment by pinching was reported to be his favorite sport.

"A-rgh! Don't ye be giving me the evil eye," the hob

objected, scratching his hairy potbelly with an offended air. "It must've been those Hyde Park Pillywiggin pixies that done it. They was sniggering about plaguing the bloody damn nobility last time I joined 'em in a tankard of wine."

She was conveying her disbelief via a scowl when Lucian snapped, "Stop dallying, Alys. We must be off. Now."

Glancing over to where he stood framed in the now open front door, she nodded. Under the cover of dropping and retrieving her reticule, she whispered firmly to the hob, "Stay here. And try to keep out of mischief. I shan't be gone long."

His thorny hand shifted from his belly to scratch his armpit. "Can't."

"You can and you will," she ordered, wondering with repugnance if there was such a thing as fairy lice.

He eyed her craftily. "Aengus said that I was to go everywhere with ye. And ye of all people should know that it ain't wise to cross his highness." Without waiting for her to reply—and indeed, what could she say?—he skipped toward the door, pausing once to stamp on Tidswell's foot. The butler flinched visibly, though whether from the abuse to his foot or from the hob's rank scent, it was impossible to tell.

Forlornly resigning herself to a wretched day, Alys followed.

The first thing she noticed as she joined Lucian outside was how pale and pinched he was looking all of a sudden. She was about to inquire if he was sickening with something when she caught a whiff of Hedley's stench and spied the little man merrily swinging from a vine near his head. Apparently the wicked hob was aware of his nauseating effect on his lordship, for he was furiously pumping his stubby legs so as to swing nearer to his face with every pass.

Alys sighed her exasperation. As if Lucian's disposition wasn't foul enough without such aggravation. Indeed, if it got much worse, even the infinitely powerful pull of destiny would be insufficient to induce a woman to love him.

Not willing to lose her immortal soul on account of

Hedley's tomfoolery, she casually reached up and grabbed hold of his vine. With the protesting hob still dangling from the end, she tossed it against the brick wall, pretending to be merely sweeping it out of the way.

There was a piercing screech, followed by a sharp "Oomph!" as the hob smashed against the wall. His face frozen into a mask of outraged astonishment, he slid to the ground where he sat shaking his head as if to jar his brains back into place.

Eyeing the greenery with disfavor, Lucian offered her his arm, muttering, "I must remember to speak to the gardener about pruning those vines. They smell as if something crawled in them and died."

Smiling blandly in agreement, Alys accepted his escort to the waiting carriage. A much subdued Hedley tagged several paces behind, muttering in hob gibberish beneath his breath.

When they reached the stylish black, green, and gold conveyance, Alys looked over her shoulder and jerked her head toward the driver, indicating that the hob was to ride outside with him. The little man pouted, but mercifully refrained from arguing. That bit of business concluded, she climbed into the carriage.

As Lucian settled into the opposite seat, he said, "The answer to your question is yes." At her querying look, he clarified, "Yes, I'm perfectly capable of dressing myself." With that he rapped on the ceiling signaling for the driver to proceed.

Though the dressmaker's shop was only a few blocks away, the crush of wagons, carts, and carriages combined with the narrowness and slipperiness of the icy streets made their progress slow.

After he'd apprised her of his ability to clothe himself, Lucian had lapsed into silence, leaving Alys free to rethink her foiled plans for the day. To her frustration, her gaze and mind kept straying to the man in the facing seat.

What was it about him that stirred her so? she wondered, remembering their collision at the foot of the stairs and how powerfully she'd been drawn by his nearness. It wasn't because he was handsome. She'd met dozens of attractive men over the centuries, a couple who, if she were to be brutally honest, had been better-looking than Lucian. Yet, for all their spectacular beauty not one had warranted more than a passing, albeit admiring, glance.

But, Lucian. Ah, well. He was a different story entirely. When he was in her presence, she couldn't seem to keep her eyes off him.

Like now. Squinting, she tried to discern his features. Between the gloom of the overcast day and the obscuring shadows from his hat brim, she was able to make out only his mouth and faintly clefted chin.

That tiny bit, however, was more than enough to distract her.

She stared at his lips as if fixated, which was exactly what she was at that moment. They were beautiful. Perfect in both size and shape. The upper one arched into a broad, well-defined bow, while the lower, more generous one swept into a sensuous curve. It was the sort of mouth that was meant to curl into a smile, the kind of lips that were created for kissing.

In that dreamy moment, Alys imagined what it would be like to kiss him; how it would feel to slowly press her lips to his and taste what lay beyond. Heat coiled deep in her belly as she imagined his tongue thrusting against hers, making her weak with pleasure as Lucan had done all those centuries ago. As she closed her eyes, licking her now tingling lips, the carriage lurched to a violent stop.

So limp from her fantasy was she that she was pitched forward out of her seat to land at Lucian's feet in a tangled heap of bombazine and wool. In the next instant, strong hands gripped her beneath her arms and she felt herself being hauled up.

"Good God! Are you hurt?" Lucian exclaimed, setting her on the seat beside him. At least that is where she assumed she sat, though she couldn't be certain. Her black velvet bonnet had been knocked over her face and she couldn't see a darn thing.

There was a plucking sensation at her hair, then her blinder was lifted. She was indeed sitting next to him. In fact, if she was to move three inches to her left, her

body could be touching his. Her toes curled from the
odd thrill of that knowledge.

"Are you hurt?" he repeated, bending nearer.

Alys looked up to say no, but the words stuck in her
throat. A hazy shaft of light filtered through the window,
illuminating his face; an impossibly handsome face that
was mere inches from hers; a face whose expression, if
she was to venture a guess, was one of grave concern.

The creases of his already furrowed brow deepening,
he cupped her chin in his palm and tipped her face into
the light to study it. As her gaze touched his, she again
felt an electrifying, inexplicable pull of attraction.

"Alys?" he uttered softly.

"Hmm?"

"Did you hit your head?"

"My . . . head?" She frowned, the exhilaration of his
nearness slowing her mind to the speed of a snail on hot
sand. "Um . . . no. Why do you ask?"

"Because you're looking at me strangely." His fath-
omless gray gaze swept her face. "Rather like a cow in
need of milking."

Alys continued staring at him for several moments as
his words fought to penetrate her foggy brain. When
they finally hit home, she jerked her chin from his hand
with an indignant gasp. A cow in need of milking, indeed! Why, the thick-skulled . . . dolt! No wonder he
was unable to find love on his own!

Insulted beyond outrage, and feeling like a ninnyhammer for even imagining herself attracted to him, she
snapped, "Of course I'm looking at you strangely. You—
you have something green stuck between your front
teeth."

To her wicked glee, he looked completely taken aback
by the notion of being less than immaculate. His expression almost comic in its chagrin, he screwed his mouth
this way and that, trying to dislodge the fictional green
thing with his tongue.

As the footman opened the door and folded down the
stairs, he tipped his face to hers and lifted his lips. "Did
I get it?"

Hiding her smile, Alys pretended to scrutinize his
straight white teeth. To her supreme discomfiture, she

couldn't help wondering what it would be like to run her tongue along those smooth, even ridges. Tempted beyond denying, she reached up and ran her gloved finger along the pearly edge, deliberately grazing the rosy lining of his upper lip in the process.

At that moment she wished as she'd never wished before that her hands were bare and that she could feel the texture of his mouth. Was it as satiny soft as it looked? Was his flesh cool as his demeanor, or was it warm with the heat of hidden passion?

"Is it gone?" he inquired from behind his bared teeth.

Distracted, as seemed to be her state every time she got near him, she frowned, slow to take his meaning. When she finally did, she snatched her hand away, mortified.

"I just got it," she mumbled. Hating herself for her weakness and wanting nothing more than to put a safe distance between them so she could regain her senses, she slid toward the door.

His hand shot out, staying her. "One moment, Alys."

Reluctantly she turned to face him, hoping upon hope that her cheeks weren't as red as they felt.

"Your bonnet," he said, reaching up to adjust her dreary mourning creation. "Charlotte would never forgive me if I let you meet London's premiere modiste looking like a hoyden." Giving the crape-trimmed brim one final tweak, he nodded his satisfaction. "There. You're ready to beard the lion in her den of fashion now."

Thus dismissed, Alys scrambled from the carriage as fast as she could. She'd rather face a whole pride of real lions than spend another moment confined in close quarters with Lucian Warre. For she knew without a doubt that the lions would be less frightening—and dangerous—than her disturbing new feelings for this man whose fate lay in him loving another woman.

Chapter 5

Lucian stared after Alys, completely dumbfounded as she flung herself from the carriage, tripping on the steps in her haste. She tottered precariously, and if not for the lightning reflexes of the footman she'd have come to grief for certain.

What in God's name is wrong with the chit? he wondered, releasing his breath in a sigh of relief as his servant navigated her safely to the walkway. One minute she was goading him until his hand itched to strangle her, only to lapse into a witless, staring stupor in the next. And now she was fleeing from him like she were a fox and he were the leader of a pack of pursuing hunting hounds. She was the queerest, most eccentric—

Eccentric! There was an awful sinking sensation in the pit of his stomach. Bloody hell. That was it. The girl was one of those dreadful sort of females who were every father's or guardian's worse nightmare . . . she was an eccentric. What other explanation could there be for her rattle-pate ways?

As if to confirm his hideous suspicion, she glanced from right to left, then hunched over and began muttering furiously to a traffic-flattened rat in the gutter. The sight made his sinking feeling bottom with a violence that left him in desperate need of a dyspepsia tonic. With his luck of late, she probably thought herself some celestial being whose divine mission in the world was to resurrect dead rats.

Seriously considering marching down to the Horse
Guards Parade and impaling himself on the first bayonet
he saw, Lucian disembarked from the carriage. Alys was
still stooped over, whispering to the rodent when he
came up behind her.

"No, no. You shall stay outside," she was directing in
a severe tone. "I shan't have you following me into the
dressmaker's and stinking up the whole shop."

He stood there unnoticed for several seconds, uncer-
tain for the first time in his life what to say or do. How
did one address a madwoman who was babbling to a
dead rat as if it were her lapdog? Should he try to return
her to her senses by pointing out that the animal was
deceased and therefore unlikely to follow her anywhere?
Or should he save himself a possible scene by humoring
her in her lunacy?

The sight of Lady Jersey, the fiercest of the Almack
dragons, stepping from her carriage just four doors down
quickly settled the question for him. It was going to be
difficult enough getting Alys to the altar, what with her
wishy-washy looks and scrambled wits, without adding
the shame of being denied a voucher to Almack's to her
ever-expanding list of shortcomings.

Praying that his ruse would work, he leaned over and
assured her in a low voice, "I believe that you've adequately lectured your friend. He doesn't appear inclined
to follow you."

She straightened up with a gasp, smashing her head
into his jaw in the process. Yelping once, he stumbled
back a step, convulsively clutching at his abused face.

Seemingly oblivious to the fact that she'd probably
loosened every tooth in his mouth, she exclaimed, "You
can see him?"

He squinted at her through a galaxy of shooting stars,
his mouth too disabled from the blow to reply. She was
gaping at him with as much amazement as he'd expect
if he had admitted to seeing a troupe of dancing fairies.

Gingerly rubbing his aching jaw, he finally managed
to grit out, "Of course, I can see him." As the words
left his mouth, his nostrils were suddenly assaulted by
an odor vilely reminiscent of the one he'd smelled by

his front door earlier. Casting the rat a jaundiced look, he added, "I can smell him too."

She hung her head as if the rat's odorous shame were her own. "I tried to get him to bathe in lavender water this morning but—" She broke off abruptly, her gaze veering sharply back to the mangled scrape of fur in the gutter. She appeared to listen to something, probably the carcass's imaginary voice, then nodded. "You're right, of course. My apologies. It was terribly rude of me. Please do proceed."

She observed the rat in silence for several moments, then looked back up at him expectantly. When he merely returned her gaze, she frowned and prompted, "Well?"

"Well, what?" he countered, praying that Lady Jersey wouldn't remove her nose from the air long enough to notice them hovering over the gutter.

She braced her hands on what, had she had a figure, would have been her hips, peering at him with marked disapproval. "Don't tell me that you don't know how to respond when someone tenders you an introduction?"

Lucian shifted his gaze from her censorious face to the carcass at their feet. Grimacing, he looked away. Surely she didn't expect him to murmur an inane pleasantry and shake the loathsome creature's death-curled forepaw?

One quick look back at her face assured him that that was exactly what she meant for him to do. Wishing that he'd followed his first instinct and sought a bayonet, he slanted a hopeful glance in Lady Jersey's direction. If the woman had already entered the shop, then he could safely put an end to this nonsense without fear of scandal.

But no. In keeping with his recent run of bad luck, she stood a scant dozen meters away, instructing her driver. Groaning inwardly, he returned his gaze to the gutter.

Hastily comparing the brief discomfort of touching a dead rat to the long-term aggravation of being stuck with Alys, he grudgingly murmured, "It is a pleasure to meet you, sir."

As he reluctantly prepared to kneel down and shake the rat's paw, she suddenly chimed in, "Hedley."

He stopped short. "Excuse me?"

"Hedley. His name is Hedley Bragg," she informed him in a matter-of-fact tone.

At a loss as how to best respond to her revelation, he vaguely replied, "That's an--ah—unusual name for a rat."

"Rat?" she echoed, gaping at him as if it were he, not she, who was crazy.

"Of course Hedley is a rat." He nodded down at the stiff creature and gave it an indicative nudge with his toe. "What would you call him?"

Her eyes widened, as if seeing the rat for the first time. Flushing a rather alarming shade of purple, she backed away from the gutter, stammering, "M-m-mouse. I thought he was a m-mouse."

Lucian watched, more confused than ever, as she flattened herself against the shop window. Rat. Mouse. The only difference that he could see was size. Apparently to her, however, the name discrepancy represented something significantly more sinister than mere physical dimensions, for she looked horrified enough to faint.

Completely at wit's end as to how to deal with the situation, he decided to gamble on changing the subject. After assuring himself that Lady Jersey hadn't witnessed his ward's peculiar performance, he offered Alys his arm, suggesting, "Shall we see what sort of finery this Madame Fanchon has to offer?"

He could have sworn that she looked relieved as she accepted his escort, though with her being mad and all he wasn't sure if her expression reflected her thoughts. At any rate she meekly followed his lead, which was all that mattered to him at that moment.

Oh, perfect! Now he thinks I'm as nutty as an almond fritter. No doubt our next errand will be to commit me to Bedlam, Alys thought, hanging her head to hide her burning face behind her bonnet brim. How could she have been such a hen-wit? Of course Lucian couldn't see Hedley.

After centuries of living in the otherworld, she knew that it was a rare human indeed who could honestly claim to have seen a fairy. The few who could did so either through the grace of the fairy himself or, as happened in two exceptional instances, because the person had a particularly sensitive soul and was therefore receptive to their presence.

Being as well aware of these facts as she was, whatever had made her think that Lucian Warre could see the hob? Especially when it was so obvious that he had neither Hedley's favor or a sensitive soul.

Wishing that she possessed Aengus's power to erase human memory, she followed Lucian through the shop door. By the look on his face just now when he'd announced that Hedley was a rat, it was clear that nothing short of magic was going to make him forget this mortifying incident. She certainly wasn't going to forget it. Not if she lived another five centuries. Not even if—

"Well, we can't complain about a lack of selections," Lucian commented, interrupting her pessimistic thoughts.

Instinct more than desire made Alys lift her head to view the contents of the shop. She blinked once to confirm that what she was seeing was real, then—

Poof! The shameful memory vanished in a puff of feminine delight.

Oh, such riches! Silks, satins, muslins, and velvets of every hue and texture were piled high on tables and shelves. Against one wall stood a cabinet whose doors were flung open to reveal roll after roll of extricate lace. Arranged neatly on a rack next to it were reels of ribbon and trims, above which were draped a kaleidoscopic array of feathered boas. In short, there was everything a woman might need to construct a fashionable gown.

Throughly entranced, Alys paused to finger a soft length of velvet, then moved on to examine a printed muslin. As beautiful as these fabrics were, they were forgotten the instant her gaze fell on a length of silk spilling across a table near the window. Suddenly blind to everything else, she walked over to it, drawn as surely as if it were calling her name.

Her breath bated with awe, she reverently lifted one corner. It reminded her of the wind-whisperers' wings:

gossamer sheer with the sparkling iridescence of a rainbow passing through a prism. It was beyond exquisite.

"Eet ees woven at a monastery in ze Himalaya mountains," informed a heavily accented female voice. *"Magnifique, oui?"*

Alys looked up to see a trim, dark-haired woman of middle years gliding through the red velvet curtain at the rear of the shop. "It's the most marvelous thing I've ever seen," she admitted.

"As eet should be. Eet takes ten years to weave enough for just one gown." Coming to a stop next to Lucian, the woman dropped a regal curtsy. "Madame Fanchon. At your service, my lord."

By the way the woman was gazing at him, you would think that he was a godlike cross between St. George and Tristam. Alys suppressed her smile. Apparently those newspaper stories had romanticized him even more than she thought.

Nodding briefly in acknowledgment, Lucian said, "And this is my ward, Miss Faire. As I mentioned in my note, she shall require a complete wardrobe for the coming season."

The dressmaker smiled at Alys. "Eet will be my pleasure to dress la petite mademoiselle. Between myself and Lady—" She paused to look around her. "But where ees your charming sister? Your note said that she would make ze selections today."

Lucian shrugged one shoulder and began to peel off his gloves. "Regrettably she was unable to accompany us today, so the task has fallen to me. With your knowledgeable assistance, I trust that we shall be able to accomplish it satisfactorily?"

"Oui! More zhan satisfactorily. As I always tell ze papas in town to catch zheir daughters ze husbands: who better to select gowns to pleeze ze masculine eye zhan a man?" Having imparted that decidedly French bit of wisdom, she returned to the curtain, her movements as smooth as if she had wheels instead of legs beneath her skirt.

Clapping loudly, she called out, "Claudine! Come at once!"

As if from thin air a rawboned, copper-haired woman

of no more than twenty materialized. It was clear from the way her face lit up when she was introduced to Lucian that the stories of his battlefield heroics were favored reading at the shop. As she stood gaping at him, her mouth ajar and her green-eyed gaze riveted on his face, Madame made a sharp hissing sound. Apparently the hiss was a reprimand of sorts, for she blushed and promptly bobbed a curtsy.

Turning from her properly chastised subordinate to Alys, who still stood by the fairy wing fabric, the dressmaker said, "Miss Faire, zhis ees my assistant, Claudine. Eef you will pleeze follow her to ze fitting room, she will help you disrobe. I will be back shortly to measure you myself."

Casting the wonderful silk one last covetous glance, Alys followed the young woman through the curtain, down a short hallway, and into a small square room dominated by a large mirror.

After taking her bonnet and helping her from her pelisse, Claudine said, "If you please, miss, I will unhook your gown now." In contrast to Madame, her French accent was barely discernible.

Alys nodded and presented the woman with her back. She was just stepping out of her gown when Madame entered the room carrying a parchment measure. The dressmaker waited until Alys was divested of her petticoat before circling around her, examining her figure from every angle.

"You are how old, mademoiselle?" she asked after her third rotation.

"Nineteen," she lied, just as Allura had told her to do. After all, she could hardly admit to being five hundred and sixteen years old, could she?

The woman eyed Alys's meager bosom critically. "I would have guessed seventeen. Ah, well." She shrugged and fitted the measure around Alys's lower hips. "Ees good. Men like zheir brides to have ze innocent looks, no?" She paused to call the measurement to Claudine, who dutifully recorded it, then shifted the notched parchment ribbon to encircle her upper hips. "With your sweet face and ze wardrobe I shall sew for you, you

will make a very fine match. And zhat will pleeze your
handsome guardian, *oui*?"

"Yes," Alys agreed. Madame had no idea just how
pleased he'd be, especially now, after the rat episode.
Just thinking about the awful incident was enough to
make her cheeks burn with shame.

A slow smile curved the dressmaker's lips as she studied Alys's face. "Aah. La petite mademoiselle turns pink
as a geranium at ze mention of her guardian. Could eet
be zhat she has tender feelings for him?" She chuckled
softly and looped the measure around Alys's waist, tugging it until it was snug. "Not zhat I blame you. He ees
most *magnifique, n'cest-ce pas*?"

Tender feelings, for Lucian? Her? Ha! How did one
say exasperating clod in French? She was about to voice
denial when Madame let out a sigh and said, "So slim
in ze waist. Ees good. Eet makes my job simpler not to
have to hide a middle like a cow." Nodding her satisfaction, she turned and chattered something in French to
Claudine.

Unendurably disturbed that anyone, even the dressmaker, might think that she was infatuated with Lucian,
she interrupted Claudine's seemingly endless reply, saying, "Er—about Lord Thistlewood."

Claudine promptly fell silent, while Madame turned
back to face her, a small, all-knowing smile on her lips.
"So I am correct. You do desire ze handsome marquess, no?"

"No. I—"

"And you want to know eef his heart ees free," she
continued on as if Alys hadn't spoken.

The last sentence froze Alys's protests in her throat.
Regarding the dressmaker with a little bit of wonder and
a whole lot of hope, she inquired, "You know about
such things?"

Madame laughed as if it were the most ridiculous
question she'd ever heard. "But of course! What do you
zhink ze ladies talk about when I fit zheir gowns?"

"They speak of Lord Thistlewood?" Alys couldn't
keep her rising amazement from her voice.

Obviously that question was more absurd than the
first, for even Claudine tittered this time. Smiling her

indulgence like a patient governess with a backward pupil, the dressmaker replied, "Zhey talk of notzhing else since his return to London."

"And what are they saying?"

"Mostly zhey wonder eef he will be looking for a bride this season, and try to guess who eet will be eef he does."

It was all Alys could do to keep from clapping her hands in delight. Such luck was almost too grand to be believed! Struggling not to appear overeager, she murmured, "Oh? And who do they think it might be? Does he appear to favor one lady in particular?" *Oh, please, Lord. Let the answer be yes.*

The dressmaker viewed her thoughtfully for a moment, then slowly shook her head. "Several names have come up, zhough his lordship hasn't shown much interest in any of zhem."

"But what about Reina Castell?" Claudine interjected. "He's shown plenty of interest in her. He bought her those—"

Madame emitted another of her hissing reprimands and shot her assistant a look that was clearly meant to silence her. The young woman flushed as pink as if she'd just committed the world's worst faux pas, and promptly bowed her head back over her writing.

"Reina Castell?" Alys quizzed, latching on to the tidbit like a terrier with a rat.

"She ees—how do I say?—a friend of his lordship. Notzhing more," Madame muttered, resuming her measuring.

Alys digested that morsel of information as she lifted her arms to allow the dressmaker access to her rib cage and chest. Friends? Hmm. She had successfully matched several couples who had started out as friends. Indeed, theirs had turned out to be some of the strongest marriages. Deciding that this Reina Castell merited further investigation, she inquired, "Is Miss, or is it Lady, Castell a patron of yours?"

Madame meticulously adjusted and readjusted the measure around her bust. When it was positioned to her satisfaction, she replied slowly, "She ees a miss, and *oui,* of late she has been a customer."

Alys waited for her to elaborate, but the dressmaker remained silent, her previously gregarious mood visibly mellowed to reticence. Not willing to relinquish the chance to learn about the woman who might be Lucian's destined true love, she prodded, "And what does Miss Castell have to say about his lordship?"

Madame darted a pointed glance in Claudine's direction. "Notzhing zhat Lord Thistlewood would wish me to repeat."

"But—" Alys protested.

"But enough!" the dressmaker cut her off. "His lordship has made eet clear zhat his relationship with Miss Castell ees a private affair, and not to be discussed. Besides, we must finish zheese measurements and rejoin him before he grows impatient." By the firm set of her jaw, it was clear that the subject was closed.

Ah. So Lucian jealously guards the details of his relationship with this Castell woman, Alys mused, straightening her spine at Madame's request. A very encouraging sign indeed. For as centuries of matchmaking had taught her: only men in love refrained from boasting about their conquest of a woman.

So certain was she that such was the case in this instance, that by the time Madame had finished measuring her, she was convinced that Reina Castell was destined to be Lady Thistlewood.

Grinning inwardly, she congratulated herself on her own cleverness. Now all she needed to do was devise a plan to bring the couple to the altar and—poof!—she had her human life back. Before she could do so, however, she must first find out more about the future bride.

But how? She stole a glance at Madame, who had taken the quill from Claudine and was now making some final notations on her chart. No. She could scratch the dressmaker off her list. Aside from asking her to lift this, or straighten that, the woman hadn't spoken to her at all as she had taken the remaining measurements.

Alys sighed and looked away. Perhaps Charlotte might be able to tell her something. Then again, probably not. If Lucian was as tight-lipped about Miss Castell as Madame had indicated, then it was unlikely that he'd discussed the matter with anyone, not even his sister.

No. What she had to do was find someone who actually knew the woman and was privy to her secrets.

"Claudine will help you dress now," Madame said, gathering up her charts and measure. "Pleeze join Lord Thistlewood and me in ze front when you are finished. We will be looking at ze fashion sketches." Giving her a warm smile, perhaps in amends for her earlier chilliness, the dressmaker exited the room.

As the door closed behind her, Claudine appeared by Alys's side holding her petticoat and gown. After neatly draping the gown over the Windsor chair that sat left of the mirror, the young assistant knelt in front of her with the petticoat. Spreading the waistband open, she held the garment at Alys's feet and indicated that she was to step into it.

Peering down at the woman with sudden interest, she obliged. Hmm. Perhaps Claudine was just the person to give her the information she needed. After all, it was she who had brought up Reina Castell. Never one to be shy when it came to anything related to fulfilling a matchmaking goal, Alys asked, "Do you assist all the ladies like this?"

The woman nodded as she drew the narrow petticoat up over Alys's hips, then moved around to her back to fasten it. "It is my job as Madame's assistant to dress and undress the patrons."

"Then you have attended to Reina Castell?"

She could feel Claudine's hands hesitate in her task of securing the petticoat. After several seconds of silence, she replied in a small voice, "Yes."

"And she has mentioned Lord Thistlewood?"

Another lengthy pause and then, "Yes." Her voice was almost inaudible now.

Alys waited until the woman had finished fussing with her petticoat and was reaching for her gown before continuing her interrogation. "Did Miss Castell, by chance, mention just how close her relationship with his lordship is?"

Apparently Madame's hisses weren't reprimands, but threats, for the girl looked terrified enough by her question to flee. Nervously smoothing the gown in her arms, she stammered, "I-I—uh—M-Madame Fanchon strictly f-forbids her workers to repeat gossip."

"But she won't know unless we tell her, now will she?" Alys retorted in a soothing tone. "And I promise you that I shan't repeat a word of anything you tell me."

Claudine looked up from the gown to meet her gaze with troubled eyes. "Excuse me for asking, miss. But are you wanting to know all this because you have feelings for his lordship like Madame said?"

"Hardly!" Alys expelled more forcefully than she'd intended.

The woman looked taken aback by the vehemence of her denial.

Cursing herself for her lack of finesse, she grappled for a way to justify her response. Thinking quickly as she spoke, she explained, "What I meant is that I wouldn't presume to think that someone of Lord Thistlewood's stature would lower himself to marry someone like me, an untitled miss." She shook her head. "My reason for asking about Miss Castell has nothing to do with me, but with his lordship's sister, Charlotte, uh, Lady Glassenbury. You know her, I believe?"

Claudine nodded. "She's most kind. She gave me three crowns at Christmas."

Alys smiled at her response. "Yes, she is a gracious lady. She's also sick with worry over her brother. That is why she was unable to accompany us here today . . . she was simply too exhausted from fretting to move from her bed."

"Oh! Her poor, dear ladyship!" The woman crushed Alys's gown to her breast in her distress. "If only there was something I could do for her."

"Ah. But there is. In truth, you might be the only one who can help her."

Claudine let out a surprised squeak and pointed to herself as if to ask, "Me?"

Alys nodded. "You see, Claudine, Lord Thistlewood has been most lonely and miserable since the war ended. Her ladyship is certain that a bride is just what he needs to brighten his life. Now since he refuses to give her so much as a hint as to what sort of woman he might favor, she has no idea where to start in her matchmaking quest.

That is why I was so interested in learning if your re-mark about him fancying Miss Castell was true."

"Oh, I—I see." Claudine chewed her lower lip for a few moments, as if torn between loyalty to the generous Countess of Glassenbury and fear of disobeying Madame's rules. Loyalty defeated fear, for after shooting a nervous glance at the door, she whispered, "Yes. It's true that his lordship fancies her."

"And what is she like?" Alys quizzed in a low voice.

Claudine slipped the gown over Alys's head. "Very beautiful. Black hair and eyes to match. It's said that his lordship prefers dark women with voluptuous figures."

"And what makes you so certain that he prefers Miss Castell to all the other pretty brunettes in London?" Alys inquired, emerging from the enveloping folds of silk.

"She says so." The girl stole another glance at the door, then leaned forward a fraction to confide in a whis-per, "And it must be true, because he paid for the last five gowns she ordered. One even had swansdown trim."

It must be true indeed, Alys thought as Claudine nim-bly fastened the row of tiny copper hooks at her back. It made sense that Lucian would want his bride to be elegantly garbed. She was just about to ask the other woman if she thought that Reina Castell would make Lord Thistlewood a good wife when there was a knock at the door.

"Claudine?" called a lilting female voice.

Claudine looked alarmed, clearly worried that their discussion might have been overheard. Biting her lip once, as if to stop its trembling, she responded hoarsely, "Yes?"

"Lady Biddleton is here for the final fitting on her riding habit. Madame has requested that you do it. I'm to finish helping Miss Faire."

Looking relieved enough to collapse, Claudine pulled the door open to reveal a thin, wiry-looking girl of about thirteen. "Miss Faire is all dressed," she said, motioning over to where Alys stood. "You have only to escort her to Madame and Lord Thistlewood."

Feeling as if this were the luckiest day of her life, and indeed it might be if her hunch about Miss Castell was correct, Alys followed the girl to the front of the shop. There she found a frustrated-looking Madame Fanchon flashing fashion sketches before the eyes of a visibly bored Lucian.

"And zhis one ees most stylish," she was saying. "See ze Ilchester braces?" She tapped the feature with one long finger and flashed him a strained smile. It was obvious that, as usual, he was being completely unreasonable.

As Alys came to stand beside his chair, the dressmaker bound to her feet, exclaiming, "Ah! Miss Faire. At last. Perhaps now zhat you are here, his lordship will see how lovely zheese gowns will look on you." As if to demonstrate, she pulled Alys to stand next to her and held up the sketch for his reference.

He merely frowned and shook his head.

The dressmaker sighed and tossed the drawing aside. After contemplating the man before her for several seconds, she snapped her fingers and uttered a triumphant "A-ha!"

Bustling to a table across the room, she picked up a bolt of rich purple velvet, on top of which she piled a length of black crepe and a long roll of tulle in a shade of purple one tone lighter than that of the velvet. Returning to Alys's side, she expertly draped the velvet over the younger woman's breasts and shoulders to form a bodice of sorts, then had her hold the crepe overlaid with the tulle in a skirtlike arrangement. That task completed, she presented the next sketch with a flourish.

"Perhaps by seeing ze fabrics on your ward, you can see how lovely she will look in zhis?" She glanced at Lucian expectantly.

The glaze had left his eyes and he looked alert for the first time since Alys had entered the room. Madame seemed to take that as a positive sign, for she further embellished, "Add ze beaded jet trim and feather boa, and voilà! Stunning, *oui*?"

With unhurried grace he rose to his feet and slowly circled Alys, his frigid gray gaze sweeping her figure with every step. When he'd made a full rotation, he said in a soft, yet unmistakably exasperated voice, "Good God, Madame. Have you looked at the girl? There's hardly anything to her. She would be lost in all this"—he waved his hand at the drawing—"fuss and feathers."

Alys glanced from the materials in her hands to the rejected sketch. As much as she liked the gown, Lucian was right. She really was much too small and youthful-looking to wear such a matronly style. Ah, well. She regretfully handed the fabrics back to Madame. There would be plenty of time to wear such gowns when she'd regained her human life. In time her girlish body would mature to match her womanly mind.

With the same air of impatience he displayed in all matters concerning his ward, Lucian picked up the stack of remaining sketches and began to sort through them. He discarded first one, then another. When he got to the third, he paused.

Handing it to Madame, he said, "We shall have this gown—" He stalked to a shelf on the far wall and pulled down a bolt of celestial blue gauze shot with gold. "Made up in this fabric." He tossed the gauze onto a worktable. In three purposeful strides he was at the rack of trims. "Embellished with this." He pitched a roll of embroidered ribbon smoothly across the room to land on top of the gauze.

That done, he turned to Madame. "Do you understand now what sort of gowns I want for Miss Faire?"

Madame chuckled and nodded. "*Oui.* You want her to look like ze angel she ees."

"Angel?" Lucian snorted. "No. I simply don't care to have her parading around looking like a little girl dressed up in her mother's finery."

If they hadn't been in such a public place, Alys would have voiced her objections to his scathing evaluation of her figure. Little girl indeed! Out of courtesy for Madame, however, she refrained from doing more than shooting him a dagger-sharp look. Lucian was making things unpleasant enough for the poor dressmaker without her adding to her discomfiture by starting a squabble.

From then on the selection process went much smoother. Madame Fanchon, now aware of Lucian's desires, produced sketch after sketch of acceptable designs. There were gowns for morning, ones for afternoon.

Three were designated as opera gowns, five as promenade dresses. Though Lucian never once bothered to
consult Alys on his selections, she could honestly say
that she was more than pleased with everything he
chose.

Just as he and Madame were trying to decide on the
fabric for her coming-out ball gown, the front door
opened and in rushed a harried-looking woman in her
mid-thirties. In with her came the unmistakable stench
of hob.

Alys groaned inwardly. Oh, perfect! Just what she
needed. Hedley wrecking havoc in the shop.

"Did you get ze thread for—" Madame began. Then
her face grew pinched, rather as if she'd eaten something
that didn't quite agree with her. "*Mon Dieu*, Lucy! Did
you step in ze horse—" She gestured to avoid uttering
the vulgar word.

Lucy shook her head, her expression of repugnance
mirroring her employer's. "I noticed the awful smell
coming from the gutter when I crossed the street earlier.
It seems to have followed me in when I opened the door
just now."

"Well, we can't have ze shop smelling like a chamber
pot every time someone opens ze door, now can we?"
Directing the woman to the back curtain with an imperious wave of her hand, Madame directed, "Tell Benjamin
that he ees to scrub ze gutter immediately."

As the woman turned, Alys caught sight of Hedley
clinging to the back of her cloak, bobbing his woolly
head in time to whatever hob tune he was humming.
When he saw Alys glaring at him, he gave her a saucy
wink and jumped down.

"What's taking ye so bloody damn long? I've only got
two centuries worth of fairy essence left, ye know," he
groused, eyeing the contents of the shop in a way that
Alys found most disquieting.

"No, that will never do," came Lucian's voice.

Both Alys and Hedley looked over to where the long-
suffering Madame was holding up a length of pink silk
worked with gilt spangles for his lordship's inspection.
He was shaking his head with a scowl dark enough to
intimidate a whole legion of footpads.

Hedley heaved a much put-upon sigh. "Oh, I see the problem. Lord Tight-Arse is being a swelled-up looby again. Ah, well. Not to worry." With a wave of his hand, he pulled a long, wickedly sharp-looking pin from thin air. Brandishing it as if it were a sword, he explained, "A few pricks with this, and he'll be agreeable just so he can leave. Whadda ye say, Alys?"

"No. Absolutely not," she hissed. Considering Lucian's contrary nature, the hob's trick would probably just make him all the more belligerent. Then what would she and poor Madame do? Shaking her head firmly, she pointed to a small sofa in the far corner, adding, "What I want you to do is to go over there and sit quietly until we're ready to leave."

"Alys?" It was Lucian's voice, and he didn't sound pleased.

Still pointing, she glanced over to where he and Madame stood staring at her as if she'd lost her mind. Oh, perfect! They had caught her scolding Hedley. Improvising to the best of her ability, she shifted her finger a fraction to point at the nearest bolt of fabric and murmured, "I said that I like that material."

By the looks on their faces, it was plain that her fabric selection had merely reinforced their opinion that she had something rattling around loose upstairs. *And no wonder,* Alys thought with dismay as she took a good look at the cloth. It was a heavy poplin in a truly hideous shade of greenish-yellow.

It was Madame who rescued her from the awkward situation. "Perhaps you didn't hear us correctly, mademoiselle. We are choosing ze material for your coming-out gown."

"Oh. Sorry." Alys smiled what was intended to be a sheepish apology. "I thought you were still selecting walking gowns."

Though Madame appeared satisfied by her reply, Lucian wasn't as easily fooled. Pointing to the sofa where Hedley was now hunched on his hands and knees examining the cover of a fashion magazine, he said, "You look tired, my dear. Perhaps it would be best if you sat down and rested while Madame and I complete our business." As usual it was a command not a suggestion.

Just as typical was how he promptly turned back to Madame and began to examine the ivory satin in her hands, clearly expecting her to obey without question.

Unwilling to be banished to the corner with the odorous hob, Alys started to protest. Then she saw the little man open the magazine and she snapped her mouth closed again. If Madame or Lucian were to look over and see the pages flipping by themselves, they'd probably accuse her of witchcraft. Wondering with horror if convicted witches were still burned at the stake, she hurried over to the sofa.

"Say, Alys," Hedley said, surveying her figure as she approached. "Ye should ask his royal clodship to buy ye one of these tit improver things." He pointed at a picture of an undergarment with bosom-enhancing padding. "Ye could use it ye know. It'd make ye look a hundred times more fashionable."

Alys snatched the magazine from beneath his elbows, upsetting his balance with her abruptness. Like she needed more reminders of her shortcomings in that department! As the little man pulled himself up from his collapsed heap, muttering something about her being overly sensitive for a five-hundred-year-old wench, she whispered furiously, "You're a great one to be criticizing another's appearance! You! A slovenly, crude . . . smelly hob! As for this—this"—she consulted the magazine in her hand—"bust improver!—making me look more fashionable, what, pray tell, do you know about fashion? You don't even wear clothes." Like all hobs, Hedley scorned clothing, depending on his natural hairiness to protect his modesty, such as it was.

The hob squawked his affront. "Better to be smelly and naked than to look like a skeleton in crow's clothes like ye. Lord Tight-Arse can dress ye up, but ye ain't gonna look no better than—" He hopped from the sofa to the abutting table upon which stood a rather emaciated-looking fashion doll in court dress. Giving the wooden doll a kick that sent her clattering to the floor, he finished, "You ain't gonna look no better than her, all titless and sour-faced." With that proclamation, he flounced off.

Alys felt both Lucian and Madame's eyes burning into

her back as she bent down to retrieve the doll. "Wonder how that happened?" she muttered, clumsily trying to stuff the doll's now detached arm back up into its sleeve.

Lucian wondered too. He'd been trying to keep Madame from noticing that Alys was whispering to herself when the mannequin had jumped off the table like a rat abandoning a sinking ship. He immediately regretted his mental simile when the scene of Alys talking to the dead rat began to reenact in his mind. As he once again saw her shrink back from the gutter, her face the color of his best port wine, a new thought struck him.

Could it be that Alys hadn't been talking to the rat at all, but to an imaginary companion? It would certainly explain her horrified reaction when he'd pointed out the rodent to her.

He cast her a speculative look as she struggled to make the doll stand again. After three tries she gave up and placed it in a sitting position on the edge of the table. Then she followed suit, sitting on the sofa with her lower lip clenched between her teeth and her hands demurely folded on her lap.

Instead of the anger he should feel at her for making such a spectacle of herself, amusement bubbled up in his chest. She looked comically like a little girl who had been caught whispering in class and was now expecting a switching. Unable to repress it a second longer, he smiled the first genuine smile he'd smiled in years.

He continued to view her over the roll of silver gauze Madame had just shoved in front of his face. In truth, Alys Faire was little more than a girl. And according to the accounts related by the married soldiers around the battlefield campfires, children were prone to flights of fancy, among which was the creation of imaginary friends.

His smile faltered as he recalled some of those tales. Yes, imaginary companions were quite common, but in five- and six-year-olds, not chits of nineteen. An inaudible sigh escaped him.

Bloody hell. No matter how hard he might try to rationalize Alys's strange behavior, it was clear that the girl was an eccentric, period. What other explanation could there be?

He paused from his musings just long enough to shake his head in rejection of the gauze. When he returned to them, a new, more edifying thought struck him.

Could it be that the chit's eccentricity stemmed not from a defect of the brain, but from mere loneliness? Considering her appalling lack of discipline, it was plain that she had been left much to her own devices growing up. That being the case, could it be that she'd created this Hedley Bragg person for lack of human companionship?

There was a unfamiliar twisting sensation in the region of his heart as he contemplated that possibility. That anyone would have to depend upon a figment of their imagination for friendship left him feeling . . . what? Lucian winced as the nameless aching sensation increased, suffusing his entire chest with indescribable pain.

For one terrifying instant he was certain that he was suffering from some fatal heart malady. Then reason prevailed and it struck him: his pain wasn't radiating from his physical heart, the pumping and beating organ, but from a place whose existence he'd always scoffed at as being mere balderdash . . . his spiritual heart. More astonishing yet was the realization that his inner hurt was in some way connected to Alys, his unwanted ward.

Unwanted. The crushing pressure from what he now identified as a foreign emotion tripled at the word, forcing him to hug his chest in fear that it would explode. *Lonely and unwanted.* The emotion burst in a breath-stealing eruption of understanding.

And for the first time in his life Lucian Warre saw another person's misery, and was strangely compelled to alleviate it.

But how? What could he do to make her feel less lonely and more wanted? He shook his head as Madame flashed a length of yellow-embroidered cambric before his eyes. It was true that he hadn't bothered to make Alys feel welcome in his home. Hell. He hadn't thought it necessary. To his way of reasoning, what she thought or felt was beneath his consideration.

Still contemplating the matter, Lucian stepped over to the next display table. When he looked down, he saw the length of iridescent silk Alys had been admiring earlier. As he lightly fingered it, he was struck by yet another notion.

Perhaps this curious business of her having an imaginary friend stemmed from his own disregard for her and her feelings. It made perfect sense when you thought about it, for she seemed to indulge in her odd behavior only when she was being ignored. Take today, for example. Aside from him ordering her to the sofa, neither he nor Madame had so much as acknowledged her presence while selecting the wardrobe.

For the first time in memory the rich and powerful Marquess of Thistlewood put himself in someone else's place and tried to understand their feelings. As he did so, he had to admit that he didn't like how he felt: insignificant and left out.

Determined to remedy the situation, though why in God's name he felt obliged to do so he couldn't say, he murmured, "Alys?"

"Yes, my lord?" By the slight quivering of her voice and the wariness of her expression, it was clear that she expected him to scold her for something.

Curving his lips into what he hoped was a reassuring smile, he gently inquired, "What do you think of having your coming-out gown made of this?" He held up the shimmering silk.

She looked so stunned that for a moment he feared she would faint. Then she rose to her feet, softly uttering over and over again, "Oh . . . oh!" If a person could float, Alys did so as she joined him at the table. "Do you mean it?" she whispered, reaching out to stroke the fabric as if it were something holy. "Can I really have a gown of this?"

"I take it that means it meets with your approval?"

"How could it not? I would feel like a fairy princess wearing a gown made of this."

"A fairy princess, you say?" His smile widened so much that his lips actually parted. "In that case, it's yours."

"Really?" she gasped.

He nodded.

The radiance of her responding smile was so luminous

that it filled him with a startling warmth that made him want to laugh, dance, and embrace the whole world at the same time. Never in his entire life had he felt so wonderful, so . . . happy.

She stared at him for several seconds, her still smiling mouth working soundlessly. Then she released a soft cry and threw her arms around him. Hugging him with a strength amazing for one so tiny, she cried, "I can't believe it! Thank you! Oh, thank you!"

Lucian chuckled, sharing her pleasure. It was a rusty sound, true, but one issued from genuine delight. "You're quite welcome, my dear." Impulsively, he returned her hug . . .

. . . and made yet another discovery. Beneath her shapeless black gown was a small, but delectably feminine body.

Chapter 6

Lucian stood with his arms stretched out behind him as his bleary-eyed valet, John Cusworth, efficiently peeled off his evening coat. It was late, long past midnight, and he'd just returned from an evening of drinking and gambling at his club.

After draping the beautifully tailored corbeau-colored coat over the dressing stand, the servant turned back to him and nimbly unfastened the buttons on his white marcella waistcoat. That done, Lucian automatically lifted his arms again to allow the man to remove the garment. Like everything else in the privileged Marquess of Thistlewood's orderly existence the nightly ritual of being prepared for bed required no second thought or spoken words between master and servant.

Tonight, however, as Cusworth silently slipped the waistcoat off Lucian's shoulders and down his arms, the sound of Alys's mocking laughter suddenly echoed through his brain. *You would laugh too if you could see how ridiculous you look. You! A grown, competent man being dressed as if he were an infant. It makes one wonder if you're ignorant of how to dress yourself and require such services not out of arrogance, but out of necessity.* The memory was enough to make his face burn with what? Fury?

No. Not fury. This feeling was something entirely different, rather as if his insides were squirming every which way. Scowling at the odd sensation, he sat down

on the edge of an armchair and instinctively extended
his leg for his servant to remove his low-heeled dress
shoe. Hell, if he didn't know better he'd say that the
chit's words had made him self-conscious, embarrassed
even, to be assisted in such a manner.

Softly he snorted his disdain at the notion. Ridiculous!
Why should he be embarrassed? It was perfectly natural
and expected for a peer of the realm to be waited on.
Nonetheless, he found himself lowering his foot back to
the floor.

"My lord?"

Lucian glanced down at the valet, who was now kneeling at his feet, peering up at him as if terrified that he'd
unwittingly committed an unpardonable act. Something
about the sight of the man's anxiety-riddled face disturbed him to the point of uneasiness. Was he really
such a tyrant that something as trifling as a change in
his routine made his servants quake with fear?

He considered the theory for a moment, then pushed
it to the back of his brain to join the rest of the Alys-
inspired absurdities congregating there. Of course his
valet wasn't afraid, he was . . . hmm . . . confused. Yes,
that was it. Confused. And with good reason. During
their ten years together, this was the first time he'd ever
broken the methodical order of their nightly routine.

Though Lucian told himself that he was satisfied with
his conclusion, his voice was uncharacteristically gentle
as he ordered, "Go to bed, Cusworth. I shall finish undressing myself."

"But, my lord!" The man looked as shocked as if he'd
said that he was going to jump off the roof to see if he
could fly.

For some inexplicable reason the servant's reaction
made Lucian defensive. Knowing full well that he was
being unreasonable, yet powerless to stop himself, he
said, "I don't know why you and the rest of the servants
persist in treating me like a half-wit child. I can dress
and undress myself, you know."

"O-of course you can, m-my lord," his valet stammered, looking as if he expected to lose his position at
any moment. "I never m-meant to suggest—"

"I know you didn't," he interjected with a sigh, immediately regretting his childish display of petulance. Whatever was wrong with him that he, the normally calm and composed Marquess of Thistlewood, would behave in such an erratic fashion? More confounded than he'd ever thought possible, he waved the man to the door, murmuring, "Just go. I'm feeling out of sorts and simply wish to be left alone." He attempted to smile his apologies.

His unusual expression seemed to alarm rather than reassure the servant. Nervously wringing his hands, Cusworth inquired, "Do you wish me to summon the surgeon, my lord?" By the way he was staring at him, it was clear that the valet thought that he was possessed by evil humors and was in desperate need of being bled.

Lucian sighed. The man wasn't too far off wrong on that account. He did have a miasma in his blood, and a poisonous one at that. And it had been injected by the sharp bite of Alys Faire's scornful words. Bloody hell! How had she managed to get under his skin, and in just four days? The woman was crazy, for God's sake!

At wit's end, he distractedly ran his hand through his hair. Yet she'd done it. She, with her imaginary companion and unpredictable nature, had somehow managed to upset his comfortably tidy existence. And he didn't like it a whit!

Vaguely he wondered if insanity, like smallpox or cholera, was a communicable disease. For Alys's madness was tainting his every thought and perversely affecting his actions.

"My lord?"

Lucian returned his gaze to his servant, who was surveying him with goggle-eyed anxiety.

"Shall I summon the surgeon?" the man repeated, the creases in his age-wrinkled brow deepening.

"No, no." He shook his head. "I'm fine. I've simply had too much to drink and not enough to eat." As if on cue, his alcohol-soured stomach gave a very unlordly rumble.

That noise did what his smile had failed to do, it relaxed Cusworth. "Ah, well. In that case, I shall wake cook and have him prepare you a tray."

Lucian pressed his fist against his midsection as his

stomach roiled with queasiness at his own reminder of his overindulgence. What he really wished was to be left alone to contemplate his difficulties with Alys. And if he sent Cusworth down for a tray, he'd have to endure his fussing for at least another hour. Finding that idea unbearable in his current state of mind, he shook his head. "No. I shall go down to the kitchen and make my own selections."

Not only did Cusworth's shocked expression reappear, he bore the aspect of one who had been stunned speechless.

Amused, Lucian started to smile but caught himself in time, not wanting to alarm the poor valet any more than he already had. The man would undoubtedly suffer a heart seizure if he was to inform him that he often passed half the night down in the kitchen, sitting by the still-warm hearth and stroking the cook's cat. It was his one guilty pleasure, a secret between him and the fat orange-striped tabby.

When the servant made no move to depart, remaining instead rooted to the carpet, gaping at him with eyes the color and shape of copper pennies, he said dismissively, "Good night, Cusworth."

Mercifully the man still had enough of his wits about him to detect the finality in his employer's voice. Snapping out of his gaping stupor, he bowed himself out of the room, murmuring, "Good night, my lord."

Once the door closed behind him, Lucian made quick work of removing the remainder of his clothes and donning a warm, wine velvet dressing gown. After slipping his feet into a pair of fur-lined slippers, he retrieved the three-branched candelabra from the bedside commode. Though the wall sconces in the hallway outside his chamber and those leading down the main staircase would still be lit, he knew from experience that the servants' back stairs would be as dark as his mood after a clash of wills with his ward.

His ward. He meditated upon the behavior of the ungovernable Miss Faire and its effects on him as he slipped from his room and sauntered down the corridor.

It was beyond perplexing that she, a chit barely out of the schoolroom, had managed to turn his well-ordered life upside down and thoroughly disturbed his piece of mind. It wasn't as if he was unused to dealing with females. He'd dealt with scores of them over the years. Yet none of them, no matter how beautiful, seductive, or, yes, infuriating they were, had warranted more than a passing thought. They certainly hadn't occupied his mind the way Alys had done this evening.

He raised the candles a fraction as he rounded the corner of the darkened west wing. In truth he'd gone to his club this evening to escape his maddeningly persistent thoughts of her, certain that a bottle of fine port and the camaraderie of his fellow clubsmen would turn his mind to other, more pleasant matters.

He'd been wrong. Miserably so. All he could think about was her. More specifically, about the way she'd felt in his arms when he'd returned her hug at the dressmaker's As brief as their contact had been, there was something about the feel of her body pressed against his that haunted him as nothing ever had; something surprisingly right and almost familiar about the way her petite form fit his tall one.

Making a derisive noise at the notion that the incorrigible Miss Faire could suit him in any way, he started down the shadowy back stairs. It was clearly time for him to visit Reina and exorcise his body of its tiresome physical urges.

Unlike most men he knew, he found sex necessary but not particularly enjoyable. To him it was rather like blowing his nose, it simply cleared up the unpleasant congestion that formed in his nether regions from time to time. Once relieved, he was free to get on with the more stimulating aspects of his life, like overseeing his fortune.

He was still cursing his body's bothersome needs when he reached the bottom of the stairs, which terminated at the far end of the kitchen. As he stepped from the stairwell, muttering to himself, he was arrested by the sight of someone sitting at the trestle table before the glowing hearth. It didn't take a second glance to identify the person. It was Alys. He groaned inaudibly. So much for his nice peaceful pilgrimage to the pantry.

Clad in a baggy nightgown and wrapper of mourning

black with her pale hair scraped back into a thick, waist-
length braid, she was the most unappealing snippet of
femininity he'd ever had the misfortune to see. At her
left elbow sat a dented pewter plate bearing the remains
of a hearty snack, in her hands was an ancient, but
vaguely familiar-looking volume bound in faded red
morocco.

As if her mere presence wasn't bad enough, she was
reading aloud, her glance straying from time to time to
the chair on her right, almost as if she were reading
to someone.

Lucian swallowed the groan that rose at the sight, not
wanting to attract her notice. She was at it again, being
eccentric, this time reading to her make-believe companion. Deciding that enduring his queasiness was prefera-
ble to dealing with Alys's queerness, he backed away
toward the stairs. He had just reached the foot of the
steps when his stomach let out an obstreperous growl.

Her head shot up and she looked sharply at the empty
chair on her right, then swiveled around to face him.
Her cheeks staining the color of the half-eaten damson
tart on her plate, she stammered, "M-my lord! What are
y-you doing here?"

Glancing longingly at his escape route, he bit out, "In
case you haven't noticed, I happen to live here."

"Of course you do," she replied with a breathless
laugh. "I just meant that you hardly seem the sort of
man to frequent the kitchen."

Lucian couldn't help noticing that she was furtively
kicking the chair to her right and making sharp waving
motions beneath the table as she spoke. Clearly she was
signaling for the departure of her invisible friend. He
sighed. Oh, well. It could be worse. At least she wasn't
spinning around the room, muttering an incantation to
make him disappear as the five-year-old son of one of
his officers had been described as doing.

Apparently her companion was in an accommodating
mood tonight, for she smiled faintly and gave a nod that
would have been indiscernible had he not been staring
at her so intently. Her pink lips still curled up at the
corners, she tilted her head to one side and peered at

him quizzically, clearly expecting him to justify his presence.

As Lucian opened his mouth to simply bid her a good night, intending to turn and leave without explanation, a hideous yowl arose from next to the stove. Before he could think, much less react, the kitchen cat hurtled across the floor and wrapped itself around his calf, clinging with all ten claws.

With a yelp, he dropped the delicate porcelain candelabra. Over the echoing crash of shattering china, he thought he heard Alys shout, "Hedley!" but her voice was drowned out by his own howls of pain as the tabby's claws dug yet deeper into his flesh.

"Bloody cat!" he bellowed, losing his balance as he struggled to detach the animal. He tottered back and forth a couple of times, then collapsed onto his backside with a bone-jarring *thud*!

Rrr! The tabby sprang from his leg. *Grr!* It darted beneath the table where it sat lashing its tail and emitting a series of gurgling hisses.

"My lord!"

Lucian looked up from the bloody scratches on his calf to see Alys dashing toward him, her face the portrait of horrified dismay. "Are you all right?" she exclaimed, coming to a skidding halt in front of him.

"Fine. I just can't imagine what could have gotten into that cat. It's usually so tame."

"You know the beastie?" she asked, her expression of dismay transforming into one of surprise as she knelt next to him.

"We're old friends. Well"—he shot the cat a disgruntled look—"at least I thought we were friends. We should be after all the nights we've passed together sharing beef chops and warming ourselves at the hearth."

"You come down here at night? To the kitchen?" Her surprise visibly heightened to shock at that revelation. Indeed, her reaction was annoyingly reminiscent of Cusworth's.

"Where else? The cat is hardly one to frequent the formal dining room," he snapped irritably. Why the hell did everyone seem to find it so scandalous that he enjoyed spending time in his own kitchen? It wasn't as if

he were down here plucking chickens and baking pies.
Growing more defensive by the minute he scowled at
Alys, waiting for her to bait him about this like she did
everything else.

To his astonishment, she smiled instead. And not in
the sneering manner he'd have expected. No. This smile
was gentle and filled with such sweetness that his defenses quickly crumbled.

Briefly meeting his gaze with eyes as warm as her
smile, she murmured, "I must confess that I've always
loved kitchens too. They're the one room that always
makes me feel at home, no matter where I am. I suppose
it's their lovely smells." As if to verify that last statement, she closed her eyes and sniffed. "Mmm." The corners of her mouth edged up a fraction. "Cloves and
cinnamon . . . like the spiced wine custard our cook used
to make at Christmas. We had such grand Christmases
at Fairfax."

Lucian stared at her wistful face, thunderstruck. He
might not be the most perceptive man in the world, but
he knew that expression. It was one he'd seen often on
the faces of young soldiers who were away from home
for the first time.

Alys Faire was homesick.

That she might miss Fairfax Castle and the friends she
had there was something he hadn't bothered to consider
when he'd had her brought to London. Hell, all he'd
thought about was himself and what an inconvenience it
was going to be to be saddled with a ward. He certainly
hadn't cared a whit for her comfort or feelings. For a
reason he was powerless to explain, he cared now. Very
much so.

For the second time that day, Lucian put himself in
Alys's shoes. As with the first, he didn't like how it felt.

Poor chit, he reflected, his entire being aching with
sympathetic emptiness. How painful to be torn from everything you know and love. How awful to be forced to
live with someone who didn't like or want you, and
made no attempt to conceal the fact.

A wave of shame—and understanding—swept through
him at that last thought. No wonder the girl behaved as
she did. She was simply responding to the shabby man-

ner in which he'd treated her. To be honest, he couldn't say that he blamed her. He certainly wouldn't be inclined to cooperate with someone who constantly criticized and disdained everything he did.

With that realization came a startling notion. If what he suspected was true, that her obstinacy was her way of rebelling against his thoughtlessness, then the task of mending her manners was going to be far less tiresome than he'd imagined. Indeed, all he needed to do was show her the consideration he expected from her, and being the reactive creature she was, she'd follow suit. It was a radical idea, but one definitely worth considering.

Lucian stared at Alys's face, his brow knitting as he contemplated the plan. As he watched, she slowly opened her eyes, sighing as if awakening from a particularly satisfying dream. When she saw him frowning at her, she gave him a tight, uneasy smile and hastily leaned over to examine his wounded leg.

"Alys?" he murmured, her obvious alarm at his frown deciding him in favor of his plan.

With visible reluctance, she looked up. "My lord?"

He curled his lips into what he hoped was a congenial smile. "I would be pleased if you'd call me Lucian. My lord makes me sound so stiff and stern."

Apparently he was starting to master the business of smiling, for, unlike Cusworth, she relaxed a bit. "Lucian," she echoed, smiling faintly in return. "I like that name. It means light."

Without conscious effort, his smile broadened. "Indeed? And how do you know that?"

"I once knew someone named Lu-uh-Lucian." She'd started to say Lucan, which also meant light, but caught herself in time.

His smile faded at her reply, his expression suddenly serious. "Alys," he said, his gaze searching her face. "May I ask you a personal question?"

A request instead of a command? Alys gaped at him, too taken aback by his gracious tone to promptly reply. When she was finally able, she couldn't help stammering, "Of course, m-my lord."

"Lucian," he gently corrected. "Perhaps in time you shall feel free enough around me that my name will fall naturally from your lips. I hope so. Since we shall be sharing a roof, at least for a time, I would like you to view me as a friend and this as your home. Which brings me to my question: Are you homesick?"

Alys couldn't have been more flabbergasted if he'd asked her to run down Pall Mall naked. That he, the king of self-absorption, would think to ask such a sensitive and, yes, perceptive question was almost too much at odds with his spiritually stunted character to be believed. Leery of his motives, she cautiously countered, "What makes you ask that?"

"It was what you said about kitchens. And the look on your face when you spoke of Christmas at Fairfax Castle. You looked"—he seemed to grapple for the correct word, then shrugged and settled on—"lonely."

There was something in the timbre of his voice, something closely akin to compassion, that made her admit, "You're right. I was feeling a bit homesick. And yes, lonely." It was true. Even after five hundred years, she still missed her home and her long-dead friends.

He nodded, his expression reflective. "In that case, we need to think of something to raise your spirits."

"Excuse me?" Alys reached up to check her ears, certain that she was hearing things. He, cheering her? Could it be that her lessons in feeling had been more effective than she'd imagined?

Apparently so, for instead of scolding her for her inattentiveness, as he habitually did, he smiled and repeated, "I said that we need to think of something to make you feel better."

"That's what I thought you said," she mumbled, far more disconcerted by his kindness than she'd ever been by his hostility. Though she knew she should be pleased with this new, more infinitely agreeable Lucian, she felt only a niggling sense of disquiet. As an incorrigible bastard, he'd given her reason to deny her attraction to him. Take that reason away and, well, however was she to keep her wits about her enough to find him his true love?

Oblivious to his effect on her, Lucian quizzed, "Was there a particular servant back home to whom you were close? Or perhaps a pet you regret leaving behind?"

Alys shook her head. Not in this century.

"How about friends? Is there someone you might like to invite to town for a visit? A girl from school, perhaps?"

Again she shook her head, realizing how pathetic she must appear not to have a living soul she could call friend. Pathetic, yes, and sadly true.

To her amazement, he didn't appear to find her lack of social alliance at all out of the ordinary. Indeed, he accepted it as matter-of-factly as if to be completely friendless was a natural state. That response made her view him with new eyes.

Was his life, like hers, void of special people with whom he could share his deepest hopes and fears? With sudden dawning, she realized that she'd been just as self-centered as he in that she hadn't bothered to learn what his life was truly like.

She gave herself a mental kick. However could she have been so stupid? In order to find him his perfect mate, she had to know more than whether he liked blondes or brunettes, ethereal sylphs or full-bodied sirens. She must first discover what sort of man lay behind his pampered, brooding facade. More importantly, she must determine what kind of person he'd be once his soul was complete. Only then would she know for certain what type of a woman would best suit him.

"Surely there must be something we can do to raise your spirits?" he inquired, interrupting her musings. "Something to make you feel more at home?"

She thought for a moment, then smiled with sudden inspiration. "You can be the friend you said you wanted to be earlier. Your sister told me that you would be escorting me to most of the social functions this season, and it would be wonderful to have someone with whom to share my thoughts afterward."

He looked nonplussed at that suggestion. "Wouldn't you rather discuss things with Charlotte? I mean"—he made a helpless hand gesture—"I'm hardly up on the latest *on-dits,* and I'm certainly not qualified to critique the ladies' gowns."

"Neither am I, nor am I interested in either." She gave her head a firm shake. "What I had in mind was that we exchange our impressions of the various events, and discuss the ideas expressed by those in attendance."

When he continued to view her doubtfully, she added, "As you pointed out yourself, we shall be sharing a roof. Wouldn't it make the arrangement more comfortable for us both if we were to become better acquainted? Who knows? We might have more in common than we suspect. We might even like each other. In truth, I find you excellent company when you're being civil as you are now."

Strangely enough, he was enjoying her company too. When she wasn't baiting or battling with him, she was a rather comfortable female to be around. Deciding that he very much liked the idea of a truce between them, he replied, "If you're willing to make an effort to be friends with me, I shall be pleased to do the same." He was about to ask her for suggestions on how to proceed when his stomach let out a voluminous gurgle.

"Sorry," he murmured, pressing his hands to his midsection to quiet the protesting organ. "I haven't eaten since luncheon. Hunger is what brought me to the kitchen."

"Oh, then you must have a slice of the meat pie cook made for dinner. It's most delicious, even cold," she replied, rising gracefully to her feet.

Speaking of cold . . . Lucian groaned softly as he followed suit, his joints stiff and aching from sitting on the chilly stone floor. Too many nights spent sleeping on the freezing ground during the war had left him permanently afflicted with sensitive joints. Feeling as creaky as the ninety-year-old head gardener at Thistlewood, he hobbled over to the table and plopped down in the chair nearest the fire. The second his backside hit the unpadded seat, Alys was there kneeling before him.

"Would you like me to cleanse those scratches for you?" she asked, clearly assuming that his groan had stemmed from pain from those slight wounds. "They're not deep, but there's no telling where that cat has been."

As Lucian looked down to reply, he noted for the first time that her hair wasn't the drab buttery yellow hue he'd thought, but a variegated blend of shimmering strands in shades ranging from moon-kissed platinum to sun-lit gold. Without thinking, he reached down and lifted her long braid from where it dangled down her back. It was really quite lovely, well, as far as blonde hair went. Especially when it was burnished by the fire-light as it was now.

"My lord?" A note of wonder shaded her voice.

Abruptly he dropped her braid, wondering what in the world had gotten into him. Since when did he admire fair hair? Masking his confusion as best he could, he frowned and corrected her, "Lucian, not my lord. Remember?"

"Lucian," she parroted. "What about the scratches on your leg? Would you like me to clean them for you?"

He lifted his leg to examine them. They'd stopped bleeding and when he touched them, they no longer hurt. Dropping his foot back to the floor, he replied, "I shall tend to them later. Right now, I think I'll have a piece of that meat pie you were praising a few minutes ago."

As if understanding his words and wanting to make certain that it received its share of the treat, the kitchen cat meowed and jumped up onto Lucian's lap. Purring frantically it rubbed against his velvet-clad chest and butted its orange-striped head against his hand. Grinning wryly, Lucian scratched it between its ears.

"Are you looking to take another pound of flesh, Prinny? Or do you wish to make up?" he inquired softly.

Alys smiled at his obvious fondness for the animal. "Prinny? Is that his name?"

Lucian shrugged without pausing from his petting duties. "I don't know what his real name is, or even if he has one. I call him Prinny because, like our Prince Regent, he's fat and smug and seems to rule the kitchen with an iron paw." Down the tabby's back his hand glided, stopping at the root of its tail for more scratching. The cat arched its back and drooled its ecstasy.

"As much as you like the beastie, you've never bothered to inquire after his name?" Alys asked, thinking that she'd never heard anything so peculiar in all her life. When she'd lived at Fairfax, she'd known the name of, or named, every cat and dog that roamed the great hall. Unable to bridle her surprise, she exhaled, "Why?"

By his expression, it was clear that he thought her question every bit as strange as she'd considered his previous response. "Because it isn't proper to be familiar with the servants." His brow creased. "Surely you know that?"

She made an incredulous noise. "Asking the cook his cat's name is hardly what I'd call being familiar."

"Considering that I've never even spoken to the cook, it would be very familiar indeed."

"You've never spoken to your own cook?" she repeated, utterly floored. Back when she was Alys le Fayre, her greatest childhood pleasure had been to sit by the kitchen hearth, listening to cook's stories and eating the gingerbread saints the woman baked specially for her. Surely the marquess had had similar experiences in his youth?

By the weight of his frown, apparently not. "Of course I haven't spoken to him. One does not speak to servants unless absolutely necessary. To do so makes them forget their places and become bold." He shook his head. "If a servant is worthy of his position, he knows his duties and therefore requires no instruction from me."

"But servants are people, just like you and I," she protested. "They deserve some sort of acknowledgment that they're human and that their efforts are appreciated."

"I pay them. That is acknowledgment enough," he stated, his words chased by another growling complaint from his stomach. Grimacing, he added, "Now if you'll excuse me, I'd like to eat before my stomach wakes the whole house with its rumbling."

Though Alys had a wealth more to say on the subject of the treatment of servants, she refrained from voicing it. No need to break their fledgling truce over something that they'd have ample opportunity to discuss in the future. Yes, better to get on with the more urgent business of getting acquainted.

Knowing from her matchmaking experience that a well-fed man was an amiable one, she nodded at the cat, who was rhythmically kneading his robe in time with its slobbering purrs, and said, "Your friend looks so content, it would be a shame to disturb him. If you like, I shall be glad to prepare you a plate."

At his murmured assent, she retrieved a pewter platter from the cupboard and set about filling it. Not certain what sort of food he preferred, for he rarely took meals with her, she quizzed him as she worked.

First selected was the meat pie. In quick succession were added two biscuits, several slices of capon, split peas with saffron, and an enormous chunk of honey and saffron cake. Alys smiled at his last two choices. Like all humans of fairy origin, Lucian appeared to have a particular fondness for honey and saffron. After setting the heaping plate in front of him, she returned to her own seat that was just opposite from where he sat.

For several moments they sat in companionable silence; he, devouring his food with the zeal of a starving man; she, trying to decide how best to begin her inquest into his life. After brief contemplation, she settled on a direct approach.

Smiling as he stuffed a generous morsel of capon into the food-frenzied cat's mouth, she asked, "Would you mind if we started getting acquainted now?"

"I thought that that was what we were doing?" he returned, his gaze still focused on the now loudly chomping feline on his lap.

"What I meant was really acquainted. You know, talk about things like where we went to school, what our childhood nannies were like. Perhaps even your experiences during the war."

He seemed to consider her request as he cut another piece of fowl and fed it to the cat. When the greedy animal had gobbled it down, he nodded and looked up. "As you wish."

In a manner that was more recitation than conversation, he proceeded to recount, "My childhood nanny was Maddie Spratling, a servant who has been with the Warre family since before my father's birth. She is a kind-hearted, but highly superstitious woman who believes in and tried to fill my young mind with all sorts of fairy nonsense."

An indignant squawk arose from next to the stove where Alys had banished Hedley. "Nonsense? Non-

sense! Who the bloody hell does Lord Tight-Arse think
he is to be calling fairies nonsense?"

His human ears deaf to the hob's protests, Lucian continued without pause, "Like most titled boys I attended
Eaton, then went on to Oxford. After graduation I
bought a commission into the cavalry where I rose to the
rank of major. Now that the war has ended, I'm here."

"And what do you intend to do in London? Look for
a wife?" she inquired boldly. *Please God, let him say yes.*

Becoming suddenly as deaf to her as he was to Hedley, Lucian turned his attention to slipping the cat another tidbit.

"Well, do you?" she probed insistently.

He released a heavy sigh and looked up. "I have no
choice but to marry. As the only living Warre male, it
is my unfortunate duty to perpetuate the family line.
And as Charlotte is so fond of pointing out, I shall be
thirty-three on my next birthday and am long overdue
to set up a nursery." By his grim expression, you'd think
that he was being commanded to present himself at
Newgate where he was to be hung at dawn.

"You might find marriage agreeable if you marry
someone you love," she pointed out gently.

He snorted. "Love? What has love to do with
marriage?"

"Love has everything to do with it. What other reason
is there to marry?"

Gone was the congenial Lucian Warre, deposed by
the disagreeable Marquess of Thistlewood. "I believe I
have already answered that question," he replied acidly.
"To beget an heir."

"Oh? And exactly how do you intend to procure a
wife for that purpose without love?"

"Simple. I find myself a placid, tractable female with
broad breeder's hips, and propose. If she's like every
other woman in London, she's not likely to say no to
eighty thousand pounds a year and the title of
marchioness."

"Are you so certain?" she challenged. "The women I
know desire and expect to receive love from the men
they marry."

His gaze captured hers then, his gray eyes so frigid

that she shivered from their chill. In a voice utterly de-
void of emotion, he stated, "Then the women in your
acquaintance are destined to be disappointed, for there
is no such thing as love."

She sighed her exasperation. "Just because you've
never experienced it doesn't mean that it doesn't exist."

"Indeed? And what proof do you have of its
existence?"

"All one need do to find proof is to consider how
many poems, songs, plays, and books have been written
on the subject throughout the centuries. Surely love must
exist for so many people to have experienced and written about it? Look here—" She picked up the book
she'd been reading earlier and handed it to him. "Even
your own ancestors experienced and recorded the
phenomenon."

Lucian took the slim volume from her and thumbed
through the pages. Emitting a disdainful noise, he tossed
it down on the table. "You call this proof? The story of
Alys and Lucan? It's nothing but a bloody fairy tale."

"It's a tale about fairies, true, but that doesn't mean
it isn't factual," she countered evenly.

He rolled his eyes heavenward and groaned. "Don't
tell me you believe in fairies?"

"As a matter of fact, I do. As do many people, which
is something you should know from your nanny's stories.
There are even those who claim to have seen the little
folk."

He ejected another noise, this one more scornful than
the last. "Well, I've never seen one. And like love, until
I have proof of their existence—solid proof—I shall continue to view them as a shatter-brained cock-and-bull
story."

"A cock-and-bull story, am I?" howled Hedley, leaping up onto the far end of the long table to glare at
Lucian.

Like all animals the cat could see the hob, and it instantly stiffened. By its defensive stance, it was apparent
that the memory of the little man ruthlessly tweaking its
whiskers was still fresh in its mind.

Before Alys could register exactly what was happening, the hob dashed across the freshly polished table

toward Lucian. With a gleeful whoop, he flopped onto his backside and slid the rest of the distance . . . landing right smack onto the cat's head.

Rrr! Sss! The tabby howled and reflexively buried its claws into Lucian's chest. "Bloody hell!" Lucian tumbled out of his chair in his startlement.

Hedley eyed his handiwork with wicked glee and cackled.

Chapter 7

A little vegetable rouge tingeing the cheek of a delicate woman, who, from ill health or an anxious mind, loses her roses, may be excusable; and so transparent is the—

Bored beyond yawning, Alys let her gaze drift from the pages of *The Mirror of the Graces* before her to the painting that hung on the opposite wall of the library. Like every afternoon during the past three weeks, as she sat in this same seat trying to muster up interest in whatever book on beauty, etiquette, or fashion Charlotte had deemed necessary reading for her coming-out education, she found her attention diverted to the picture. It was a portrait of Charlotte and Lucian, painted when she was nine, and he only five.

As always she let her gaze skim past the laughing girl embracing a wiry brown dog, to stare at the dark-haired little boy lounging against a chair next to her. Dressed as he was in a gay red and brown skeleton suit with a toy knight dangling from one hand, he was the very portrait of carefree childhood . . . until one looked at his face.

His was a face compellingly old for one so young; old in that it lacked the lively animation that all children possess before time and experience lower their sphinxlike mask of adult stoicism. Alys had spent hours trying to decide exactly what it was that made him appear so. Was it the set of his lips, so tight and solemn? Or the inscrutable stare of those cool gray eyes?

Thoroughly captivated by the pigment and linseed-oil image, she braced her elbows on the table and rested her chin atop her interlaced fingers. Had he truly been such a grim child? Or had the artist simply caught him in a pensive moment? Knowing the adult Lucian as she did and about the diminished state of his immortal soul, she'd have bet her chance at regaining her humanity that the former was the case.

That certainty wrapped her in a weighty blanket of remorse. That he'd been incapable of enjoying the sweet frivolity of childhood because of her treachery in his previous life riddled her with a guilt almost too painful to bear.

Someday, she silently promised herself and the morose boy in the painting, someday soon she would make it up to him. She'd see that he wed a woman who would bring him all the laughter and jolly times he had missed in his youth. She would see him blissfully matched, and not just because she was required to do so to regain her human life. In truth, she wanted him to be happy.

That last startling revelation gave her pause. That she actually cared about Lucian Warre and his feelings beyond the consideration demanded of her to find him a wife caught her completely off guard. In all her centuries of matchmaking, she'd never felt more than a vague fondness for any of the men and women in her charge. Indeed, there were a few she'd positively loathed.

So what was so different about Lucian? Why did she care so desperately about him? More puzzling yet, what was it about him that stirred such a fierce sense of protectiveness within her? It wasn't as if he'd given her any reason to feel as she did. If ever there was a man firmly in charge of himself and his future, it was Lucian Warre.

Yet . . . yet there was something in his very strength, something in the remoteness of his autocratic command, that made him seem touchingly vulnerable to her. True. His arrogance exasperated her at times, often with a vehemence that made her yearn to shake him like the child she doubted he ever was. Yet always, no matter how infuriating he might be, she felt a niggling sense of warmth for him that made her long to draw him into her embrace and hold him until he experienced the emotion that only his destined love had the right to teach him: tenderness.

Inexplicably depressed by that last thought, she dropped her gaze from the portrait to the yellow damask sofa below, beneath which Hedley lay curled up asleep. His grizzled head was pillowed on the open pages of *A Social Guide to Deportment and Etiquette for Gentlemen of Refinement,* and in one hand he loosely grasped the crumbling remains of a Shrewsbury cake.

Despite her melancholy, Alys smiled. Since their trip to the dressmaker's the hob had developed an inordinate preoccupation with fashion and society, and had since read every book in the library pertaining to the subject. Indeed, he was far more schooled in what lay between the covers of the manuals Charlotte had given her than she, a fact that he was quick to point out whenever she voiced her objections to him correcting her in her dress or deportment.

As irritating as his all-knowing posturing was, however, something good had come from his new avocation: he'd started to bathe. Not a morning had passed during the last two weeks when she hadn't been awakened to the sounds of him splashing around in her washbasin, humming hob tunes. This morning he'd even gone so far as to finish off with a dab of scent he'd filched from Lucian's dressing table.

Muttering something in his sleep about the correct application of pomade rouge, the little man flopped over onto his back, sending the partially eaten cake flying from beneath the sofa in the process. Those unconscious words served as a much needed reminder for Alys to resume her studies. Charlotte was due to arrive at four to help her practice her curtsy for her court presentation, and would undoubtedly quiz her on what she'd learned.

Casting the childhood portrait of Lucian one final glance, she bent back over her book. She'd just gotten to a section entitled "Female Charms, Their Use and Abuse," when she heard a muffled string of curses emanating from the fireplace. There was a peculiar scraping sound, followed by more cursing, and then a pained yelp.

Curious as to who could be causing such a raucous in Lucian's normally tomb-still home, she stepped over to investigate. The fire, lit earlier in the day, had exhausted its wood and was now little more than glowing embers and silvery ash.

As she knelt upon the hearth in preparation to peer up the flue, her ears were abused by yet another flurry of crude oaths, this time followed in quick succession by a *thud!* and the echoing cry of "Ow!" There was a wild *scratch! scratch!* chased by a harsh duet of screeched "Aarghs!" and *thump!-thumps!* Then, in a heavy downpour of thick, black soot, the flue spit forth a small, howling urchin . . . howling that increased from loud to earsplitting as his half-naked form landed hard on the hot embers.

Mindless of everything but pulling the now howling child from the fireplace before he was badly burned, Alys grasped him by his sticklike arms and dragged him up against her. Ignoring the fact that she was wearing a new white cambric gown and that he was caked with grime, she pulled him onto her lap to comfort him.

"There, there. You're safe now," she cooed, looking over his heaving shoulder to assess the damage to his bare back. He was so filthy, it was impossible to tell anything. Gently cupping his small chin in her palm, she lifted his face to peer down into his bloodshot blue eyes. "Are you badly hurt? Would you like me to summon a surgeon?"

Sniffling noisily, he squirmed away. " 'E's gonna beat me as 'tis fer makin' this mess," he muttered, his wizen little face contorting with terror as he viewed the soot frosting the fine Persian carpet. " 'E'll murder me if 'e 'as to pay fer a leech."

"Who's going to beat you?" Alys asked softly.

He sniffled again and scrubbed away a tear with the back of his hand, exposing a patch of ashen skin beneath the soot in the process. "Moles."

"Moles?"

"Me master, the chimney sweep. And 'e's gonna be mad as hops when 'e sees this mess. 'E's gonna tan me hide fer sure this time, tho' it ain't really me fault that I fell." Wincing violently as he struggled to his feet, he added more to himself than to her, "If 'e 'adn't been 'ittin' me with 'is broom, I'd never of slipped in the first place."

"He was hitting you?" Alys gasped. The boy was so thin, it was easy to imagine a single blow breaking him in half. "That—that's—unspeakable!"

He shrugged. "It ain't no worse 'an when 'e pokes pins into me feet."

"He sticks pins into your feet!" Alys echoed, her outrage growing with every passing second. "Why would he do such a thing?"

" 'Blimey gor! Ye don't think I go up burnin' chimneys 'cause I want to, do ye?" he retorted, eyeing her like hers was the stupidest question he'd ever heard. "It's 'ardly wot I'd call pleasant to 'ack and cough and 'ave me eyes burned by smoke, and me elbows and knees scraped raw by the walls. I could even get stuck and suff-y-cate like me good chum, Eddy, did last week."

Before Alys could respond to that last appalling piece of information, the library door burst open and in stalked a lumbering brute of a man carrying a long-handled broom. Behind him, objecting in a most strident tone, was a harried-looking Tidswell.

"If you please, Mr. Moles. You must wait in the hall and let me retrieve the boy for you," he was saying.

Moles, having spotted his quarry, let out an enraged bellow and lunged at the climbing boy. "Blighted little bugger! I'm goin' ta teach ye ta be so bloody clumsy!" With a blow that reverberated through the whole room, he struck the boy with his broom, catching him in his thin ribs. Whimpering breathlessly, the boy fell to his knees, his tears streaking through the filth on his cheeks as he clutched his abused side.

"I must object, sir!" Tidswell gasped, while Alys froze, too horrified by the man's display of brutality to move.

"It whar an acc-y-dent, Moles," the boy sobbed, shrinking into a tight, cringing ball. "I swear it whar. It won't 'appen again."

"Yer damn right it won't 'appen again!" Moles thundered, clubbing him with the broom, this time about the head and shoulders. The child screamed and collapsed sprawled across the soiled carpet.

"Sir! I really must protest this display!" Tidswell remonstrated again, this time more forcefully. "The young miss—"

Ignoring the butler, the chimney sweep gave the sobbing boy a vicious kick in his bony backside, snarling, "Now ye get off yer worthless arse and back up that chimney. I won't 'ave it said that Moles don't run the finest sweepin' bizness in London."

Valiantly the climbing boy struggled to obey. When he was slow to attain his goal, Moles raised his broom again.

Something inside Alys snapped at the sight. "No!" she screamed. Lunging to her feet, she grabbed the filthy brush end, halting its vicious descent. Her wrists aching from the force of the sweep's thwarted swing, she berated, "What kind of monster are you to treat a child so cruelly? Why, just look at him!"

Still clutching on to the broom, she jerked her head to where the sobbing boy lay huddled by the hearth. "He's so thin it's a wonder he can stand, much less climb! Especially after falling down the chimney and into hot ashes. There's no telling how badly he's burned, covered as he is in filth. If you had even a shred of human decency, you'd take him home to bed and summon a surgeon!"

"Pardon me, miss. But I don't see how this is any of yer bizness," Mole retorted, casting her a look that was nothing short of insolent.

Alys snorted her disgust and dropped her end of the broom. Kneeling down beside the piteously weeping climbing boy, she snapped, "It's everyone's business to protect children from brutes like you, and that's exactly what I intend to do." With that, she pulled the boy into her soothing embrace, glaring defiantly up at the chimney sweep over his thatch of matted hair.

A growl emanated from the brute's throat. "Little bugger's me apprentice, and it's me bizness to see that 'e does 'is job. And I intend ta do jist that!" Dropping his broom, he swooped down and ripped the boy from her arms.

The climber howled and kicked him in the shin, a bit

of rebellion that earned him a backhanded slap across the face.

Shrieking her rage, Alys jumped to her feet and grabbed on to the boy's flailing left arm. "You let him go this instant!" she screamed, giving his arm a yank in a desperate attempt to pull him free.

Moles counterpulled on his opposite arm. " 'E's mine and I'll do wot I damn well please with 'im. Now if ye really care about the little bugger, ye'll let go afore I break 'is arm." As if to demonstrate the validity of his threat, he gave the climber's right arm a wrench that made him scream a curse no child should know.

With a roar completely at odds with his staid appearance, Tidswell surged forward and grasped on to the same arm Alys was clutching. "You will unhand the child and leave this house immediately," he commanded.

"Oh? And who's goin' ta make me? Ye, ye crabbed old quiz?"

"What the hell is going on here?" demanded a frigid voice from the doorway. All heads swiveled toward the newcomer, though Alys knew who it was without looking. It was Lucian. All it took was one glance to see that he was furious.

Lucian was furious, livid, if the truth must be told. He'd happened upon Lord Atwood outside of Angelo's, where he and Stephen practiced their fencing every Thursday afternoon, and had invited the young man back to the house under the pretext of showing him the new stallion he'd purchased. Being that the cub was one of the three eligible bachelors on his list, his real purpose, of course, was to introduce him to Alys.

Clad in a filmy white frock with a pink ribbon sash, his ward had looked surprisingly winsome when she'd joined him for breakfast this morning. So pleasing was her appearance that he'd had visions of the callow Lord Atwood taking one look at her and instantly falling into a gawking, infatuated stupor.

Lucian slanted a glance down at the young lordling, who'd moved to his side. He was gawking all right, but in goggle-eyed horror, not calf-eyed infatuation. And with good reason. The scene they had arrived to was reminiscent of a St. Giles street brawl.

Alys, with her gown and face liberally streaked with soot, was engaged in a tug-of-war with a burly chimney sweep over a filthy ragamuffin of a boy, screeching like an irate fishwife. Doing nothing to enhance the shocking display, the normally unflappable Tidswell had joined in the scuffle and was adding his bellows to Alys's shrieks with a volume that made him long to slap his hands over his ears.

Gritting his teeth in fury, Lucian stepped into the room. Not only had Alys turned his orderly life upside down, she'd managed to turn his peaceful house into bedlam. Firmly affixing his gaze on to the object of his displeasure, he growled, "I want an explanation for this disgraceful spectacle, and I want it now."

Alys opened her mouth to reply, but her voice was superseded by that of the red-faced chimney sweep. "I was tryin' ta teach me apprentice a lesson, when them, there"—he jerked his head at Alys and Tidswell—"decided that they dinna like the way I was teachin' 'im, and interfered."

Alys let out an indignant squawk. "A lesson! He was beating the poor child horribly, with this"—she gave the filthy broom on the floor a indicative kick—"just because he lost his hold in the chimney and fell into the fireplace."

Lucian transferred his gaze to the muck-crusted urchin, whose arms were still being stretched to either side by the opposing factions. Pursing his lips with distaste, he inquired tersely, "Are you hurt, boy?"

The boy darted an anxious glance at the scowling chimney sweep, then shook his head. "Naw. I'm all right, guv'na."

"Your lordship," Tidswell corrected sternly.

The ragamuffin ducked his head in deference. "Sorry, yer lordship."

"Of course he's hurt. How could he not be? He fell into the hot embers," Alys piped in, successfully tugging the boy from the sweep's slackening grip and dragging his small form protectively against hers. "Though it's impossible to tell through all the dirt, I'm certain he was burnt, not to mention the bruises and heavens knows what other kind of injury he received from his"—she

stabbed the chimney sweep with her accusing gaze—
"lessons. He's simply too afraid of the brute and what
he might do to him to say so."

"It's true, my lord," Tidswell corroborated, joining
Alys in glaring at the sweep. "The man is a savage beast
who was abusing this poor child in a most unspeakable
manner."

" 'Tweren't abusin' I were doin', but discipline," the
man protested. "Look what 'e did ta yer fine rug." He
indicated the soot-smeared rug, as if its sorry state could
escape even the most casual notice. "Ye don't want me
to let the little bugger get away with doin' that, now
do ye?"

All four pairs of eyes were fastened on Lucian's face
now, clearly expecting a response.

Lucian groaned inaudibly. The last thing he wanted
was to get involved in this disagreeable business, and he
would be involved if he stated an opinion. And as he
knew from experience, involvement led to consequences,
consequences that in this instance promised to be very
unpleasant indeed, no matter whose view he took.

If he sided with the sweep, agreeing that the boy deserved punishment for soiling the rug, then he'd undoubtedly be forced to bear the brunt of the
forementioned pair's displeasure for God knows how
long. If he were to take their part against the sweep,
then he might be forced to see to the urchin's welfare, a
thought that he found singularly intolerable. He detested
children and had thus far scrupulously avoided taking
any under his roof.

Desiring to keep his house free of children without
taking the sweep's part, he decided to do what he'd have
done had he been facing the predicament alone: he'd
simply ignore the boy's plight and order the filthy duo
from his house. He was about to do just that when his
gaze fell on Alys's face.

He'd intended to stare in her eyes as he gave the
order, to warn her with his glare that he'd not brook
such bothersome interruptions in the future. Instead the
words died in his throat. No one had ever looked at him
like she was doing now.

Her expression was not one of petulant demand as

he'd expected, nor was she giving him one of those annoying dewy-eyed looks of pathetic appeal like most females were wont to do. No, she was gazing at him with an expression of absolute faith; faith that he'd do the right and compassionate thing; faith that he had it in his heart to be merciful.

As he stared at her too taken aback to speak, a very small, very sweet smile of encouragement sketched across her lips. That anyone who knew him would credit him with having a single humanitarian bone in his body was almost too astounding to be believed. That he found that fact suddenly disturbing was more astonishing yet.

He gave his head a small shake. This whole situation was too ridiculous to countenance. Why did she expect him to act in a charitable manner? And why, in God's name, should he extend such benevolence to the boy? He was nothing but a member of the lower class, one of the thousands of unwashed minions who had always been beneath his notice. So why should he be expected to notice now? Despite what Alys seemed to believe, he was in no way responsible for the boy.

Yet . . . yet, for some reason, one completely at odds with his dispassionate nature, her confidence in the generosity of his spirit made him desire to be the noble knight she credited him with being. In truth, he was actually tempted to champion the climber . . .

Which meant that in all probability he'd end up stuck with the boy. Bloody hell! Certain that one glance at the creature's dirt-smudged face would instantly dispel him of his gallant notions and bring him back to his senses, he shifted his gaze downward.

The expression on the boy's face merely deepened his altruistic urge. His was a look of misery-laced resignation, one that, unlike Alys's, clearly said that he held out no hope of being rescued from his wretchedness, especially by a member of the nobility. To Lucian that look was like a reprimand of how often he'd ignored the plight of London's ill-used street children, too selfish to acknowledge their grievous condition, too unfeeling to care.

Remembering all the times he'd had his footman push starving young beggars away from his coach, or how he'd averted his gaze from the sight of a freezing child huddled in a doorway for warmth, stirred up a singularly unpleasant emotion. To say that he felt ashamed would have been too mild a description for the cringing pain he felt inside. For unlike simple shame, this feeling triggered an almost uncontrollable impulse to make amends for all the times he should have cared and hadn't.

But you can't save all of London, he reminded himself, the disdainful aristocrat in him rebelling against the notion that he, the rich and powerful Marquess of Thistlewood, was in any way obliged to notice, much less acknowledge and help, anyone below his station.

No, but you can save this boy, an unfamiliar part of him countered.

Before Lucian knew quite what was happening, he was saying, "I do not believe in beating children, no matter what their crime. And I shall not tolerate you doing so beneath my roof." Encouraged by Alys's radiant smile, he added, "Now Mr. . . . ?" He glanced at Tidswell to provide the man's name.

The butler was looking at him with approval, a sentiment he'd never thought to see on the man's dour face. "Moles, my lord," he supplied, the corners of his mouth curving up.

Lucian nodded, illogically pleased by the servant's favorable regard. "Mr. Moles, I shall give you exactly one minute to leave this house, then I shall summon my footmen to throw you out."

"Suits me fine. I'll jist take me apprentice and be on me way. Plenty of other people with dirty chimneys who ain't so particular about hows they get cleaned." With that, he grabbed the boy and roughly jerked him away from Alys.

"No!" she cried, catching on to the boy's arm again. This time the child's thin hand wrapped around her wrist to aid her in her efforts to stay him. Turning her imploring gaze to Lucian, she beseeched, "Please, my lord. Don't let the monster take the boy. He'll beat him, maybe even kill him!"

" 'E's me apprentice all proper and legal," Moles snarled. "You take 'im away, and I'll see ye before the magistrate ta answer for it. Ye may be a bleedin' lord, but ye ain't above the law."

"Then by all means take me to court. The boy shall remain here," Lucian mandated, barely able to believe his ears as he listened to his own words. Had he really said that? Keep the filthy urchin? Whatever had possessed him?

One look at Alys's face, so tender and filled with gentle pride for him, and he knew the answer to the question. He'd done it for her. Done it because, by simply believing in him, she had brought out a benevolence in him he'd never suspected he possessed.

"Pardon me if I don't jump to do yer biddin' like old spindle breeches there." Moles jerked his head at Tidswell. "Bart, 'ere, is the best climbin' boy I've got, and yer damned cracked in yer high and mighty head if ye think I'll leave 'im because ye says so."

"Then you should have considered his value and treated him accordingly," Lucian informed him icily. Nodding to the butler, he said, "Please bid the footmen to show Mr. Moles out, Tidswell."

Tidswell actually grinned. "My pleasure, my lord."

"Yes. Go summon the bleedin' footmen," Moles mimicked, tearing the boy's arm from Alys's clasp and dragging him toward the door. "We'll be long gone to whar you'll nivver find us by the time they get here."

Lucian stepped back to block the doorway. "You're not going anywhere with that child."

Clamping the struggling boy's neck in a stranglehold to subdue him, the sweep hauled him to where Lucian stood firmly rooted to the threshold. "Oh? And who's gonna stop me?" he snarled, his gin-fouled breath striking Lucian in the face as he spoke.

Lucian looked him straight in his bloodshot eyes. "Me."

"Ye and what bloody army?" he challenged, the menace in his voice unmistakable.

"Me and"—he smashed his fist into the man's smirking face—"this."

The sweep howled his pain and outrage, his grip on the boy's neck slackening in his surprise. Adding insult to injury the climber kicked his master in the knee, then ducked out of his hold and scampered to Alys, who shoved him protectively behind her. Cursing in a manner that Lucian found offensive, even after years in the cavalry, the man lunged at him.

Lucian countercharged, violently knocking the sweep backward. The veteran of untold street fights, the man grabbed him around his waist, dragging him to the floor with him. The second their bodies hit the carpet, the sweep rolled on top of him, viciously elbowing him in the belly in the process.

Lucian grunted as nauseating pain exploded up through his torso. Too stunned to strike back, he lay there simple warding off the punishing blows raining down on his face and upper body. Through the din of the man's curses and Tidswell's shouts for the footmen, he heard Alys shrieking. Then he saw a small form fly onto the sweep's back, where it clung like a monkey to a banana tree.

It was the boy. With language every bit as foul as his master's, he began boxing at the man's ears, screaming his rage. It only took Lucian a moment of listening to his words to realize that the boy's fury stemmed not from his own abuse, but from that being heaped on his new benefactor. That the child, as fragile and malnourished as he was, would unselfishly risk serious bodily harm to come to his aid filled him with irrational warmth. It also made him cease worrying about protecting his face in favor of overpowering the sweep before he could retaliate against the boy.

Thus resolved, he violently arched his body, intent on bucking the sweep off him as if he were an unbroken stallion and the man an inexperienced rider. It didn't work. Though he and the sweep were evenly matched in height, the other man outweighed him by at least two stones. Pile on the additional weight of the climber, as slight as it was, and his torso and lower body might as well have been shackled to the floor.

Without a conscious change of tactics, Lucian reflexively slugged the sweep in his midsection. No sooner had his fist made contact than he heard a loud crash followed by a downpour of bits and slivers of something hard and white. The sweep grunted once, then slumped forward, burying him beneath his flabby form.

Laboring to catch his breath, Lucian shifted his head slightly to the right to peek over the unconscious man's shoulder. Hovering above them holding what was left of his ancient Grecian urn vase—the rare one dating from 600 B.C.—was Alys. Next to her, clapping his hands and jumping up and down, was the climbing boy. For some strange reason, he felt like applauding as well, though he knew he should be furious at Alys for using the most valuable piece of art in the room to fell the chimney sweep.

"My lord! Are you quite all right?" Tidswell exclaimed, leaning into his line of vision. Though his craggy old features were tainted with concern, there was something suspiciously like a smile tugging at his lips.

"I'm fine," Lucian grunted, nudging at the sweep's inert form. Without the weight and worry of the climbing boy, he easily shoved the man off him.

As he rolled over onto his belly to push himself up on his knees, he found himself nose to toe with a particularly fine pair of boots. He groaned aloud as he looked up into their owner's horror-struck face.

Bloody hell! He'd completely forgotten Lord Atwood. At a loss as to what to say, he ran his hand through his mussed hair and said what one normally said to afternoon guests, "You shall stay for tea, shan't you, Atwood?"

Chapter 8

"Ouch! Jesus," Lucian muttered, wincing as Charlotte dabbed at the bloody cut above his eye.

"Pshaw! It's nothing but a scratch. Hardly worth all this fuss and bother," she chided, smiling in a way that completely belied the sternness of her tone. She was so proud of her brother that she'd have hugged him if she thought he'd allow it.

When she'd arrived at the house twenty minutes earlier, the first sight to greet her eyes had been a very flustered Lord Atwood. His homely face flushed a blotchy red, he'd stuttered something that sounded oddly like "row," then had dashed down the front steps as if the hounds of hell were loose and he were their midnight prey. As if that weren't irregular enough, her knock was answered not by Tidswell, but by a contingent of grinning footmen bearing a groggily cursing ruffian, who they cheerfully tossed into the street.

Though these untoward incidents had alerted her that something was amiss within the walls of her brother's house, they hadn't prepared her for the shocking sight that had met her eyes when she'd entered the library.

Lucian, with his hair standing up on end and his perpetually immaculate clothing rumpled beyond redemption, was on his knees with a ragamuffin of a boy clinging to his neck. More remarkable yet, he was smiling. That her brother would smile at a child, not to mention allow one to touch him, made her wonder if she was having one of those dreams where one thought they were awake, but were in reality still asleep.

She wondered all the more seriously if that was the case when an equally disheveled Alys explained in a breathless jumble how her child-loathing brother had rescued the boy from an abusive chimney sweep. It was Lucian's grumbling after Alys and the ragamuffin had been led away that had convinced her that this was no dream.

And he was still at it. "I'm going to be stuck with her for certain after this," he groaned, pushing her hands away from his face to rise. As he was wont to do these days, he began to pace.

Charlotte straightened up, frowning. "Whatever do you mean?"

"Atwood," he moaned, as if it were the most tragic word in the English language.

Her perplexity deepened. "Atwood?"

"He witnessed the entire debacle." Lucian pivoted smoothly on his heels as he reached the Chippendale desk, retracing his steps without pausing in his explanation. "I brought him home to meet Alys. Bradwell and Stanton mentioned that his father is badgering him to marry, and I thought they would suit."

"Alys and Atwood? Suit?" Charlotte couldn't keep the amazement from her voice. "Whatever gave you such a bird-witted notion?"

That last question drew a dark scowl from Lucian. "Hardly bird-witted when you think about it. Atwood is young and rich. And he'll be an earl someday. As for Alys, well"—he reversed directions again—"her Surrey property borders his."

"And you think those reasons enough to deem them suited?"

"Many a solid marriage has been based on less."

"And many a life has been ruined by such unions," she countered sharply. "Really, Luc! How could you even consider Atwood as a possible husband for Alys without first seeing whether or not they liked each other?"

He shrugged. "What's not to like? They are both

young and both need to get married. I don't doubt that they would have done well enough together."

Charlotte sighed her exasperation and plopped down into the chair Lucian had vacated. "You really are a bird-wit. Doing well enough together is hardly what I'd call a good marriage. As for the chances of Alys fancying Atwood, well, he's as suited to her as"—she gestured helplessly as she tried to think of a completely unseemly person to illustrate her point—"as—as Tidswell is."

One dark eyebrow rose in sardonic amusement. "Isn't comparing Atwood to Tidswell rather like comparing figs to turnips? At least Atwood is young and of noble birth."

"And Tidswell can string more than three words together at a time, and his face isn't covered with spots," she volleyed back. Shaking her head, she asked, "Can't you see what I'm saying?"

He stopped his pacing midstride to stare at her. "You want Alys to marry Tidswell?" His voice and expression were so bland, it was impossible to tell whether or not he was joking.

Charlotte returned his inscrutable gaze as she tried to ascertain, then gave up with a snort. Knowing her brother, he was probably serious. For all that he could speak six languages and was a genius at mathematics, he was a complete nodcock when it came to understanding matters of the heart. Despairing as much over his ignorance as his reply, she snapped, "I was simply using Tidswell as an example to show you that a few good qualities don't necessarily make a man an appropriate suitor for Alys's hand." She shook her head to emphasize her point. "No. And I think that if you were to give the matter serious thought, you'd see how truly incompatible Atwood and Alys are."

He pivoted to begin his fifth trek across the room. "What makes you so certain they would be incompatible?"

Charlotte marked his progress with irritation. She might as well be talking to the wall for all the impression her argument was making on him.

"Well?" he demanded.

She made an impatient noise. "Well, for one thing,

Alys likes intelligent conversation, something she would never get from Atwood. Another is that her favorite pastime is dancing, and as I and my poor feet can attest, he has no skill whatsoever in that direction. She's also a skilled horsewoman, and in case you haven't heard, Atwood has yet to traverse Rotten Row without being thrown. No." She gave her head one adamant shake. "They would never suit. Alys should have a charming, intelligent, virile beau. One with whom she can experience marital pleasure . . . in and out of bed."

Lucian's pacing came to an abrupt stop, and for the first time in Charlotte's recollection, he looked embarrassed. To her amusement, he actually blushed. "Bedding is hardly an appropriate topic of discussion between brother and sister," he informed her stiffly. "Nor is it something to be considered when appraising a man's qualifications as a prospective husband."

She laughed. "Wherever do you get such quaint notions, Luc? Clayton's virility had a great deal to do with me choosing him, as did his handsome face and fine figure. Women and men aren't as different as you think in their criterion for selecting a mate. Ask Alys. I'm certain that she'll have plenty to say about your plans for her and Atwood, and none of it favorable."

"There are no plans for her and Atwood. Not after today," he growled, resuming his agitated pacing. "Nor, I doubt, with anyone else once the scandal of what happened here this afternoon gets out."

"And who, pray tell, is going to gab about it? Not Atwood. We both know that he's completely tongue-tied in company. And certainly not the servants. By the worshipful way they were looking at Alys for crowning that chimney sweep, I don't doubt they'd follow her lead and do the same to any one who dared say a wrong word about her. And, of course, your secret is safe with me."

Lucian sighed and dropped into the well-padded chair opposite of where she sat. "I only pray that you're correct. It would be a sad state of affairs if Alys were to be branded an incorrigible hoyden before she had a chance to make her bow into society."

"I'm certain no one will breathe a word. And if they do"—she shrugged—"you shall simply deny it. Whether or not they believe you, no one is going to dare call the almighty Marquess of Thistlewood a liar."

He eyed her dubiously. "You truly think so?"

"I know so," she affirmed, gesturing dismissively. Without giving him a chance to respond, she slyly added, "Anyway, since we're discussing society, I would like to tell you of my plans for Alys this season."

As always, Lucian's eyes visibly glazed at the mention of the upcoming season. "If you must."

It was on the tip of Charlotte's tongue to scold him for his indifference, but she stopped herself, knowing that it would only be a waste of breath. Confining her displeasure to a frown, she began, "As you know"—she injected a note of accusation in those first three words—"Alys has yet to make the acquaintance of any of the other girls coming out this season. I thought we might remedy that situation by having an informal tea here next week. What do you think?"

Lucian rubbed his temples as if just the thought of a dozen misses and their mamas taking tea in his drawing room gave him a raging headache. "Do as you wish," he finally murmured. "I shan't be here next week, so it makes no difference to me."

She arched one eyebrow in question. "Oh? And where exactly will you be?"

"Thistlewood Castle. I received a message this morning informing me that there was a fire in the village the day before yesterday. I need to go and assess the damage. I shan't be away any longer than a fortnight."

"You intend to run off to Sussex and leave Alys all alone in London." It was an accusation, not a question.

He snorted. "Being in a house with eighteen servants is hardly what I'd call alone. Besides, you visit her every day."

"True. But that's hardly the same thing as being under the protection of a guardian. What if she were to become ill, or something were to happen to her that required a decision from you? You are legally responsible for her, you know." When he remained unimpressed, she added, "Why, just look at the incident with the chimney sweep! What would have happened if you hadn't been here?"

"I wouldn't be stuck with a muck-crusted street urchin, that's what," he grumbled, though one corner of his mouth twitched upward as he uttered the words.

"That's not what I meant at all, and you know it!" she exclaimed, utterly exasperated. "I was referring to the chit's high-spirited penchant for getting in the briers, and your need to be on hand to extract her."

"I can hardly leave my burned-out tenants freezing in the fields while I stay in town to play nursemaid to a willful hoyden."

"And you can hardly leave her unattended," she countered.

"So what do you expect me to do?" He made a disdainful noise. "Take her with me? I'm sure she'd be thrilled to death to be pulled from the excitement of London to rusticate in Sussex."

Charlotte seemed to consider his flippantly uttered words, something she wasn't supposed to do. Worse yet, he could see the slow dawning on her face that always heralded the emergence of an idea. From the look in her eyes, he got a niggling hunch that he wasn't going to like what she was about to suggest.

His hunch proved correct. Clapping her hands in delight, she cried, "Oh, but of course! Why didn't I think of it earlier? We shall have a small house party at Thistlewood. We could invite Lord and Lady Newcombe and their daughter, Marianne. And, of course, Diana Ramsey and her father. Perhaps even—"

"No!" Lucian practically shouted the word, appalled at the suggestion. Thistlewood was his haven of calm, his peaceful sanctuary. The last thing he wanted was to have his refuge invaded by a bevy of green girls and their matchmaking mamas. Alys might make friends, true, but he would be forced to spend the fortnight dodging the traps set by this mother or that in hopes of capturing their daughter a wealthy marquess. "No," he repeated, this time more softly.

"Why ever not?" she asked, looking truly taken aback by the vehemence of his veto. As he tersely explained his reason, that alarmingly devious look seeped across her face again.

"Ah! But don't you see, little brother?" she exclaimed

in response. "What's sauce for the goose is sauce for the gander. While Alys and I entertain, you and my husband shall invite a few of the more eligible bachelors down to hunt, or fish, or whatever it is you men find amusing. The men and women, of course, shall mix and who knows? Alys might make her own match."

Reluctantly, Lucian had to admit that her idea had merit. Indeed, after a moment of further contemplation, he found himself chuckling dryly. "You truly are a scheming little vixen, Lottie."

She inclined her head in acknowledgment. "I shall take that as a compliment."

"In this instance, it was meant as one. Your plan is quite ingenious. I'm surprised I didn't think of it myself."

"You didn't think of it because you're a complete looby in matters of the heart," she retorted with a sniff. "It's a good thing you have such a shrewd sister, eh?"

"I shall reserve that judgment until after the house party." With that, he rose to his feet and extended his arm. "Now, Sister Sly-boots, shall we retire to my study and compose a list of likely victims for our upcoming matchmaking trap?"

It was well into evening when Charlotte departed to dine with her husband. Alys, who developed a headache after the library fiasco, had been served her dinner in her room, leaving Lucian to sup alone in what suddenly felt like the huge green and gold formal dining room. This was the first time in the past two weeks he'd eaten his evening meal without Alys sitting on his right, prattling about whatever fanciful notion happened to be on her mind. To his astonishment, he found that he missed her chitchat very much. So much so that he spent the entire meal thinking of her, course after savory course recalling some of their more whimsical discussions.

As a footman set his dessert before him, a bowl of Loundes pudding, his thoughts shifted erratically from her queer differentiation between trolls and goblins to her confrontation with the chimney sweep that afternoon. The remembrance set a muscle twitching in his cheek.

For all Miss Faire's milk-and-water looks, she had the heart of a Trojan. Indeed, once the wreckage in the library had been cleared and the smarting from his bruises had subsided, he'd grudgingly had to admit that for all her eccentric ways, her actions had been downright heroic.

What started out as a tic in his cheek ended up as a smile as he visualized Alys brandishing the remains of his precious urn with the climbing boy bouncing up and down next to her, raucously cheering her on. What a strange pair of little monkeys they were! Especially the boy. That he'd retained his spirit in the face of so much suffering was nothing short of miraculous.

Lucian's smile faded at that thought. Poor miserable creature. He was all skin and bones, and at last glance so covered with soot that it was impossible to tell his coloring or true physical condition. Vaguely wondering how the child fared, he picked up his spoon. In his pre-occupation with his and Charlotte's plans for the house party, he'd neglected to ask after his new . . . what? Guest? Servant? He shook his head. Whatever was he to do with the boy?

An orphans asylum, perhaps? he considered, skimming a spoonful of red currant sauce off his pudding. Illogically that idea led him to remember the fragile feel of the boy's body as he'd thrown himself against him, clutching at his waistcoat and sobbing his gratitude. That memory made him put down his spoon, his dessert unsampled.

No. An orphans asylum was out of the question, as were the almshouses and foundling hospitals. When he'd rescued the child from the sweep, like Alys, he'd become his responsibility. And part of that responsibility was to see that he thrived, something that in his pitiful physical condition would be impossible at one of the dreary charitable institutions. Besides, if he was to be scrupulously honest with himself, he'd admit that he rather admired the chimney climber.

Admire? . . . a filthy, stinking street urchin? the haughty aristocrat in him gasped, utterly appalled. As if it wasn't shocking enough that he'd stooped to notice the boy, not to mention engage in fisticuffs over him.

For a reason that completely eluded him, Lucian did as he'd done that afternoon: he pushed aside his blue-blooded prejudices and separated the boy from his social class. What he found, once he'd stripped away the stigma of poverty, was a bright, heroic child who was far more deserving of his admiration than the selfish, indolent lords and ladies he counted as his peers; a child who deserved a kinder future than that previously planned by fate.

Suddenly nothing in the world seemed as important or urgent as discovering where the boy was and how he fared. Anxious to do just that, Lucian picked up his bell intent on ringing the footman and sending him to inquire. Like the spoon, he set the bell down unused. He didn't want to hear about the boy, he wanted to see him.

Mystified as he was by his own strange turn of mind—he, the Marquess of Thistlewood making a sickbed visit to a chimney climber?—Lucian didn't stop to ponder his actions as he pushed away from the table. Like much of what he'd done and thought in the past few weeks, he simply attributed this new bit of idiosyncracy to Alys's curious influence. He was halfway to the door when he was halted by a new concern.

Where had Tidswell taken the boy? He thought for a moment. Hmm. Probably downstairs where the servants slept. Or did they sleep upstairs, in the attic? As enormous as the house was, he'd never noticed, much less cared enough to ask where the servants quarters were located. This time when he picked up the bell, he rang it.

Instantly the footman appeared. "My lord?"

"Yes—" Lucian looked at the servant blankly, realizing that though the man had been in his employ for over five years, he'd never bothered to learn his name. Hell, he'd never even spoken to him beyond a curt yes or no. Like his odd impulse to see the boy, he suddenly had a burning desire to know his servant's name. "What is your name?" he blurted out bluntly.

The man looked as stricken as if he'd just been sacked. "Hendricks, my lord. Melvin Hendricks."

Lucian nodded and smiled. As with Cusworth, his smile seemed to terrify rather than reassure the man. He sighed. Was he really such an ogre that the servants quaked at his attention? If so, why had he failed to notice this problem earlier?

He shook his head as the disturbing answer came immediately to mind. Why would he notice it? Aside from paying their wages, up until now he'd barely been aware of their existence.

"M-my lord? Is something w-wrong?" the footman stammered.

"Wrong? No. The meal was excellent." As an afterthought, he added softly, "As was your service, Hendricks."

The man appeared momentarily nonplussed, then a look that Lucian easily recognized as pleasure flushed his face. "Why, th-thank you, my lord."

Lucian's feigned smile stretched into a genuine one at the sight of his servant's delight. He felt so good inside that you would have thought that it was he, not the footman, who'd received the praise. To his surprise, Hendricks gave him a shy grin in return.

Feeling the same foreign, but enjoyable sensation he'd felt when the boy had hugged him that afternoon, he inquired, "I was wondering if you know where Tidswell has taken the chimney sweep's assistant?"

"He charged one of the upper housemaids with the little lad's care. Last I saw she was tucking him into bed in the attic." His grin broadening almost to his ears, he added, "If I might be so bold, my lord, it was jolly excellent what you did for the lad. All the servants think so."

The man's accolade made the joyous bubble in Lucian's chest swell until he was certain he would burst from it. Accepting the compliment without questioning why a mere servant's approval made him feel so splendid, he inclined his head in acknowledgment. "Now, Hendricks, if you would be so kind as to tell me where I might find the boy, I would like to look in on him myself."

The footman bowed. "If you please, my lord, it would be an honor to guide you there myself."

Lucian nodded his acquiescence.

With a lively spring in his step completely at odds with his normally formal, dignified gait, the footman led Lucian up to the attic and through the seemingly endless maze of corridors. From time to time they encountered one of the servants who, without exception, gaped at him with bulging-eyed surprise, only to drop into a shaky curtsy or bow when he nodded pleasantly in passing. After walking what felt like a mile, the footman stopped before a slightly ajar door.

"Shall I announce you, my lord?" he inquired solemnly.

Lucian shook his head. "This is a casual call. No need to alarm the boy with formalities."

A smile touched the man's lips. "As you wish, my lord. I shall await you here to direct you back to the dining room."

Lucian nodded and pushed the door open. The room within, though small and sparsely furnished, was surprisingly cozy. Someone, probably the woman who sat by the bed mending what appeared to be a sheet, had added several colorful pictures and a braided rug, transforming it from a rough garret cubbyhole into a homey retreat. Silently giving his surroundings his stamp of approval, Lucian focused his attention on the bed. By the stillness beneath the mountain of covers, it was clear that the boy slept.

Quietly, so as not to disturb his slumbers, Lucian approached the bed. *Creak!*—he stepped on a loose floorboard. The woman looked up expectantly. Like the rest of the servants, her face twisted with shock the second she laid eyes on him. "My lord!" she gasped, tangling in the sheet and falling to her knees in her haste to rise and curtsy.

Without thinking about the lordly impropriety of his actions, he rushed over and helped her to her feet. "Ssh," he cautioned, "we don't want to wake the boy."

Her mouth opened and closed soundlessly several times, then she blurted out, "Did I do somethin' wrong, milord?"

"Ssh," he repeated, jerking his head toward the coat. "And no, you've done nothing wrong." He paused to cast an approving eye at the boy's well-scrubbed face and neatly combed light brown hair. "By the looks of our young guest, I'd say that you have done your job very well." From beneath all that grime had emerged a singularly attractive child. Indeed, looking as he did now, he could easily have belonged to any one of his titled friends.

Attractive child? he repeated to himself incredulously. Now there as an oxymoron for the books. Since when did he consider children anything but a noisy, annoying, necessary evil?

"Was there somethin' you required, milord?" the maid asked.

He smiled and nodded. Apparently the key to this smiling business was to give the recipient a compliment first, for the maid was the first servant who didn't look ready to swoon at what he considered his most amiable expression. Delighted at his success, he replied, "I was wondering if the boy is well."

A frown crinkled her brow as her gaze settled on the boy's pale face. "As well as can be expected, I suppose. He's been starved and beaten somethin' awful. Thought I'd cry when I saw all the bruises and scars beneath the dirt."

Lucian's eyes narrowed as he returned his own gaze to the boy. "Was a surgeon summoned?"

"Aye, milord."

"And?"

"And he said that with plenty of good food and fresh air, he'll be right as rain in a few weeks time." Without warning her face crumpled as she looked back up at Lucian, her eyes shimmering with unshed tears. "He's such a nice little boy, milord. Please don't send him to the workhouse. Peggy, the chambermaid, and me, well, we'll see to it that he ain't no trouble if you let him stay. We'll even work extra hard to pay for his food and keep. I promise—"

Lucian laid a soothing hand on her shoulder. "It's all right—" He sighed at his own ignorance. "What is your name?"

"Tillie, milord. Tillie Digbie."

"I have no intentions of sending the boy to the work-house, Tillie. And I most certainly don't expect you and Peggy to pay for his keep. I—"

"Milord?" came a groggy voice from the cot.

Without sparing the maid another glance, Lucian

closed the short distance to the bed in two strides. "Yes. I'm here—"

"Bart," Tillie supplied automatically.

"Bart is it?" Lucian gently inquired of the boy.

He nodded against the pillows. "Bartholomew Brumbley. At yer service, milord."

Lucian smiled at the fierce pride in his voice. "Bartholomew. A fine name. Very fine indeed."

"Aye. I always liked it meself," he retorted without conceit. "Me mum named me after the Bartholomew Fair."

"And where is your mother?" Lucian inquired.

Bart shrugged. " 'Ere and there, I suppose. Ain't seen 'er since I whar five . . . not since she sold me to Moles."

"She—sold you?" Lucian repeated with horrified fascination. At the boy's nod, he bit out, "What sort of mother would sell her own children?"

"A mum wot has nine children. She hawked us all. The girls went to Mother Blackfrair. They whar virgins, or at least Mum said so, so I guess they whar probably whored to rich swells who's scairt of catchin' the clap, or 'ave an itch fer little girls. As fer the rest of the boys—" He shrugged again. "They was gone long afore I whar born."

The matter-of-fact way in which he explained his sisters being sold into prostitution chilled Lucian to the very core of his soul. That a young child would know about such evil, much less accept it as a normal part of life, was unspeakable. Without thinking, he reached down and lightly stroked the boy's thin cheek, as if by doing so he could erase all the bad memories. "How old are you, Bart?" he murmured.

"Nine."

"Nine?" Lucian echoed, unable to keep the dismayed surprise from his voice. By his size, he'd guessed him to be about seven.

Mistaking his surprise for displeasure, Bart struggled to his elbows, imploring, "Please don't turn me out, milord. I know I'm young. But I'm smart and I'll work 'ard fer ye if ye'll let me stay! I don't eat much and I'll sleep—"

"Hush. Ssh," Lucian soothed, gently coaxing him back

down to his pillows. "I have no intentions of turning you out."

The boy stared up at him as if he were afraid to believe his rare good fortune. "Ye don't?"

Lucian shook his head firmly.

"Nivver?"

"I'll make you a bargain, Bart," Lucian responded slowly. "You promise to eat until you can't stuff another morsel into your belly, and to sleep in the nice room I'll have Tidswell give you, and you can stay here as long as you like. Do we have a deal?"

With a sob, Bart threw himself at his savior, hugging him with all his might. "Oh, yes! Yes, milord! I'll do anything ye say! Jist ye wait and see. I'll be the bloody best, most loyal servant ye ever 'ad!"

Lucian felt a peculiar dampness in his eyes as he returned the boy's hug. "I don't doubt that you shall be," he murmured sincerely. And if a human heart could truly melt, the Marquess of Thistlewood's did at that moment.

Chapter 9

Three days after her encounter with the chimney sweep, Alys found herself ensconced in Lucian's luxurious traveling chariot, headed for Thistlewood Castle. Charlotte shared the coach with her, while Lucian and Clayton rode alongside on a pair of mounts they'd purchased at Tattersall's only the week before. Bringing up the rear of their small procession was a Fourgon bearing their luggage and the town servants they'd elected to bring along.

Charlotte, who was exhausted from attending a pre-season ball the night before, slept, leaving Alys free to reflect on their destination.

Thistlewood. Her heart contracted painfully at the name. How she dreaded seeing it again. Though it had been almost five hundred years since she'd last beheld its massive ashlar walls, her shame and guilt over what had happened there was as fresh as it had been all those centuries ago; her pain over Lucan's death as raw.

Blinking away the tears that always formed at the thought of Lucan, she rested her cheek against the icy window glass and stared out at the winter-raped landscape beyond. However was she to survive the next two weeks living beneath the roof of the place that held such sorrowful memories for her? Everything about it, no matter how altered it was by man and time, would remind her of Lucan.

She would feel his gentle presence in the stone and

timber of the castle; she would hear his seductive murmur in the whisper of the night wind. Most disturbing
of all, she would smell him in the ghost scents of the
thyme, agrimony, and speedwell that proliferated across
the Sussex downland in spring. Lucan had always
smelled of sunshine and the Thistlewood downs; fresh
as innocence, yet sensually earthy. And from the first
unforgettable moment when he'd held her close, she'd
been unable to draw a breath at Thistlewood without
aching to feel his arms around her.

Alys closed her eyes, her lips parting in a silent sob.
If anyone were to ask her at that moment if she knew
the whereabouts of hell, she'd have answered without
hesitation: Thistlewood Castle. For where but hell was
every sight and sound a heartache, every breath a
torment?

Apparently she looked as awful as she felt, for Charlotte, upon waking, leaned over from the opposite seat
and laid a hand on her cheek. "Are you feeling quite
all right, dear?" she inquired, frowning as she slid her
smooth, cool palm from Alys's cheek to her forehead.
"You're not getting ill from the motion are you?"

Alys smiled faintly at the other woman's solicitude.
Charlotte was the dearest person she'd met in centuries,
one with whom she looked forward to remaining friends
once she regained her humanity. Taking Charlotte's
hand from her forehead to enfold it in her own, she
reassured her, "I'm fine, Lottie. I was just thinking."

"They must be very gloomy thoughts indeed for you
to look so wretched," the other woman observed, cock-
ing her head in a manner that clearly invited Alys's confidence. Before Alys could respond, she added in a
breathy gush, "Ah! But of course! We're passing
through Surrey now, and if I recall correctly, your home
is just a few miles from here. Is that what has you in a
fit of the dismals?"

"Yes," Alys lied. Well, she could hardly tell Charlotte
that she was mourning for the man her brother had been
five hundred years ago, now could she?

Charlotte nodded sympathetically. "I remember how
terribly homesick I was for Thistlewood when I was first
married. No doubt I would have pined away completely

had Clayton not taken me there for frequent visits during that first year. If you like, I shall ask Lucian if we might stop at Fairfax on our way back to London."

"No!" Alys protested, more sharply than she'd intended. At Charlotte's startled look, she added, this time softly, "No, I—I don't want to be a bother." The truth was that the single night she'd spent at her old home waiting to leave for London and Lucian had been sheer misery; as she was certain would be the case at Thistlewood, everything she saw at Fairfax had reminded her of her human life and all the suffering she'd caused.

Charlotte made a clucking noise. "I realize my brother isn't exactly a paragon of warmth and thoughtfulness, but he's not such a heartless beast as to deny you a visit to your home if you so wish it."

Alys shook her head again. "Perhaps I'm the heartless beast for, in truth, I have no wish to visit Fairfax. As terrible as I know it sounds, I find that I'm exceedingly anxious to return to town and all the excitement of the coming season." It was no lie. She truly was eager to get back to London and get started on matching Lucian with Reina Castell.

Charlotte chuckled and pressed a kiss to Alys's hand, which she still held. "You're not heartless, my dear, merely young. And it's only natural for you to want the excitement of parties and outings, as well as to crave the company of others your own age. Lucian and I considered those things when we decided to come to Thistlewood, which is why we planned to surprise you with a house party. We thought you might enjoy getting acquainted with some of the other girls before the start of the season. Lucian and Clayton have also invited a few of the young men down for hunting, so you shall have an occasion to practice your dancing and conversation before the social rounds begin."

"A house party," Alys echoed, her mind working fast and furiously. "With other young women?"

"And men," Charlotte reminded her.

"Yes, of course," she murmured absently. If Lucian had had a hand in making up the guest list, it was very possible that Miss Castell had been included. That being the case, this would be the perfect opportunity to further

her matchmaking cause. With that design in mind, she
inquired coyly, "Would you mind telling me who you've
invited, and perhaps a bit about each guest so I won't
feel quite so awkward when we're introduced?"

"That's exactly what I intended to do." Opening her
reticule, Charlotte extracted a piece of paper. After un-
folding it, she read the first name. "Lord Langley, and
his daughter, Miss Diana Ramsey." Looking up, she
elaborated, "They're Lucian's Thistlewood neighbors.
Though Diana is older than you—she turned twenty-four
last month—I'm certain you'll enjoy her company. Like
yourself, she's an excellent horsewoman. She's also the
best hunter in the county. She's beat the men to the
fox at the annual hunt at Thistlewood two years in a
row now."

"I'm sure we shall get on famously," Alys assured her,
her palms itching to rip the list from Charlotte's hands
to see if Miss Castell was on it. Instead she slaked her
urge by prodding, "Have you invited anyone from
London?"

Charlotte looked up from the list to eye her curiously.
"Was there someone in particular you wanted to meet?
A young man, perhaps?"

It was on the tip of Alys's tongue to come right out
and ask about Miss Castell. Then it occurred to her that
she might be expected to reveal where she had heard of
the woman and the nature of her interest. Remembering
her promise to the dressmaker's assistant not to repeat
her gossip, she fibbed, "I thought it might be nice to
have a friend who I might visit once we return to town."

Satisfied by her response, Charlotte consulted her list.
Her index finger sliding down the page, she mused,
"London. Let's see now . . ." Her finger paused. "Ah,
yes. Lord and Lady Wakehurst, and their daughter, Cassandra. They have a town house in Mayfair. Cassie is a
dainty creature of eighteen . . . quite refined and ladylike. Between you and me, I've always thought her
rather lacking in spirit, but Lucian thought you might do
well to emulate her ways. Then there is—"

Without so much as a shout of warning the coach
lurched to an abrupt stop, causing both women to grab
for their holders to save themselves from being flung to

the floor. From outside arose a cacophony of babbling voices, accompanied by the high-pitched screams of a horse.

"Whatever could be happening?" Charlotte exclaimed, straining to see out the window. As if in reply, there was a loud *thump!* . . . then Lucian's riderless stallion streaked past the window in a blur of sleek mahogany. For a long moment both women sat staring blankly after the animal, too stunned by the significance of the sight to respond. Then Charlotte uttered a piercing cry of "Luc! Dear God, Luc!" and flung herself from the carriage. In a flash of jonquil-yellow cashmere, she sprinted down the frosty road.

Alys was after her in a twinkling. That Lucian might be injured, or possibly worse, sent her panic-stricken heart crashing to the pit of her stomach. Chanting over and over again, "Please, Lord. Please let him be all right," she raced to where a small knot of servants were clustered in the middle of the road.

Ahead of her, Charlotte shoved through the crowd, shrieking Lucian's name. In the next instant, her wail rent the air. Filled with terror, not for herself and what she would lose if Lucian died, but for Lucian himself, and his imperiled soul, Alys followed the other woman's example and rudely elbowed her way through the tightly packed wall of humanity. When she reached his side, she froze.

Crumpled on his back with his limp limbs tangled in the folds of his black traveling cloak and his head lolling loosely on Charlotte's lap, Lucian looked dead. Too numb with horror to react, she merely stood there gaping down at his ashen face.

It was the screech of "Gor blimey, milord! Are ye kilt?" from Bart, paired with the jostling she received as he hurled past her and planted himself on his benefactor's chest, that snapped her out of her stupor.

"Lucian?" she whispered brokenly. Then she collapsed to her knees in the muddy snow, her legs suddenly too weak to hold her. Her ragged sobs mingling with those of Charlotte and Bart, she reached down and gently touched his pale cheek.

Over the past few weeks, he'd come to mean so much

to her. More than she'd ever imagined possible. She thought about him constantly during the day, she dreamed of him at night. If she didn't know how impossible the notion was, she'd have said that she was falling in love with him.

So tender were her feelings for him at that moment as she lightly caressed his cheek that she'd have gladly traded her immortal soul for Aengus's power of healing. Willingly she'd have agreed to be banished to the underground kingdom, hopeless and doomed, living a shallow imitation of life until she turned to dust and simply ceased to be. Anything to save Lucian.

As if someone, Aengus, or perhaps even God, had heard her heart's anguished plea and had granted it, Lucian's thick dark lashes fluttered once, then he slowly opened his eyes. For a brief second he stared up at her, his slate-gray eyes blank and unfocused. Then he muttered in what at that moment Alys considered to be his wonderfully irritated voice, "What the hell is everybody wailing about? Can't a man take a spill from a horse without having it treated like a national tragedy?"

"Oh, Luc!" was all Charlotte managed to choke out as she swooped down to cover his face with kisses.

"For God's sake, Lottie!" he sputtered, struggling to rise in an attempt to escape her affectionate assault. To his supreme frustration his efforts were foiled by a squirming weight on his chest. "What the—" he began, only to break off midsentence at the curious sight of Bart clinging to his coat, keening as if he'd just lost his best friend. "Bart?" he murmured, lightly touching the boy's thin, heaving shoulder.

Bart looked up rather blankly. In the next instant he let out a hoarse screech and scrambled off him, eyeing him with as much amazement as if he'd just arisen from the grave. His first words confirmed that that was exactly what he was thinking. "Yer-yer not kilt?" he gasped.

Lucian frowned, but not unkindly. "Of course I'm not 'kilt.' Since when do dead men sit up and speak?"

"You may not be killed, Luc. But it's possible that you were injured in your fall," Charlotte cautioned, laying one gloved hand on his chest to stay him as he again attempted to rise. "You should lie still, at least until we're certain that nothing is broken."

"I can assure you that I'd have noticed immediately if anything were broken," he informed her dryly. Nonetheless, for all his protests to the contrary, he let out a hiss of pain as he sat up. Though it was true that no bones appeared broken, everything else felt to have been bruised black and blue.

"Luc—" Charlotte protested, reaching out to grasp his shoulder.

He grunted his annoyance at her coddling and shrugged her away. "For the last time, Lottie. I'm fine." Determined to prove his claim, he started to stand, only to fall back down with a yelp as brutal pain lanced through his right ankle. Inaudibly gritting out a particularly vile curse, he gingerly massaged his throbbing limb through the stiff leather of his riding boot.

"You really are the most pigheaded man I've ever had the misfortune to know," Charlotte exclaimed, rising to her own feet to peer down at him with marked displeasure. Ignoring the humiliating fact that the servants were well within earshot, she braced her hands on her hips and proceeded to scold him.

"I told you that you were probably injured. But did you listen? Of course not! Like most men you had to find out for yourself, quite possibly causing yourself further harm in the process. It would serve your stubbornness right if you were forced to hobble about on crutches for the next few weeks. I remember—"

"Enough!" Lucian roared. Determined to regain the upper hand, and what little dignity he had left, he added in his most lordly tone, "There is no call to be such a scold. I twisted my ankle, nothing more," all the while flexing the anatomy in question to assure himself of the validity his claim. To his relief, his foot wiggled within his boot, though every movement was torture.

Obviously his face reflected his discomfort, for his unchastened sister snapped, "It might not be broken, but from the way you're wincing and grimacing, it's bad enough that you should ride the rest of the distance in the coach." With that, she imperiously signaled for the footmen to help him stand.

Lucian opened his mouth to protest his need for assistance, but a moan issued forth instead as the servants carefully levered him to his feet. Manfully stifling his next moan behind his clenched teeth, he gratefully grasped the shoulders of the flanking footmen. If he hadn't experienced a broken ankle in his youth and the agony that accompanied it, the pain he was experiencing now would have made him seriously wonder if his injury was worse than he'd first suspected.

Instead of easing his mind as he'd hoped, the memory of that miserable experience merely made him all the more aware of his discomfort. Desperate for something—anything!—to distract his thoughts, he glanced at the assembly around him.

What an odd cortege they made! Charlotte hovered near his right, in turn scolding and cautioning the supporting footmen, while Alys, her expression as somber as if they were escorting him to his grave instead of his coach, kept pace on his left. Trailing behind was the retinue of servants. And bringing up the rear, carrying his hat with the reverence of a bridesmaid bearing the train of a bridal gown, was Bart.

To his surprise every pair of eyes was leveled in his direction, the compassion in their gazes undeniable. That the servants sympathized with and were concerned about his discomfort was a startling revelation. In all his years as their employer, he'd never much thought about their feelings for him. They had never seemed important. But now, as he was being aided with genuine kindness by the very people he'd until recently dismissed as insignificant, he saw that it mattered very much indeed.

In truth, he found the thoughtful manner in which the footmen coaxed him over the road ruts and the smiles of encouragement from the rest of the servants humbling to the extreme; humbling in that he knew that he didn't deserve anything more from them than their requisite services. He certainly hadn't done anything, like double their wages or increase their Christmas boon, to earn such a generous wealth of compassion.

It wasn't until Bart scampered to his side and slipped his mitten-clad hand in his to administer his childish brand of comfort that he understood their change of demeanor. By the expression of tender pride reflected on every face, it was clear that their feelings had nothing to do with money, and everything to do with his charity toward Bart.

Completely baffled, Lucian dropped his gaze from his smiling servants to the small boy looking up at him with big, adoring eyes. That something as seemingly insignificant as an act of kindness could reap such enormous rewards was almost too incredible to believe. Especially when that act was one that brought him such extraordinary pleasure.

"Careful there, milord," cautioned the footman on his left, fortifying his support as he eased him over a particularly slippery patch of ice in front of the coach door.

Lucian glanced up to meet his gaze, smiling. "Thank you, Dinsmore." Just the look of pleasure wreathing the man's face made the trouble he'd gone to to learn the servants' names worthwhile.

As he waited for one of the other footmen, Cutler, if he remembered correctly, to open the door, Bart gave his hand one final squeeze and then, with visible reluctance, started to pull away. Smiling gently down at the boy's wistful face, he tightened his own grasp to stay him.

"Would you do me the honor of riding in my traveling chariot with me, young man?" he inquired. "I find that my ankle hardly hurts at all when you hold my hand like this." And it was true. As distracted as he was by the joyous feelings warming his heart, he barely noticed his injury.

Like Dinsmore, Bart's face lit up as if illuminated by a hundred candles. "I'll 'old it all the way to Sussex, milord, and with pleasure," he exclaimed with a fervency that left no doubt that he would do as exactly as he promised.

Lucian was about to respond when he noticed that Alys had wandered over to the edge of the road where Clayton and the groom were attempting to calm his furiously kicking and bucking stallion. From where he stood, he could see that she was frowning. It only took a second for him to realize that she wasn't frowning at his seemingly possessed horse, but at the road. He groaned inwardly when in the next instant her lips began to move.

Bloody hell! Alys was babbling to her imaginary friend again. Clenching his teeth against his pain as the footmen helped him step into the coach, he vowed to somehow banish—what was his name again? Hmm. Ah, yes. Hedley. He'd banish Hedley back into the realm of Alys's imagination from whence he'd sprung.

At that moment, Alys herself would have heartily agreed to banish Hedley, preferably to somewhere far, far away. "You could have gotten his lordship killed with your stupid tricks," she hissed, gesturing to the maddened horse whose mane and tail were being mercilessly tweaked by a pair of giggling pixies.

The hob sullenly stabbed at the snow with one of his two stumpy toes. "Don't ye be giving me the evil eye. Ain't my fault that the pixies attacked Lord Tight-Arse's horse."

"Oh, really?" she intoned, raising her eyebrows in a show of sardonic disbelief.

"Oh, really," he echoed, "and ye ain't got no evidence proving that I had anything to do with it."

"Don't I? If I'm not mistaken that's Beacon tangled in the horse's mane,"—she nodded at the tiny, green-clad man kicking at the animal's neck—"and Scur swinging from his tail." Her head shifted to indicate the mischief-maker's identically attired companion. "Both who are, if I recall correctly, friends of yours."

Hedley's beady-eyed gaze shifted guiltily from her face to the hole he was digging with his toe. "So? That don't prove a thing."

"It most certainly does. Those two are Kent wood pixies, and I happen to know that we're in Surrey."

"So?"

Bracing her hands on her hips to glare down at him in a manner reminiscent of Charlotte scolding Lucian, she rebuked, "You must think me a complete fool if you believe that after five hundred years I don't know that wood pixies never leave their own forests without specific instructions to do so. They most certainly don't go about bedeviling horses in foreign woods unless, of course, that is the mission that drew them there in the first place."

Hedley sniffed. "So?"

"So. Since you're the only other world folk I know who bears ill will toward Lucian, who else could be responsible? I can assure you that there isn't a single fairy in England who would dare play such a hazardous prank on Aengus's reborn son for the sake of their own amusement." When he didn't reply, she demanded, "Well?"

By now the hole in the snow was large enough to encompass his entire foot. "Just wanted to teach him a lesson for calling me a bloody damn cock-and-bull tale," he grumbled without looking up.

"Teaching Lord Thistlewood is my job, not yours," she pointed out severely. "Your duty is to assist me, and right now I demand that you do so by sending your friends back to Kent."

He slanted her a mutinous glower.

She tossed down her trump card. "Either you do as I say, or I shall be forced to summon Allura and have her report to Aengus that you almost got his son killed again. I also expect you to promise to refrain from playing such dangerous tricks in the future."

The hob actually looked alarmed by her threat. "Dinna mean to hurt the pompous clodpate, just embarrass him," he mumbled, kicking snow into the hole.

"Unfortunately you succeeded on both counts. Now—"

"Alys!"

Alys sighed and looked over to where Lucian was leaning out the coach door, impatiently gesturing for her to return to the vehicle. "Coming!" she shouted back. Returning her gaze to Hedley, she ordered, "Now send those pixies back to Kent, and do it now."

While Hedley ran in circles around the frenzied stallion, shouting something in a fairy language she didn't understand, Alys stripped off her kid gloves and knelt down. By the time she'd finished stuffing the gloves with clean white snow, the pixies had disappeared and the horse, though shaking and lathered, was calm. After ordering the hob to ride with her so she could keep an eye on him, she returned to the waiting coach.

Compared to the biting cold outside, the interior of the conveyance was warm, deliciously so. Lucian, minus his boot and stocking, was settled in the seat opposite Charlotte with his injured ankle propped up on her lap. Next to him, Bart sat patting and stroking his hand like a doting mother soothing her fitful child. And curled up beneath their seat mumbling something, probably insults about her, was the sulking Hedley.

As Alys slipped into the seat next to Charlotte, the woman looked up from examining her brother's ankle to inquire, "Whatever were you doing out there? I was beginning to worry that you'd frozen to death."

Alys held up her snow-filled gloves. "I was making ice packs for Lucian's' ankle. I thought they might help numb the pain."

"As if my leg isn't cold enough," Lucian muttered, casting a jaundiced eye at her offering.

"Oh, stop being such an ingrate, Luc. I think it was very sweet of Alys to sacrifice her gloves to make you the packs," Charlotte admonished unsympathetically. "And if anyone has call to whine about the cold, it's she. Why, just look at her poor hands." She lifted the appendages in question from Alys's lap to chafe between her warm palms. "They're like blocks of ice from digging in the snow."

To Alys's astonishment, Lucian didn't make one of his derogatory noises, nor did he shower her with dark scowls. No. After viewing her thoughtfully for a moment or two, he smiled faintly. "You're absolutely right, Lottie. It was considerate of her." His smile widening into one of heart-stopping beauty, he shifted his smoky gaze to Alys, murmuring, "Thank you."

Alys stared back, too overwhelmed by his magnificence to reply. Scowling, he'd been a handsome man; smiling, he was a devastating one. Bowing her head to hide the heated flush she felt creeping across her face, she somehow managed to croak, "You're welcome. W-would you like me to apply the—um—packs for you?"

"If you would be so kind. Yes."

It was then that she glanced at his injury. "Oh, Lucian!" she wailed, gently touching his angrily swollen ankle. "How awful! Are you sure it's not broken?"

"Positive." He wiggled his toes to demonstrate, though the display made him wince. "It looks much worse than it is. I can assure you that it shall be completely healed in a few days."

Alys eyed him dubiously. "How can you be so certain?"

"I had two similar injuries during the war, though neither," he justified wryly, "was caused by a spill from a horse."

"So why were you thrown this time?" Charlotte cut in. "You haven't lost control of a horse since you were, oh—" She indicated a very small child with her hands.

"I don't know. One minute Clayton and I were"—he sucked in a hissing breath as Alys laid the packs over his damaged ankle—"trotting along discussing Lord Conaway's prime new cattle. In the next instant, Charlemagne reared up and dashed off in a mad frenzy. If I were prone to superstition, I'd say that the animal was possessed."

"Superstitious or not, it wouldn't hurt to use a rowan switch instead of a crop the next time you ride that overgrown brute," Charlotte declared, tucking a woolen lap robe over Alys's handiwork to keep the uninjured parts of his bare foot and lower leg warm.

Lucian looked at her as if she were as deranged as his horse. "Why should I do a thing like that?"

"Don't you remember Lady Tremaine?" she countered.

His brow furrowed. "Lady Tremaine?"

"Oh! Of course you don't remember her. How foolish of me. You were just a baby when father gave her to me," Charlotte replied, giving his leg an apologetic pat. "Lady Tremaine was my very first pony. I received her as a gift for my fourth birthday. To make a long story short, she turned out to be an exceedingly wicked beast, biting anyone who came within arm's length of her and bucking me off every chance she got. Father was seriously considering putting her down when Nurse Spratling suggested that I use a rowan switch to discipline her instead of a crop. She said that rowan switches drive out evil spirits and control bewitched horses."

"Did it work?" Bart piped in, his small face screwed up in an expression of complete mystification.

Charlotte grinned and winked at him. "Like a charm. Two whops on her rump, and she became the most obedient horse in the stable."

Predictably enough, Lucian was incredulous. "Rowan branches? Evil spirits and bewitched horses? Bah! Superstitious stuff and nonsense. Next you'll be telling me to tuck a four-leaf clover in my hat and dance around a fairy ring."

"You do that only if you wish to see fairies," Alys impulsively corrected him.

He transferred his disdainful gaze from his sister to her. "Oh? And what would you have me do? Sprinkle my horse with holy water and have the pope spit in its eyes?"

Alys bristled at his sneering tone. "Of course not. Now you're being completely ridiculous."

"Ah. Let us heed the voice of sanity," he mumbled, just barely loud enough to be heard.

"Really, Luc. Just because you're in a foul mood from falling from your horse gives you no call to be rude," Charlotte chided. Fixing her brother with a condemning look, she said, "Please do tell us what you would do about the horse, Alys. I find the subject of spells and charms exceedingly fascinating."

Lucian snorted and closed his eyes as if the whole topic induced him to nap.

Alys shrugged. "Simple. I'd hang an iron bell around its neck."

Charlotte looked intrigued. "Why a bell?"

"The problem with Lucian's horse isn't evil spirits, but mischievous pixies. Wood pixies to be exact. And fairy folk hate both iron and bells."

That drew another snort, a softer one, from Lucian.

Which Charlotte ignored. "I remember Nurse Spratling mentioning their dislike of iron . . . but bells?" She shook her head. "Why do they hate bells?"

"Because they associate the ringing of bells with churches. Fairies are terrified of God and anything that has to do with him."

Bewilderment creased Charlotte's brow as she absorbed that bit of information. "They fear God? How very odd!"

"Why'd anyone be 'fraid of God?" Bart quizzed, his expression mirroring Charlotte's.

"According to legend, the very first fairies were angels who were cast out of heaven," Alys explained, glancing from woman to child. "As a result of being shunned by God, they have no immortal souls and anything related to religion reminds them of that dreadful fact."

"I can't say that I blame them," Charlotte commented with a delicate shudder. "How singularly terrible not to have the hope of heaven."

Bart seemed to consider Alys's explanation for a moment, then blurted out, "Why'd God toss 'em out? Whar they so awful wicked?"

Alys smiled at his youthful curiosity. "They weren't exactly wicked, Bart. Their crime was that they let themselves be beguiled by Satan. Now while beguilement didn't make them bad enough for hell, they certainly weren't good enough to remain in heaven. So God cast them all to the earth. Wherever they were when heaven's gates closed was where they were forced to remain forever. That explains why some fairies live in the air, while others in trees, water, or even in the bowels of the earth."

"If fairies ain't good 'nough to go to 'eaven, or wicked 'nough for 'ell, wot 'appens to 'em when they die?" Bart inquired solemnly.

"Instead of souls, they have what they call fairy essence. When it runs out, usually after about a thousand years, they simply fade away and cease to be."

That last explanation drew a derogatory noise from Lucian. "I wish those ridiculous legends would follow suit and disappear as well." Opening his eyes to shoot Alys a look of pure irritation, he grumbled, "Now if it isn't asking too much, could we please change the subject? It's bad enough knowing that I shall probably have to endure the Thistlewood tenants' fairy tomfoolery without having more of the same inflicted on me all the way there."

"You see," Charlotte began, her lips twitching with suppressed amusement as she turned to Alys. "The tenants believe that Lucian is one of our ancestors, a knight named Lucan from the thirteenth or fourteenth century who—"

"She's already read the tale," Lucian rudely cut her off. "So why don't we close the tedious subject by simply saying that my tenants believe me to be Lucan come back to save his soul."

"A belief which will probably strengthen to certainty when you show up with a lovely young lady named Alys," Charlotte pointed out with a chuckle. "I don't doubt that their minds will have you two married and your soul saved before the end of our visit."

Lucian looked as shocked as Alys felt at the notion of a marriage between them. *Not that being wed to him would be so awful,* she mused, lowering her eyelashes to add stealth to her gaze as she appreciatively scrutinized his elegant face and form. *No, not awful at all.* Just impossible.

Clearly Lucian thought the idea not only impossible, but distasteful to the extreme, for he was quick to retort, "Even my tenants, as fanciful as they are at times, aren't jingle-brained enough to think that Alys would ever suit me."

For some reason, his brusque intimation that he could never in any way be attracted to her stung Alys more than she would ever have believed. Not, of course, that she wanted him to view her as a possible bride. It was just that she found it disheartening to the extreme to be perceived as unworthy by a man to whom she was admittedly attracted. It shook her faith in herself, making her seriously wonder if, despite Charlotte's frequent reassurances to the contrary, she was lacking not only in appearance, but in character and demeanor.

Her mood suddenly as deflated as if someone had punched a hole in her spirit and drained out her happiness, Alys sighed. Ah well. What did it really matter what the haughty Lord Thistlewood thought of her anyway? He would soon be happily wed to Miss Castell, and she would be free to find a man with less exacting standards.

Or maybe not. Somehow the thought of wedding and bedding a man who wasn't Lucian left her feeling nothing short of miserable. If possible her spirits depressed a fraction more. That she desired Lucian was a dismal truth that was growing more and more impossible to deny as the days sped by.

But I shall deny it! she vowed, straightening her spine with resolution. Not that she had any choice in the matter. Even if she dared to act upon her feelings, which she didn't, Lucian had made it abundantly clear that he had no interest in her save getting her married and off his hands. It was remembering his matchmaking plans for her that reminded her of her own for him.

With a determination born of hopelessness, she savagely shoved aside her futile desires and abruptly asked Charlotte, "Would you finish telling me who will be attending the house party?" The sooner she matched Lucian, the sooner she could get away from him and the unsettling emotions he roused within her.

"I assume that you have no objections to us discussing the party?" Charlotte in turn asked Lucian, her voice edged in sarcasm.

In an imperious display of boredom, he tipped his head against the petit-point squab and closed his eyes, muttering, "Be my guest."

At his less than gracious consent, Charlotte retrieved her list from the coach floor and began to read. When she laid the paper down a half hour later, Alys couldn't help frowning.

"Why, you looked distressed, dear," Charlotte observed. "Is there someone on the list you find displeasing?"

Lucian's eyes slitted open to join his sister in her interrogative scrutiny.

Alys shook her head, her mind searching frantically for a diplomatic way in which to question the exclusion of Miss Castell.

"Then what is the matter?" Charlotte prodded gently. "Did you perhaps think of a friend you might like us to invite?"

"Not a friend, but, well, there was someone I would like to meet," Alys ventured tentatively.

"And who might that be?" This was from Lucian,

who, surprisingly enough, was now viewing her with genuine interest.

Unable to meet his querying gaze as she uttered the name, she busied herself with checking her makeshift ice packs. "Reina Castell."

Her reply was greeted with absolute silence. After an overlong moment of such, she hazarded a glance up. Charlotte was gaping at her in horror, while Lucian looked as unpleasantly surprised as if he'd just sat on a thorn. As his piercing gaze stabbed into hers, his perturbed expression slowly dissolved into one she knew all too well: disapproval. After another tense beat, he ground out, "What do you know about Reina Castell?"

Seized by a sudden fit of trepidation, she nervously scooted her gaze back to the ice packs. "Not much. I overheard it mentioned how very popular she is, and I thought—well—" she grappled for a plausible explanation, "I thought that she might teach me a trick or two to attract suitors." Perfect!

Lucian released a sharp bark of laughter. "Oh, she knows plenty of tricks to attract men, but none I wish you to learn."

"But why ever not? You have made it abundantly clear that you're eager to marry me off. Don't you want me to have every possible advantage so I can make a good match?" she appealed, returning her earnest gaze to his now turbulent one.

He in turn shifted his to Charlotte, who held up both hands and said, "Oh, no, Luc. You deal with this."

When he finally glanced back at her, he seemed at a loss. After a moment of contemplation, he cleared his throat twice and muttered, "Reina Castell is a ladybird."

"A . . . ladybird?" she repeated, puzzled. Was ladybird a term of endearment like lovebird?

"You know." He gestured rather helplessly. "A demi-rep."

She tilted her head to one side, waiting for him to further clarify his meaning.

He gestured again. "A *fille de joie.*"

She shook her head. "I'm sorry. I'm afraid I'm not very good at French."

"Oh, botheration! She's Lucian's mistress," Charlotte blurted out in an exasperated tone.

Alys gasped her dismay. "M-mistress?"

"For God's sake, Lottie. Must you always be so blunt?" Lucian growled, his face darkening with something suspiciously like a blush.

"Pshaw, Luc! Don't be such a ninnyhammer. Alys is bound to hear gossip about such things when she gets out into society, so we might as well tell her about them now."

With a terrible sinking sensation deep in her chest, Alys glanced from Charlotte's vexed face to Lucian's suddenly inscrutable one. Then she sighed.

So much for an easy match.

Chapter 10

"Thistlewood Castle," Charlotte announced, lightly thumping the window with her index finger as she pointed.

Bart obligingly pressed his face to the glass to look. "Blimey gor! 'Tis a bleedin' palace!" he exclaimed in the next instant, his voice breathless with awe.

"Gentlemen do not say blimey gor or bleeding," Lucian quietly corrected him.

The boy turned from the view, his expression earnest as he peered up at his hero. "Wot'd a gentleman say then?"

Lucian considered the matter for a moment, then replied, " 'By Jove, it's a genuine palace,' would be a fine response."

"By Jove, 'tis a genny-un palace," Bart echoed. Then he grinned. "I like that . . . by Jove. By Jove!"

Chuckling as Lucian launched into a lesson on socially acceptable oaths, Charlotte turned to Alys. "What do you think of your home for the next fortnight?"

Wishing upon wish that she were alone and thus able to view the castle without an audience, Alys reluctantly glanced out at the dusk-grayed landscape. In the distance, rising from the dark mirror of a moat, its buttressed battlements silhouetted against the dying glow of the setting sun, was Thistlewood.

The sight left her as stunned and breathless as if she'd been struck squarely over her heart. It looked exactly as it had the first time she'd seen it all those centuries ago, on that joyous evening when she and her father had arrived at the castle to partake in a banquet celebrating her betrothal to Lucan. Such powerful feelings of déjà vu did the scene invoke that when she closed her eyes to shut it out, she saw Lucan as he'd looked that night, galloping out to meet them.

His armor, all gold and glittering in the light of day, was bleached ghostly silver by the rising moon; his fluttering green mantle captured the twilight gloom, darkening until it was as black as a midnight grave. When he was but a scant yard away, he reined his pale gray destrier to a prancing halt.

For several interminable seconds he sat there, perfectly still. Then, in a blurred chain of motions, he yanked off his helm and threw back his coif, revealing hair like wet ebony.

Alys gasped. Lucian.

Or was it? Though the knight's features perfectly mirrored Lucian's, his expression was impossibly unlike any she'd ever seen on the face of the self-possessed Marquess of Thistlewood. This Lucian looked haunted, tragically so, like a man who was doomed and knew it.

Blanketed in an odd, achy sense of foreboding she slowly opened her eyes. "Oh, Lucian," she mouthed, resting her forehead wearily against the frosty window glass.

For a long moment she stared out at the road, bleakly watching a Mail coach approach at breakneck speed. It wasn't until the vehicle had passed and was little more than a distant twinkle of lamplight that she began to understand the significance of her dark vision.

She'd known that seeing Thistlewood again would be a torment, but she'd seriously misjudged the depth and nature of her pain. While it was true that she grieved for Lucan, tenderly and with the poignancy that comes with the finality of death, that grief had somehow become eclipsed by the deepening sense of anguish she felt over Lucian's precarious state. The strange knight was simply another of her conscience's many cryptic reminders that what she'd done here at Thistlewood might possibly have damned Lucian to a fate every bit as awful as Lucan's.

As if she needed a reminder. Struggle though she might, a strangled sob slipped out.

"Alys?" Charlotte murmured. When Alys didn't reply, she cupped her chin in her palm and turned her face toward her, tipping it up into the flickering light from the coach lamp. What she saw made her frown. "Why, whatever is wrong?"

Alys shook her head, squeezing her eyes shut to halt the fall of her burgeoning tears. But it was too late. A bead of damp sorrow had already escaped and was slipping down her cheek.

"She's crying, Luc," Charlotte announced, her tone clearly commanding her brother to do something to remedy the situation.

There was the sound of movement on the opposite seat, then another hand, this one larger and stronger, took her chin from Charlotte. "Alys? What's the matter?" this was from Lucian.

Too distraught to concoct a plausible reply, Alys screwed her weepy eyes yet tighter and croaked, "Nothing."

He made an impatient noise. "Of course something is wrong. I know you well enough to know that you wouldn't turn into a watering pot without cause. Clearly something is plaguing you, and unless you tell me what it is, I shan't be able to remedy it."

When she merely shook her head again, he sighed. There was a beat of silence, then, "As my ward, it's only proper that you confide your troubles to me . . . even those you think I might find silly or trifling. By the same token, I give you my most solemn vow to do my duty as your guardian and counsel you to the utmost of my ability."

She heard the soft murmur of fabric against flesh, then she felt his warm breath tickling against her ear. "Besides, poppet, if I remember correctly, we agreed to become better acquainted," he whispered. "And how, pray tell, am I to do so if you refuse to trust me?"

Poppet. More than his words, as encouraging as they were, it was his unexpected use of that charmingly quaint endearment that made her open her eyes to look at him. He appeared concerned, genuinely so, his gaze warm and reassuring as it touched hers.

With a smile that reflected the kindness in his eyes, he gently wiped away her tears with his kidskin-gloved thumb. "Will you tell me, or shall we play charades so I might hazard a guess?"

The teasing note in his voice completely melted her already softening defenses, and before she knew quite what she was saying, she blurted out, "I'm afraid."

That confession seemed to give him pause. "Afraid?" His dark brows drew together. "Afraid of what?"

"I think it's perfectly obvious what," Charlotte replied for her. "She's afraid of the castle. The poor child took one look at it and was seized by the vapors."

Lucian stared at his sister thoughtfully, as if considering her summation, then looked back at Alys, whose face he still held. "Is that true?"

Slowly she nodded. It was true. Her fears were all rooted at Thistlewood.

For a moment he seemed at a loss as to how to respond, then his expression visibly softened and he smiled. "I realize that the castle is old and looks quite ominous, but I can assure you that no boggles or ghosts lurk within its walls." His smile broadened into a grin. "However, if one should choose to make an appearance during our visit, you tell me straightaway and I shall chase it away."

As Alys gazed at his face, one made all the more handsome by the humor crinkling his eyes and curling his lips, she found that she truly believed his words. If anyone could put her ghosts to rest, it was he. For who, but he, had the power to distract her penitent thoughts from Lucan. Who, but he, could strengthen her faith in her own ability to redeem his soul? Indeed, he was presently doing both very well with his uplifting display of newfound compassion.

Feeling suddenly better than she'd felt in centuries, Alys shyly returned his smile. "Thank you, Lucian. I shall remember that and be less frightened knowing that you stand ready to champion me against whatever might lurk in the shadows."

Chuckling, he released her face and fished his handkerchief from his pocket. "Sir Bogy-slayer, at your service, my lady," he quipped, presenting it with the air of a knight favoring a maid with a victory token.

She accepted with a regal incline of her head.

"Well done. Very good, indeed," Charlotte said, eyeing her brother with sisterly pride. "If I didn't know better, I'd say that you were beginning to sprout a heart."

How Lucian responded, or even if he in fact did, was lost to the deafening clatter of the wheels as the coach started across the causeway spanning the moat. Not that Alys would have marked his words had she heard them, she was spellbound by her immediate view of Thistlewood.

Built in a symmetrical foursquare, the castle was as impressive today as it had been five hundred years earlier. Round, turreted towers joined the four corners, square ones rose at strategic intervals along the walls. A great gatehouse, crowned with a parapet and stabbing aggressively into the star-flecked sky, fortified the entrance. At first glance it appeared as if time had passed it by. Then they pulled through the gatehouse and Alys saw how vastly it had changed.

Apparently every generation of Thistlewood heirs had seen fit to leave their mark, for the once spacious central courtyard was all but engulfed by structural additions in a patchwork of styles. To the right was a gallery in the Tudor style, to the left a wing from the Italian Renaissance; both leading from the castle to an immense Jacobean edifice with Gothic and Rococo embellishments.

As if reading her mind, Lucian nodded at the buildings and more groaned than said, "Hideous, isn't it?"

"The additions are rather—uh—startling," she replied diplomatically. "Though I imagine that the castle would be quite lovely without them."

"My thought exactly, which is why my contribution to the glorious heritage of Thistlewood Castle shall be to tear them down and restore the original structure."

Charlotte laughed as the door was pulled open and the steps folded down. "What, Luc? No Grecian temple or Indian cupolas?" she teased. "How very un-Warre-like of you."

From then on everything was a blur of activity and motion. The first to disembark was the still sulking Hedley, who cast Alys a single glare before dissolving into the courtyard shadows. Lucian, braced between two beefy footmen, exited next and was promptly whisked upstairs, accompanied by an ancient minikin of a woman who lost no time in chiding him for being a "careless sprig."

"Nurse Spratling," Charlotte whispered, her eyes dancing with mirth as she and Alys followed Bart down the steps to the slippery cobblestones below. "She still views Luc and I as children in need of a firm hand."

As if to prove her point, the frail-looking woman paused on the front steps to holler in a startlingly robust voice, "Stop yer dawdling and come along now, Lottie. Ye know the night air gives ye the grippe." She started to turn, then paused. After a brief instant, she added, "And bring yer friend. She looks none too hale and hearty either."

"I haven't had the grippe since I was five," Charlotte protested, though too faintly for all but Alys to hear. Nonetheless, she grasped Alys's elbow and towed her toward the door, as directed.

Assured of her charge's obedience, Spratling scurried off after Lucian, undoubtedly bent on blistering his ears with more scolding.

Once inside, a round, rosy housekeeper who was as jolly as Spratling was crusty showed the women to their chambers. Alys's room, though located on the second floor of the Jacobean monstrosity, was surprisingly taste-fully appointed.

In the grand tradition of the seventeenth century, the walls were paneled in richly carved walnut. The parquet floor, in a stunning lozenge pattern, was scattered with a quartet of green, brown, and salmon patterned rugs. A massive Tudor-style tester bed with green draw cur-tains and a patterned coverlet abutted the east wall, across from which stood a fireplace masterfully adorned with plasterwork.

Relieved not to be housed in the castle, Alys dropped

into a Restoration-style chair by the hearth and removed
her damp half boots. As she raised her icy feet to warm
them by the fire, she mentally ticked off, *One day down,
thirteen more to survive.*

Alys was just finishing her breakfast the next morning
when there was a knock at her bedroom door. It was
Charlotte, an exceedingly radiant Charlotte who stood
on the threshold smiling as if she'd just captured the
leprechaun's treasure.

Always smartly attired, today she looked as fresh and
cheerful as the first blossom of spring. Her gown, a
sunny creation of pale yellow poplin, was dramatically
piped and banded with puffings of brilliant violet satin.

Taking both her friend's hands in her own, Alys pulled
her into the room. Holding her at arm's length to admire
her ensemble, she exclaimed, "Why, Lottie! You look
absolutely stunning! Thistlewood clearly agrees with
you."

Charlotte smiled and gave her a quick hug. "By the
roses in your cheeks, I'd say that it agrees with you as
well."

Tactfully refraining from informing her that her roses
had nothing to do with Thistlewood and everything to
do with her box of rouge, Alys returned both her smile
and hug without comment.

Taking her silence for a harmonious response, as Alys
had intended her to do, she continued, "I thought you
might like a tour of the castle before the rest of the
guests arrive. Once the besiegement begins, I doubt we
shall have time to do more than exchange a few rushed
words in passing."

Though Alys would have preferred to have suffered
her initial impressions alone, she arranged her face into
a bland mask of concurrence and nodded. To say no
might wound her friend's feelings, and she would go to
any lengths, even endure what was bound to be a pro-
tracted tour of Thistlewood, to avoid doing something
so unkind. So she tamped down her disquiet, draped a
shawl over her shoulders, and followed Charlotte into
the hall.

To her surprise, the next two hours passed most pleasantly. Snickering like schoolgirls with mischief on their minds, they explored the hodgepodge of annexes, poking fun at every turn. They reached the height of their hilarity when Charlotte, upon contemplating a frightful cherub-infested dome, ceremoniously dubbed the collective additions the Thistlewood Goiter.

From hall to gallery to wing they wandered, carved paneled walls giving way to grim murals depicting bloody battles, which in turn yielded to intricately detailed plasterwork friezes and medallions. There were comfortable rooms from Elizabeth's reign, stark ones from the time of the Commonwealth. Here was the gilt of Louis XIV, there the chinoiserie introduced by William and Mary.

It wasn't until they stepped into the original castle that Alys was plagued with her first twinge of genuine dread. Soon they would walk through the hall where she and Lucan had plighted their troth, all too unbearably soon they would ascend to the tower where he had died.

The warmth of her previous pleasure chilled at that thought, seeping away like melting ice. Clutching her shawl tighter to her chest, as if by doing so she could somehow rekindle the heat within, she followed Charlotte into what had once been the retainer's hall. Instead of the long, rough tables where the serfs had once dined, the room now housed a sumptuous display of tapestries.

Instantly she was drawn to the tapestry that had once hung over the dais in the Great Hall. Loomed in a rainbow of still vibrant colors, it was a magically wrought masterpiece portraying the romance of Aengus and Rowena.

" 'Twas a wedding gift to my parents from the fairies," Lucan had said, his aqua gaze worshiping not the genius of the otherworld artisans, but the contours of her face.

Later, a century or so into her captivity, Allura had shown her the fragmentary tapestry the fairies had started to weave in honor of her and Lucan's betrothal. It too was to have been glorious, though now tragically doomed to remain unfinished forever.

The emotional strain of that last memory sapped Alys's strength, and she collapsed upon a nearby marble bench.

"This is the Tapestry Gallery," Charlotte was saying, her back still to Alys. "This piece"—she pointed to a faded tapestry depicting a hunting party—"and that one"—she turned to indicate Lucan and Rowena's wedding gift—"date from the early fourteenth century."

Apparently Alys looked as fragile as she felt, for the instant Charlotte caught a glimpse of her, she rushed over, clucking, "You look tired to death, dear. Perhaps we should save the tour of the old castle for another time."

It was on the tip of Alys's tongue to agree, to flee from her memories like a coward from a fight. But something inside stopped her; a voice that reminded her that no matter where she went or how much time elapsed, she could never escape her Thistlewood past. Not until she resolved it. And as she knew all too wretchedly well, to do so she must first face it.

But could she do it? Did she truly have the strength of will to do something so contrary to her every instinct? She was about to say nay, never, when she remembered her purpose for being there.

And that purpose was to help Lucian ... something she couldn't do if she spent the next fortnight dodging and cowering from the reminders of her past.

It was remembering her mission and all that was at stake that made her square her shoulders and stand on her rather wobbly legs, declaring, "I'm fine. Truly, I am. Please, do let's continue."

Charlotte hesitated, clearly not convinced of her professed soundness.

Forcing herself to smile, Alys grasped her friend's hand and pulled her toward the arched stone doorway. "Come, Lottie," she urged, injecting a false note of gaiety into her voice. "I'm fairly bursting to see the castle you and Lucian so love."

Charlotte resisted a second more, then reluctantly obliged. It took only for her to show Alys what was once the retainer's kitchen and was now a cozy parlor for her to become caught up in her role of guide again.

Room by room, floor by floor, tower by tower, they toured the much altered castle. Unlike the "Thistlewood Goiter," however, these renovations had been thoughtfully and aesthetically done. Indeed, so fabulous was this new Thistlewood that in her wonder Alys all but forgot where she was.

It wasn't until they stood before the spiraling staircase leading up to the west tower that her earlier anxiety crowded in on her again. At the top of those stairs was where Lucan had lain suffering during those last tortured hours of his life. It was where he'd died, his last breath spent whispering her name; it was where Aengus, maddened with sorrow and terrifying in his wrath, had smote her with his vengeful curse.

It was the cradle of her pain, sorrow, and remorse. And now was the time to face the child of her treachery.

Pushing away her panicked impulse to run, she picked up one suddenly leaden foot and planted it firmly on the bottom step. As she struggled to force the other one to follow suit, Charlotte grasped her elbow to stay her.

"No, Alys. We mustn't go up. Those are Lucian's chambers, and he doesn't take kindly to being disturbed."

Alys froze, gaping at her in mute horror. Lucian . . . dwelling in that tragedy-scourged tower? That news escalated her panic to such an intense degree that for the first time in her life she felt on the verge of fainting. His taking quarters there was like a dark omen, a sinister portent that history was on its way to repeating itself.

"Why?" she finally managed to croaked.

Charlotte frowned slightly, her eyes narrowing as she studied her face. "I'm not really certain why he's such a bear about being disturbed. He's been that way for as long as I can remember."

Alys shook her head in vigorous jerks, her alarm doubling with every heartbeat. "I meant, why did he select such isolated chambers? Surely it must be an inconvenience for him—"

"Are you quite all right?" Charlotte interrupted, her voice laced with urgency. "You're growing paler by the second."

Alys pressed her palm to her cheek, as if by doing so she could somehow discern her own pallor. "Am I? Oh. Well, I must admit that I'm a bit dizzy from looking up at that coil of steps," she replied, surprising herself with the smoothness of her falsehood.

Charlotte nodded, visibly mollified by her response. "But of course. That staircase does have that effect on a great many people at first."

"Even Lucian?" she asked, though why she wanted to know she couldn't say.

"My guess is no, though I truly can't say for certain. My intrepid little brother was crawling up those stairs long before he knew the words to state his feelings one way or another." She released a soft peal of laughter. "He was so drawn to that tower that Spratling, fanciful old dear that she is, used to say that he must have spent many a pleasurable hour there in another life to love it so in this one."

Those last words gave Alys pause. Allura said that Lucian's soul had retained fragments of the emotions once experienced by Lucan. Could it be that it remembered the tower, recalling it not with the agony of Lucan's last hours, but with the joy from the years before? The more she thought about it, the more sense it made. And the more sense it made, the more relieved she grew.

If what she suspected was true, Lucian hadn't been drawn to the tower to fulfill some dark legacy. He was attracted by an unconscious desire to recapture the joy he'd experienced there; a joy that by all indications was missing from his present life.

Alys smiled with sudden understanding. Ah-ha! Now it was clear what his next lesson should be: how to have fun.

"There is one room left to see," Charlotte said, breaking into her ruminations. "And that is the old nursery in the northwest tower. However, if you don't feel up to tackling the stairs we can return to the 'goiter' and take some refreshment."

Nursery? What better place to find clues as to what Lucian might find fun? With that pragmatic thought in mind, Alys hastily replied, "Please, let's do visit the nursery. I'd love to see where you and Lucian spent your childhood."

Unlike the nurseries Alys had seen in the past, most of which had been little more than dreary, cramped garrets, much thought had gone into making this one comfortable.

Cheerfully decorated in scarlet, blue, and ivory, this room, like the rest of the castle, had been renovated beyond recognition. The walls, once of hard, cold ashlar, had been plastered over and were illustrated with wonderful murals depicting enchanted forests. Carpet covered the rough plank floor, and the ceiling was painted to resemble the sky on a perfect spring day.

Two small beds, now stripped of their coverings, stood parallel with their half-tester headboards butted against the north wall. Across from them, directly in front of the colorfully tiled fireplace, was an ancient-looking swinging cradle. By the scores of toys scattered across the tables, shelves, and floor, it was clear that the Warre children had been much loved by their parents.

"Oh! How wonderful!" Alys exclaimed, practically flying across the room in her haste to examine an enormous toy castle. It was an exact replica of Thistlewood, the way it had looked before the Warre family had begun their disfiguring quest to perfect that which was already perfect.

Filled with childlike delight, she dropped to her knees before it. It was nothing less than exquisite. As she reverently touched one of the carved wood stones, Charlotte knelt next to her.

"Father had it made for Luc the Christmas he was five," she explained, smiling at Alys's wonderment. "How he loved it! He used to sit here for hours surrounded by his toy knights, planning sieges and fighting battles. I shall never forget how he looked at his play, so grave and intense. It was almost as if he'd forgotten that the knights were of wood, and that he was but a boy."

"Perhaps his imaginary warfare is the reason he did so brilliantly in the cavalry," Alys suggested, running her fingertips along the battlements. When she came to the latch that opened the front of the castle, she slanted a querying glance at Charlotte. "May I?"

"Please do. The knights should be inside."

And they were. Two dozen brilliantly painted ones in

various poses of combat, some even mounted on prancing destriers.

"This was his favorite," Charlotte said, picking up a
knight and handing it to Alys. "No one but he was allowed to touch it."

One glance, and Alys almost dropped the figure in her
astonishment. From his gold armor to his green mantle
and silvery steed, he bore a starting resemblance to
Lucan.

"Poor knight," Charlotte crooned, gently touching his
chest. "He was the hero of every battle, only to die in
a tourney at the end of each day."

So Lucan's soul does remember, Alys thought. She
stared at the figure another brief instant, then reverently
set it back into place. Suddenly too emotionally drained
to continue facing such a powerful reminder of her past,
she turned from the castle, murmuring, "What was your
favorite toy?"

"Mine?" Charlotte sat back on her heels to gaze
around the room. After a moment her face lit up. "Lord
Woodywig!" In the next instant, her brow puckered.
"Why, I wonder what happened to his lordship's
clothes?" Shaking her head in wonder, she rose and
moved to a small table at which three wooden dolls and
an earless stuffed dog sat taking tea. One of the dolls, a
large male one carved with an enormous court wig atop
his rather narrow head, was completely naked.

Alys joined her as she picked him up. "He used to
have the most beautiful velvet coat," Charlotte
mourned. "Royal blue, with an ivory silk waistcoat and
trousers to match. Miss Coquette"—she nodded at a female doll in a pink satin shepherdess-style dress—"used
to find him quite dashing."

Alys was about to comment when she heard a vulgar
noise, followed by, "Bibble-babble! Tittle-tattle! Can't
ye stupid cows shut up and let a hob get his beauty
sleep?"

She glanced sharply around the room. No Hedley in
sight. Come to think of it, she hadn't seen him since the
night before when he'd stomped off in a huff. There was
another sound, this one reminiscent of an elephant with
flatulence. She followed the noise with her gaze, her eyes

narrowing on the hearth. If she wasn't mistaken, it was coming from the cradle.

After duly complimenting Lord Woodywig's fine carving, she feigned an interest in the old cradle. As she wandered toward it, expressing a desire for a closer inspection, Hedley popped his head up over the side and wagged his tongue at her.

She rolled her eyes toward the heavens in exasperation. What she wouldn't say to the nasty little beast if Charlotte weren't present! When she drew close enough to actually look down into the cradle, her annoyance escalated to outrage. Hedley had literally stuffed himself into an overly small suit of clothes . . . Lord Woodywig's clothes by the look of the blue velvet coat.

Lying back upon a linen blanket, his arms folded behind his head in a pose of studied nonchalance, he drawled, "How do ye like my new clothes?"

"Those aren't your clothes and you know it," she whispered, leaning over the cradle as if to examine its silk-draped hood.

"Well, they oughtta be. They look a damn sight finer on me 'n on old Lord Wormywood over there."

"It's Woodywig, and you shall return them to him the instant Charlotte and I leave the room."

The hob countered her stern scowl with a belligerent glare. "Why'd I do a dung-brained thing like that?"

"Because they don't belong to you, that's why."

He grunted. "So?"

"So. Even a loutish little savage like you knows that it's wrong to steal. And I'm warning you, Hedley, if you don't—"

"What was that you said, dear?" Alys heard Charlotte say from directly above her. She tipped her head back to see her friend standing over her, peering down at her quizzically.

"I was—um—just wondering how old this is," she hastily fabricated, gently thumping one of the two trestle-footed suspension posts.

Charlotte sank to her knees next to the cradle, her saffron skirts pooling around her like a ring of summer sunlight. Gently rocking it, she murmured, "According to legend, it's as old as Thistlewood Castle. It is said to have first belonged to Lucan and Elinore."

"And you believe it?" Alys asked, eyeing her curiously.

"How can I not? Just look at how wide it is."

Alys did as she was directed, pointedly ignoring Hedley who was making an obscene hand gesture at her. It truly was wide, at least twice the width of any other cradle she'd ever seen.

"Just the right size for twins, wouldn't you say?" Charlotte inquired slyly.

Alys nodded. "Have there been many pairs of twins born at Thistlewood?"

"Just one, and that was Lucan and Elinore." She smiled rather smugly. "If you ask me, that small fact proves the legend a truth."

Indeed it did. Suddenly as interested in the cradle as she'd pretended only moments earlier, Alys dropped to her hands and knees to examine the carving on the side panels. Yes. She recognized those pagan symbols. They were fairy blessings.

"All the Thistlewood children have slept in this cradle. My grandfather. My father. Even Luc and I, though my mother desperately wanted to purchase a grand new one for us. I always dreamed—" Charlotte's voice broke then, strangled by something that sounded curiously like a sob.

Alys glanced up in question. Charlotte was staring at the bed, her face as forlorn as if she'd just lost the love of her life. "Why, Lottie. Whatever is wrong?" she exclaimed softly.

Charlotte blinked rapidly, clearly trying to hide the tears Alys could see shimmering in her eyes. "I—it's just that—oh, I'm being a weak, foolish female, that's all. Please forgive me," she murmured, turning her face away.

Alys straightened up and looped her arm around her friend's waist to draw her near. Affectionately nudging Charlotte's head with hers, she said, "The only bit of foolishness I can see is that you've forgotten how very much I love you and are refusing to tell me what has you so downhearted."

Charlotte looked back at her then, smiling faintly amid her tears. "I haven't forgotten. I just think it inappropriate to lament my barren state to an unmarried miss . . . no matter how much I love her in return." She lightly counterbutted Alys's head.

"Then you truly are a foolish woman, for it is always appropriate for friends to confide in each other, no matter how delicate the nature of their troubles," Alys mildly chided her. "Besides, how can you be so certain that you're barren?"

"After sixteen years of marriage, I would have borne a child by now if it were not so."

Alys stared at her friend's profile, her heart breaking for her. By the quiet sorrow woven through her voice, it was tragically clear that her childlessness caused her unspeakable anguish. Feeling more helpless than she'd ever before felt in her centuries of life, she vainly sought to reassure her. "You might bear a child yet, you know. It's not completely unheard of to conceive after years and years of fruitlessness." She nodded her encouragement, though even to her her words rang hollow.

Charlotte gave her a thin smile and pressed a kiss to her brow. "You're very kind, my dear, but Clayton and I gave up hope long ago."

"Milady?"

Both women followed the voice to where a neatly uniformed maid of no more than sixteen stood on the threshold. The instant she gained their notice, she bobbed a curtsy.

"Yes?" Charlotte inquired.

"It's sorry I am to be disturbin' ye, milady. But Lord Langley and Miss Ramsey 'ave arrived."

"Thank you, Mary. I shall be down directly to greet them."

The maid curtsied again and departed.

"Well, it seems the besiegement on Thistlewood has begun," Charlotte commented, standing up and smoothing her skirts. "Would you care to meet Diana Ramsey now, or would you prefer to wait?"

"I'm certain that Miss Ramsey would like to freshen up before being introduced. Besides, I would like to spend a while longer up here looking at the toys. That is, with your permission?"

"You have my permission to spend as long as you like looking at whatever catches your fancy here at Thistlewood," Charlotte returned with her usual graciousness. Alys expected her to rush off then, but she instead reached down and gave her shoulder a light squeeze. "Please, Alys, don't waste your pity on me. I've learned to accept my childless lot long ago." With that, she exited.

Alys sat back on her heels staring sadly at the open door, though Charlotte had long since disappeared from sight.

"Too bad she don't know any Nibelungens," Hedley muttered.

Alys glanced down, startled, having all but forgotten his presence in her preoccupation with Charlotte's tragic plight. He was sitting with his chin propped up on the side of the cradle, his expression uncharacteristically thoughtful.

"Nibelungens?" Alys echoed, frowning. She vaguely recalled the name. They were a reclusive fairy race, goldsmiths, if she remembered correctly, who lived in a subterranean world somewhere beneath the Nordic countries. What they had to do with Charlotte and her barren state, she couldn't imagine. When she said as much, Hedley made a disdainful noise.

"Thought ye knew everything about fairies, dinna ye?" He cackled. "Well, for yer bloody damn information, Miss Fount-of-All-Fairy-Knowledge, the Nibelungens make golden rings that can make a barren female fertile."

"Truly?" Alys exclaimed breathlessly, his words sending her low spirits soaring to optimistic new heights. Why, all she had to do was get one of those magic rings, then Charlotte could be the mother she so desperately desired to be.

But how? She had no links to the fairy world other than those given to her by Allura and Aengus. Her spirits came crashing down again as she eyed her present link. She had about as much chance at getting Hedley to grant her such a favor as she did at marrying the pope. Her eyes narrowed slightly. Perhaps if she bribed him . . .

"Now don't ye be staring at me like that," he squawked, sinking back down into the cradle. "I ain't gonna go looking for those spiteful, gold-mucking Nibelungens, not for nothing. That's just asking for trouble."

"Not even for a suit of clothes of your own?" she tempted.

The hob's head popped back up again. "Brand-new, made-to-measure clothes?"

Alys nodded.

"Can I have a dark blue coat with gold buttons like Lord Tight-Arse were wearing last Tuesday?"

"You may have any color and style you like. If you get the ring before the end of the fortnight, you shall also have a pair of those Hessian boots you so admire," she promised, though where she'd find such a tiny pair, she hadn't a clue.

His face took on a dreamy, faraway look. "Blue coat . . . gold buttons . . . Hessian boots." He sighed his rapture. "I'll be the finest hob in the whole frigging world."

"Indeed you shall be," Alys agreed, hard-pressed to hide her glee. She was just congratulating herself on a bargain well made when Hedley moaned and flopped back down again.

"Can't get the bloody damn ring even if I do find the Nibelungens," he wailed. "We ain't got nothing to pay for it."

Alys's brow puckered as she considered the problem. "What payment will they demand, do you suppose?"

"Gold," came his mournful reply. "Ten times the weight of the ring. Them Nibelungens are a greedy lot."

She stared at the side of the oak cradle with dismay. Wherever was she going to get such a piece of gold, unless . . . ? She twisted the end of her shawl, tormented by a sudden fit of indecision. There was always her treasured bracelet.

She shifted her gaze to her bare wrist, visualizing it banded in gold and rubies. She'd been wearing the bracelet when she was abducted into the otherworld, and

it was now all she had left of her life as Alys le Fayre.
To part with it would be to sever her last tangible tie to
who she once was.

Then she thought of Charlotte, her dear, sweet friend,
and the terrible heartache in her voice as she confessed
her barren state. As she again saw her face, so tragic
and shadowed with despair, remembering who she had
once been suddenly seemed much less important than
simply being who she was now. And the woman she had
become desperately wanted to help the first real friend
she'd ever had. Laying her hand over her wrist to bid
her old life a silent farewell, she asked, "Would they be
satisfied with my gold and ruby bracelet?"

There was a long silence, then Hedley's head slowly
emerged over the side of the cradle, his mouth agape.
"Y-ye'd give up yer bracelet so Lord Tight-Arse's sister
can have a babe?" By the shock in his voice, you'd have
thought that she'd offered to hack off both hands and
an ear.

Knowing that her former selfishness had prompted his
incredulous response and shamed by the fact, she repeated, this time more forcefully, "Is it enough?"

He thought for a brief moment, then nodded. "More
'an enough. Enough for two fertility rings and a cure for
blindness, I'd say."

Alys smiled her relief. "I just need the one ring. If
you go now, you may do whatever you wish with the
balance." She didn't have to offer twice. He disappeared
almost the instant the words left her mouth.

Still smiling, she reached out and gently rocked the
empty cradle. Soon, very soon, it would be filled.

Chapter 11

By late afternoon all the guests had arrived. After introductions were made and an informal dinner served in the pale blue and gold "Little" dining room, the ladies withdrew to the cozy first floor "Crimson" drawing room where they proceeded to share the latest *on-dits* with tittering zeal.

Since Alys knew none of the unfortunates about whom they gossiped and found their chatter dull to the extreme, she occupied herself with trying to ascertain if any of the five marriageable young ladies present might suit Lucian.

Cassandra Thorndike and Susanna Trumball she dismissed out of hand. While both were eminently suitable, the former being the daughter of an earl and the later a duke, they were blondes. And the dressmaker's assistant had quite specifically stated that the discriminating Marquess of Thistlewood had a marked preference for brunettes. That left raven-locked Gemma Hartley, mahogany-tressed Gloriana Seymour, and Diana Ramsey with her chestnut curls.

Her options thus narrowed, she let her gaze wander from face to face, listening carefully as each woman spoke. Though not particularly clever, blue-eyed Gemma was by far the prettiest, while the green-eyed Gloriana was the wittiest. Brown-eyed Diana, while attractive enough, seemed rather retiring, sitting slightly apart from the group and adding little to their gleeful character assassinations.

Retiring? Alys intensified her scrutiny of the woman. Was this the same Miss Ramsey whom Charlotte had described as being a bold huntress and a neck-or-nothing rider? Why, she seemed positively timid. Unless . . .

Her gaze sharpened as the object of her contemplation glanced at the door for the tenth time in half as many minutes. Unless, like herself, the woman was bored half to death by the gossip and was therefore eager to escape. The more she considered the likelihood, the more sense it made. After all, Miss Ramsey lived here in Sussex, so it was possible that she too was unacquainted with the scandalmongers' victims.

She was thus about to dismiss the woman's lack of animation as simple disinterest when Miss Ramsey raised her demurely lowered lashes and Alys saw that instead of being glazed with tedium, her eyes were overly bright.

Instantly Alys dropped her own lashes to disguise her perusal. Hmm. Perhaps she wasn't so very bored after all. As she watched, Miss Ramsey began to clasp and unclasp her hands in a nervous, fidgety sort of way. And her biscuit and cream zephyr skirts began to stir slightly, as if she were either tapping her foot or her knees were shaking. That last notion gave way to a new theory.

Could it be that Diana Ramsey was anxious over the impending arrival of the gentlemen? Was she, perhaps, ill at ease around members of the opposite sex? That would certainly account for both her retiring manner and her visible agitation.

Yet, that too made no sense. A woman timid of men would hardly relish and excel in a male-dominated sport like riding to the hounds. Alys frowned inwardly as Miss Ramsey glanced at the door yet again, this time heaving an inaudible sigh as she looked away. It was then that it stuck her: Diana Ramsey wasn't dreading the gentlemen's appearance, she was eagerly awaiting it. She clearly fancied one of the male guests.

Alys gave herself a mental kick. After four hundred and eighty years of matchmaking experience, how very witless of her not to have recognized the signs of infatuation. They were all there. The bright-eyed impatience, the trembling anticipation, and—Alys smiled to herself as the woman reached up and touched one of the glossy ringlets framing her face—the self-conscious primping.

Still smiling, she looked to where Miss Trumball was recounting some ridiculous incident involving the Regent and a goat. It would be intriguing to see which gentleman had won her heart and to mark the progress of her chase. If the woman pursued her man as relentlessly as she did her foxes, she'd doubtlessly have him bagged before the end of the fortnight.

As it turned out, the lovesick Miss Ramsey wasn't kept waiting long. Less than an hour after the ladies had withdrawn, the eleven gentlemen, three of whom were the fathers or guardians of the same number of girls, joined them. From matchmaking habit, Alys watched Miss Ramsey as the remaining eight gentlemen, all bachelors save Charlotte's husband, filed into the room.

The young woman sat completely indifferent, until Lucian, in the company of his best friend, Lord Marchland, appeared. Then she dropped her gaze, her cheeks flushing a very becoming shade of pink.

Ah-ha! So it was Lord Marchland she favored. Alys didn't even try to disguise her smile. Now there was a match truly made in heaven. Lord Marchland, or Stephen, as he'd insisted she address him, was an outstanding horseman, an excellence reportedly shared by Miss Ramsey. Add that to the fact that they were both avid hunters, were both tall and had more than a hint of red in their hair, and it was clear that they were destined for each other.

"Pray, do take a turn around the room with me and tell me what you find so amusing," Charlotte begged, coming to stand next to her chair as the rest of the party broke into groups. "I fear I shall disgrace myself by falling asleep if I am obliged to play dumb-crambo or whist."

Laughing at her friend's wry tone, she stood up and took her proffered arm. As they began their leisurely promenade around the ostentatious crimson and gold room, Charlotte prompted, "Well?"

"Well, what?" Alys teased, though she knew exactly what her friend sought with her single word query.

"Well, what has you so very amused? You were clearly entertained by something, and I wager that it wasn't anything said by those dull little prattle-boxes."

"What?" Alys drawled in mock amazement. "Are you telling me that you didn't find it exceedingly diverting to hear how Miss Dimrumple's garter slipped to her ankle during some assembly?"

"About as diverting as that bit about Lady Hamilton's pug dog fouling on Lord Nesmith's new boots," Charlotte retorted with equal irony.

Alys laughed. "Indeed? I'm afraid I quite missed that charming little tale."

"So I noticed." Charlotte slanted her a shrewd glance. "You seemed inordinately engrossed in observing Diana Ramsey."

Alys sobered instantly. And here she'd thought she'd been so sly in her scrutiny.

Apparently her face reflected her chagrin, for Charlotte laughingly assured her, "Oh, don't fret. I seriously doubt anyone else noted your gawking. Not even Diana herself, though I must say that she was not at all herself this evening. She's usually such a lively, original chit."

"So you said, which is why I was staring at her," Alys admitted, following Charlotte's example and nodding as they passed Lord and Lady Shadwell, Gemma's parents. "I was waiting for her to display the rare wit you so praised. When she failed to do so, I found myself trying to ascertain why."

"Oh? And what did you discover?" Charlotte inquired, inclining her head at Susanna, who was flirting with Lord Vardon, a fair-haired young man with singularly beautiful blue eyes.

Alys followed suit, then replied, "It is my belief that she was on tenterhooks over the appearance of the gentlemen. If I don't miss my guess, your Miss Ramsey is in love." She gestured with her head toward where Diana Ramsey sat on a small gold brocade sofa, wedged between Cassandra and Gemma. "Just look at her. It's as plain as the nose on her face."

And it was. Instead of joining her giggling teammates

in guessing what word the broadly gesturing Lord Walby was acting out, she was gazing longingly toward where Stephen, Gloriana, and several pairs of parents were following the badly limping Lucian into the adjoining music room.

Charlotte followed Alys's gaze with her own, glancing first at Miss Ramsey, then at the musically inclined party. "You're very perceptive for one so young and inexperienced, Alys," she murmured. "For indeed you are correct. Diana does fancy herself in love. She's had the most dreadful crush on Lucian since she was thirteen."

"Lucian?" Alys echoed, coming to an abrupt standstill.

Charlotte stopped as well, eyeing her curiously. "Of course, Lucian. Who did you think it was?"

"I—" She shrugged helplessly. "I just assumed that it was Lord Marchland. From what I know of him, and from what you've told me of Miss Ramsey, it seems only natural that they would suit."

Charlotte seemed to consider her words, then slowly nodded. "Perhaps they might at that, if she ever really saw him. But since he is always in Luc's company when they meet, she's hardly aware he exists." She chuckled softly and pulled Alys over to sit on a bench beneath the portrait of some long-dead Warre soldier. "Indeed, Diana has cared for Luc for so long and with such rare devotion that I sometimes wonder if perhaps she were born to love him."

Perhaps she was, Alys mused, watching as Miss Ramsey excused herself from the dumb-crambo game and wandered over to stand near the music-room door. Perhaps she was his destined true love. With that promising notion in mind, she gently prodded, "And how does Lucian feel about her? Does he in any way share her feelings?"

Charlotte shrugged. "You know Luc. He's singularly stupid when it comes to matters of the heart. While he likes Diana and has on several occasions declared her to be exceedingly jolly company, he's blind to her more tender feelings for him. How he cannot see them, I don't know. But he doesn't."

Alys glanced from Miss Ramsey, who was now leaning

against the doorjamb and gazing wistfully into the music room, to Charlotte. "Do you think that he might love her in return if he were to perceive her feelings?"

It was Charlotte's turn to stare at Diana. "She has a better chance than most, I suppose. At least he doesn't find her intolerably silly and boring the way he does most women. And she is quite lovely. Indeed, she was such a success during her first season that she received a half-dozen very handsome offers, all of which she declined. Between you and me, I credit her refusals to her steadfast belief that Luc will someday come around and return her love."

She seemed inclined to add something more when a footmen bowed before her and relayed the message that the cook urgently needed to speak with her. After promising to meet with him directly, she turned back to Alys.

"Poor cook. He's so used to cooking for just Luc that he's quite at wit's end as to how to feed this throng. Now, if you'll excuse me"—she gave Alys a quick kiss on the cheek—"I must go see if I can calm him down enough to prepare supper."

Alys sat there for a long while after Charlotte departed, considering the intriguing possibility of a match between Lucian and Miss Ramsey. It made perfect sense, really. For not only did she love him and he like her, both steps in the right direction, her father's estate bordered Thistlewood. As Charlotte had pointed out, they seemed fated to fall in love and marry.

Now, if only Lucian would open his eyes and see it as well.

Alys considered the problem a moment, tapping her foot impatiently as she thought. Then a slow smile crept across her face. How could he not see how perfect Diana Ramsey was if she were constantly in his company? And what better way to throw her in his path than to befriend her and insist that she accompany them to all the upcoming season's festivities?

Feeling as if a burden the size of the world had been lifted from her shoulders, Alys smoothed her skirts and wandered over to where Miss Ramsey still stood at the door, staring into the music room as if transfixed. The instant Alys followed her gaze with her own, she saw why.

Never had Lucian looked more romantically handsome than he did at that moment sitting at the pianoforte, playing a hauntingly beautiful, yet unfamiliar air. Alys smiled, thrilling with the sheer pleasure of just looking at him.

His hair, gleaming like polished ebony in the candlelight, tumbled in thick, glorious waves over his forehead and collar, emphasizing both the perfection of his profile and the stunning breadth of his shoulders. By the expression on his face, so dreamy and faraway, he appeared to be lost in the lyrical kingdom of his melody. Enhancing his darkly quixotic portrait was his attire.

As if painted in a moody study of fading light, he was garbed in a trio of hueless tones. His coat, exquisitely cut and tailored to accent his athletic torso, was of fine black wool; his snugly clinging trousers of pearl-gray kerseymere. Like his frilled cambric shirt, his damask waistcoat was white, the two garments visually distinguishable only by their contrasting sheens and textures.

While most men so tall and powerfully built looked awkward when seated at a pianoforte, Lucian somehow managed to project a grace that was at the same time elegant and masculine. With the mastery of a born musician his strong fingers stroked the keys, firmly yet eloquently coaxing music from the responsive instrument.

Across from her, Alys heard Miss Ramsey sigh and felt inclined to follow suit. He truly was magnificent, and getting more so by the day as his soul grew and his demeanor softened. Before her very eyes he was transforming from an arrogant, insensitive autocrat into a charming, thoughtful man who any woman, even herself, would be delighted to call her own. For one brief instant, as Alys stood gazing longingly at Lucian, she allowed herself to imagine what it might be like to be loved by him.

How splendid the privilege to touch him, to stroke, fondle, and caress him at will. How blissful to kiss his lips and taste the rapturous sweetness of his answering passion. What heaven to lay in his arms, flesh against

flesh, sharing the intimacies that were as of yet to her
vague images invoked by the amorous whispers of lovers. How very . . .

   . . . impossible her desires.

Her longing pulsing like a dull ache in her soul, she
tore her gaze from him. No! He wasn't for her, he never
could be. Not even if by some miracle he fell in love
with her and both their hearts willed it so. His future
lay with a mortal woman, one whose love would grant
him eternal salvation. And if she truly cared for him,
she'd forget her dangerous infatuation and focus her en-
ergies on thrusting him into the arms of his savior.

Feeling suddenly leaden and emotionally used up, she
forced herself to turn to that savior and say, "I had no
idea he played so very well."

The other woman started, blinking rapidly as if chasing away a dream. Staring at Alys as if seeing her for
the first time, she murmured, "I'm sorry. Did you say
something?"

Alys's lips curved into her most cordial smile. "I said
that he plays very well."

"Yes," Miss Ramsey agreed, her gaze straying back
to the object of their mutual adoration. "But then, his
lordship does everything well. He is quite a remarkable
man, though I fear few people realize just how truly
wonderful he is." This was said proudly and with unapol-
ogetic admiration.

"I do," Alys countered with quiet sincerity. "I find
him exceptional."

That drew a sharp glance from the other woman. By
the wariness in her previously amicable gaze, it was apparent that she'd perceived Alys's response not as re-
spectful praise from a grateful ward, as she was meant
to do, but as the worshipful simpering of a possible rival.
"Indeed?" she intoned, a chill icing her voice.

"Oh, yes," Alys replied, hastily assuming the demeanor of a guileless schoolgirl. "Though I must confess
that I did find him rather fierce and frightening at first."
She giggled. "Aren't I the silliest creature in England?"

Miss Ramsey thawed but only slightly. "His lordship is
rather given to barking and brooding, something which a
young chit such as yourself might understandably find

alarming. But as you have discovered for yourself, he possesses many fine qualities which quite outweigh that unfortunate tendency."

Nodding, Alys delivered her coup de grâce to the other woman's lingering suspicions. "Yes. Indeed, he's become so dear to me over the past few weeks that I've come to view him as a comfortable surrogate for the brother I lost at Waterloo."

Like a warm fire chasing away a deep winter chill, her comment melted the remainder of Miss Ramsey's icy reserve. Her expression softening into one of infinite compassion, she clasped both Alys's hands in hers, softly exclaiming, "As well you should, Miss Faire. Lottie told me of your brother's heroic sacrifice, and it's only right that Luc—um—his lordship should step into your brother's boots and assume his role to the best of his ability."

She gave Alys's hands a gentle squeeze. "I also want you to know that as a long-time friend and neighbor of his lordship that I too stand indebted to you. And if I can ever in any way be of service to you, please feel free to ask me."

"Perhaps you can help me," Alys replied, lowering her lashes to hide the cunning she was certain showed in her eyes. "You see, this is my very first party and I'm not quite certain how to go about things. Lottie's been helping me as best she can, but as you can imagine, she is very busy."

"But of course, Miss Faire—"

"I would be honored if you would call me Alys."

"Only if you agree to call me Diana." She grinned suddenly. "Oh, Alys. I do so hope that we shall be friends."

"I would like that. Aside from Lottie and Lucian, I have no friends here . . . or in London." Alys slanted her a querying look. "You shall be coming to town for the season, shan't you?"

Diana shrugged. "My father still holds out hope that I might make a match, and therefore wishes me to go. I, however, am not so certain that I wish to endure yet another season of being gaped at and appraised like a horse at Tattersall's."

"Oh, but you must!" Alys exclaimed. "Lucian and I

shall be attending all the festivities, and it would be so comforting to have a friend from whom I might seek advice. Especially one like you, who is experienced in the ways of the ton."

The other woman looked positively stunned by her words. "Luc shall be participating in the season? How very irregular of him! I had assumed that he'd cajoled Lottie and Clayton into taking you about, since they are so fond of the parties he loathes."

Alys shook her head. "My brother left his lordship charged with the duty of finding me a suitable husband, and I must say that he's taken his duty very much to heart. Indeed, he gave me a list of possible suitors to consider the second day I was under his roof."

Diana stared at her for several seconds as if utterly shocked, then burst into laughter. "How very like Luc to treat marriage as if it were an agreement to purchase cattle! And what did you say, pray tell?"

Alys gave a nonchalant shrug. "I tore up his silly list, telling him that I was perfectly capable of selecting my own husband and that I wouldn't marry without love."

Diana's mirth escalated to the point of hilarity. "Oh, Alys! I see that we shall be very good friends indeed!" she gasped out between her laughter. "Perhaps I shall come to town for the season after all. How exceedingly diverting to watch Luc muddle about the marriage mart with you foiling him at every turn. Almost as amusing as seeing how he eludes the scores of matchmaking mothers who will no doubt attempt to trap him for their daughters."

"No doubt," Alys agreed, well pleased with the turn of conversation. "Though they will probably be wasting their time. Aside from yourself and Lottie, his lordship seems to find women singularly silly creatures."

"H-he's spoken of me?" Diana stammered, her cheeks growing very pink.

"Oh, yes. He spoke of you on the way here. It appears that he thinks very highly of you. Indeed, he told me that I was to observe you and follow your example." All right, so it was a lie, but one ground in truth. For according to Lottie, he did admire Diana, though he'd never so much as acknowledged his acquaintance to the woman in her presence.

When Diana seemed at a loss as to how to reply to that flattering bit of news, Alys continued, "He also bid me to be my most charming to the gentlemen, though I must confess that I feel quite at a loss around them. As Lottie might have told you, I spent the last few years at a rather strict boarding school in Bath, and have therefore had little contact with men."

"They really aren't such a frightening lot once you get accustomed to them," Diana assured her, looping her arm around Alys's waist and turning her from the music room to face the merry assembly behind them. "Just see how easily the other girls are conversing with them."

And indeed they were. Though most of the younger set had never met before that afternoon, they were chattering away as if they'd all known each other forever. All except for the foppish Lord Drake, that is, who stood before a mirror at the far side of the room, frowning at his immaculately arranged neckcloth.

Alys studied him for a brief instant, vaguely remembering seeing his name on Lucian's list before she tore it up. Though slightly too modishly dressed for her taste and a bit taken with herself, he wasn't unpleasant to look at. Indeed, many would call him handsome.

Apparently she was staring more blatantly than she'd imagined, for Diana released a low, throaty chuckle and said, "So it's Lord Drake, is it?"

"Excuse me?" Alys murmured, pretending not to have understood the other woman's comment.

Diana inclined her head faintly in the direction of the object of her scrutiny. "Do I detect a glint of interest in the elegant Lord Drake?"

Alys smiled coyly, a new idea striking her. "He was on Lord Thistlewood's list as a possible suitor."

"Was he indeed?" Diana paused to regard the young man, then inquired, "And you find him an agreeable candidate?"

Alys bowed her head as if in maidenly reticence. "Well, he is very handsome. And I couldn't help but to notice what fine brown eyes he has."

Diana chuckled again. "Not to mention his equally fine brown hair and fashionable wardrobe, eh?"

"Yes. He truly is a splendid man," she murmured. She counted to three, then heaved a dejected little sigh. "Far too splendid, I fear, to ever take notice of a plain creature such as myself."

"Plain? You?" Diana softly exclaimed, her voice laced with amazement. "Why, wherever did you get such a bird-witted notion?"

Alys gestured toward where Gemma and Cassandra were still engrossed in their game. "Just look at how pretty the other girls are. I feel quite drab by comparison." She shook her head mournfully. "However will his lordship see me when I'm in such stunning company?"

"Very easily, I'd guess," Diana replied. "For not only are you the prettiest girl in the room—no,"—she raised her hand to silence Alys, who'd opened her mouth to protest—"it's true. Not only are you the prettiest here, you're a blonde. And it's widely known that Lord Drake has an eye for pretty, fair-haired misses. I also hear tell that he's in the market for a wife this season. All things considered, I'd guess that you have an exceedingly good chance at bagging him if you play your cards right."

"But as I've already explained, I don't know how to play that game," Alys protested, carefully baiting her hook.

Like a trout tantalized with a fly, Diana immediately snapped. "Then I shall teach you. It isn't so very hard, and I don't doubt that you shall be an excellent student. Between the two of us, I wouldn't be at all surprised if you're at the altar with Lord Drake before summer's end."

"Then you shall be coming to town after all?" Alys inquired, hard-pressed to keep the triumph from her voice.

"I suppose I shall," she replied as if just realizing what all her plan entailed. Then she smiled in a soft, secretive way that left little doubt in Alys's mind that she was thinking of Lucian and the possibilities of the coming season. "Yes," she quietly mused. "I do believe I shall be coming to town."

Alys returned her smile. Someone would be at the altar by the end of the summer, but it wouldn't be she and Lord Drake.

Chapter 12

"Then I said, 'My dear Weston, you really must nip the waist in a fraction more. It is so terribly *du vieux temps* to wear one's coat so loose.' And do you know what he said?" Lord Drake paused to peer at Alys through his ever-present quizzing glass, clearly expecting her to guess.

"I haven't the slightest notion. Pray do tell," Alys murmured, struggling hard to repress her yawn. A two-topic man, namely fashion and himself, his lordship had been prattling about his tailor since they had begun their walk a half hour earlier.

It had been six days since the party's arrival at Thistlewood, and the weather had taken an unseasonal turn for the better. Indeed, today was so fair that the bulk of the guests were outside riding, walking, or simply sitting in the courtyard enjoying the clement temperature.

Diana, who had very much taken to heart her promise to help Alys snare Lord Drake, had used the fine weather as an excuse to invite that same gentleman to accompany them on a stroll around the moat. Alys, in turn, had teased Lucian into joining them, declaring it only proper that each lady have an escort. By the look of keen amusement that passed between him and Diana, it was clear that both thought her ruse one to assure that she'd have Lord Drake all to herself. Accordingly, they now strolled several yards in front of them.

As Drake outlined the challenges of fitting a coat

when a man's shoulders were as wide as his and his waist as trim, Alys let her gaze stray to the couple ahead of her.

Unlike herself, Diana seemed to be enjoying her escort's company. Filled with wistful envy, Alys watched as Lucian bent his glossy sable head close to Diana's shiny chestnut one, whispering something into her ear. She laughed, low and husky, then said something in return that made him expel a very unlordly guffaw.

Instead of being thrilled that her matchmaking plans showed such promise, she felt lonely, rather as if she were excluded from a club to which everyone else happily belonged. And perhaps she was, for all the others in their party were free to seek and share love as they pleased, while her curse prohibited her from engaging in such delightful pursuits.

Inwardly sighing her desolation, Alys slanted a glance up at her escort, who had concluded his discourse on the fit of his coat and had launched into an oration on his valet's miraculous boot polish. While it was true that her curse banned her from participating in love's sweet games, it didn't deny her the simple pleasure of a man's company and conversation; pleasure that was markedly absent at that moment.

Lord Drake, catching her glance and mistaking it for interest in his topic, smiled and pointed to the boots in question. Resolved to play out her game, for Lucian's sake, she returned his smile and pretended to study the mirrorlike sheen of his Hessians.

Too bad she hadn't known what an out and out bore he was before she'd contrived this scheme. At least then she'd have had the foresight to feign infatuation for a more amusing gentleman, say, Lord Ardell. Though not as physically prepossessing as Lord Drake, he had a great charm and wit about him that would have at least made him good company. Then again, he wasn't on the infamous list of suitors, so Lucian might have refused to participate in Diana's matchmaking machinations had she selected him instead.

Ah, well. Alys expelled a gusty breath as she looked up from Lord Drake's gleaming boots, nodding her admiration. She'd survived boredom before, she'd undoubtedly do so in this instance as well. After all, it wasn't as if she were actually required to marry his tedious lordship. No indeed. She had only to tolerate his company until Lucian married Diana, then she'd use her matchmaking skills to find him a woman who would genuinely love him and vice versa. That way, no one would be hurt by her game.

Except herself. She shook her head, pushing away, as she constantly did of late, her ever-encroaching feelings for Lucian. Like her boredom, she'd survive the heartache of seeing him wed to Diana. Besides, she mustn't forget the positive aspect of all this: she'd regain her humanity, thus acquiring the mortal life she was presently only playing at possessing.

Who knows? Perhaps in time, long after she'd escaped Lucian's dazzling presence and her heart had healed, she might find a man of her own to love. Not that she expected the grand passion one found with their destined true love. As she knew all too well, a person was granted only one such love per lifetime, and her shallowness had killed hers almost five hundred years earlier.

"I got it! I got the bloody damn ring!"

That crowing declaration snapped Alys out of her misty-eyed reverie. Blinking twice to clear her vision, she gazed to her left, the direction from which the voice had come. There, balanced on a rough masonry embankment, triumphantly waving a thick gold band, was Hedley.

As she and Lord Drake strolled past, he hopped from his perch to the ground next to her feet. His stumpy legs pumping hard to keep pace, he cantered at her side, grumbling, "Nasty lot, them Nibelungens. Threatened to stake me down with horseshoes in a barn full o' cats if I dinna leave their fusty old caves immediately."

It was all Alys could do not to gasp aloud at the horrific nature of that threat. Nothing rendered a hob powerless quicker than a horseshoe, and to be left thus in a den of cats, the fairies greatest nemeseses, could have proved disastrous, even fatal to Hedley. And despite his nasty temper and crude ways, she had become rather fond of him.

"Yea. Old Hedley, here, would've ended up hob meat

if he hadn't been so bloody damn quick-witted and told 'em that he were a messenger from King Aengus." He cackled. "Them Nibelungens might be yakkedy-gop Norse trolls, but they're still under Aengus's rule. And since they ain't been in his good graces for nigh on two centuries now, they changed their tune quick 'nough. Got the ring and the spell, but we gotta do the spell tonight, on the first eve of the new moon, or it might not work."

Spell? Alys ached to inquire, though, of course, it was impossible to speak to Hedley in Lord Drake's presence. She'd assumed that Charlotte had only to wear the ring during marital relations in order to conceive. Hoping upon hope that her expression would be enough to prompt the hob to elaborate, she furrowed her brow and frowned to convey her mystification.

But he was no longer looking at her. He was skipping backward in front of them, eyeing her escort with the awe of an art student viewing the work of a great master for the very first time. He continued on like that for a long moment, then, in a wickedly faultless imitation of a Bond Street fribble, whom he delighted in studying, he drawled, " 'Pon my honor, my dear Miss Faire. He is a devilishly fine dresser, ain't he? Charming fig'er, quite the thing. Lord Tight-Arse would do well to follow his example. Dull dresser that Tight-Arse. Could do with a bang-up waistcoat like that."

Grinning in a way that always boded ill, he hopped like a frog on a hot hearth, then leaped up to dangle from the edge of the scarlet, blue, and gold striped garment in question.

Lord Drake broke off from whatever he was saying to gape down at his waistcoat, where Hedley hung squiggling his fingers against the fabric as if testing its quality. Though he was unable to see the hob, by his faint squirming it was plain he could feel him.

"Cassimere," Hedley announced with the smug self-assurance of a connoisseur. Indeed, he had become a bit of an expert on such matters, what with all the time he spent reading fashion periodicals and scrutinizing the public at large. "Very expensive cassimere," he elaborated with the emphasis on expensive. "And ye'll be

buying me one exactly like it if ye want my help in
casting that spell tonight. Don't forget that ye promised
me my pick of clothes if I helped ye with this baby-
getting business."

What choice did Alys have but to nod? She certainly
couldn't order him to get down and stop poking at his
lordship as she longed to do. Ah well. She smiled wanly
up at Lord Drake, who had valiantly resumed his conversation, despite his twitching discomfort. Perhaps the
naughty hob would become so enthralled with the notion
of his new waistcoat that he would take himself off to
plan the remainder of his promised ensemble.

Unfortunately, such was not the case. Upon receiving
her surreptitious agreement, he balled up his free hand
and punched his victim in the midsection, grimacing as
his fist made contact. His poor, beleaguered lordship
stopped abruptly in his tracks, convulsively dropping her
arm to scratch at his middle.

"Ah-ha. Just as I suspected. He's wearing a corset,"
Hedley crowed, dropping down to swing from Drake's
trouser falls. "Want one of those too." Having voiced
that demand, he turned his attention to testing the fabric
beneath his hands.

Alys glared at the hob, only to look away in the next
instant, flushing when she realized exactly where she was
staring. Mercifully, at least for her, his lordship was too
immersed in his own itching misery to notice her unladylike breach; an itch that had no doubt migrated to a
lower, more taboo region of his body.

Alys watched with sympathy as Lord Drake's hips
began to jerk and his handsome face flushed a mottled
scarlet. Poor, poor man. Being the gentleman he was,
he'd no doubt allow himself to be driven mad by the
tickling before scratching himself down there in her
presence.

Fortunately, or unfortunately, for Lord Drake, depending on how one viewed the matter, Hedley deemed
his trousers dashing and then, with a propelling kick to
his fashion idol's groin, sprang up to straddle his shoulder. Ignoring his lordship's obvious discomfort, he
rapped his fist against his cheek-high collar, his intent

expression bringing to mind a carpenter testing the soundness of a questionable wall.

"Stiff as iron," he marveled. "And his points—" His admiration visibly rose to adoring new heights as he fingered the precisely starched triangular edges. "Sharp as daggers, see?" To prove his claim, he grabbed one of the corners and gave his now grimacing lordship a sharp jab in the cheek.

His grimace mutated into a look of surprise liberally mixed with pain. "What the h—" he ejected, his hand flying from his midsection to cup his abused face.

"Is something amiss, my lord?" Alys queried, her sweet tone belying her furious urge to throttle the hob.

Gingerly rubbing his cheek, he murmured, "I don't know what's come over me. I suddenly seem to be feeling—"

"Hedley!" Alys hissed, her outrage overriding her discretion as the hob grasped the other point and prepared to repeat his wicked little demonstration.

Drake frowned, his hand stilling on his cheek. "Hedley?"

"Badly. I said that you look as if you feel badly," Alys fibbed, slanting the hob a threatening look. "Perhaps our walk has been too much exertion for you after so many days of being confined to the castle."

Hedley smirked and inched the point nearer to his victim's cheek, blatantly baiting her.

"Perhaps you are correct. I do find all this fresh air and exercise a bit—ah—fatiguing," Drake admitted with a wan smile.

"In that case, we must return to the castle so you can rest." The sooner she removed him from Hedley's injurious presence, the better.

Her escort's faint smile broadened into a cloying one. "You are most understanding, my dear Miss Faire," he cooed, lifting her hand to press a kiss to her palm. As he drew his lips away, murmuring something about the incomparable benevolence of her heart, she saw Hedley's knotty arm muscles flex, clearly signaling his intent to stab.

Tweaked beyond reason, she reflexively swatted at him. *Smack!*—

"Oww!" Drake howled as her hand connected not with Hedley, but with his already maltreated cheek. *Clunk! Tinkle!* His quizzing glass went flying from his face, shattering as it dashed upon the cobblestones at their feet.

From the walkway below, she heard a chortle. "Na-ha! Missed me!" But she was too appalled by her own reckless actions to give the troublesome little man the kick he so richly deserved. Still sniggering, he disappeared.

Gazing numbly up at Drake, who was clutching his cheek and eyeing her with scowling resentment, she stammered, "M-my lord. I'm—"

"What the devil is going on here?" interrupted a tight, furious voice that Alys knew oh-so-well.

Her mind frantically groping for an explanation, she bit her lip and reluctantly turned to face Lucian. He looked as incensed as he sounded, glaring from her to Drake, and then back again, as if trying to decide which one to throttle. "I—I—" she sputtered. Oh, perfect! Her mind was blank.

"She slapped me," Lord Drake supplied, fixing her with an accusing stare.

Lucian's stormy gaze shifted from her to Drake, his glittering eyes narrowing as he focused on his face. "So I saw," he ground out. "What I want to know is why."

So ominous were both his tone and demeanor that Alys thanked God that they weren't directed at her. *At least not yet,* she reminded herself, her flesh prickling as she ventured another glance at Lucian's grim face. No doubt all that raw anger would be redirected at her the instant her escort reported her shocking behavior. Heaving an inaudible sigh, she miserably shifted her gaze to Lord Drake, waiting for him to utter his condemnation.

Unlike herself, he was holding up admirably beneath Lucian's intimidating regard, a truly astonishing phenomenon given his foppish appearance and mien. Indeed, he seemed utterly composed as he said, "I can assure you, Thistlewood, that I did nothing whatsoever to offend the gel. Quite the contrary. I was merely expressing my admiration for her sweet nature when she slapped me."

Lucian stared at him for another unnerving moment, then slowly dragged his gaze over to Alys to impale her with his displeasure. "Is what he says true?" he growled.

Alys opened and closed her mouth soundlessly several times before she finally managed to croak, "Yes."

"And he in no way insulted or offended you?"

"N-no."

His eyes were like burning slits now, searing hers with his ire. For several heart-racing beats he stared at her, then his lips flattened into a hard, tight line and he commanded, "Apologize to Lord Drake this instant."

Alys swallowed so hard, she was certain that everyone within a ten-mile radius heard her gulp. Searching her numb mind for a plausible way to excuse her actions, she turned her gaze to the equally stony-faced Lord Drake, mumbling, "I truly am sorry, my lord. I-I can assure you that it was a complete accident. I—" Irrationally the vision of him wiggling beneath Hedley's torment popped into her mind. With it came inspiration. Her faltering voice instantly regaining its strength, she finished, "I was simply trying to swat a spider from your hair when you moved, making me slap you instead."

Drake's eyes widened and his face blanched to an odd, ashy color. "Spider, you say?"

She nodded. "A fat brown one, about, oh"—she indicated a length of about an inch and a half between her index finger and thumb—"this big."

"That big, eh?" His shoulders began to twitch and when he smoothed the front of his already immaculate coat, she noted that his hands trembled. "Did you—uh—did you by any c-chance get it?"

"I believe so," she replied, watching with dismay as he convulsively poked his sleeve, then swatted his side.

"Y-You believe so, but y-y-you're not"—he clawed at his midsection—"absolutely certain?"

"As certain as I can be," Alys assured him, patting his arm in a feeble attempt to calm him.

He yelped and batted her away, clearly so unnerved by her story that he'd mistaken her hand for the spider in question.

"Good heavens! Are you quite all right, Lord

Drake?" This was from Diana, who was just joining them.

"Spiders. Must have walked through a whole bloody nest of them," he muttered, his body jerking in earnest at that notion. "Thought I felt something crawling on me earlier, but I—" His eyes bulged as he slapped at an imaginary spider on his neck. "I—oh!" Panting with terror, he more shrieked than said, "Please excuse me!" Then went dashing off toward the front of the castle as if pursued by a whole fiendish legion of the creatures.

Alys started after him, horrified by the panic her tale had wrought, but Lucian grasped her arm, stopping her. Capturing her rueful gaze with his darkly flickering one, he gritted out, "Miss Ramsey. Would you please be so kind as to follow Lord Drake and make certain that he gets back to the castle safely? My ward and I have something pressing we must discuss."

"But of course," Diana replied, peering curiously from guardian to ward, before hurrying after Drake. When she was well out of sight, Lucian rounded on Alys.

"What the hell kind of game are you playing?" he spat, his hands punishing as he grasped her upper arms and gave her a savage shake.

She stared at him wordlessly, too shocked by the intensity of his fury to respond.

Clearly he didn't expect or even particularly want a response, for he continued with barely a pause. "I knew you were a stubborn, wayward little hellion, but never— ever!—did I credit you with being cruel."

"Cruel?" she exclaimed, flabbergasted by his accusation.

"What the hell would you call what you just did to a man whom you damn well know is terrified of spiders?" He didn't utter the words, he snarled them.

Alys shook her head once. "But I didn't know! How could I?"

"Like hell, you didn't. In case you've forgotten, I was in the coach when Charlotte went over the list of guests. And I distinctly remember her gossiping at length about how an almost fatal bite as a youth has left Drake deathly afraid of spiders."

Alys probed her mind, desperately trying to recall

hearing such a thing. But she drew a blank. She'd been so preoccupied with worrying over the exclusion of Reina Castell from the list of female guests that she'd been completely deaf to what was said about the male ones. Feeling as wretched as if she were confessing to murder, she haltingly admitted to her inattentiveness.

Snorting his disgust, Lucian released her arms and pushed her away, the force of his thrust almost toppling her backward. "Of course. How very stupid of me. I should have remembered that woolgathering heads your regrettably long list of faults." He paused a beat to rake her with his scornful gaze, then looked away, heaving what sounded like a sigh of defeat.

"Whatever am I to do with you, Alys?" he continued, rubbing at his temples as if just the thought of her made his head ache. "No man in his right mind is going to marry you. Certainly not the sort your brother would have deemed suitable. As for me being stuck with you indefinitely, well, that is a notion too hideous to be entertained."

That he thought so poorly of her dealt Alys's heart a deep, mortal blow. While she knew that he would never love her as a man did a woman, she'd hoped that he might at least come to regard her as a friend. Indeed, she'd made every effort to build such rapport between them. And by the way he'd responded, smiling at her quips and readily accepting her invitations to partner her at cards, she'd thought herself successful. Apparently she'd been wrong.

It was her turn to sigh. As with everything else involving Lucian, it seemed that she'd somehow muddled her attempts to gain his friendship. Feeling like the world's biggest failure and at a loss as to how to turn herself around, she whispered the only thing she could think to say, "Please Lucian. Please believe me when I say that I am truly sorry about Lord Drake."

"Sorry?" he scoffed, his face reflecting the contempt in his voice. "There are some instances when merely saying you're sorry is inadequate, and I'm very much afraid that this might well be one of them. It is entirely possible that Drake is even now regaling our guests with tales of your forward conduct, in which case you shall undoubtedly be ruined by the time we return to the castle."

"But that's ridiculous!" she exclaimed, stunned by his words. "I did nothing but chase a spider from his lordship's hair!"

"Swatting insects from a suitor is hardly the act of a well-bred miss," he pointed out dryly. "One which could easily get that same miss branded as the worst kind of romp. As a man of the world, Drake knows this, just as he knows that polite society is unlikely to countenance a miss reputed as being such. Therefore, he might label you a romp in hopes that you will be shunned by the ton, thus rendering you powerless to pass gossip about his cowardice."

Alys hung her head, too miserable to respond. She'd really made a mess of things this time. If she were banished from society, then her opportunities to thrust Diana into Lucian's company would be reduced to few or none. Then how would she ever get them together?

Fumbling for a way to salvage the potentially disastrous situation, she cast him a repentant look and suggested, "What if I were to assure him of my silence on this matter? Surely he could bear me no malice then?"

"Couldn't he?" Lucian emitted a disdainful noise and crossed his arms over his chest, staring at her as if she'd just said the stupidest thing in the world. "Do you truly expect to appease him by drudging up what was bound to be one of the most humiliating episodes of his life, and swearing secrecy to his shame?" He shook his head as if overwhelmed by incredulity. "If so, then we must add dull-witted to your rapidly expanding list of faults."

Dull-witted, indeed! Alys opened her mouth to protest his rude assessment, but before she could say anything, he continued, "Don't you see that by acknowledging his shame, you will also be conceding your own understanding of how injurious your information might be? A man like Drake is bound to see that as a threat, no matter how pretty your apology. And he'll ruin you rather than be at the mercy of your discretion."

He seemed about to add something else, then stopped short, his eyes narrowing as if struck by a new thought. Staring at her in a way that made her uncomfortably certain that he could see all the way into her soul, he finished, "But then, perhaps you've already ascertained all that yourself."

"W-what?" she sputtered, taken aback by his odd twist of reason.

He chuckled, but in a dry, humorless way. "Come, come now, Alys. Don't insult my intelligence by playing coy with me. I'm beginning to see quite clearly now what you're about."

Alys gaped at him, genuinely baffled. "Excuse me?"

"Lest you've forgotten, you were more than a little vocal in your objections to marriage when we discussed the matter."

"It wasn't the notion of marriage I found disagreeable, but your presumptuous list of bachelors." She shook her head, her bewilderment deepening. "However, even if it were marriage to which I objected, I fail to see what it would have to do with any of this."

"What indeed?" He arched one eyebrow in sardonic query. "Tell me, my dear Miss Faire. What are the chances of a ruined young lady receiving an offer?"

The scandalous intimation of that question threw her completely off balance. "You honestly believe that I would ruin myself to escape marriage?" she gasped. "Why that's"—she flung her hands up—"that's preposterous!"

"Is it? First you chase off Atwood by engaging in a scuffle with a chimney sweep, now you scare Drake off with tales of rampaging spiders. What have you planned for suitor number three? A lit match to the boot, or a handful of leeches in his trousers?"

Alys snorted her exasperation. "Of course not. And you know perfectly well that I didn't deliberately discourage either of those other two gentlemen. Both incidents were simply the result of unfortunate—misunderstandings."

His lips curled into a tight sneer. "It seems to me, my dear, that you are particularly prone to being misunderstood, especially by bachelors of my choosing."

She returned his arrogant smirk in kind, embellishing it with a haughty sniff. "Then perhaps, my lord, you should stop choosing. I've already informed you that I shall select my own husband."

"Then I suggest that you get busy selecting." He more spat than said the words. "For be warned, my dear ward: you shall be married before the end of the season, even if I have to pay some penniless old roue to take you off my hands. I shall not be saddled with you for a single day longer than necessary, do you understand? I shan't!" He practically shouted that last sentence.

The vehemence of his cruel proclamation struck hard at the core of her being, making her yearn to scream her fury at the resulting agony. She'd been trying to tell herself that his hatefulness stemmed from his anger over Drake. But it was clear she'd been wrong, wretchedly so. He despised her, profoundly and undeniably despised her. How else could he speak to her so?

For a long moment she stood frozen by emotion; pain exploding into rage, her rage escalating into an almost mad desire to hurt him as badly as he'd just hurt her. But, of course, doing so was impossible. For how did one strike at the heart of a man who had no heart to wound?

Lowering her lashes to hide her tears, she murmured with as much dignity as she could muster, "I understand perfectly, Lord Thistlewood. Please be assured that I shall find a way to relieve you of my odious presence as soon as possible, even if I must run away and live on the streets to do so. For despite your low opinion of me, I have much too much pride to stay where I'm not wanted." With that, she picked up her skirts and bolted off down the fairway, her hurt dissolving into wrenching sobs as she ran.

Chapter 13

"Alys," Lucian whispered, offering his turned-up palm in a gesture of contrite appeasement. But it was too late. She had already stumbled up the embankment and was rapidly moving out of sight. Finger by finger he slowly curled his hand into a fist, dropping it to his side when it was a taut, trembling ball.

Dear God. What is happening to me? he agonized, tipping his head back to stare at the infinite smear of blue above. *Why am I being tormented with these strange and unwelcome feelings?* One minute they were stunning him with their rawness, the next they confused him with their conflicting nature. Always, their intensity made him long to fall to his knees, screaming for deliverance from their terrifying grip.

He closed his eyes and gave his head a hard shake, as if by doing so he could jolt his emotional equilibrium back into balance. Worse of all, these damnable feelings compelled him to behave in irrational, often reckless ways that bewildered and distressed him. Which is exactly what had just happened with Alys.

Never in his life had he experienced such mindless rage as he had when he saw her slap Drake. Indeed, he'd been so besieged with protective instincts that it had taken every last ounce of his self-control not to throttle the man first and ask questions later.

Why? He clenched his fists tighter. Why had he, who was known far and wide for his unflappable reserve, al-

most resorted to violence over a presumed slight to a
woman he didn't even like? It wasn't as if he were gallant by nature. To him, gallantry was a sentiment best
left to poets and fools, especially when it involved a
scuffle over a woman. For aside from his late mother
and, of course, Lottie, he could think of no woman with
honor worth defending.

That being the case, why did he suddenly have this
burning need to champion Alys?

Slowly he opened his eyes and tilted his head down
to stare at the emptiness where only moments before
she had stood. Why indeed? The chit was incorrigible, a
regular menace. He sighed.

Life had been so peaceful before she'd arrived, so . . .
simple. During the days he'd gone about his business,
doing the same thing at precisely the same time, automatically performing his lordly duties. At night he'd
gone home to his perfectly run house where he'd follow
his time-honored routine of dinner, then brandy and a
cigar, followed by reading or perhaps a conversation
with Stephen should he stop by, concluding with bed.
No surprises, no disruptions, no upsets. Just the same
patterns day in, day out, just the way he liked it.

Then Alys had come into his life and home, bringing
in her wake trouble, chaos, worry . . .

And this awful emotional upheaval. Lucian's mind
froze, paralyzed by that observation. Alys was responsible for these troubling new feelings and thoughts? Ridiculous! How could she, a mere slip of a schoolgirl, so
powerfully influence him, a hard, autonomous man of
the world?

Utterly perplexed, he removed his hat to run his hand
through his hair. Well, she was certainly different from
any young miss he'd ever met, that much was for sure.
She was impulsive, stubborn, eccentric to the point of
oddness, opinionated, and brash. He smiled faintly at
that last. She had to be brash to stand up to him as she
did; he, who had the ability to silence a dissident voice
in the House of Lords with just a frown.

Slowly his smile faded. She was all those unfortunate
things, true; yet despite those faults, she also possessed
many traits that he couldn't help but to admire. For one,

she was valiant. Hadn't she shown herself as such in the
matter of the climbing boy? And she was generous, almost to a fault. Why, he'd lost count of the number of
times she'd emptied her purse in the palms of a hollow-
eyed match-seller or chilblain-plagued beggar. She was
also witty, making him laugh even when he was disin-
clined to do so, and fanciful in a way that was as
thought-provoking as it was delightful.

And last, but not least, despite his infuriated claims
to the contrary, she was clever; far too clever to do
something as harebrained as ruin herself to escape marriage. Knowing Alys's lively imagination, she'd dream
up an ingenious and undoubtedly successful plan to discourage her suitors without bruising either her reputation or their pride . . .

. . . something he'd known even as he'd leveled his
churlish accusations to the contrary.

That shameful admission made him long to crawl into
the nearest foxhole and hide. How could he have been
so unjust? So cruel and hurtful? He'd had no call to be
so angry with her, not after she'd explained her actions.
True her inattentiveness to Charlotte's instruction had
warranted a reprimand, but she most certainly hadn't
deserved to be insulted and made to feel like a
pariah . . .

. . . something that he'd realized even as he'd done so.

His bewilderment outstripping his shame, he asked
himself why. Why, knowing as he had that what he was
doing was wrong, had he done it?

Why indeed? Lucian cringed in both heart and flesh
as the truth tore forth from his soul: he had behaved as
he had out of fear and confusion. He was confused by
his urge to protect her, and afraid of the weakness that
that impulse implied. And because he had been at a loss
as to how to deal with those emotions, he'd resorted to
anger. Anger he knew well. It was comfortable.

Comfortable, true, but not particularly pleasant, he
glumly reminded himself. Certainly not as pleasant as
sitting by the kitchen hearth at night with Alys, sharing
not only the heat of the fire, but the warmth of
companionship.

For an instant he pictured her face as it looked on

those occasions, smiling and full of youthful vivacity.
Then he pushed the vision away, groaning. After the
way he'd treated her, he doubted if she would ever again
join him in another of their delightful midnight raids
on the pantry. That prospect left him with a haunting
emptiness, making him feel . . . what?

He furrowed his brow, forcing himself to examine the
emotion. He felt . . . lonely. Yes. Devastatingly so. Indeed, the notion that he might never again share another
of their special moments was one that he found unbearably wretched.

His frown deepened then as he was gripped by yet
another sensation, one that closely resembled a defini-
tion he'd been forced to memorize at Eton: regret: to
miss very much; to be very sorry. Yes. It must be regret
he was feeling, for he was very sorry indeed for the way
he'd spoken to Alys and he would most definitely miss
the amusement her company provided.

That admission clarified a new, more startling insight:
he liked her.

And she no doubt hated him. He expelled a long,
gusty breath. If only there was something he could do
to make amends. Something that would restore her confidence in him and replant the uprooted shoots of their
fledgling friendship. But what?

He could apologize. He paused, taken aback by that
new and decidedly alien notion. Apologize? Aside from
murmuring a shallow pardon for a social faux pas such
as spilling a drop of wine or accidentally bumping someone on the street, he'd never apologized to anyone in
his life. However did one go about it? Somehow, simply
saying he was sorry seemed inadequate.

He mulled over his dilemma for a moment, then his
mind flashed back to Alys and her apology to Drake.
She'd said she was sorry, yes, but she had also explained
her actions so they could be understood and forgiven.
And despite his own unreasonable claims to the contrary, there was no doubt in his mind that Drake had
forgiven her for slapping him.

But would that same tactic work for him? Indeed, was
he even capable of expressing the feelings that had
driven him to such behavior? He ran his hand through

his hair once more, this time to smooth it, then replaced
his hat. He had to try. He valued Alys's company far
too much to lose it over his own fear-induced stupidity.
Thus determined, he went after her.

But she was nowhere to be found. He searched for
her in all her usual haunts: her chamber; the picture
gallery, where she and Diana often met to promenade
and gossip; both Charlotte's and Diana's rooms; even
the kitchen. But to no avail. No one could recall seeing
her return to the castle. He was about to order his horse
saddled, certain that she'd made good her threat to run
away, when a footmen informed him that a maid had
reported seeing her mounting the stairs to the old
nursery.

With relief blossoming in his chest, Lucian hurried to
the northwest tower, taking the corkscrewing steps two
at a time in his rush to see Alys. He was three quarters
of the way up when he came to an abrupt half, frozen
by sudden apprehension.

What if she refused his apology? Like an untimely
shift from day to night his glowing eagerness darkened
to dread. People, women in particular, did reject apologies, he knew that much from the buzz at White's. What
he didn't know was what the rejected party did to make
further amends.

Cursing himself for disregarding his fellow clubsmen's
never-ending chatter on male atonement to females, he
practically dragged himself the rest of the way up the
stairs, stopping only when he reached the open door at
the top. As tense as an unruly schoolboy summoned to
the headmaster's office, he peered into the room.

Sitting on the floor with her head slightly bowed and
her hands clasped to her chest was Alys. To her right
lolled a resplendently garbed doll, Lord Woodywig, if he
remembered correctly; to her left lay a pair of well-used
battledores and a sorry-looking shuttlecock. In front of
her hulked his old toy castle, which she was contemplating with such a faraway expression that for one brief
instant he wondered what she saw when she looked at
it. Dragons, knights, and imperiled princesses, perhaps?

Despite his anxiety, Lucian smiled. Never had she
looked so young and innocent as she did at that moment,

garbed in a simple white frock, surrounded by play-things. Indeed, had he not known better he'd have taken her for the rightful occupant of the nursery.

His smile broadened as he imagined her indignation were he to voice that observation. Of late she'd tried so hard to look and act grown-up. Yet, despite her pains-taking efforts, he found himself incapable of viewing her as anything other than a child.

A rather pretty child, he added with some surprise as she tilted her head, thus presenting him with her delicate profile. His bemusement growing by the second he sur-veyed her face, his gaze appraising as it traced the dainty contours of her throat, jaw, and chin, scanning up until it came to a mind-jolting halt at her mouth.

Those lips. His eyes widened as if seeing them for the first time. Since when had they become so pink, so—generous? And her nose. He blinked twice in disbelief. Why, it wasn't nearly as unremarkable as he'd supposed. Indeed, from this angle it looked almost classical, pleas-ingly so.

Classical and pleasing? Alys? He rubbed his eyes, hop-ing that by doing so he would clear away whatever was transforming his plain ward into a vision of loveliness. But it was to no avail. No matter how hard he rubbed, his former duckling remained a swan.

Amazing. He dropped his hands back to his sides, shaking his head in astonishment. So miraculously im-proved was her face that had it not been for her unfortu-nate hair color, he might be tempted to pronounce her pretty.

Unless, of course, like her face he'd grossly misjudged her hair? That suspicion prompted him to glance at the golden curls framing her brow. Hmm. Perhaps it wasn't so very bad after all. Not once one got accustomed to it. He tilted his head to one side, viewing those silky little ringlets through new eyes. Indeed, if he were to be brutally honest, he would have to admit that he was beginning to find blonde women rather appealing.

Smiling faintly at his astonishing new predilection, he dropped his gaze to let it sweep along the graceful line of her cheek. Of course, in order to be truly attractive, a fair-haired woman must have a complexion like fresh cream and rose petals . . .

. . . like Alys.

And it certainly didn't hurt if she possessed a pair of fine blue eyes . . .

. . . like Alys.

His jaw dropped then as he mentally added up his ward's attributes and realized their sum: Alys Faire wasn't merely pretty, she was beautiful. And when she turned abruptly, probably in response to his shocked intake of air, he saw that she wasn't the child he'd deluded himself into perceiving, but a woman. A stunning and desirable woman.

For a long moment they stared at each other; she, visibly tense and defensive, doubtlessly expecting him to resume his diatribe; he, too astounded by his discovery to speak.

It was she who looked away first, but not before he noted the dampness shimmering in her eyes, betraying the hurt she was clearly trying to hide. That he was brute enough to so savagely wound an innocent girl shamed him to the deepest fibers of his being.

More desperate than ever to make amends, he whispered, "Alys, I—" then fell mute, at a loss as to how to proceed.

Alys remained motionless for several seconds, damning him with her silence. When she finally did look up, her face was as dispassionate as if he were a footman summoning her to dinner. "My lord?" she murmured, her voice mirroring her expression.

With growing urgency, Lucian returned her impassive gaze with his pleading one. Never had he felt so helpless, so frustrated, as he did at that moment as he grappled for the words to express his remorse. "I—I—" he choked out, but again his voice failed him.

Damn you! Say it! he commanded himself, his urgency spiraling toward panic. Obediently his mouth opened, but nothing came out. For several agonizing beats he fought to free the imprisoned words, releasing captive sobs in their stead. "I'm—" he finally croaked, his voice breaking from strain and emotion, "sorry."

She gasped, looking so shocked that for one unnerving

moment he wondered if he had unwittingly uttered his self-directed curses rather than his well-intentioned apology. "You're . . . sorry?" She wasn't just echoing his words, by her tone she seemed to be marveling over them.

He nodded, smiling his relief. To his amazement, she returned his smile. It was a small one, true, but it was enough to release him from his emotional paralysis.

Closing the distance between them in four long strides, he exclaimed in a pent-up rush, "I am sorry, Alys. My behavior was truly reprehensible. I had no call to speak to you so harshly, and if you choose never to forgive me, well"—he made a helpless hand gesture as he dropped to his knees beside her—"I cannot say as I blame you."

She contemplated him gravely, as if considering whether or not to accept his apology. After what felt like an eternity, she nodded. "Of course, I forgive you."

He stared at her, not quite daring to believe that he'd heard her correctly. "You . . . forgive me?"

She nodded again.

"Why?" he blurted out. That she could forgive him without pleas, or at least an explanation as to why he'd acted as he did, puzzled him beyond his reasoning.

She smiled faintly. "Because you said you were sorry."

"But it seems so little, I mean"—he shook his head as he tried to find a way to convey his thoughts—"I mean, how can you forgive me so much, so easily? All I did was utter two small words."

"Not so small when they come from here." She laid her hand over his heart. "Each word is worth a thousand pretty phrases when spoken with as much sincerity as you did just now."

Lucian stared down into her luminous blue eyes, his jaw dropping slightly as he tried to comprehend that foreign notion. He'd never considered the way in which words were spoken to be important, only the meaning of the words themselves. That something as seemingly trivial as timbre and inflection could so empower even the simplest utterance was a concept beyond his scope of imagining.

Yet, it must be true, he mused. It had to be for her to look at him like she was, so sweetly and with a charity he still wasn't certain he deserved.

Just then she started to pull her hand from his chest. Impulsively he seized it and lifted it to his lips. He might not be deserving of her forgiveness now, but he would be. No matter what it took, he would make amends and prove himself worthy of the gift of her friendship. With those vows echoing through his mind, he pressed his lips to her palm, murmuring, "Accept not only my sincerest apologies, but my equally sincere promise that I shall never again speak to you in such a manner."

"Not even if I do something terribly naughty and deserve it?" There was a teasing note in her voice that made him glance up in surprise. Though she was trying to look serious, the corners of her mouth were twitching and her eyes sparkled with barely contained deviltry.

"Not even if you put a spider in Lord Drake's snuffbox." He shook his head, the return of her high spirits lifting his own solemn mood. "I shall simply turn you over my knee and administer the paddling I've been threatening to give you since your arrival."

"Oh, dear. In that case, I shall have to put that spider back in the garden where I found it," she murmured, freeing her tethered smile. It was a warm, genuine smile; a dazzling rarity in a society where every expression was the unnatural result of much thought and training.

To Lucian, it was the most charming smile in the world, one far more enticing than the tight-lipped simpers most women seemed to think seductive. It was too enticing.

Swallowing hard, he tore his gaze from her face, tempted almost beyond redemption to pull her into his arms and ravish her innocently curved lips with his suddenly needful ones. That he, who prided himself on his immunity to desire, should feel such strong attraction to any woman was startling; that he should feel it for his ward was disgraceful. No, it was worse than disgraceful: it was obscene. Her brother had entrusted him to protect her, and on his honor he would not violate that trust by seducing her.

"Lucian? Are you all right? You're so flushed and quiet all of a sudden," Alys said, her concerned voice breaking into his thoughts.

Lucian started to glance up, to smile his reassurance, but caught himself in time. No, it was best if he didn't look at her face until he was certain he had regained his control. Shifting his gaze from here to there and back again in an almost frantic attempt to find something— anything!—to distract his mind from his unseemly thoughts, he muttered, "I'm fine." It wasn't until he spied Alys's hand resting on her lap that he was successful.

Loosely cradled in her palm was a toy knight, a magnificent one armored in gold and mantled in green. He smiled faintly, all thoughts of kissing and other fleshly delights fleeing as he recognized it as his childhood favorite. Though it had been more than two decades since he'd played with it, the remembrance of the many scintillating hours he'd spent sitting here, engaging that knight in imaginary battles, infused him with fierce pleasure.

Filled with a wonder he hadn't felt since those days, he took the figure from her hand and held it up to examine it with jaded adult eyes. It was still wonderful. Lovingly tracing the knight's upraised shield with his thumb, he murmured, "Where in the world did you find this? I'd thought it lost years ago."

"Here." She opened the front of the castle to reveal his once cherished army of knights, all lined up with military precision. "Aren't they beautiful?"

"Beautiful?" He chuckled. "I always imagined them to be quite ferocious. Some days, even bloodthirsty. Especially this one." He picked up a knight arrayed all in black, and held it up for her scrutiny. "Sir Diabolus. He coveted the castle, which belonged to Sir Stoutheart"— he indicated the golden knight by jerking the hand that held it—"and was constantly waging war to win it."

"Did he ever succeed?"

"Only when I was in a foul mood."

"You? In a foul mood? Surely you jest!" she quipped, laughing.

He grinned, not at all offended by her good-natured allusion to his saturnine disposition. "As Spratling was constantly pointing out, I was an exceedingly dour child."

"How could anyone be dour living in such a splendid nursery, filled with"—she gestured to the castle and knights—"such glorious toys? Why, if all this were mine, I'd have smiled so much that everyone would have thought me feebleminded."

There was a wistful note in her voice that made him venture a glance at her face. She was gazing at the castle with such abject longing that he was forced to ponder why. Had her childhood been deprived, or in some way unhappy? That hers or anyone else's youth might not have been as privileged and carefree as his was something he'd never stopped to consider. Now that he was considering it, he was curious.

"Your nursery wasn't comfortable?" he inquired, bluntly voicing that curiosity.

She shot him a sharp glance, as if taken aback by his question. "Well, yes . . . yes . . . of course it was. It just wasn't as sumptuous as yours."

"And your childhood, was it"—he paused a beat to think of an appropriate word—"pleasant?"

She smiled at him, in a gentle, dreamy way that inspired not desire, but a softer, deeper emotion. "Oh, yes," she replied on a sigh, "it was wonderfully pleasant."

Something about that enigmatic smile made Lucian suddenly eager to learn everything about her. Secretly vowing to do just that, he quizzed, "And what sorts of things did you do?"

She shrugged. "That was centuries ago . . . uh . . ." she flushed a becoming primrose pink, "at least it feels like centuries."

"It was almost yesterday," he quietly contradicted. "The letter I received from your brother's solicitor said that you were just recently home from school."

"Yes, though I was more a boarder than a student the last two years I was there. Since we had no one at Fair-fax my brother deemed suitable to chaperone me, he thought it better that I remain at Wickington until he returned from the war."

He frowned. "Wickington? Isn't that a religious institution of sorts?"

She nodded. "It caters to the daughters of men in the hierarchy of the Church of England. My parents sent me there in hopes that what they saw as my wayward tendencies might be curbed. My childhood ended the day I entered that school. I was only ten at the time, so you see, it truly has been a long while since I was a child."

At his querying look, she elaborated. "The teachers were extremely strict, demanding that we behave like sedate little adults at all times. Childish nonsense was not tolerated, and games, except those based on the teachings of the Book of Common Prayer, were strictly forbidden. Not," she hastily reassured him, "that I'm complaining. I took great pleasure in my spinning, weaving, and needlework."

"I'd be complaining very loudly if I were you," he countered. "Spinning, weaving, and needlework? Religious games Bah! Dreary pastimes for a child! And here I thought Eton was a grind."

"What was Eton like?"

"Hard. At times even miserable. But at least we were allowed to play."

She tipped her head to one side, her gaze as inquisitive as he was certain his own must be. "What sort of games did you play?"

"Cricket, hide-and-go-seek, skittles, and, of course, battledore-and-shuttlecock. I was the undefeated champion at the last," he declared with not a small measure of pride.

"Battledore-and-shuttlecock?" she repeated slowly, then shook her head. "I'm afraid I'm not familiar with that game."

"What? You've never played battledore-and-shuttlecock?" His shock was genuine. "Remind me to write the Wickington School a scathing letter the instant we return to London. They've left you with a woefully incomplete education, my dear."

Alys dropped her gaze, a tiny smile playing on her lips. "As my guardian, I believe that it is your duty to fill the gaps."

He studied her a moment, not certain if that last was a statement or a hint. Then she slanted him an expectant look from beneath her lashes. "Well, my lord?"

A hint. He grinned. "You are quite correct. It is my duty to see you versed in all aspects of life," he concurred, pleased by her wish to learn the game. After all, what better way to foster a friendship than by playing together? Finding the idea more appealing by the second, he seized his and Charlotte's old battledores and announced, "Miss Faire. School is in session."

To Lucian's delight, Alys proved an apt student, quickly mastering the game. And after only a quarter hour of instruction, he found himself engaged in a fiercely competitive match.

"A-ha! Take that!" She slammed the cork and feather shuttlecock with all her might, sending it flying over his head.

With a proficiency born of experience, he easily caught it with his racket and smacked it back, laughing, "You're going to have to do better than that if you want to win!"

She redoubled her efforts, this time swatting it so far to his right that he practically had to fly to return it.

Back and forth they volleyed, running, sometimes even jumping as each sought to be the victor of their match. Once, in her zeal to avenge a particularly sly move on his part, she dropped her racket. To his amusement a mild oath slipped from her scowling lips, making her blush and him roar with laughter.

It wasn't until they neared the end of their game that he was struck by a startling revelation: he was having fun; giddy, unadulterated fun; something he hadn't experienced in decades. Just as astonishing, he craved more and was now frantically trying to think of a reason to prolong their lesson. So stunned was he by his own uncharacteristic frivolity that he failed to notice Alys standing to his left as he sailed in that direction after the shuttlecock.

"Oomph!" They collided. For an instant they teetered unsteadily, clinging to each other in a frantic attempt to steady themselves. Then they lost their balance and went tumbling to the floor, where they landed with his tall body sprawled atop hers. So dazed and breathless was Lucian that it wasn't until he felt Alys move beneath him that his sense and awareness returned.

Or rather, his body's awareness to her soft form alerted his senses. *What the hell is wrong with me today?* he wondered, thunderstruck by the sudden tightening in his groin. First he'd been tempted to kiss Alys into submission, now his male parts were aching with that awful congested feeling they got when he neglected to visit his mistress.

But this is impossible, he told himself, appalled to feel himself harden completely. He'd visited Reina the night before he'd left for Thistlewood, and a single visit was normally enough to afford him relief for a whole month if necessary.

Again Alys squirmed. This time her belly brushed against his arousal.

Dear God! He caught a hissing breath, his teeth clenching as fire streaked through his loins. What was happening to him? He'd never had this problem just a week after being relieved. Hell, he hadn't been this aroused when he'd mounted his first woman. Like desire, lust had simply never been a problem for him.

Until now.

"Lucian, you're crushing me," Alys murmured, giving another wiggle that almost drove him over the edge.

"Sorry," he groaned, rolling off her. He wanted to help her up, to apologize for his clumsiness and assure himself that she was unhurt. But he couldn't. Aside from muttering a hoarse inquiry as to her well-being, he could do nothing but sit with his knees drawn up and legs together, hiding his wretched condition.

As he sat there miserably watching her straighten her skirts and smooth her hair, he tried to rationalize his erratic behavior. Was he perhaps sickening with something? Or could it be that he was overly tired? No, no. It must have something to do with the fresh country air. He sighed. Again, no. He'd spent much of his life at Thistlewood, and it had never affected him like this.

That left only one explanation, the logical one he so desperately wanted to deny: he was losing control. And heaven help him, he hadn't a clue how to regain it.

Chapter 14

His face was so close, she could have counted his eyelashes had she wished. Smiling at that fancy, Alys gently ran her fingertip along their inky length, admiring their fanlike fullness. Like everything else about Lucian Warre, they were magnificent.

"Alys," he sighed, his eyes closing beneath her adoring touch.

Her toes curling in rapturous response, she twined her arms around his neck and buried her face into the warm hollow at the base of his throat. For a long while she stood like that, savoring the feel of his body. He felt so good, so right, his tall form fitting her small one as perfectly as if he were her destined true love. And the way he smelled—

She nuzzled against his thundering pulse point, inhaling. He smelled like fertile earth kissed by thyme, agrimony, and speedwell . . . like Thistlewood in the spring. She released her breath on a hushed moan, only to draw another, deeper one, in the next instant.

Mmm. Yes. Like Thistlewood, but with a sublime difference. Beneath the innocent perfume of the Sussex downs lurked a subtle, more provocative scent; one so musky and potently masculine that she was powerless to resist its seductive beckoning. It was the fragrance of heated male flesh; the essence of Lucian himself.

Tempted beyond denial, Alys hungrily pressed her lips the length of his throat, half kissing, half caressing up over his jaw, stopping only when she came to his ear. For the briefest of moments she studied it, then tentatively licked the shell-like lining.

He gasped and lolled his head nearer. Eager to oblige his voluptuous urging, she sucked his lobe into her mouth, teasing it with her teeth and tongue until his quivering gasps erupted into explosive pants.

"I love you, Alys! Dear God, I love you!" he cried, his voice a spasm of raw desire.

"I love you too," she whispered between nibbles, letting her breath tickle his ear as she spoke.

He shuddered in response, strangled groans issuing from his lips. Thrilling at her feminine power, she gave his ear one final nip, then softly kissed across his lean cheek. Over the bridge of his nose she kissed, leisurely meandering her way across his face to his other ear. For several sizzling moments she ravished it, alternately licking and biting it until he squirmed against her, writhing in his passion.

"Let me love you—" he begged, his plea terminating in a sob.

"Soon," she purred, her mouth skimming the strong angle of his jaw. Feature by elegant feature her lips worshiped his face, kissing him everywhere but his moan-parted mouth. His flesh was warm, its texture smooth, like time-softened silk dried in the hot summer sun. It wasn't until she'd paid homage to every enticing hollow and plane that she turned her attention to his neglected mouth.

Her fingers trembling with her own need, she traced its fascinating shape, time and again dipping between his lips to caress the moist pink lining.

With every touch he moaned, each sensual utterance more impassioned than the last. When he could bear the exquisite torment no longer, he seized her marauding hand by the wrist and crushed it to his chest. "Look at me," he commanded, his voice as rich and steamy as hot chocolate.

She did, melting against him as their gazes united. Never had his eyes been so adoring, never so warm and inviting. One glance and she was enslaved. Seconds raced by on heartbeats as he inched his lips toward hers,

her craving to taste him building until she was tempted
to seize his head and brazenly crush her mouth against
his. Just when she was certain she could bear the anticipation no longer, she felt his breath fanning across her
cheeks.

"Lucian," she sighed, her lips parting to receive his
kiss.

"Will ye get yer frigging arse out o' bed and come
on?" he replied.

"Lucian?" she repeated, this time in query. Whatever
had happened to his voice? He sounded almost like—

There was a smack against her cheek. "Do I sound
like Lord bloody damn Tight-Arse to ye?"

Like the night haze burning away at dawn, her pleasurable dream dissipated, then vanished. Groaning her
chagrin, she flopped over onto her belly and buried her
face into her pillow, desperately trying to recapture it.

This time the hob kicked the back of her head. "Will
ye get up? We got work to do."

"Go away. I'm mad at you," she muttered, her eyes
still screwed close. To open them, even for an instant,
would be to break her last tenuous hold on her dream,
and then she would never get to taste the lips forbidden
to her in life.

There was a grunt close to hear ear. "Fine with me.
Last thing I want to do is stand around all night sprinkling magic dust on a pair o' humping swells."

Magic dust? Humping swells? She furrowed her brow
against her pillow, her mind still drifting in a more romantic realm. Whatever was the hob babbling about
now?

"And don't think ye won't owe me new clothes if
Tight-Arse's sister don't get a baby," he continued, leaning against her shoulder. "Ye will, 'cause it'll be yer own
lazy fault."

Sister? New clothes? She gasped then, and bolted up.
The spell! Wildly she looked around her bed, searching
for the hob, but there was no sign of him. "Hedley?"
she called, hoping upon hope that he was near enough
to hear her.

"Down here, ye clumsy cow," came a grumbling reply
from the floor. "Where do ye think I'd be? Brighton?"

Almost weak with relief, Alys leaned over the edge of the mattress, squinting as she peered into the gloom below. There was just enough light from the hearth to illuminate the hob, who lay sprawled on the carpet, rubbing his forehead.

He returned her gaze with a particularly evil glower. "What the hell were ye doing tossing me off the bed like that? Trying to kill me?"

She gaped at him, momentarily nonplussed. Then it dawned on her what had happened: when she'd leaped up just now, she'd inadvertently knocked him to the floor. Smiling her apology, she reached down and offered him her hand. "Of course not. It was an accident."

He slapped her hand away. "Yer bloody accident almost broke my neck."

"You can't break your neck, or anything else," she pointed out in a reasonable tone. "Fairy bones don't break."

He shrugged and pulled himself into a sitting position, now massaging the anatomy in question. "Well, there's a first time for everything, ye know."

She opened her mouth to issue a caustic retort, then hastily closed it again. No, arguing with the belligerent hob was not the way to help Charlotte. If she provoked him further, he might vanish and stay away for several days. Then what would she do?

Deciding that another bribe was in order, she offered him her hand again, saying, "I truly am sorry that I hurt you, Hedley. To prove just how sorry, I'm going to buy you a nice walking stick to go with your new suit."

His eyes brightened visibly. "A polished blackthorn one with a gold top and tassels?"

She nodded. "Whatever you wish." Thus appeased, he latched on to her hand and allowed her to hoist him back up to the bed. "Now then," she said, gently depositing him on her pillow. "I suppose we should get busy on our baby-getting spell. What do we do?"

"Ye stand outside Lord Tight-Arse's sister's door holding this"—he pulled a lit green candle out of thin air—"chanting, 'Goosle, goosle, bumby mag. Mombo, kimbo, unke boo.' I'll go into the room and sprinkle them with magic dust while they hump."

Alys's face flamed with mortification for her friends, though, of course, they'd never be aware that their love-making had been observed. Embarrassed to ask, but compelled to do so, she murmured, "What if they're not—uh—humping right now?"

He cackled. "One sprinkle of dust and they'll be at it like a couple o' ballybogs drunk off elderberry wine." He stopped laughing then, as abruptly as he'd started. "Ye did get Tight-Arse's sister to wear the ring, didn't ye?"

Alys nodded as she pulled her bedside candle from its holder and fitted the magic one in its place.

"What'd ye tell her?"

"The truth," she replied, sliding from the bed to retrieve her dressing gown.

"Ye told her it was a magic ring?" the hob squawked, his eyes bulging in astonishment.

"I told her that it was an ancient fertility charm. Lottie . . ." she paused as she pulled on her rose cashmere robe, "loves folklore and fairy tales. So when I told her that it was a magic ring, she put it right on. She vowed not to remove it until she'd conceived."

Hedley shook his head, as if he couldn't quite believe what he was hearing. "Smart wench. Guess stupidity ain't a Tight-Arse family curse after all." With that, he somersaulted off the bed, landing lightly on his feet on the carpet below. "Well, don't stand there gaping like a netted selkie. Come on!"

Down the hall and stairs they crept, down to Charlotte's rooms that were located on the ground floor of the wing linking the old castle to the Jacobean annex. As luck would have it, the guests were exhausted from their day spent outdoors and had retired early. The servants appeared to have followed suit, for they didn't encounter a single soul as they went. Thus unimpeded, they quickly reached their destination.

"Now, do ye remember the chant?" Hedley asked, turning from the carved paneled door to peer up at Alys.

She knelt down, whispering, "Goosle, goosle, bumby mag. Mombo, kimbo, uncle—"

"Unke! Not uncle!" he squawked.

"*Unke*," she repeated, then finished, "boo." At the

hob's insistence she repeated it several more times. When he was satisfied that her recitation was perfect, he produced a gold silk bag and faded through the door.

Feeling suddenly very much alone in the dark, drafty hall, Alys straightened back up into a standing position and began to chant. For the first few minutes she nervously glanced this way and that, wondering how in the world she'd explain herself should she be discovered. Then it occurred to her that it was unlikely that anyone save Charlotte, Clayton, or Lucian would be in this part of the castle at this hour of night. And since the former two were soon to be otherwise occupied, and the latter undoubtedly slept, what was there to worry about?

What indeed? Grinning at her own foolishness, she pushed aside her worry and began to chant in earnest.

Lucian held his hand to the candle, shielding the flame from the draft as he stepped into the Italian Renaissance wing. As he'd hoped it was cool here, it usually was in the winter. Still tending his flame, he paused before one of the ill-fitting floor-to-ceiling windows, letting the trespassing night chill seep over him. He was hot, feverishly so, his body burning from his erotic dreams . . .

. . . dreams about Alys. From the moment he'd closed his eyes to sleep, his mind had replayed the disturbing scene from the nursery. Over and over again he'd fallen on top of her, the tension in his groin deepening and tightening each time she in turn squirmed beneath his weight. Indeed, so intense was his arousal that it was the wrenching ache of his need that had finally awakened him.

And it still plagued him. Groaning his discomfort, he pressed his face against the cold window glass, desperately trying to banish the lingering image of Alys lying beneath him. She looked so beautiful, so very tempting. He groaned again, this time letting his hand stray from the candle flame to massage the source of his need through his dressing gown. If only he were in London. Reina would set him right quick enough.

Well, you're not in London, he reminded himself, *and aside from releasing yourself, the only way you're going to rid yourself of your problem is to get walking.*

Release himself? Lucian dropped his hand to his side,
his cheeks burning as he realized where it was and what
it was doing. Bloody hell. He'd never succumbed to that
particular indignity, not even when he was at Eton, and
he wasn't about to do so now.

Which left walking. Sighing his resignation, he pushed
himself away from the window and stalked down the
hall. He was halfway to the Jacobean annex when he
saw a feeble light glimmering in the distance. He paused
a beat, his eyes narrowing as he made out a shadowy
figure lurking at his sister's door. By the size and shape,
it was clearly female. Charlotte, perhaps?

Of course it was Lottie. Who else would be in this
part of the house at this time of night? For the first time
since his miserable awakening, Lucian smiled. And who
better than his sharp-tongued sister to distract him from
his nagging lust? More eager for conversation than he'd
ever been in his life, he hurried toward her, the thick
carpet runner silencing his footfall as he went. It wasn't
until he was a few feet away that he began to doubt the
shadow's identity.

This woman was smaller, slighter in build. And when
she bowed over her candle, light haloed her head, illuminating hair braided in a rope of moonbeams and
sunshine.

Lucian halted in his tracks, his eagerness turning to
shock. It wasn't Lottie, but Alys, the person he least
desired to see at that moment. Who else had hair like
that?

Stifling his urge to moan aloud, he instinctively backed
away. What was she doing at Lottie's door at this time
of night he didn't know, and he most certainly had no
intention of finding out. Not garbed as he was in only
his woolen dressing gown with his arousal jutting against
the folds.

Utterly unnerved by the thought of an encounter, he
took another step backward, followed by another. Just
a few more and . . .

Clink! Tinkle! . . . He backed against a crystal candle
branch, setting the delicate pendants clanging against
each other.

Alys spun around, a small cry springing from her lips.

"W-who's there?" she whispered, shrinking against Lottie's door.

A frustrated noise escaped Lucian. Bloody hell! He was trapped. Seeing no other choice, he reluctantly moved toward her, holding his candle up to illuminate his face. "It's me, Alys," he said. Was that really his voice, so rough and tight?

She held her own candle aloft, squinting slightly as she peered up at him. Instead of looking relieved, as he'd expected, she looked dismayed, almost . . . guilty. Casting the door behind her a furtive glance, she squeaked, "Lucian?"

He frowned. What in God's name was wrong with the chit? She was acting most peculiar. He almost laughed aloud the instant that thought formed. Hell, Alys wasn't acting peculiar, she *was* peculiar. And for her, her current behavior was perfectly normal. Still . . .

Remembering his duty as her guardian, he felt obligated to inquire, "What brings you here at this time of night? Are you ill?"

"Ur—" She lowered her lashes and slanted another glance at the door, squirming slightly as if caught in an illicit act.

Illicit act? His gaze sharpened with sudden suspicion . . . and something else; something that gnawed at his belly like a dagger-toothed demon. Was this wing the rendezvous place for a midnight tryst with a suitor? Drake, perhaps? It was clear from the way he and Alys were huddled together after dinner, laughing and cooing like a pair of mating doves, that they had come to terms over the afternoon's debacle.

The remembrance of that scene coupled with the thought of her seeking greater intimacy with the simpering, dandified blood provoked his inner demon into a gut-shredding fury. "Well?" he snarled.

She looked up, her eyes wide, visibly taken aback by the savagery in his voice. "Uh—I'm—um—fine," she murmured.

"And?' Lucian met her gaze over the flickering flames of their candles, his eyes boring into hers, demanding an answer.

Her brow knitted. "And what?"

"If you're not ill and seeking Lottie's aid, what are you doing here?"

She returned his gaze for several moments, her expression tense and hunted. Then she replied in her odd, halting manner, "I-I couldn't sleep, so—uh—I was taking a walk, and . . ."

A duet of moans exploded from behind Lottie's door, tailed by a feminine cry. To Lucian's seasoned ears it was obvious that his sister was being pleasured, and in a very fine fashion indeed.

Alys, of course, hadn't his sexual experience. "Listen! That noise!" she softly exclaimed, jabbing her thumb at the door. "I heard it as I was walking by, and stopped."

A series of groans, these masculine, volleyed out into the hall. Her eyes widened a fraction more. "There it is again. You don't suppose someone has broken into the house and is robbing them, do you?"

Lucian met her guileless gaze for a beat, then looked away, at a loss for a reply. Damn that school. Damn those Bible-brandishing teachers for leaving her so unprepared to face the world. What the hell was he supposed to do now? Though his arousal had substantially subsided, the last thing he wanted to do was explain sex to the chit who had put him in his heat in the first place.

For one cowardly instant he considered ignoring her question and ordering her back to her room. Then his mind flashed on Drake and his own initial suspicions, and he knew that he couldn't leave her vulnerable to the silver tongues and seductive wiles of unscrupulous rakes. And they would pray upon her, there was no doubt about it. She was simply too desirable to be resisted by men as weak of flesh as they.

Slowly he raised his gaze, this time to study her face. She was still staring at him, awaiting his response. The question now wasn't what to do, but how to do it.

He thought for a moment. One way would be to fob the noises off as nightmares, and then beg Lottie to explain matters to her in the morning. Another would be to insist that she read the book his father had given him on his fourteenth birthday.

In turn he weighed each alternative, finally discarding both with a sigh. While Lottie might be able to explain what went on in the marriage bed, he doubted if she would fully impress upon Alys the dangers represented by rakes. As for the book, well, in order to understand the contents, one needed at least a rudimentary knowledge of sex, something that she clearly did not possess.

That left only once choice, the one he was loath to consider: he could talk to her himself. Though he'd have liked to discard that option as well, he couldn't. Not in good conscience. For as she had pointed out just that afternoon, it was his duty as her guardian to augment her woefully inadequate education.

Not quite certain how he was going to do so, yet honor-bound to try, he grasped her elbow, murmuring, "Clay and Lottie are . . . fine. However, I do think we need to have a talk." With that, he gave her arm a gentle tug, urging her to accompany him. Where, he wasn't certain, just somewhere away from his enraptured sister's door.

She didn't budge. "Can't it wait until morning? I find that I'm exceedingly"—she yawned—"tired all of a sudden."

He shook his head. Wish though he might that it could wait, he knew that he'd find an excuse to cancel their talk should he have the whole night to think. And the results of that failure could be disastrous.

Shooting the door one last glance, as if not quite convinced of her friend's well-being, Alys allowed herself to be led away. After a brief contemplation, Lucian escorted her to the library.

Spacious, but cozy, the library was lined with books from ceiling to floor, its air redolent with parchment and leather. Scattered throughout were plumply stuffed chairs, two of which sat before an impressive stone fireplace with a cluttered tea table between them. Apart from his tower chamber, this was Lucian's favorite room at Thistlewood.

After he'd settled Alys in a chair by the hearth, stoked the fire, and lit the lamps, he strolled over to the side table where he stood pretending to study the wine and liquor-filled decanters. Stalling for time while he searched for a way to broach the delicate subject, he inquired, "Would you care for something to drink? A glass of brandy to help you sleep, perhaps?"

She shook her head, her flaxen braid bouncing on her shoulder as she moved. Urgently in need of fortification himself, Lucian poured a liberal measure of port, his motions as slow and exacting as if he were doling out the elixir of life. When he'd delayed the inevitable as long as he could, he took the seat next to Alys.

For a long moment he sat staring at the contents of his glass, making one last attempt to concoct an opening line. Finally he sighed and forced himself to meet her gaze. "God help me, Alys. I've tried and tried, but I simply can't think of a delicate way to ask what I must. So please pardon my bluntness, but I must know: what knowledge have you of matters of the flesh?"

She tilted her head, eyeing him as if not quite certain she'd heard him correctly. "Excuse me?"

He gritted his teeth and clarified, "Did that school teach you anything of sexual matters?"

Alys stared at him for several seconds, speechless, then dropped her gaze, heat rising to her cheeks. Oh, perfect! Because of her feigned ignorance, he now thought it necessary to explain what had been going on behind Charlotte's bedroom door.

"Well?" His voice was gentle, yet demanding.

She chewed the inner lining of her lower lip, fraught with indecision. Should she confess her understanding and nip what was bound to be a disturbing conversation in the bud? Or should she continue to pretend innocence as befitted her schoolgirl guise?

As she struggled to decide, wavering back and forth between her options, she was struck with a new and very intriguing notion: if she were to allow him to explain love, marriage, and all related matters as he saw them, she might gain a better understanding as to how to go about matching him to Diana.

Instantly taken with the idea, she made a helpless hand motion and stammered like an embarrassed Bath miss, "I know that . . . um . . . s-sexual matters often result in babies."

"And do you know why?"

She shook her head, her lashes still demurely lowered.

He sighed. "You do know the manner in which men's and women's bodies differ, I trust?"

"Men are taller and—uh—let's see now—they're stronger." She slanted him what she hoped was a suitably timid look. "Oh"—she gestured to his stubbly chin and jaw—"and they have whiskers."

His shadowed jaw visibly tightened. "Anything else?"

"No . . . no. At least not that I can think of."

He was staring at his glass now, lightly tracing the rim with his thumb. "Have you never seen an unclothed male, or perhaps a painting of one?"

"No." A lie, for she had once spied on a trio of knights bathing in a stream back when she was Alys le Fayre.

He released another sigh and quaffed his port, draining the entire measure in one smooth swallow. Dropping his empty glass to the table between them, he muttered, "I see that you're more innocent than I feared."

For several beats he simply stared at the glass, as if at a loss how to proceed, then he heaved himself to his feet and stalked to the bookcase comprising the north wall. After a rather lengthy search, during which he remained silent, he pulled a thin, gold-bound volume from the shelf.

Leaf by leaf he flipped through it, pausing now and again to examine a page. It wasn't until he neared the end that he found what he sought. Nodding once, he lifted his gaze to meet hers.

"You reminded me this afternoon that it is my responsibility as your guardian to improve your education," he said, his strong fingers tightening on the book as he spoke. "And as I can see from your reply just now, it needs considerable improvement in the areas of anatomy and the related sciences."

A half-dozen long strides and he was by her side. "Since I deem it crucial that you have at least a rudimentary understanding of these subjects, I see no alternative but to teach them to you myself. I also see no reason not to start our lessons now, since we're mutually plagued by sleeplessness." With that, he placed the open book in her hands. "For our first lesson, I want you to examine the sketch on the left-hand side and tell me what you observe."

Obediently Alys did as directed, a hot wave of embarrassment sweeping her from hairline to toes when she saw what she was to study. It was an anatomical chart of a man . . . a detailed one.

Leaning over her shoulder to join her in her scrutiny, he quizzed, "Well?"

"Um . . . it's a man."

"And?"

Her cheeks heated to the point of burning, she averted her gaze from the chart to stare at the carpet. "He's . . . n-naked."

"Yes. And aside from being taller, stronger, and having whiskers, how does his body differ from that of a woman?"

Her, and her brilliant ideas! Alys squirmed self-consciously, desperately regretting her lie. Why hadn't she had the good sense to confess her understanding of sexual matters and be done with it? As meticulous as Lucian was about everything else, she should have guessed that he would be equally so in teaching her this.

Certain her face matched the beets they'd had for dinner, she glanced back at the picture and gingerly laid her fingers on the man's chest. "He's . . . f-flatter."

Lucian's head was so close to hers, she felt the motion of his head as he nodded. "Correct. What else?"

Half expecting to die from her mortification as she did so, she let her fingers slide lower to the point at the sketch man's groin. "He's got a . . . um . . ."

"A penis," he supplied, his voice as impassive as if he were referring to an ear. "And those"—he reached over her shoulder and pointed at the globular sac between the man's legs—"are his testicles. These organs"—he drew an invisible circle around the sum of manly parts—"are what a man uses to plant a baby in a woman's belly."

Struck mute by her embarrassment, Alys nodded faintly, hoping upon hope that he'd close the book now and be done with the disturbing lesson. But, of course, he wasn't finished. Indeed, from the way he moved from behind her chair and began to pace before the hearth, it appeared that he'd just begun.

Deeper and deeper she shrank into her chair, growing more discomfited by the second as he delved into the mysteries of those masculine parts and their functions. Though she knew the rudiments of the sexual act—how could she not after hundreds of years of matchmaking?—she had never bothered to ponder the mechanics it took to perform it. Now that he was explaining them, she understood why: they were too amazing to be imagined. Especially what he was describing now, how the male member grew and stiffened in response to physical stimulation or lustful thoughts. An erection, he called this hardening. Hmm.

As he expounded upon erections, how they occurred and their purpose, she found herself stealing glances at the sketch, her toes curling as she wondered what Lucian would look like naked and aroused. His body would be magnificent, of that she was certain. She'd felt his muscular strength as he'd lain atop her in the nursery; she had admired the lithe symmetry of his body beneath his elegant clothes.

Her belly suddenly tight and achy, she closed her eyes and imagined touching him in the manner of which he spoke. Oh, what joy to bring him such pleasure, to fondle and tease him until he lay inflamed and writhing. What rapture to have him caress her in return, stroking that secret place that now tingled and throbbed.

Just the thought of sharing such intimacies with him sent a flood of liquid warmth gushing to her woman's parts; parts that grew ever hotter as he explained the male need for regular sexual release. Wantonly emboldened by her passion, she opened her eyes and inquired in an oddly husky voice, "What of you, my lord? Are you too plagued with such . . . needs?"

He paused his pacing midstride, visibly taken aback by her question. For several tense moments he stared at her, his expression inscrutable, then replied, "I'm a man aren't I?"

He most certainly was. The handsomest, most desirable one she'd ever met. He was everything a woman could wish for and more. Much more.

And he could never be hers.

As disheartening as that reminder was, it did little to crush her sensual yearning. Quite the contrary. It made her long all the more to learn of that which she would never experience, to know of him and his most private desires.

Such personal knowledge would also help her match him to Diana. Or so she tried to tell herself in a desperate bid to justify her licentious curiosity. Justifiable or not, she was helpless to stop herself from asking, "And do you seek release?"

He was silent for so long that she was beginning to doubt that he would answer when he quietly replied, "I do find it necessary to seek release, yes, though not as often as most men I know. I pride myself on my control over such matters."

"But who do you . . ." she blurted out, then stopped short when she realized what she had started to ask.

"Who do I go to for release?" he finished for her.

Utterly mortified, she nodded.

He shrugged, seemingly unabashed by her indelicate question. "Men of means, such as myself, keep mistresses for that purpose. Others find relief with prostitutes."

Reina Castell, of course. Alys could have kicked herself for her stupidity. Charlotte had said that the woman was his mistress. And though she hadn't previously been quite as informed as to the specifics of a mistress's duties as she was at that moment, she did know that they were engaged to satisfy a man's baser instincts. Where was her mind not to have remembered that?

It was, of course, lost in the fog of her own desire; a desire so intoxicating that it robbed her of all reason and propriety, compelling her to probe into affairs that were none of her business. Suddenly far more embarrassed by her brazenness than she'd been by Lucian's talk of the male members, she hung her head, chastised by her own shame.

When she'd remained still for several moments, he resumed both his pacing and his discourse, progressing from the sexual practices of ordinary men to the lecherous machinations of rakes. From there he went on to warn her of the dangers of seduction and instructed her how to protect herself against falling victim to such. Then he fell mute.

For a long while they remained silent; he, still pacing back and forth before her; she, now composed and waiting for him to continue. Though he'd told her more than she'd ever need to know about lust, seduction, and sexual performance, he'd said nothing of love. At least not yet.

And so she waited . . . and waited . . . until it became clear by his continued silence that their lesson had ended. She frowned then, puzzled. How odd. Considering how remarkably his soul and his capacity to feel had grown since her arrival, she'd have thought that he'd have gained some concept of love. At least enough to acknowledge it as a reason to engage in sexual relations.

As she mulled over that troubling detail, she was suddenly reminded of Allura's warning: not only had Lucian's half soul shriveled during its torturous limbo between heaven and hell, it had been wounded and scarred. Could the results of that damage be the problem? Had his ability to love been crippled beyond repair?

Horrified by that very real possibility and of the tragic consequences should it be true, she asked point-blank, "But what of love, my lord? Surely the acts you described are more satisfying when performed with one you love?"

Instead of halting, as she expected, his easy, loping stride quickened into an agitated march. "Love?" He made a disdainful noise as he turned on his heels and retraced his steps in front of the hearth. "Love is simply the respectable name for lust . . . the genteel excuse men and women use to hide their shame of their own carnal urges."

"No . . . oh, Lucian . . . no!" She shook her head, her panic mounting in the wake of his callous response. "Love, true love, has nothing whatsoever to do with the selfish physical gratification of which you spoke." Desperate to make him listen, to prove that his ability to love still lived, she reached out and caught his flowing dressing-gown sleeve as he passed, forcing him to halt.

Clinging to his arm as if his understanding were her last hope for salvation, and indeed it might well be, she gazed up into his stony face and quietly enumerated, "Love is the tenderness with which a mother holds her child; it's the loyalty between friends, and the kindness a man shows a less fortunate stranger. It's the joyous union of hearts, minds, and bodies in marriage; it's the devotion with which a husband and wife cherish each other. Love—"

"Is a myth," Lucian interjected, impatiently disengaging his arm from her grip. "At least your rhapsodic nonsense about husbands and wives. As I've told you time and again, love has nothing to do with marriage, nor, I feel compelled to add, is the union of bodies in the marriage bed a particularly joyous event. Marriage is simply the pairing of two people from like stations with the sole purpose of uniting fortunes and perpetuating family lines." He crossed his arms over his chest. "From what I've heard, the act of perpetuating is a most unsatisfying experience."

Alys stared up into his chilly gray eyes, despairing for both their souls. "But . . ." She made a feeble hand motion, grappling for an example of love between man and wife. "But what of . . ." Ah, yes! "What of Charlotte and Clayton? Not only are they married, they obviously love each other in the way I described. As for the marriage bed, well, from the noises we heard coming from their chamber, I'll wager that what they were experiencing was supremely satisfying."

He returned her gaze for several seconds, his dark eyebrows raised in sardonic amusement. Then he laughed. "You're a clever little poppet, I'll give you that. You grasped my lesson well to discern what those noises were and what they meant."

"Then you admit that what we heard were most probably sounds of sensual pleasure?" she countered, a faint hope glimmering in her chest. If she could get him to acknowledge love, he might become curious enough about the emotion to explore it.

"Probably."

"And that in some instances, Lottie and Clayton being

a prime example, that love can exist within marriage?"
she persisted.

He tilted his head to one side, his expression thoughtful as he considered her question. "Lottie and Clay are
fond of each other, yes," he finally allowed, "and devoted. If that's what you mean by love, then I suppose
it does exist within their marriage."

Alys stared at him for several beats, his reply opening
her mind to a new and very encouraging possibility.
Could it be that his emotional void sprang not from an
inability to feel love, but from a failure to recognize it?
If that were the case, then it was clear what his next
lesson must be.

Her lips curving into a faint smile, she murmured, "It
seems, my lord, that you're as ignorant about love as I
am about matters of the flesh."

He shrugged one shoulder. "Only because I've never
deemed the specifics of love necessary knowledge."

"Well, I do deem it necessary, as does most of the
rest of the world," she retorted softly. "And if you'll
allow me, I'd be honored to teach you what I know of
the subject."

Lucian gazed at her, bewildered by his strange desire
to play student to her tutor. While he'd had scores of
women lecture him on love over the years, he'd never
cared enough for any of them to listen to what they said.
Alys, however, he admittedly liked, and for that reason
he was intrigued to hear her views on the subject he'd
always dismissed as boring drivel.

"Please?" She held out her hands, her eyes begging
him to take them. "It's the least I can do to repay you
for your kindness these past few weeks."

Lucian stared at her upturned palms, moved by the
enormous significance of her simple gesture. From the
way she was offering her hands, she clearly begged not
only for his forbearance, but for his trust. And in return
she promised her own.

He stood motionless for several moments, caught completely off guard by her mute petition. To him, trust was
the ultimate expression of friendship; it was the pinnacle
of respect, and the mark of absolute unity. And aside

from Lottie, he'd never given his to a woman. He'd never found one he deemed worthy.

Until now. With an unfamiliar warmth kindling in his chest, he stepped forward and slowly laced his fingers through hers, eagerly accepting her gift and gladly bestowing his own. For a long while he remained like that, his large hands clasped in her small yet strong ones, entranced by the current of goodwill flowing between them.

Lulled by the spiritual caress of her favor and feeling more at peace than he'd ever dreamed possible, Lucian Warre did another first: he sank to the floor to sit at her feet. Never in his life, not even as a child, had he, the dignified Marquess of Thistlewood, done anything so shockingly subservient. Yet at that moment, it felt right . . . natural, not at all demeaning.

Smiling his bemusement at his own unprecedented action, Lucian settled himself on the hearth carpet, his fingers still twined with hers. No doubt the ton's eyebrows would rise right off their faces if they were to see him sitting at his ward's feet like a well-trained dog. Not that he cared. He'd have done the same had the whole of London been watching.

When he was comfortably situated with his feet tucked beneath him and his right shoulder resting against the arm of the chair, she gave his hands a squeeze and inquired, "Shall we begin our lesson, my lord?"

Though he'd have been perfectly content to sit there in silence, holding hands and watching the fire, he nodded.

She smiled and nodded back. After a beat, where she seemed to consider how best to begin, she said, "The most important thing to remember about love is that it isn't one grand, sweeping emotion as personified by poets." She shook her head. "No. It's more a . . . a hodgepodge of good feelings, deeds, and thoughts, all directed toward one person."

He stared up at her, incredulous. "I frequently direct all three toward Turk. Are you telling me that I'm in love with my horse?"

She laughed. "You might possibly love him, yes. It's not uncommon to love a horse, a dog, or even a house.

But you're not *in* love with him. Being in love takes two people. And the feelings I'm referring to are a different sort of good . . . special . . . they're . . ." He could almost see her mind working as she struggled to think of the right word. Finally she shook her head, surrendering her mental battle with, "Perhaps it would be easier if I gave you examples."

"You're the teacher."

She flashed him a smile. "Let me see now. An example of love. Hmm." She frowned. "Oh, yes! Perfect!" The smile was back. "When two people are in love everything in the world seems new and wonderful. The mundane things in life, like eating breakfast or riding in the park, are suddenly special, just because they're done together." She glanced down to meet his gaze. "Do you understand what I mean?"

Genuinely puzzled, Lucian started to shake his head, then he saw the fire gleaming in her eyes and stopped short. How many times as they sat laughing by the kitchen hearth had he seen the fire reflected in her eyes like that? As he always did when he thought of their midnight forays, Lucian smiled. Ah! Now there was an excellent example of mundane moments made special by the company . . . though, of course, the feeling stemmed from friendship rather than love. Yet, that difference aside, was the sensation similar to that of which she spoke? Judging the two close enough, he changed his head shake to a nod.

"Good!" she praised, her face glowing with approval. "Very good indeed! Do you think you're ready to move on to a more advanced example?"

At his nod, she stated, "Love is a sense of being linked to your special someone, even when you're apart."

"Linked?" He frowned, utterly perplexed.

"Yes, linked . . . here." She raised one of their still joined hands and laid it lightly against his heart. "Linked is . . . well, an example would be looking across a room full of people and seeing only the person you love. It's a—um—a spiritual intimacy that makes you feel like you're the only two people in the world, even when surrounded by a crowd."

Lucian stared at her, her illustration merely deepening

his bewilderment. Looking across a crowded room and seeing only one person meant that you were in love with them? Absurd! There had been many a night since arriving at Thistlewood when he'd sat among their guests and seen only Alys. But it wasn't because he loved her. No, of course it wasn't. It was because she was the most vivacious chit in the room and naturally drew the eye.

"Lucian? Do you understand?" Alys's voice invaded his thoughts. By her prodding tone it was clear that she was repeating her question.

He nodded, not because he understood, but because he was too discomfited by the reason for his confusion to discuss it with her. Keeping with his lie, he smiled faintly and murmured, "Have you other examples?"

She returned his meager smile with a generous one, visibly pleased by his interest. "Love joins your two souls, giving you an awareness of how the other person feels and what they need without you ever having to ask. It's the faith to confide your deepest hopes and fears, no matter how impossible or ridiculous they might seem, and know intuitively that your special someone will understand. It's utter and complete trust; it's the unconditional acceptance of each other."

As she ticked off her examples, Lucian found himself mentally comparing each to parallel fragments of their friendship. In every instance, he found them disturbingly similar. Take what she said about being aware of each other's feelings.

While he wasn't by nature an insightful man, of late he had grown sensitive to Alys's moods. And though he'd never stopped to consider his motive behind his consequential actions, he could see now that they were unconscious attempts to coddle her feelings.

Yet, all that had nothing whatsoever to do with love. It was simply a result of the familiarity that had sprung from their friendship . . . as was their habit of confiding in each other. And they did confide in each other, exactly as she described. Indeed, sharing their hopes and fears had become one of the most pleasurable parts of the kitchen raids. But again, it wasn't because they were in love, but because . . .

. . . they trusted each other. And trust was a natural

part of friendship. So was accepting each other's idiosyncrasies, which they did with ease these days. In truth, he now found her eccentricity rather charming. Even her occasional tête-à-têtes with her imaginary friend no longer gave him pause. She, in turn, refrained from tweaking him for his stiff-rumped pomposity, and it had been a goodly while since she'd deliberately provoked him.

They went on like that for a long while: she, dispensing examples of love; he, comparing them to their friendship, and in every instance discovering close parallels. It wasn't until she'd concluded her discourse and they had sat in silence for several moments that he finally spoke.

Utterly confused by her lesson and disturbed by the questions it roused regarding their own relationship, he quietly inquired, "Where did one so young learn so much about love?"

"Oh. I . . . uh . . ." Her cheeks flooded with color. "Um . . . from listening to couples in love, and . . . ur . . . reading . . . and watching my parents," she stammered out in her peculiar manner.

"And you believe that the examples you related are true indicators of love?"

She nodded firmly. "I know so."

"How can you be so certain?"

"Because everyone I've ever known who was in love expressed these same feelings." She frowned suddenly. "Why? Do you doubt what I've told you?"

"No." He slowly shook his head. "It's just that I wonder if there might perhaps be . . . ah . . . exceptions to the meaning of some of your examples." He hoped so . . . there had to be. God help him! He wasn't falling in love with his ward, was he?

Chapter 15

"You look perfect!"

Alys turned from the mirror to grimace at Charlotte, who stood framed in her bedroom door. "I look ridiculous," she contradicted, waving her hand at her outlandish attire. And she did. Between her outmoded hoop skirt gown and enormous plumed headdress, she looked like a pouter pigeon on the verge of laying a dozen eggs.

A pigeon with a misplaced tail, she added wryly to herself, shoving one of the eight white ostrich feathers from her eyes.

"Yes, you do look ridiculous," Charlotte agreed with a laugh as she moved into the room. "Which is why you're absolutely perfect. Looking absurd is a requisite part of a court presentation."

Alys's frown deepened, as did her puzzlement. "I always assumed a court presentation to be a grand and ennobling experience."

Charlotte released another musical laugh. "As one who has endured the experience, I can state with authority that it is neither grand nor ennobling. It's simply a trying but necessary ordeal a young lady of good birth must suffer in order to make a proper bow into society." She came to a stop a couple of feet from where Alys stood. "Now, I want you to turn slowly so I can inspect you from every angle."

Suddenly nervous—for what if she committed an unpardonable faux pas while at court, or in some way reflected badly upon Lucian and Charlotte?—Alys did as directed. Now and again her friend stopped her to puff her pale blue silver-shot tissue overskirt or to straighten her lavishly embroidered and spangled satin petticoat. When she'd made a full pirouette, Charlotte took two steps back where she stood tapping her finger against her chin, evaluating her overall appearance. Instead of smiling and nodding, as Alys would have expected given her earlier praise, a frown knitted her brow.

"Is something wrong?" Alys anxiously inquired, her friend's obvious dissatisfaction doing nothing to boost her flagging confidence.

"Oh. No." Charlotte shook her head, though her brow remained puckered. "I was just wishing that I'd thought to bring my diamonds for you to wear. All the other girls shall no doubt be decked out to the point of collapsing beneath the weight of their mother's jewels. Perhaps . . ." She glanced down at her own heavy gold collar set with amethysts and diamonds as if considering its loan, they shook her head. "No. It will never do. You need diamonds, sapphires, or aquamarines . . . even pearls would be better than nothing."

"But I do have diamonds and pearls. See?" Alys pushed aside her bobbing plumage to display a modest diamond and pearl headband. "Diana lent me the tiara she wore for her presentation . . . for luck."

"It's lovely, as are you," the other woman returned, though it was clear from her expression that she was far from pleased by the meager display. "I especially like what Miss Deakins has done with your hair. Those little ringlets on your brow quite bring out your eyes, and the way she braided and coiled the back high on your head makes your neck look exceedingly long and elegant."

Lettie had done a splendid job, Alys admitted to herself as she turned back to the mirror to examine her abigail's handiwork. Indeed, it was the only part of her appearance she found pleasing. Charlotte, however, looked more than pleasing, she noted as the other woman joined her in the mirror's reflection. She was nothing short of radiant, glowing in a manner that made her feel quite drab in comparison. When she said as much, her friend blushed and lowered her lashes.

"Can you keep a secret, Alys," she murmured, slowly opening the circular fan dangling from her wrist.

"You know I can."

Charlotte stared at the scene painted on the ivory fan sticks as if seeing it for the first time. "I think . . . I'm not positive, mind you, but I think that your magic ring might have worked."

Alys gaped at her, speechless with joy. She'd spent the past seven weeks fretting that Lucian's untimely interruption might have ruined the spell. Hedley, as was typical of his pessimistic nature, was certain of it. "Oh, Lottie!" she finally exclaimed, her words tumbling out in a breathless rush. "How very wonderful!"

The other woman closed her fan, only to unfurl it again in the same motion. "As I said, I'm not certain. So please don't tell Luc or Clay. I don't want them to be disappointed should it turn out that I'm wrong." She snapped the fan closed again.

"But you think it likely?" Alys gently quizzed.

Charlotte nodded. "Very likely. My menses are three weeks late and . . ." She looked up then, he gray eyes sparkling like silver stars. "Oh, Alys! I've never been late before. Never!"

"Then it must be so. I shall pray that it is," Alys declared, sweeping her friend into her arms for a fierce hug.

"Your gown!" Charlotte protested, though she was smiling as she pushed her away. "You must take care not to crush your skirts. It wouldn't do to arrive at court all rumpled."

Alys grinned as Lottie repaired the damage, making clucking noises beneath her breath as she worked. "When will you be certain enough to tell Clayton?" she inquired.

"After I've been examined by the doctor."

"And when will that be?"

Charlotte's fingers stilled on her overskirt. After a beat, she looked up, her gaze suddenly bleak. "I don't know. I'm . . . afraid. I'm not at all certain that I shall be able to bear the disappointment should he prove me wrong."

"But if you are correct, you need to be taking special

care of yourself," Alys gently reminded her. Smiling her most reassuring smile, she lifted her friend's hands from where they still clutched her skirt and clasped them in her own. "If you like, I'll visit the doctor with you. We shall tell Clayton and Lucian that we're going shopping. That way, if we find that you aren't with child, the only ones to suffer disappointment will be you and me"

After a beat, Charlotte returned her smile with a tremulous one of her own. "I . . . I would like that very much."

Alys nodded. "Then shall we agree now to pay the doctor a visit on Friday next at, say, one o'clock?"

For several seconds they stood in silence, their fingers laced and their gazes locked in womanly communion; Charlotte, mutely conveying her hope-spawned dread; and Alys soothing it with her quiet strength.

Finally Charlotte inclined her head in agreement and disengaged her hands. "It's so very queer," she murmured, resuming her puffing of Alys's hug-crushed overskirt. "But sometimes I get the oddest impression that you're far older and wiser than I." She released a short, breathy laugh. "Silly creature, aren't I? Especially considering that you don't look a day past sixteen." Grinning at her own foolishness, she straightened back up. "There. Perfect. Now fetch your fan and we shall parade you past Luc for a final inspection. He and Stephen are in his study waiting to admire you."

Her hands suddenly cold and trembling, Alys snatched her fan from her dressing table and followed Charlotte from the room, frantically trying to remember the court protocol she'd so dutifully memorized. To her consternation, she couldn't remember a single rule.

"Miss? Might I be so bold as to tell you that you look positively splendid?"

Alys glanced up at Tidswell, blinking twice in her surprise at finding herself at the bottom of the curving staircase. However had she gotten there? As with her diligently studied court etiquette, her mind drew a blank.

Distressed though she was over her sudden memory lapse, she somehow managed to smile her acknowledgment of the elderly butler's compliment. "Thank you, Tidswell. But the credit for my appearance should go to Miss Deakins and"—she gestured to where Charlotte stood, smiling—"Lady Glassenbury."

Tidswell grinned a surprisingly boyish grin for a man of his age and distinction. "Their efforts are but the gilding on the lily of your youthful beauty."

Charlotte chuckled. "Why, Tidswell! I had no idea that you were a poet."

To Alys's amazement, the stuffy butler laughed. It was little more than a rusty cackle, true, but a laugh nonetheless. "Only when I'm inspired by such loveliness, my lady." He seemed about to add something, but the sound of footsteps reverberating from the right-hand corridor distracted him. An instant later two footmen emerged, stopping and bowing just inside the foyer when they spied the ladies.

"Well?" he inquired, his clipped tone returning.

"We passed 'is lordship's inspection. 'E said we look fit to accompany the ladies to court," one of them, Watson, if she remembered correctly, replied.

Viewing them as they stood at attention beneath Tidswell's critical eyes, Alys couldn't help but to agree with Lucian's assessment. Attired as they were in their green and gold State livery, complete with freshly powdered wigs and lavish lapel bouquets, the men looked very grand indeed.

"And where is the third of your number?" Tidswell demanded harshly, though Alys could have sworn that she detected a smile lurking at the corners of his sternly set lips.

"I believe that he's fetching something," replied Burke, the second footman. "He said—" He glanced over his shoulder as the pounding of rushing footsteps emanated from the hall behind him. "Ah! Here he is now."

"He" was Bart, dashingly garbed in a livery exactly matching that worn by the two footmen. He even wore a small wig and silk hat, the latter of which he swept off the instant he saw the ladies. After sketching a rather awkward bow, he walked in a measured pace over to Alys. Clearly struggling to bridle his urge to grin, he pulled his hidden right hand from behind his back and with a flourish presented a flawless white rose.

"If ye . . . *you* please, miss. I would be 'onored—er—*honored* if you would accept this t-t—" He glanced briefly at Tidswell who silently mouthed a word. "Token. I would be honored if you would accept this token of my good wishes on this grand occasion." His smile broke loose then, as did those of Tidswell and the footmen.

Alys returned the boy's pleased smile with her proud one. "Gallantly said, Bart," she praised, marveling, not for the first time, at his stunning improvement. Between the maids' nurturing, constant feeding by cook, and Lucian's and Tidswell's gentle tutoring, he was rapidly becoming a perfect gentleman. Indeed, so amazing was his progress that had she not witnessed his remarkable metamorphosis herself, she would never have believed that the bright-eyed, pink-cheeked child before her had until recently been an ill-used climbing boy.

Accepting the rose with a curtsy, she murmured, "I shall carry this with pride and feel all the braver for knowing that you hold me in such high esteem." With that, she leaned over and pressed a gentle kiss to his pleasure-flushed cheek.

"A-hem!" Tidswell cleared his throat, his expression every bit as gratified as Bart's. "Lord Thistlewood directed me to present you ladies to him the instant you came downstairs. And since we all know how his lordship feels about being kept waiting—" He gestured for the women to follow him.

With every step Alys took, her anxiety mounted. What if, unlike the footmen, Lucian didn't approve of her appearance? As hard as she tried to convince herself that it wouldn't matter, that this was all nothing but a part of her matchmaking duties, she couldn't help wishing to see his eyes light up with admiration when he saw her.

So great did her desire become that as they waited for Lucian to respond to Tidswell's discreet scratch, she found herself praying, *Oh, please, Lord! Just this once, please make him say that I look beautiful. If you do, I shall never ask another thing for myself as long as I live. I promise.*

At Lucian's command to enter, the butler swung open the door and ushered them in. Not daring to look at the man whom she sensed sat behind the imposing desk,

Alys allowed Charlotte to lead her to the center of the
room and pose her as if she were a fashion doll. For a
long while she remained thus arranged, her face tilted
to a profile with her gloved left hand holding the rose
and resting lightly against her overskirt and the raised
right one holding her open fan.

When there was no comment from either man, Charlotte querulously inquired, "Well?"

The heavy silence continued for a moment longer,
then a voice that Alys readily identified as belonging to
Stephen exclaimed, "Deuced if you aren't passing fair,
Alys! A regular diamond of the first water. Rather re-
sembles that sculpture of Diana we saw in the Duchess
Street gallery, don't you think, Luc?"

Bolstered a fraction by his effusive praise, she ventured a glance out of the corner of her eye. Stephen
lounged in a chair before the desk with his dusty riding-
boot-shod feet casually propped up on the glossy desktop, eyeing her with unmistakable appreciation. When
he caught her looking at him, he winked and grinned.
She shifted her head to smile back, her self-assurance
rising yet higher . . . high enough to risk a peek at
Lucian.

One look and her fledgling confidence plummeted, this
time to an all-time low. He sat behind his desk with his
hands steepled beneath his chin, his eyes narrowed, and
his lips pursed as if he didn't at all approve of what he
saw. After a few beats, he crossed his arms over his
chest and murmured, "She looks well enough."

Alys sagged as if gut-punched. Well enough? Looking
"well enough" was a far cry from looking beautiful.
"Well enough" was what one said when they couldn't
think of anything nice to say. Heaving a mental sigh she
closed her fan and dropped her pose. She was a fool to
have expected anything more. For while Lucian had
been quite attentive of late, squiring her around London
and showing her the sights, he'd never so much as hinted
that he found her the least bit attractive.

"Well enough?" Charlotte echoed, a rising note of
indignation in her voice. "Is that the best you can do?"

He shrugged. "She lacks sparkle."

Alys stiffened, thoroughly affronted. She'd like to see

just how much he sparkled after spending four torturous hours being squeezed, poked, pinched, powdered, and curled.

"Of course she lacks sparkle. She has no diamonds," Charlotte retorted, viewing his criticism in an entirely different light. "I, for one, think it a disgrace that the Marquess of Thistlewood's ward has no jewels to wear for her court presentation. So will the rest of the ton when it becomes known."

To Alys's astonishment, the eternally calm and collected Lottie actually wrung her hands. "Oh, the scandal! Just imagine how tongues will wag. If only there were time to send for my diamonds. If only—" She broke off abruptly then, slanting her brother a look that was nothing short of calculating. "Ah! But of course! She must borrow Mother's diamonds. You do keep them at the house, I trust?"

Lucian, who'd been watching his sister's theatrics with an air of amused indulgence, shifted his gaze back to Alys, letting it sweep her from the top of her plumed headdress to the toes of her silver-shod feet several times before finally shaking his head.

"No. Mother's diamonds would never suit her. The settings are too massive and the style too ostentatious. Miss Faire is much too young and small to wear such imposing jewels to good effect."

Charlotte released an unladylike grunt. "I agree that they are far from ideal, but they're better than nothing."

Again Lucian shook his head. "No. Alys should have her own jewelry; jewelry that emphasizes rather than detracts from her delicate, youthful beauty."

Delicate, youthful beauty? Alys's heart gave an exhilarated jolt. His off-hand admission that he found her just a wee bit attractive was more precious to her than all of Charlotte's and her mother's jewels combined.

Charlotte, however, was not as easily placated. Her hands braced on her hips, she glared at her brother, exclaiming, "Agreed. Unfortunately we haven't the time to dash off to Ludgate Hill and purchase what we need. That being the case, I see no choice but for her to borrow Mother's diamond court set. I will not allow the poor girl to suffer the indignity of attending her presentation as plain as a pauper. If you refuse to—"

"Enough," he commanded, raising his hand to silence her. "I didn't say that she wouldn't have diamonds to wear to court, just not Mother's." With that he opened his top drawer and removed a box approximately a foot square.

"I may be ignorant of the more trifling aspects of good ton, as you're so fond of pointing out," he continued, raising his gaze from the box to cast his sister a wry look. "But I am aware of the importance of jewelry for a court presentation. How could I not be after witnessing the endless fuss you and Mother made over the matter in the weeks prior to your presentation?" Chuckling as if amused by the memory, he beckoned to Alys. "Come here, Miss Faire."

It was more the gentleness of his smile than the temptation of the green leather box in his hands that drew her to him. As she came to a stop next to Stephen, who now sat up straight and was gaping at his friend as if he'd sprouted a third eye, Lucian moved from behind the desk to stand on her other side.

Holding out the box, he said, "This is for you . . . a coming-out gift of sorts."

Handing Bart's rose to Charlotte, who had followed her over, she took the offering from him. Even without seeing the name Rundel & Bridge stamped in gold on the top, she would have known from the feel of the box that it held something unimaginably expensive. Stunned that he would think to buy her such a gift, or any gift at all for that matter, she stood simply holding her treasure, staring up into his handsome face with wonder.

And there was so much to wonder at. Never had his gaze been so tender, never had his face held such fondness. Indeed, he was looking at her in much the same manner she'd seen countless men look at the women they loved. Confused, and not just a little unsettled by what had to be her own silly imagining, she dropped her gaze to stare at the box.

After several beats, he prompted, "Open it."

Once, twice, thrice, she fumbled with the clasp, but her efforts came to naught. Her discomfiture had rendered her hopelessly clumsy. After her fourth failed attempt, Lucian gently pushed her fingers away and opened it himself.

Stephen, who'd half risen to view the contents of the box, fell heavily back into his chair, letting out a long, low whistle. Charlotte gasped aloud. As for Alys, she stood staring with her mouth ajar, utterly thunderstruck.

Never in all her centuries had she seen anything as exquisite as the necklace, earrings, and bracelet before her. Each silver link of the necklace was set with a small diamond, the chain broken at intervals with small blossoms of round diamonds with marquis-cut ones forming the leaves. In the very center hung a dazzling diamond rosette, a design that was echoed by the matching drop earrings.

"Oh, Lucian," she whispered, reverently running her finger across the bracelet. It reminded her of a May Queen's flower crown rendered in diamonds. "They're . . . oh!" She tilted her head to meet his glowing silver gaze with her flabbergasted one. "I've never seen anything so wonderful. Thank you."

"The instant I saw them, I knew they were for you," he murmured, returning her gaze with a warmth that made her flush and look hastily back at his gift.

Dear God! Whatever had gotten into her? Why had she suddenly become so fanciful, reading passion in his every glance? Embarrassed at even having imagined such foolishness, she said rather inanely, "No doubt the other girls will turn green with envy when they see these."

"Well, well, Luc. Perhaps there's hope for you yet," Charlotte remarked, taking the box from Alys to subject the contents to closer scrutiny. After a moment, she nodded. "A perfect selection."

"We shall soon see, shan't we?" Lucian countered, lifting the necklace from the box and unlatching the clasp. Holding it before Alys, he politely inquired, "May I?"

At her nodded consent, he draped it around her neck, his supple fingers grazing her collarbone as he first straightened a blossom, then adjusted a link. Casual though his touch was, it sent intense frissons of pleasure quivering up and down her spine, forcing her to curl her toes to keep from squirming. So great was her sensual agitation, that by the time he'd latched the clasp and stepped around to take the bracelet from Charlotte, she was certain that her toes were cramped into a permanent curl.

"There!" Charlotte exclaimed, after the last earring was in place. "Tell me that she doesn't sparkle now, Luc!"

Gently, Lucian cupped Alys's chin in his palm and tipped her face up. For what felt like a breathless eternity, he studied her, his eyes aglow with the admiration she'd so fervently prayed to see. Just as her toes began to curl again, he softly conceded, "She sparkles enough to dazzle a blind man." To Alys's surprise, and apparently Stephen's as well, for she heard him ejaculate "My word!" beneath his breath, he dipped down and dropped a light kiss on her cheek.

As she stood there, flushing with delight at his compliment and something much more wicked at his kiss, he pressed his lips close to her ear to whisper, "You're right, poppet. The other girls will be green with envy, but not of your jewels." Before she could respond, he stepped away, quipping, "Now off to court with you two. Stephen and I have some serious drinking to do if we're to be properly primed for your coming-out ball tonight."

Stephen smiled, amused by the sight of the urbane Marquess of Thistlewood doing the pretty for his ward. Damn if he didn't resemble a love-struck cub, fawning over the chit as he was. Chuckling to himself, he wondered if his friend was even aware of his own enamored posturing. Probably not. While he was awake on just about every other suit, he was a regular nodcock when it came to recognizing his own feelings.

And he did have feelings for Miss Faire, that much was obvious. Lucian Warre, self-proclaimed skeptic of love, had finally lost his heart, and to his dreaded ward, no less. Gleefully deciding it his duty as Luc's best friend to open his eyes to that fact, he waited until the ladies had departed, then commented, "I must say, Luc. Miss Faire traps out quite nicely."

Lucian grunted, his gaze still riveted to the door through which she had exited.

"Ghastly shame about her hair, though," he continued, deliberately baiting his companion. "Be a real out and outer if it weren't for that unfortunate hair."

That remark had its calculated effect: it drew a reaction from Lucian. A swift one. Indeed, his head whipped around so fast in his haste to fix his friend with his glare that Stephen wondered if the move had left him dizzy. His eyes little more than glittering slits, he growled, "What the hell is wrong with her hair?"

"It's blonde."

Lucian's gaze didn't waver. "So?"

He shrugged. "About as exciting as a bowl of cold gruel, fair-haired women. Sallow-faced, colorless creatures, every last one of them." He feigned a grimace. "Rather do without than bed one."

Surveying him as if trying to decide whether to throttle him on the spot or to challenge him to pistols at dawn, Lucian gritted out, "Perhaps you should spend less time with your bloody horses and more time in the company of humans. You've clearly lost your eye for women if you judge Miss Faire either sallow-faced or colorless."

Spoken like an affronted lover, Stephen noted, hard-pressed to hide his amusement. Unable to risk a retort for fear of chuckling aloud, he merely intoned, "Oh?"

Lucian jerked his head to the affirmative as he rose. "A man with any taste whatsoever would have noticed Miss Faire's extraordinary coloring right off," he snapped, sweeping up the glass he'd drained earlier and striding across the room to the wine sideboard. "Surely even you must have observed what fine eyes she has?"

Stephen bit his lip, struggling to suppress his mirth. After a moment he released it just enough to mutter, "Blue, aren't they?"

"Blue, yes. A bright, clear sapphire with just a touch of violet," Lucian elaborated, lifting the port decanter. Apparently deciding that the discussion warranted something stronger, he set it back down again and poured brandy in its stead.

After holding up the flask to Stephen, who nodded,

he stalked back over to the desk with his full glass in one hand and the container of brandy in the other. "As for her being swallow-faced," he continued, seating himself, "well, if you'd get your mind off your new blood foal long enough to actually look at her, you'd see that she possesses a singularly lovely complexion. All pink and ivory, rather like—" He waved his hand, description eluding him.

"Like a painting by Mr. Gainsborough," Stephen supplied, sliding his glass across the wide desktop for his friend to fill.

Lucian smiled faintly as he obliged. "You did notice that much, I see." He slid the now full glass back. "Next time you see her, I suggest that you make that same effort to observe her hair. It's quite extraordinary, really. Like—" Not normally given to waxing poetic on any subject, words again failed him.

And again Stephen came to his rescue, "Like saffron satin, perhaps?"

Lucian sipped his brandy, his expression thoughtful as he considered the description. Slowly he shook his head. "No. Nothing so mundane as that. It's brighter . . . richer."

"Brighter and richer, eh? Hmm." To him, Alys's hair was simply yellow. Delightful, yes, but nothing remarkable. Lucian must indeed have lost his heart to see it as exceptional. Thrilled that his friend had at last discovered love, and with a girl who, by all appearances, fully shared his feelings, he playfully mused, "If not saffron satin, then perhaps a king's ransom of gold spun into silken filaments?"

As seriously as if they were discussing investing a fortune, Lucian contemplated his friend's revised description. At length, he nodded. "Add the sun, moon, and stars, and you'd be correct."

For a long while after that, they sat in a companionable silence, drinking their brandy; Lucian, staring off into the distance with an uncharacteristically wistful expression; Stephen, calculating how to point out what his friend had just proved beyond all doubt.

Finally judging directness his best tactic, he took one last swig from his glass, a deep, fortifying one, and said with a sigh, "Fetching as Miss Faire is from the neck up, there's still the problem with her figure."

Lucian's thunderous scowl was back in a flash. "And what, pray tell, is wrong with her figure?"

"All straight lines and no bosom to speak of," he replied, repeating the words his friend had used after his first interview with the girl.

Lucian's face turned so red that had he not been young and obviously fit, Stephen would have feared he was about to succumb to apoplexy. Slamming his glass to the desktop with a force that would no doubt leave a mark, he bit out with ominous calm, "You might be my oldest and dearest friend, Stephen. But I will not allow you to discuss my ward as if she were some bit of muslin you were considering for a mistress." He slowly rose to his feet, the challenge in his rigid stance clear. "I will not allow it. Do you understand?"

Stephen grinned. "Better than you imagine."

Impossible though it seemed, Lucian's face darkened a shade. "Oh? And what exactly do you mean by that cryptic remark?"

"Only that I can see from our present conversation that you've changed your mind about your ward."

Lucian snorted his impatience. "Stop being obtuse."

"Seems to me that you're the obtuse one. 'All straight lines and no bosom to speak of' are your words, not mine. In case you've forgotten, that's how you described Miss Faire after your first encounter." He raised one eyebrow and fixed his companion with a knowing look. "Not quite as opposed to her as you were at first, eh, Luc? My guess is that you've developed a tendresse for her."

Lucian couldn't have looked more stunned if he'd announced that he was going to aid Napoleon in escaping from St. Helena. Indeed, his intense flush slowly drained from his face until he was blanched to the sickly grayish-white of cold ash. "Tendresse?" he repeated, a faint frown worrying his brow. "Me? For Miss Faire? Ridiculous!"

"Is it? Seems to me that you've been paying a jolly lot of attention to the chit of late."

He shrugged. "It's my duty as her guardian to see to her welfare."

"And you consider jaunts to the theater, Vauxhall, and Week's Mechanical Museum a part of seeing to her welfare?" Stephen quizzed, his grin broadening to face-splitting proportions.

Lucian countered his grin with a scowl. "What would you have me do, leave the poor girl languishing about the house? Contrary to what you seem to believe, attending to a ward's welfare goes beyond merely feeding, housing, and clothing her. She's a person, and as such requires companionship and diversion. As her guardian, it's my obligation to see that she has both."

"According to Miss Faire, you've provided both in abundance."

Lucian shrugged again. "I simply take her along with me whenever I attend an amusement which Charlotte deems appropriate for a young lady. Nothing more. It isn't as if I've gone out of my way to entertain her."

"Haven't you indeed? In that instance, I must assume that you've developed a sudden fondness for Astley's," he drawled, watching with wicked amusement as his friend's face began to darken again. "When I ran into Lottie and Miss Faire at Gunter's on Monday, your charming ward emptied the bag about your visit to the amphitheater last Thursday. Claimed that you quite enjoyed the performance. Considering your loathing for the place, I must say that the news came as a bit of a shock."

If his eyes didn't deceive him, the imperturbable Marquess of Thistlewood actually squirmed as he gritted out, "The chit had her heart set on going, and being the stubborn baggage she is, she teased me until I consented to take her. I only went so that I might have a moment's peace."

Stephen guffawed at that. "Fess up, Luc. No woman has ever been able to tease you into doing anything you didn't want to do. You went because you wanted to please her, and you wanted to please her because you're in love with her."

"Damn it, Stephen!" He slammed his palm hard against the desktop. "Once and for all, I am not in love with the chit. I care for her as a friend and nothing more. End of discussion!"

Stephen nodded once and bowed his head over his brandy, hiding his smile. It might be the end of their discussion, but it was no doubt just the beginning of Lucian's thoughts on the matter.

She looked beautiful.

Lucian jostled through the crush, his gaze riveted on his ward as she gaily stepped through the figures of a quadrille. Never had she been so radiant, never so desirable as she was tonight. Without glancing away from the entrancing sight, he murmured an apology to whoever's foot it was he'd just trod upon, then stepped to the edge of the dance floor where he was afforded an unobscured view of Alys.

She looked like a fairy bride, garbed as she was in diaphanous white. Completely enchanted, he let his spellbound gaze sweep her length, taking in every delicious detail of her appearance. Her plumed monstrosity of a headdress had been removed, replaced by a delicate wreath of silk flowers, lace, and pearls. More pearls were braided through the shimmering circlet of her hair, a jewelry theme that was echoed by her earrings and necklace.

He smiled faintly as his gaze touched first her gold filigree and pearl earrings, then the magnificent matching pendant, remembering his mad dash up to Ludgate Hill to purchase them. Odd impulse, that purchase. He'd been on his way to visit Reina that afternoon, whom he'd all but neglected since his return from Thistlewood, when he'd impetuously and rather incongruously decided that Alys's new diamonds weren't at all the thing to compliment her ball gown.

That he'd even considered such a matter was perplexing, though not nearly as puzzling as his sudden disinterest in Reina. By all rights of God and man, he should have been eager to visit her and relieve himself of what had recently become his chronic lust.

Yet, as his carriage had wended through the streets toward the house he'd leased for her, he'd felt nothing but a slight distaste for what he was about to do. In truth, he no longer found Reina's dark, voluptuous beauty to his taste, wishing instead for a small, willowy maiden with hair like the sun, moon, and stars, and eyes the color of the Thistlewood harebells. Therefore, when he'd been faced with the choice between seeking sexual release from Reina and purchasing a gift that was certain to make Alys smile, he'd easily and without regret selected the latter.

At least he hadn't regretted his choice until Alys, in her excitement over his gift, had hurled herself against him and hugged him repeatedly while squealing her thanks. Ah, well. He let his gaze touch and then linger on her gloriously flushed face. The satisfaction he'd derived from her pleasure was far greater than any he'd ever found in Reina's arms, and well worth the brief episode of lustful discomfort he'd suffered as a result.

Indeed, watching her float across the dance floor now in the exquisite iridescent silk gown she'd fancifully dubbed her fairy-wing frock, Lucian decided that no price would be too dear to pay for the joy of seeing her smile. As he stood there admiring the way her face-framing ringlets bobbed against her cheeks, a voice penetrated the dreamlike fog of his mind.

"You're gawking, Luc," it said, the utterance faint and muted, as if coming from a great distance.

Lucian blinked twice. What the—

In a chaotic rush of sights and sounds, his awareness of time and place returned. How very odd. He frowned at the laughing, chattering horde around him and gave his head a sharp shake. How very odd indeed. For several moments there it was as if the rest of the world had faded away, leaving only Alys and him.

Love makes you feel like you're the only two people in the room, even when surrounded by a crowd. His eyes narrowed as he easily identified the source of that sudden thought: it was one of the examples of love Alys had quoted him that unforgettable night in the Thistlewood library. A creeping sense of uncertainty stole through him as he remembered that intimate interlude and how it had made him feel; a sensation that was at the same time terrifying and exhilarating.

Could Stephen have been correct in his assessment of

his feelings for Alys? Had their friendship transcended into that mysterious emotion called love? Having never experienced love, he wasn't at all sure. Yet, when he examined his feelings and honestly compared them to all he'd read and heard of the emotion, it seemed possible. Hell, more than just possible, it was probable. Blissfully so.

"Luc?" It was the same voice as before, only this time loud and clear, and edged with mirth. "Are you quite all right?" Someone clapped him on the shoulder. "You look rather flushed there, old fellow. Shall I fetch you a drink?"

Lucian smiled then, suddenly placing the voice he'd never before failed to recognize. Speak of the devil . . .

He turned and nodded cordially at Stephen, his smile broadening as he noted that, for once, his friend didn't look as if he'd just tumbled off a horse. Quite the contrary. Clad as he was in full evening attire with his dark auburn hair brushed into an artistic tousle, he cut a very grand figure indeed. One that by the admiring glances being slanted at him over their fans, was much appreciated by the ladies.

The music ended then, and Lucian's attention was diverted from his friend to his ward, who was being claimed by Lord Drake for a minuet. As Drake bowed and Alys curtsied, Stephen drawled, "Make a fine couple, Miss Faire and Drake. Don't you agree?"

Lucian shrugged, not at all pleased with the way Drake was eyeing Alys's bodice. Lascivious fop. He ought to take him out and toss him into the nearest spiderweb for leering at his ward as if she were a dollymop for hire.

"The betting book at White's favors him twelve to five to win her hand before the end of the season," Stephen continued, "though I have my money on someone else entirely."

That report shocked Lucian's thunderous glare away from Drake and onto the bearer of the news. "They're betting on who will win Alys's hand?" he ground out, incredulously.

"Mmm—yes."

"And who the hell is responsible for starting that par-

ticular wager?" He'd tear the bastard limb from limb
with his bare hands.

Stephen graced him with his sunniest smile. "I am."

"You?" he choked out, wondering if, considering the
circumstances, a court of law would convict him of murder if he throttled Stephen right then and there.

Stephen nodded. "Grown rather fond of Miss Faire,
you know. Wanted to make certain that her debut was
a success, so I placed a bet that you would declare yourself to her before the end of the season. Thought it
might lure the ton here to see—"

"Me!" Lucian roared the word so loudly that several
people turned to stare.

"Tsk! Tsk! Luc," Stephen playfully chided, nodding
and smiling at their gaping audience. "You're making a
spectacle of yourself."

"I told you this afternoon that I'm not in love with
Miss Faire. And I most certainly shall not be proposing
to her," he hissed, in no mood to admit to his change
of heart.

"That has yet to be seen," his friend countered with
a nonchalant shrug. "Whatever the outcome, my ploy
has had the desired effect." He gestured to the mob
milling around them. "Looks like the entire ton turned
out to catch a glimpse of the paragon who's captured
Lord Thistlewood's icy heart."

When Lucian remained unappeased, he slapped him
on the back, quipping, "Give a lift, Luc! Drake was at
the club when I made my bet and declared his own intention to court her. No doubt he'll win her before the
close of the season and put an end to the wager."

"That coxcomb? Win Alys?" Lucian bit out, transferring his murderous thoughts from Stephen to Drake.
"They would never suit."

"You thought they suited well enough to put him on
your list of potential husbands," Stephen pointed out.

"Yes. But that was before I became fully acquainted
with him. Now that I am, I've changed my mind."

Stephen chuckled and slanted him that all-knowing
look he was beginning to find most annoying. "Seems to
me that your change of mind came not from getting to
know him, but her." He seemed about to add something

else in that same vein, when the music ended. "Ah!" he ejected, straightening his already immaculate neckcloth. "You'll have to excuse me now. Miss Ramsey promised me this dance. Ripping gel that Miss Ramsey." He tugged at his gloves. "Can't imagine why you didn't introduce us years ago."

Lucian eyed his friend incredulously, wondering if he'd taken one too many spills from his horse. "I've introduced you to her on countless occasions," he reminded him. "If memory serves me right, I've even gone so far as to suggest that you two might suit. As you've probably discovered for yourself, there's no better horsewoman in England than Diana Ramsey. She also knows more about the care, training, and breeding of prime blood than the grooms at Tattersall's."

"That she does," Stephen heartily agreed, scanning the crowd for the object of his admiration. "No silly gossip or prattling of bonnets from Miss Ramsey. No indeed. Showed me a new way to clean and file horses' teeth when I called on her last Wednesday."

"You're calling on Miss Ramsey?" Lucian echoed, grinning his delight for both his friends.

Stephen returned his smile faintly. "Yes, though I'd appreciate it if you didn't bandy the news about. She has yet to give me a sign that she cares for me beyond her enjoyment of our conversations on horses."

"You know that I'm hardly one to gossip," he retorted. "However, if it will make you rest easier, I promise not to breathe a word of your interest in the beauteous Miss Ramsey until after you've announced your engagement."

"I must say that you're more optimistic about my chances with her than I am," Stephen replied, his tone uncharacteristically glum.

"That's because I know you both and see how very well suited you are." He gave his friend a heartening slap on the back. "By the way, I was wrong this afternoon when I accused you of losing your eye for women. It's obviously improved. There's no prettier or finer woman in all of England than Miss Ramsey."

"Except perhaps Miss Faire?"

Lucian stared at his friend, rendered temporarily

speechless by the sudden turn of conversation. After a moment of thought, he carefully replied, "Even if I did feel more for Miss Faire than mere friendship, and I'm not saying that I do, we mustn't forget that I'm her guardian. As such, I would be honor-bound to put aside my feelings for her and find her a suitable husband, as requested by her brother."

"Indeed?" Stephen mused, that knowing look creeping back across his face. "And who is more suited to be her husband than you? Not only are you young, rich, and titled, you clearly care for the girl. By the way she looks at you, I suspect that she has feelings for you as well." With a single nod to emphasize his point, he strolled off to claim his dance partner.

Alys? In love with him? He stared after his friend, utterly thunderstruck. Could it be true? Slowly, for in his shock he was unable to think with any haste, he considered what it might mean if Stephen was correct in his assumption. If it was true that Alys loved him, then perhaps it might not be a bad idea to court her. As Lottie was constantly pointing out, he was long overdue to marry and set up a nursery. And he did genuinely like the girl. Enough, in fact, that he could easily imagine himself spending the rest of his life with her.

Suddenly wanting nothing more than to get a drink and find a place where he might ponder his thoughts of Alys in peace, he turned from the dance floor and pushed his way through the crowd. He was halfway across the room when he was accosted by Lords Stanton and Bradwell. Mentally groaning his dismay, he nodded to the gossipy pair, muttering, "Stanton. Bradwell."

"Excellent ball, Thistlewood!" enthused Bradwell, lifting his quizzing glass to survey the packed ballroom. "A regular crush."

"Yes," Stanton agreed. "Told Bradwell here that it's the biggest crush so far this season. At least one hundred more people here than were at Lord Massey's gel's debut last week."

"Indeed?" Lucian intoned, desperately trying to think of a way to extract himself from the prattling pair.

They nodded in unison. "I must say, my dear fellow, Miss Faire is everything you said she was and more.

Already been a dozen toasts proposed to her charm and beauty." This was from Bradwell.

"Heard at least that number of bucks declare their intention to call on the chit tomorrow," Stanton added, not to be outdone. He chuckled and clapped Lucian on the back. "Seems your days of peace and quiet are done, Thistlewood."

Chapter 16

Stanton's prediction proved correct. Lucian's days of peace and quiet were numbered. Alys was a success, a brilliant one, and as a result the house was under constant siege by her would-be suitors. Indeed, since her debut the week before, not an afternoon had passed when he hadn't returned from his club to find a horde of eager bucks lingering on the stoop, with a half-dozen more inside dancing attendance on his ward.

Pausing before the foyer table, Lucian glared at the morning's offerings of posies and beribboned boxes of bonbons. Bloody hell. The house was beginning to look like a cross between a hothouse and a damn confectioner's shop. Emitting a derisive snort, he turned on his heels and stalked off down the hall, cursing the fates who had seen fit to bless Alys with her dazzling success.

Oh, he knew he should be pleased. A proper guardian would be thrilled beyond elation that his ward was the reigning toast. Yet, he felt nothing but a niggling sense of panic; panic at the thought of losing Alys; panic at his own inability to keep her from slipping away. And she was slipping away from him, that fact was undeniable. Indeed, if the rumors circulating around his club proved true, she would receive a dozen proposals before the end of the season, ten of them from imminently suitable young men, including that of Lord Trumbold, heir to the Dukedom of Trevandale.

His frown deepening into a scowl at that prospect,

Lucian stepped into his study, slamming the door behind him in his agitation. Damnation! The situation was hopeless. How could he, a stiff-rumped marquess of thirty-two, hope to compete with a gay and charming duke-to-be of twenty-four? In all honesty, what chance did he have against any of her younger suitors? By comparison he was singularly old and dull. Hardly the answer to a maiden's dream. At least that's the way he'd felt the night before at the theater.

Muttering an oath he'd never have voiced in public, Lucian slipped into the chair behind his desk and picked up the *Morning Post,* resolved to banish the galling incident from his mind. The episode was trifling, really, he told himself. Hardly worth fretting over.

Yet, try as he might to concentrate on the headlines, his thoughts kept straying back to it. After his eighth fruitless attempt to read an article on America's proposed import tariff, he spat a curse and tossed the paper aside. His mood growing more foul by the second, he heaved back into his chair and succumbed to his ungovernable urge to brood.

Dismal though yesterday evening had been, it had started out pleasantly enough. Hell. It was better than pleasant, it was splendid . . . the best time he'd had with Alys since her debut.

As they had been driven to the theater, comfortably ensconced within the cozy confines of his town coach, they had chatted with their previous ease, sharing their thoughts and laughing together, just as they had before her coming-out ball. Indeed, so intimate was their talk that had it not been for their evening attire and the occasional lurch of the coach, he could easily have imagined them sitting before the kitchen hearth.

Heaving a soundless sigh, he paused to mourn their merry midnight rendezvous, which had ceased in the wake of her newfound popularity. So in demand was his lovely ward that they seldom arrived home from their dizzying rounds of balls, soirées, and routs before three in the morning. When they did, she was so exhausted from the previous night's activities that she went straight up to bed. On those nights he would sit by the kitchen hearth, hoping upon hope that she would join him, his lonely ache deepening each time she failed to appear.

Having thus been deprived of her company and sorely feeling the loss, he'd looked forward to their evening at the theater and the prospect of having her all to himself. Especially in light of Stephen's suggestion that she might welcome his attention. In truth, he'd hoped to use the occasion to initiate their courtship.

But—damn it!—he'd never gotten his chance. The moment they'd stepped from the carriage the bucks had merged on them, fluttering around Alys like butterflies attracted to a particularly sweet flower. As if that wasn't bad enough, they'd turned his theater box into a regular crush during intermission. What disturbed him most about their intrusion wasn't that they had thwarted his courtship of Alys, but the way they had summarily dismissed him as a possible rival. By all but ignoring his presence, they had effectively banished him into the background as if he were an unwanted maiden aunt.

To Lucian's consternation their snub not only infuriated him, it made him, for the first time in his life, question himself and his own attractiveness to women. And he still did.

Oh, rationally, he knew that he was in his prime. Indeed, every affair saw hordes of matchmaking mamas throwing their marriage market offerings in his path. As for the chits themselves, it was clear from the way they fluttered and flirted that they found his person every bit as pleasing as their mamas found his fortune and title. That being as it was, he had absolutely no call to doubt his own desirability.

Yet, for a reason he was powerless to explain, Alys's suitors' easy dismissal of his status as one of London's most eligible bachelors had made him doubt it very much. Indeed, the more he thought about it, and he had considered the matter at length, the more he wondered if they were perhaps correct in their assumption that he was too old and stodgy to win her affections. After all he was fourteen years her senior and her guardian to boot.

Guardian. Just thinking the word left a bad taste in his mouth. Damn Bevis Faire for cursing him with the title; damn him for all but destroying his chance of winning the only woman for whom he'd ever cared.

With a groan that gave voice to his despair, Lucian buried his face in his hands. What he wouldn't give to have met Alys at her debut like her other beaus. What he wouldn't do for the chance to call on her as befitted a proper suitor. No doubt then those damn green cubs would take him seriously.

But would she? For what felt like the millionth time since Alys's debut, he cursed Stephen for planting the notion of courting her in his mind. Now that it was there, it had taken root and overgrown his other desires, strangling them out until all he could think of was her. So fervent had his longing become that ofttimes during the day he caught himself daydreaming what it would be like to be loved by her. He'd even gone so far on an occasion or two to imagine what their children might look like.

Dreams. Wishful dreams. And by all indications, fruitless ones. Making a frustrated noise, he dropped his hands from his face to the desk, flexing them as he visualized them wrapped around Stephen's neck. He could throttle his friend for fostering this obsession. Indeed, so dark was his mood at that moment that had Stephen been in London, he might have ridden over to his bachelor quarters and done just that. Fortunately for his friend and unfortunately for him, Stephen was in Sussex.

Two days after Alys's debut, Diana Ramsey had received news that her stable of prized blood horses had been laid low by a mysterious fever. Being the horsewoman she was, she'd naturally rushed home to nurse them.

While Stephen understood and heartily approved of her decision, he was nonetheless devastated to see her go. So much so that after three days of watching his friend mope over his lost would-be love, Lucian had suggested that he go stay at Thistlewood where he could call on Diana and help her tend her sick horses. Naturally he'd accepted, leaving Lucian to deal with his foundering courtship alone.

Briefly Lucian considered riding to Thistlewood and venting his frustration to his friend. Stephen could al-

ways be counted on to hear him out and offer advice
that was as soothing as it was rational. Tempting though
the thought was, he promptly discarded it. He couldn't
leave London. Not with the way Drake had taken to
hovering over Alys of late. No doubt the popinjay would
swoop down on her the instant he left town and insist
on serving as her escort. And he refused to give him
such an advantage.

Drearily resigning himself to the fact that he had no
choice but to woo Alys as best he could and pray that
he didn't make a fool of himself, he picked up the *Morning Post* again. Unlike before, this time he eventually
succeeded in distracting his mind with his reading. Page
after page he browsed, skimming over advertisements,
poring over an article on the slave trade, and studying
the latest offerings from Tattersall's.

He was just finishing an account of a particularly grue-
some murder in St. Giles when he chanced to glance at
the advertisement below it. As was his habit with public
notices, he arbitrarily discounted it and was about to
turn the page when the word faeries caught his eye. Instantly thinking of Alys and her fascination with the
whimsical creatures, he read on.

It was an announcement for an improving lecture and
art exhibit titled *The Lore and Legend of Faeries of the
British Isles,* to be presented at Winkley's Museum of
Curiosities on Tuesday afternoon next. A slow smile
curving his lips, he carefully tore the announcement from
the paper. Perfect. Not only was Alys sure to enjoy the
lecture, they were unlikely to encounter any of her
plaguesome suitors there. His mood suddenly better than
it had been in a week, he rose from his desk and went
to find his ward, eager to invite her to attend the lecture.

With every step he took, his own excitement mounted.
It wasn't that he had developed a sudden interest in
fairies, no, he still considered them the most ludicrous
of ludicrous myths. His delight stemmed from the prospect of making Alys happy. To him there was no greater
thrill than seeing her eyes light with pleasure. And her
smile! Watching her sweetly bowed lips part and curl
did such strange and wonderful things to his insides.

Grinning his anticipation, Lucian hurried toward the

parlor. If he was lucky, she might even hurl herself at him in her delight, hugging and kissing him the way she had when he'd presented her with the pearls. His grin grew wicked at that thought. Like her smile, the feel of her body pressed against his did strange and wonderful things to him, though the effect was much more physical.

Ready to burst with eagerness, he rushed from parlor to breakfast room to garden, searching for Alys. He was charging for the stairs, certain she was in her chamber primping, when—

"Oof!" He plowed smack into Tidswell.

"My lord!" the precariously teetering butler gasped, his gnarled hand latching on to the newel post to steady himself. Rapidly regaining both his equilibrium and composure, he added in the next beat, "My fault entirely. Please forgive me, my lord."

Completely unfazed by their collision, Lucian grinned and clapped the elderly servant on the shoulder. "It was my fault and you know it, Tidswell. I shouldn't be racing about the house without looking where I'm going. Nurse Spratling would no doubt bend my ears for my recklessness if she were here."

"No doubt," Tidswell agreed, a ghost of a smile playing on his lips.

Lucian glanced up the stairs, then back at the servant, who waited obediently to be either commanded or dismissed. With a nod, he started to do the latter, then changed his mind, inquiring instead, "Do you, by chance, know where Miss Faire might be?"

"Miss Faire?" the time-etched furrows of Tidswell's forehead deepened. "I believe . . . yes . . . she's gone out—"

Out? The word hit him like a pail full of icy water. In his ecstatic delirium, it had never occurred to him that Alys might not be home to share in his excitement. Like a lump of sugar in a pot of acrid tea, his high spirits dissolved, leaving behind the bitter dregs of disappointment.

"—though I can't say where she's gone," Tidswell was saying. "Cook had a squabble with Mr. Watkins, the butcher, and he refused to deliver the lamb for dinner.

I was attending to the matter when she left, and was therefore away from my post."

Out. Probably with that coxcomb Drake, Lucian continued to fume, only half listening to the servant's explanation. His fury banked at that thought, its heat searing away his disappointment. No doubt the fop had taken her driving in that stupid high-wheeled phaeton of his, and they were even now dashing about Rotten Row.

"Hendricks was tending the door in my absence. If you like, I shall seek him out and ask him where Miss Faire went, with whom, and when she's expected to return," the butler finished.

Suffocating with anger now, Lucian glared at the man as if he, and he alone, were responsible for his ward's truancy. His voice little more than a breathless hiss, he replied, "Don't bother." Ignoring the butler's startled expression, he pivoted on his heels and stalked off. He was halfway across the foyer when he paused, commanding without turning, "Send Miss Faire to me the instant she returns. I shall await her in my study."

Restraining his urge to smash his fist against the wall as he went, he gritted his teeth and resumed his infuriated trek. Damn the chit! How dare she go gadding off without his permission? He clenched his teeth so hard, his jaw ached from the tension. Well, he'd put an end to her devil-may-care ways quick enough. By the time he was done with her, she'd think twice before so much as setting foot outside the house without first consulting him. Thus resolved, he stepped into his study, slamming the door behind him with a force that made it shudder on its hinges.

One hour ticked by, then another as Lucian awaited Alys's return. Just before three, Tidswell offered to serve him his luncheon in his study, but he testily declined, his ever-escalating wrath completely robbing him of his appetite. By the time the clock chimed four, he was on the verge of exploding. Where the hell was she? If she had merely gone driving with Drake, she'd have returned hours ago.

Not one normally given to flights of fancy, Lucian's imagination nonetheless ran wild as he considered scenario after scenario involving her and Drake, each more vexing than the last.

Had they stopped at Gunter's for an ice, where they now sat exchanging calf-eyed glances over their frozen confections? Or could it be that they dallied in some secluded part of the park, robbed of all sense of time and place by their burgeoning passion?

If such a thing were possible at that point, his fury rose a notch as he pictured Drake pulling Alys into his embrace to steal a kiss. The worse part about the scene was that she enjoyed and hungrily returned it. He was just imagining her sighing and swooning against the bastard's overstarched shirtfront when there was a scratch at the door.

"What!" he roared, the word accompanied by his fist slamming against his desk.

There was a lengthy silence, as if whoever was at the door was having thoughts about responding, then Tidswell's voice replied, "Miss Faire, my lord."

And no doubt flushed from pleasure with her lips swollen from Drake's kisses, Lucian thought darkly. His eyes narrowing on the door, he growled, "She may enter."

Her face was flushed, all right, just as he'd imagined. Worse, her eyes sparkled with a starry radiance that he could never, not even in his most wishful dreams, hope to duplicate with his own kisses. That thought sent his fulminating rage bursting through the brittle wall of his composure.

As she glided across the room toward him, her step as light as if she walked on clouds, which in her mind she no doubt did, he bellowed, "Where the hell have you been?"

She stopped short, her rapturous expression mutating into one of startled confusion. "Lucian, what's wrong? Has something happened?" She advanced another step, her gaze anxious as it searched his face. "Are you all right?"

He made a derisive noise. "As if you care."

"Whatever makes you say such a thing? Of course I care. You know I do," she protested, visibly recoiling from his bitter reproach.

"Oh? Do you always treat people you care for in such a thoughtless manner?" Without pausing to allow her to defend herself against his unreasonable charge, he added with a snort, "No wonder you have no friends in Surrey."

She paled at his cruel reminder. Indeed, so crestfallen did she look that had he not been so incensed, he'd have no doubt felt shame for causing her pain. In his present state of mind, however, all he felt was an ungentlemanly and admittedly irrational need to punish her for making him feel as wretched as he did. By the distress on her face as she advanced toward him, it was clear that he was well on his way to satisfying that need.

Swallowing repeatedly, as if fighting to dislodge a lump from her throat, she admitted in a strangled voice, "You're right. I have no friends back home, which is why your friendship means so much to me." Her muslin-draped thighs touched the edge of the desk then, halting her. "Please, Lucian," she implored, extending her hand to him. "If I've inadvertently done something terrible to you, please tell me so I might make amends. I value your friendship far too much to lose it over some misunderstanding."

Friendship? *Friendship?* He fixed her proffered hand with a contemptuous stare. Damn it! He didn't want to be her bloody friend. He wanted to be more, much more. With a disdainful grunt, he looked away.

"Lucian, please." Her voice was barely above a whisper now.

"You still haven't answered my question," he snarled, pushing aside her plea as if he hadn't heard it. "Where the hell have you been?"

There was a pause, too long a pause in his opinion, before she replied in her peculiar, halting manner, "Out . . . with Lottie. We were . . . shopping."

If ever he'd heard a falsehood, this was it. More convinced than ever that she had been dallying with Drake and was now trying to hide her guilt, he latched his gaze on to hers, ruthlessly probing her eyes for the truth as he interrogated, "Where did you and my sister go?"

She blinked once and glanced away, a faint blush staining her cheeks. "Oh, er, we went to the Arcade."

"What did you buy?"

She bit her lower lip. "Nothing. I just went along to . . . to keep Lottie company."

"Company? Hmm." He leaned back in his chair and folded his arms across his chest, his gaze never wavering from her averted face. "How odd," he murmured.

He saw her steal a peek at him out of the corner of her eye. "What is odd?"

"Your mention of company made me realize how odd it is that my sister didn't come in to take tea with us. She always does after your shopping excursions, you know, usually to nag me into buying some gewgaw or another she's certain you can't live without."

Alys made a hand motion that was as jerky as the laugh that accompanied it. "She had nothing to nag you about. She didn't find today's offerings particularly interesting either. Besides, she was anxious to get home to Clayton."

Lucian's eyes narrowed as he watched her flush creep over her ear and down her neck. Never in his life had he known a female to go shopping and not see something she wanted. Especially his sister. If Clay hadn't had such a generous income, she'd have no doubt spent them into the poorhouse by now. That fact in itself would have been enough to convince him that Alys lied. Couple it with the way she was blushing and stammering, and only a fool would be beef-witted enough to believe her tale.

And Lucian Warre was no fool. He was also a man who loathed liars. Determined to expose her explanation for the falsehood it was and demand the truth, he inquired with lethal calm, "Shall I tell you why neither of you saw anything of interest?"

She let out another shaky laugh, one that damned her all the more in his eyes. "No doubt you're going to say it's because we've already bought out all the shops." She glanced at him then, as if to gauge his reaction to her quip.

He wasn't amused. Indeed, he'd never been so out of humor as when he snarled back, "The reason you saw nothing of interest was because you didn't go shopping."

"How did you . . ." She gasped and clamped her

mouth shut. But it was too late, those three words had revealed her perjury. By her horrified expression, she knew it.

"Ah. I see I am correct in my conjecture that you lied about your whereabouts."

"Lucian—" she began.

He cut her off with an imperious wave of his hand. "My guess is that you also lied about being with my sister."

"No . . . oh, no! I truly was with Lottie! I swear it!"

So fervent was her vow that he was almost tempted to believe her. Almost. Snorting his incredulity, he rasped, "Unless Lottie has taken a lover, which I strongly doubt, and you went along to act as go-between, I can't imagine what you could have done with my sister that would compel you to lie."

"Lucian, please—"

"No," he barked, silencing her as much with his wrathful gaze as with his words. "My guess is that you weren't with Lottie, but with one of your tiresome suitors. Considering the way he's constantly sniffing after you, probably Drake. The fact that you're lying about your outing makes me wonder what questionable activity you were engaged in." He leaned forward then and inquired darkly, "Tell me, my dear. Shall I post the banns or call the bastard out?"

Her jaw dropped and she turned so red that he half expected her to succumb to a fit of hysterics. After several tense moments, where she stood opening and closing her mouth like a grounded trout, she gathered her composure and replied with an aplomb he had to admire, "Your first option is out of the question my lord, and unless you wish to challenge your sister to pistols at dawn, so is the second. Contrary to what you seem determined to believe, I truly was with Lottie."

"Shopping I suppose?" He practically spat the word shopping in his frustration. Damn her stubbornness! When she merely shrugged, he bashed his fist against the desk and stood up, roaring, "You will tell me where you've been and with whom. I demand to know. Now!"

"Demand," she echoed, tipping her head back to fear-

lessly meet him eye to glittering eye. "You have no right
to demand anything from me."

"I have every right," he flung back. "As your guardian, it's my right to regulate all your actions."

"And as a living, breathing, thinking, and, yes, *free*
person, I have every right to tell you that it's none of
your business!"

"Living and breathing?" He stared at her furiously
heaving chest for a moment, then released a dry chuckle.
"Obviously. Thinking?" He raised his gaze to her face,
one eyebrow lifting in sardonic query as he studied it.
"That, my dear, is debatable. As for your declaration of
being free, well, until such a time as you see fit to tell
me the truth, you shall be confined to this house and
receive no callers."

Something about the expression in her eyes as she
returned his gaze sent a sudden niggling sense of disquiet
crawling up his spine. Oh, he'd known she'd look angry
and she did, but this wasn't the petulant high dudgeon
he'd expected. No, this was different. Hers was a look
of anguished betrayal, one disturbingly like that which
he'd seen reflected in his own mirror when he'd caught
a soldier he'd once called friend selling British intelligence to the French.

For the first time since he'd begun his tirade, Lucian
wondered if he'd perhaps misjudged her actions. Could
it be that her stammering confusion stemmed not from
her grappling for lies, but from fear in the face of his
wrath?

The notion wasn't so farfetched, not when you considered all the times he'd reduced his worldly peers to
cringing bullyrags with the same brand of intimidation
he'd just used on her. In truth, the fact that she had
enough conviction to bear up so well against it spoke
volumes in favor of her innocence.

"Since I am to be your prisoner, I assume that you
have no objections if I confine myself to my chamber?"
she finally replied. Without waiting for his permission,
she turned on her heels and strode from the room.

Something about the quiet dignity of her voice paired
with the regal lift of her chin made him question all the

more seriously if his allegations might indeed be
unfounded.

He knew they were unfounded an hour later when
Charlotte came bursting into the room.

"Luc! Thank God!" she gasped, dashing over to
where he'd been pacing for the past half hour.

Lucian paused midstride, taken aback by his self-possessed sister's flustered state. Never, not even on the
dark day when she'd come to Oxford to tell him of their
parents' deaths from smallpox, had he seen her in such
a nettle. Something terrible must have happened, something unspeakably horrific. And there was only one thing
he could think of catastrophic enough to discompose
her so.

Holding out his arms as she flew at him, he caught
her by her shoulders, exclaiming, "Dear God, Lottie!
What has happened?" He paused a beat to search her
flushed face, praying without real hope for a negative
response to the question he was about to ask. Steeling
himself for the worst, he whispered, "Is it . . . Clay?"

"Y-yes!" she wailed and threw herself against him.
Flinging her arms around him with a strength that forced
a grunt from him, she buried her face against his shirtfront, muffling her words as she pleaded, "Promise you'll
help me! Please! I have no one else to turn to."

Lucian stared down at his sister's disheveled head, at
a loss as to how to proceed. Never in their almost thirty-
three years as siblings had she sought solace from him.
After an awkward moment during which he struggled to
remember how Nurse Spratling used to ease her distress,
his brotherly instinct took over and he folded her into
his embrace. Clumsily patting her back, he soothed,
"Ssh. There now, Lottie. Of course I'll help you. Why
don't you tell me what's happened. Was there an
accident?"

Charlotte shook her head against his chest. "Worse."

Worse? A numbing shaft of pain lanced through his
chest. Worse meant that Clay, a man whom he was
proud to call brother, was—

"He's at his club," she moaned as if revealing the
most lamentable of tragedies.

So incongruous was her tone to her words that Lucian

was certain he'd misheard her. Frowning, he stared down at where her face was still buried in his shirt. "Excuse me?"

She lifted her head to meet his gaze, her eyes feverishly bright. "He's at his club. I rushed all the way home to tell him my news, but—oh! the infuriating man—he wasn't there! I thought I'd die from disappointment! Rutherford said that he's at his club and isn't expected home until supper." Lucian had discarded his coat, so she clutched at his waistcoat in her urgency. "I can't wait that long, Luc. I simply can't! You must go fetch him for me."

Lucian blinked down at his sister, struggling to make sense of her incoherent babbling. "Then nothing awful has happened to Clay?"

"Awful?" She let out a shaky little laugh. "Awful? No." She shook her head with vigor that made hay of her already mussed curls. "Quite the contrary. Something wonderful has happened to him. He just doesn't know it yet. That's why I must see him immediately."

"How can something wonderful happen to a person without them knowing it?" he asked, his brow furrowing as he tried to make sense of her last garbled piece of information.

She regarded him as if judging him against some secret measure, then hopped up onto her tiptoes and planted a playful kiss on his lips. "I was going to come by and tell you the marvelous news this evening, but since I'm already here, well . . ." She pulled away, grinning. "How does the title uncle suit you?"

It took a moment for her words to hit him. When they did, he could only stand there, gaping at her as if seeing her for the first time. And indeed he was.

She wasn't just Lottie, his bossy yet devoted older sister, she was a woman; a strong, extraordinary woman who, considering the way matters stood between him and Alys, might very well be carrying the next Marquess of Thistlewood.

And she meant the world to him.

Lucian gave a mental start at that last. Until that instant he'd never given much thought to his feelings for his sister. She was simply a presence in his life; a con-

stant, ofttimes steadying presence whose love and loyalty
he'd always taken for granted. Why hadn't he realized
years ago how much he loved her?

Smiling with all the warmth he felt inside, he gathered
her tenderly in his arms, murmuring, "I shall cherish the
title uncle as much as I do that of brother, and strive to
be worthy of it." Impulsively he dropped a kiss on her
cheek. "Congratulations, Charlotte. This truly is the best
of news."

"Isn't it?" She gave him a delighted hug. "I was certain the whole of London heard mine and Alys's whoops
when the doctor told us the news this afternoon."

Lucian's heart froze in his chest. "Alys was with you?
At the doctor's?"

"It was she who insisted that I be examined."

"She . . . did?" Dear God! What had he done?

"Oh, Luc! You can't imagine how frightened I was.
I've longed so for a child, and I was certain I couldn't
bear the disappointment should the doctor prove my suspicions wrong. When I confided my fears to Alys, she
made me see how important it was for me to learn the
truth, good or bad. When we—" She broke off, frowning. "Luc? Whatever is wrong? You look as if you've
just lost your best friend."

Shattered by remorse, he bleakly returned her gaze.
She was regarding him with such tender concern, such
soul-felt love and compassion, that for the first time in
his stoic life he completely lost control of his emotions.
With a sob that gave voice to his despair, he sagged into
her waiting embrace and buried his face against her hair.
"I have, Lottie. Heaven help me, I have."

Chapter 17

Her dallying with Drake? How dare Lucian have so little faith in her! Snorting her aggravation, Alys flopped over onto her back where she lay glowering at the shadowy canopy above. It was insulting, that's what it was. Insulting that he would think her capable of such fast behavior, especially after all the trouble she'd gone to to win his respect.

Or so she'd thought she'd won it. She let out another snort, this one more forceful than the last. Apparently she'd been wrong about that, just as she'd been wrong about the progress of his soul. It was plain that it hadn't grown nearly as much as she'd assumed. Why else would he have behaved as he had? She grunted her frustration.

"Ye sound like a bloody damn hog at the trough the way you're snorting and grunting over there."

"I can't help it. I've never been so furious in my life," she fumed, raising up on one elbow to scowl at Hedley, who sat on the dressing table curling his newly shorn hair. "How dare his hateful lordship accuse me of impropriety with Drake! How dare he! I could just—ooo!" She punched her mattress, pretending it was Lucian's belly.

"Rant, rave, gripe," the hob grumbled, thrusting the tweezers he was using as a curling tong into the candle flame. "That's all ye've done for the last six hours. Can't see why yer so friggin' boggled by any of this. Ye know as well as me that Tight-Arse ain't exactly what any-one'd call an amiable fellow."

"Of late he's been quite amiable, even charming," she countered, wondering even as she uttered the words why she was coming to his defense. She was mad at him, remember?

"Charming? Lord Tight-Arse?" Hedley made a vulgar noise and pinched the last newspaper-wrapped coil of hair with the hot tweezers. "Got the temper of a troll and a personality to match."

For a reason Alys was powerless to explain, his scorn-ful assessment of Lucian annoyed her. While it was all right for her to vilify him, Hedley doing so was quite another story. Eyeing the little man in a way that clearly expressed her displeasure, she snapped, "I hardly call it daft to apply the term charming to a man who is always laughing, smiling, and teasing."

It was no lie. Lucian had laughed and smiled often during the past few weeks, though she had to admit that it was his more and more frequent teasing that she found most endearing. There was something about his expres-sion at those times, a look of anxious uncertainty as if he wished very much to be amusing and feared he'd failed, that went straight to her heart. He seemed so vulnerable, so unlike his normally confident self, that it took every last bit of her restraint not to gather him into her arms and reassure him.

Picturing his face as it had looked the night before as he'd delivered a particularly droll quip, she again won-dered what had wrought his drastic change. Could it be that his soul had not only not grown as much as she'd thought, but that something had happened that had made it start to shrivel back to its previous wasted state? Her abating anger cooled to a chill as she considered the devastating consequences of such an occurrence.

As if sensing her foreboding thoughts, the hob paused from removing his cooled curling papers to meet her gaze in the mirror. His tone surprisingly gentle, he said, "Just because he's being a grumpity-growl don't neces-sarily mean that there's something wrong with his soul."

"There has to be," she moaned, shaking her head. "What else could make him behave like such a beast?"

"Seems to me that yer expecting an awful lot from old Tight-Arse."

She frowned, puzzled by his odd remark. "Whatever do you mean?"

He shrugged and resumed his task. "Just that he's human, and that humans, even saints, carry on like sods sometimes. Saw yer goody-good Lucan throw a few tantrums that'd put a troll to shame."

"So?"

"So. It don't usually mean nothing when a human acts crazy, it's just their nature. They're a difficult bunch of snarly-snots . . . moody and unpredictable. I avoid 'em as much as I can."

Alys eyed him thoughtfully, too struck by his logic to take offense at his scathing appraisal of her race. For once he made sense. Lucian was human, and as such could be expected to succumb to the dark moods that plagued all humans. In her urgency to heal his soul, she'd lost sight of that fact.

"If ye ask me, and ye never do"—there was a note of condemnation in the hob's voice as he uttered those last four words—"something's touched a new part of him, something he don't like. As ye know, his lordship don't deal so good with new feelings, especially those that ain't comfortable. Remember what a cross-patch he was back when ye first started working on him?" Having had his say, he turned his attention back to his hair.

Alys lay in silence for several moments, watching him finger-comb his curls into a fashionable tousle. Though what he said made sense, she was unable to think of a recent incident that might have evoked an unpleasant new feeling in Lucian. Unless . . .

Her heart skipped a beat. Unless he was out of sorts over Diana's return to Sussex. The more she considered the possibility, the more certain she became that that was the case.

Of course he missed Diana. How could he not? At her insistence the woman had been their almost constant companion during the past few weeks and, according to Lucian, a most excellent one. "As good of company as one could wish," he'd pronounced her on several occasions, then had gone on to express his gladness that she found her so as well. That all being as it was, what else but her absence could have put him in his current pet?

What indeed? She remained frozen with jubilation for a moment, then bolted up from the bed, gasping, "Oh, Hedley! I just might succeed in my mission after all!" Executing two pirouettes and a hop, she danced over to the dressing table where she seized the hob and planted a kiss on his carefully coiffed head.

"Watch the hair! Watch the hair, ye slobbering cow!" he squawked, furiously kicking his dangling legs.

"Sorry," she murmured, setting him back down. "It's just that I'm so happy."

He grunted as he turned to the mirror to assess the damage. "Bloody damn crazy human," he muttered, tugging at his kiss-crushed curls. "One minute yer mad enough to split a gut, the next yer as tickled as an elf drunk on elderberry wine."

"I am tickled," she admitted, clasping her hands to keep from seizing him again in her excitement. "I'm almost certain that Lucian's foul mood is due to Diana Ramsey returning to Sussex. If I don't miss my guess, he's got feelings for her."

"Of course he's got feelings for her. The way ye've been shoving her in his face every time he turns around, he probably feels sick at the sight of her."

Alys rolled her eyes at his typically pessimistic response. "If you spent more time with Lucian and less time lounging about the Bond Street shops, you would know how much he enjoys her company. Not only has he admitted that he likes her, he's never once denied my request to include her in our outings."

Hedley sniffed as he lifted his dark blue coat from the scent flask that served as his clothes horse. "That last don't prove diddly-squat. He never denies ye nothing anymore."

"He doesn't deny me because I never make unreasonable requests," she retorted, doggedly clinging to her optimism. "And the fact that he considers inviting Diana to accompany us a reasonable request proves that he cares for her. You know as well as I that his lordship never does anything he doesn't want to do."

"He is a stubborn sod," the hob agreed. Shoving the

last gold coat button into its mooring, he turned and struck a dandified pose. "So? How do I look?"

"Like a fop," she pronounced, eyeing the exaggerated flare of his collar points. And he did. Garbed in the modish blue, gold, and scarlet suit of clothes she'd commissioned from Madame Fanchon, dolls clothes, she'd told the bewildered modiste, he was the very picture of dandification.

Apparently foppery was his goal for he preened as if receiving the greatest of compliments. "Excellent! Then, I'm off."

"Off?" she echoed, incredulous that he'd even consider leaving at such a critical moment. "You can't go off. I need you to help me plan how to advance Lucian and Diana's romance. We need to think of a way to make Lucian go to Thistlewood."

"Dreadfully sorry, my dear Miss Faire," he drawled, perfectly emulating the cultured tones of his beloved haut ton. "But I have a spot of romance to attend to myself."

"Romance? You?" She couldn't keep a rising note of amazement from her voice.

"Umm. Yes," he murmured, carefully balancing his tall silk hat atop his curls. "Courting a passing fair pillywiggin named Tansy. Squiring her to a ball at the Hyde Park flower walk this evening." He picked up a tiny pair of gloves that she had never seen before. "Well, mustn't be late." With that, he disappeared.

"You come back here this instant!" she commanded, though she didn't really expect him to comply. Of course he didn't. Sighing her exasperation, she plopped down onto the bench before the dressing table. To the devil with the hateful little beast! She didn't need him anyway. She was perfectly capable of finding a way to bring Lucian up to scratch by herself.

After what felt like an eternity of sitting there, alternately tapping her bare feet and drumming her fingers against the table as she schemed, she came up with what she saw as a perfect plan: she would have Hedley cast a spell on the Thistlewood stables to give the illusion that Lucian's horses suffered from the same fever as Diana's. When Stephen, whom she'd been told was at This-

tlewood purchasing a foal, discovered the illness, he
would no doubt summon Lucian posthaste. Once in Sussex, Lucian would naturally consult Diana on cures. And
as she knew from her matchmaking experience, nothing
brought two people together quicker than a common
purpose. Of course the animals would be none the worse
for their enchantment.

Too excited to even consider sleep, she decided to
celebrate her brilliant plan. And what better way than
with another slice of the almond cake Tidswell had
slipped her after she'd refused her supper? Suddenly
famished at the prospect of food, she donned her dressing gown and slippers and hastened to the kitchen.

Down the hall she rushed, her hand shielding her candle from the breeze of her motion as she went. She was
just starting down the pitch-dark servants stairs when
she heard the longcase clock in the hallway above boom
the time. One. Two. Three—

Oh, perfect! she thought, counting out twelve strokes.
It was late enough so that the servants would all be abed
and early enough so that Lucian was probably still at his
club. That meant that she would have the kitchen to
herself . . . which meant that she could eat without any
witnesses to her gluttony.

Her mouth watering in anticipation, she skipped down
the last five steps and waltzed from the stairwell toward
the pantry. Since she was casting aside her ladylike deli-
cacy, she might as well have two slices of cake. Yes,
and some of that gingerbread she'd smelled baking that
morning. She was halfway across the kitchen, wondering
if cook had made any jumbles, when a faint movement
by the hearth caught her eye.

She stopped midstride, her heart jumping to her throat
as her gaze darted to a figure slumped in a chair by the
fire. Who the—

Lucian? She squinted into the shadows. Of course it
was Lucian. Who else's form was so long and elegant?
Who else had such broad, magnificent shoulders? Nobody but Lucian . . .

And she was mad at him.

Or so she tried to tell herself. Yet, struggle though
she might, she was unable to rekindle her previous fury.

Oh, it wasn't that she thought he no longer deserved her wrath. He did. Or that she'd forgiven him. Well, perhaps she had, but just a little.

No. What stifled her anger was the pervading sense of sadness she felt at seeing him there, sitting by the hearth as he so often did during their jolly midnight tête-à-têtes. If her plan succeeded, and for his sake she prayed it would, this might very well be the last time she saw him thus. For once he married Diana, he would be far too busy at night to sit by the kitchen hearth exchanging confidences with her.

Filled with a crushing sense of loss she advanced toward him, not certain what to say or do, knowing only that she had to be near him. If this was to be their last night together, how could she let it pass in anger?

Yet, it seemed doomed to do just that. From the way he remained motionless at her approach, pointedly ignoring her presence, it was clear that his temper hadn't cooled an iota. Indeed, if his appearance was any indicator, his mood had gone from bad to worse.

Always immaculately groomed, his normally perfect hair was tousled and wild, as if he'd spent the past few hours running his hands through it. His dressing gown, a costly looking garment of black, gold, and copper patterned silk, was haphazardly wrapped and tied; peeking from beneath it were baggy trousers in dire need of ironing. More startling yet, he was barefoot.

At a loss as to how to proceed, Alys paused a scant yard away, staring at where his collar was carelessly twisted and half tucked into the neck of his robe. How she ached to straighten it, to feel the silken warmth of his skin as she worked. She longed to smooth that errant strip of velvet over his shoulder and savor the strength beneath. Most of all, she yearned to see his smile of thanks when she finished.

More anxious than ever to make peace, she softly uttered his name, hoping without really believing that he was lost in his thoughts and was thus oblivious to her approach.

Still nothing. She might as well have been as invisible as Hedley for all the response she received. She waited a moment longer, then sighed. Ah, well. Perhaps it was for the best that they remain at odds. Why torment herself by nurturing her hopeless love? Feeling as if her heart were being ripped from her chest, she forced herself to turn away.

"Don't leave. Please." The words were little more than a ragged whisper.

She froze in her steps. After a beat, she pivoted back to Lucian. He hadn't moved. Indeed, there was no outward sign that he'd even spoken. Baffled, she stood staring at his bowed head, wondering if she had perhaps imagined his words. Just as she was about to turn away again, he slowly lifted his face into the light.

If ever a man looked crushed by life, it was Lucian Warre. He looked defeated, hopeless, as if he'd lost his whole world and despaired at ever finding it again. It shattered her to see him so.

Wanting to weep at the sight of him, she rushed to his side, mindless of everything but her own need to hearten him. Dropping to her knees in front of his chair, she lifted his limp hands from his lap and clasped them to her breast. "Don't look so sad. Surely nothing can be so awful as to merit such gloom?" she crooned, tipping her head back to look up into his eyes.

For an instant their gazes touched and she saw a grief so deep that it could only have come from his soul. Then he sucked in a shuddering breath and looked away, murmuring, "The thought of losing you is that awful, and worse."

"Lose me?" she echoed, completely caught off guard.

He bowed his head. Or was it a nod?

"Please talk to me, Lucian," she implored, her hands tightening around his. "I want to understand, I— Oh! Are you worried that I might run away or do something silly because of this afternoon?"

"No, though after the despicable way I treated you, I wouldn't blame you if you did. I was a bastard and deserve your scorn. In truth, I'm surprised you're still speaking to me. I was certain you must hate me."

"I doubt if I could ever hate you," she sincerely replied.

"You should. At the very least you should spurn my company until I apologize."

Had she been in a smiling mood, Alys would have smiled then. That he would even acknowledge that he owed her an apology showed how far he had come. Curious to find out just how far that was, she murmured, "How long shall I be required to wait before you do so?"

He sighed. It was the saddest sound she'd ever heard. "It's not that I don't want to apologize now. I do, more than anything in the world. I just don't know how. I've racked my brain all evening, but I simply cannot find the words to adequately express my remorse. Somehow, simply saying I'm sorry doesn't seem enough."

"Sorry is always enough when it's uttered with sincerity," she reminded him. "I told you so at Thistlewood. Remember?"

His brow furrowed. After a beat it smoothed again and he nodded. "So you did. It was in the nursery if I remember correctly."

"Yes. The nursery. And like then, I forgive you now," she said, thinking back on that moment and the merry battledore-and-shuttlecock lesson that had followed. What she wouldn't do to see him smile as he had that day. Perhaps—

She slanted him a speculative look. Perhaps not. Unlike that afternoon at Thistlewood, restoring their friendship now clearly hadn't lightened his spirits in the least. Puzzled, she continued to gaze at him, trying to fathom his odd mood. Just when she was about to give up, she remembered his earlier comment and the anguish in his voice as he'd uttered it.

"Lucian?"

He made a distracted mmm noise.

"You said something earlier about losing me. What did you mean?"

There was a long pause, so long that she was beginning to doubt he would answer. Just as she opened her mouth to prompt him, he replied, "I meant that I see you slipping further and further away from me every day, and that it tears me apart knowing that I'm losing you."

Alys froze, stunned as much by the despair in his voice as by his words. She'd known that he was fond of her, that he counted her among his favorite companions. Yet, never once had he said or done anything to make her suspect that his feelings ran deeper than mere friendship. Surely he wasn't trying to tell her now that they did?

"I hate your suitors," he continued, the savagery in his voice giving testament to the truth of his words. "I hate them for their youth and charm, for I know that I lack both and can never compete against them for your affections. I hate them for their privilege of courting you, because as your guardian, I cannot do the same. I hate them—all of them—because someday you shall fall in love with one of them and marry him."

"Lucian—no," she protested.

But he went on as if he hadn't heard her. "It was my jealousy that made me behave as I did this afternoon. Every time you go driving, riding, or even walking with one of your cursed suitors, I'm terrified that he might ask for your hand and that you might accept. If I could, I would lock you away from the world where I might keep you all to myself."

Before she could think, much less react, he pulled his hands from hers and dragged her up onto his lap. "Dear God, Alys. What am I to do?" he asked, his voice little more than an agonized whisper.

"Lucian—" she tried again, not certain what she would say, knowing only that her weakening resolve would crumble if he continued.

But continue he did. "I love you. I love you so much that I sometimes want to weep from the wonder of it. You're my joy, my comfort . . . my everything. For the first time in my life I feel alive, truly alive. *You* make me feel so. How am I to—" he faltered then and it was with obvious strain that he finished, "—live without you?" His voice broke completely on the last word.

Silenced by his emotion, he mutely sought her gaze, his unspoken longing reflected in his eyes as he captured it. For a heartbeat he held it, then, with a sob that expressed the pain his fractured voice couldn't, he crushed her against him and buried his face in her hair.

A sob, softer yet every bit as anguished as his, escaped Alys. Oh, how she longed to confess her own feelings and ease his torment! Three words, that's all it would take. Just three . . .

I love you.

Three words that would surely doom them forever. Not that she cared what happened to herself. Indeed, if it were only her soul at stake, she would gladly risk it for a taste of the paradise she knew she would find in his arms. For she would rather have one splendid moment of loving him than the eternity of emptiness she faced without him.

They remained like that for a long while: she, half lying, half sitting on his lap, lightly stroking his back as she mourned their love; he, with his face buried in her hair, clinging to her as if she might disappear should he ease his hold. Though he made no sound, she could feel his sobs in the heaving of his chest against hers.

At length, she felt his face move against her hair. An instant later he lifted it. Instinctively she looked up and met his gaze in the flickering firelight. Though there was no telltale dampness on his ashen cheeks, she could see that his eyes were red. It was as if his soul wept and his body had yet to learn how to follow suit. It was terrible to see.

His expression grave, as if he'd just committed an unpardonable act and was shamed by it, he dropped his arms from around her, murmuring, "I'm sorry, Alys. Please forgive me. It was wrong of me to speak of my feelings as I did."

Alys knew she should rise from his lap then, that she should nod her forgiveness and march directly to her room. But she couldn't. Heaven help her! She couldn't. She simply hadn't the strength to walk away and leave him so crushed and humbled.

Too caught up in his apology to notice her breach, he continued, "I spoke with Charlotte this afternoon. We—"

"I assume she told you the wonderful news?" Alys cut in, eagerly grasping for a happy subject with which to distract him.

He smiled faintly, though there was no real joy in his expression. "Yes, she did. And I'm thrilled for her." Having expressed that rote sentiment, he let the curled-up corners of his lips flatten back into their previous straight line. "I also told her of my feelings for you and confessed to letting my jealousy get the better of my good judgment this afternoon. She suggested that, under the circumstances, it might be best if you stay with her and Clayton for the remainder of the season. Considering what just happened, I have to agree."

Something inside her, perhaps the last of her resolve, snapped at the thought of leaving him. Before she could shore up the fierce torrent of emotions that cascaded forth, she blurted out, "No, Lucian! Oh, no! Please don't send me away. You can't! I can't bear to leave you."

He couldn't have looked more stunned if she'd come right out and confessed her love. Or more elated. "Are you saying that you share my feelings?" he whispered, his voice breathless with awed wonder.

Never had Alys been as torn as she was at that moment, watching his somber face light with a radiant smile. She knew she ought to deny her love, that she should make an excuse for her hasty words, but she couldn't. How could she when doing so meant watching the joy drain from his face?

Feeling the weight of her curse more keenly than ever, she dropped her gaze from his, desperately seeking a solution to her quandary. Surely there must be a way out of this without destroying either his heart or their souls?

If there was, she couldn't find it, though her failure to do so most certainly didn't stem from a lack of trying. At wit's end, she gave up. That brought her back to her only possible option: she must break his heart. Perhaps if she was clever, she might compel him to turn to Diana for solace.

As she struggled to reconcile herself to doing so, he gently cupped her chin in his palm and lifted her face. His gaze dark and penetrating, he repeated, "Do you share my feelings?"

Her eyes must have said what her lips dare not, for he moaned once and swept her into his embrace. Slowly inching his face down to hers, he murmured, "I've wished and hoped, but never did I truly believe that you could be mine. I'm half afraid that this is all a wondrous dream from which I shall awake at any moment."

His mouth was close to hers now, so close that his warm breath caressed her lips as he spoke. "Tell me, sweet Alys, are you real? Or are you merely a tantalizing figment of my imagination?" he quizzed, his voice hushed to a black velvet whisper. "Perhaps I should kiss you and find out." Without waiting for her response, he swooped down and claimed her lips with his.

There was no gentleness in his kiss, none of the courtly reverence with which Lucan had kissed her. There was only passion; a raw, demanding passion beneath whose thrilling assault she was powerless to do anything but surrender. And surrender she did, easily and without so much as a whimper of protest.

Oh, rationally she knew she should struggle, that she should shove him away and flee as fast as her feet could carry her. But—God forgive her!—she hadn't the fortitude. The temptation to sample his ravishing ardor was simply too irresistible to deny.

One taste, she promised herself, that's all she'd take. Just one taste to sustain her for the rest of eternity. Surely they wouldn't be damned for stealing just one brief moment of rapture? Not if she made things right tomorrow.

Tomorrow . . . yes, tomorrow, she pledged, the last of her lingering qualms melting beneath his kisses. Tomorrow she would find a way to undo the damage she did tonight. Tomorrow she would redouble her efforts to match him to Diana. But tonight . . .

Alys twined her arms around Lucian's neck and recklessly met his passion with hers. Kiss for ravenous kiss she matched him, thrilling to every responsive move of his mouth. Never had she known such desire, never had she felt such urgency as she did in that instant as she sampled the forbidden sweetness of his lips.

Groaning her name, he pressed her yet nearer, holding her so close that her soft curves molded to the hard contours of his body. His mouth fiercely possessive, he claimed her savage passion, taming it with a mastery that sent shivers of pleasure shooting along her nerve endings.

Over and over again they kissed, his every sensual nip and brush intensifying the humming excitement in her blood. Driven by her ripening need, she parted her lips, beckoning him to taste the honeyed warmth beyond.

Half sobbing, half moaning his own desire, he eagerly answered her brazen summons. His strokes aggressive and insistent, he thrust his tongue between her lips, probing and plundering with a boldness that sent heavy jolts of sensation streaking through her body.

In a frenzy of heated response she clung to his neck, melding her mouth to his, matching his tongue stroke for inflammatory stroke. Sometimes they plunged deeply, others they teased each other with shallow little licks; every time his touch sent electrifying sparks shooting through her veins. So hot was their passion that Alys swore she could feel steam rising from their lips.

As their long denied hunger flared and exploded, Lucian pressed his chest hard against hers, forcing her back until she arched over his arms. Growling in a way that gave voice to his desire, he ravished her mouth one last time, then pulled away. His breath coming in ragged pants, he gazed down at her face, his expression one of such seductive tenderness that she was left with no doubt as to the depth of his feelings.

Overcome with her own burgeoning emotions, she reached up and gently stroked his cheek. Once. Twice. Three times she caressed it, memorizing the texture of his skin, engraving it upon her heart. It felt even nicer than she'd imagined, satiny smooth with just a hint of stubbly beard.

Cheek to brow, brow to eyes, eyes to nose, nose to mouth, she traced each exquisite feature, committing them to memory. As her fingers drifted downward to acquaint themselves with the strong angle of his jaw, he turned his head and pressed his lips to her palm.

For a brief instant their gazes met over the top of her hand; his, smoldering with unslaked desire; hers, slightly unfocused with kiss-drugged passion. Then he released a hoarse cry and buried his face against her throat. His mouth hot and urgent he worshiped her arched neck, erotically nibbling here, kissing there, stopping only when he reached the prim neckline of her dressing gown.

Growling his impatience, he ripped the frog fastenings from their loops and flung the garment open, revealing the gentle slope of her bosom above the low frilled neck of her nightdress. For a long moment his gaze roved over her exposed flesh, lust raging visibly on his face. Then he tipped his head forward and resumed his amorous odyssey.

Down he kissed, across her collarbone and over her cleavage, the moist heat of his mouth sending shiver after delicious shiver racing through her. Softly moaning her pleasure, she surged against his lips, greedily urging them lower. Her breasts felt heavy, aching for his touch. Maddened with a need that was as frightening as it was exhilarating, she dragged his arms from around her and guided his hands upward to cup her breasts.

With a strangled groan, he accepted her offering, crushing the hard evidence of his own desire against her as he did so. His touch gentle yet persuasive, he fondled her through the thin fabric of her gown, teasing and tweaking her sensitized nipples until she was certain she'd die if he didn't continue.

Never, not even in her most heated fantasies, had she dreamed that loving him would be so exquisite. She'd guessed it would be pleasurable, even rapturous . . . but ah! Imagining sensations as heady as these went far beyond the scope of her untried fancies. Suddenly greedy to discover all of love's torrid secrets, those held by his body as well as hers, she tugged loose the tie at his waist and feverishly thrust open his robe.

As with everything else in her dreams of Lucian, the reality of his bare torso was far more splendid than that of her imaginings. With his hard-sculpted chest and lean, sinewy waist, he was sheer perfection.

Awestruck by his beauty, she reached out and reverently traced the muscular contours of his chest, thrilling at the feel of him. He felt as good as he looked, like granite sheathed in silk, with a sprinkling of dark hair that tickled sensuously against her fingers with every caress. So tantalizing was he to her touch, that she let her fingers drift lower, eager to experience every magnificent inch of him.

Down they meandered, down over his strong ribs and tapering waist; down across his flat, rippling belly until they were halted by the edge of his trousers. Yearning to touch that which lay sheathed within, yet too shy to do so, she wistfully traced the line where flesh met fabric.

Gasping and moaning in turns, he writhed beneath her sensual ministrations, time and again butting his arousal against her backside. Just the feel of him, so hard and rampant, made her throb with the need for greater intimacy. Issuing a soft sound from the back of her throat, she ground against his thrusting hardness, brazenly tendering a wanton invitation.

She didn't have to ask twice. Hoarsely whispering words of love, Lucian slipped his hand beneath her gown. Up her thigh, over her hip, and across her belly it brushed, leaving tiny ripples of delight everywhere it went. For one sensually charged moment he tickled her navel, then his fingers snaked lower to tease her secret curls.

Her body taut and expectant, she rubbed against his hand, gasping his name. Breathlessly moaning his own need, he dipped lower, grazing the pulsating bud of her desire. She shrieked, startled at the intensity of the resulting sensation. Claiming her lips once again with his, he deepened the intimacy of his caress, masterfully rubbing, stroking, and parting her flesh.

Time and again she cried into his mouth, her body jerking and writhing as hot, shivery sensations streaked through her belly. When she was certain she could bear the erotic torment no longer, his fingers stilled and he pulled from their kiss.

His eyes glistening pools of desire, he rested his forehead against hers, demanding in a fierce whisper, "Say that you love me, poppet. Promise me that you'll be mine forever."

She emitted a soft moue and gyrated against his motionless hand, desperately seeking to relieve the ache between her legs.

Grinning in a way that was nothing short of wicked, he stroked her inflamed flesh once, then drew his fingers away again. "Say it," he directed again.

Too dazed by desire for prudence, she twined her arms around his neck and confessed between kisses, "I love you, Lucian Warre. Now and forever!"

The instant the words left her mouth, she felt an all-too-familiar force pulling at her body. Before her eyes, Lucian's smiling face wavered, rippling and distorting like a reflection in a windswept pond. Then it exploded into a hundred fragments of colored light and she was hurled into a vortex of endless darkness.

Screaming Lucian's name, she kicked and clawed at the nothingness, desperately seeking to halt her descent. In the next instant, she was struck by a blinding flash of pure white light.

Thud! She landed in an ignoble heap at Allura's feet.

Chapter 18

Too stunned to speak, Alys simply lay there, staring up at Allura. The fairy looked every bit as surprised as Alys felt, an expression that she found distinctly unsettling. If Allura hadn't transported her back to the otherworld, then Aengus had. And if Aengus was responsible, she was in serious trouble.

With dread slithering up her spine, she peered fearfully around Allura's office, expecting the wrathful fairy king to materialize at any moment and condemn her as he had the night of Lucan's death. And like that night, what could she possibly say in her own defense? Now, as had been the case then, she was guilty of wronging his son. This time, however, it was tragically possible that she might have sealed his doom. Forever.

As happened with disturbing frequency, Allura seemed to read her mind. "Aengus isn't here," she murmured, her musical voice shattering the leaden silence. "He's been on a sojourn since you went up to the mortal world."

"Not here?" Alys echoed. "Then who . . . ?" She gestured to her surroundings in bewilderment.

"Oh, you're correct in believing Aengus responsible for transferring you back here, though it was through no conscious act on his part. You're here because of the codicil he added to the spell he used to send you above . . . a safeguard, if you will."

"A safeguard?" Alys's brow knitted at the peculiarity of Aengus doing such a thing. "I don't understand."

"No, of course you don't. But before I attempt to explain, let me ask you a question: Are you in love with Lucian Warre?"

Feeling more wretched than she'd have ever believed possible, she nodded her guilt.

"And did you confess, or perhaps demonstrate your feelings?" By the way the fairy was eyeing her disheveled state, it was clear that she suspected the latter.

Thus reminded of her wanton disarray, Alys shoved herself up into a sitting position and self-consciously tugged her dressing gown closed. Seeing no need to elaborate on the obvious, she merely nodded again.

Allura sighed. "Aengus was afraid this would happen." In the blink of an eye, the fairy was perched upon the purple and gold striped sofa against the far wall. Patting the cushion beside her, she bid, "Come. Sit, and I shall explain as best I can."

Though it took Alys a good deal longer than a blink to do so, she did as she was directed. As she settled herself, Allura began, "You see, Alys, despite the ill manner in which you used his son, Aengus believes that you genuinely loved Lucan. Granted, it was a shallow, prideful sort of love, not at all the kind he needed to save his soul, but it was love nonetheless. And when people love to any degree, be it the loyalty between friends, the devotion of a child to his parents, or the passion between man and woman, their souls are connected for all of eternity."

"Then that's why I was so attracted to Lucian, even in the beginning when he behaved in a singularly unattractive manner," Alys mused.

The fairy nodded. "Aengus feared that you might feel so, just as he feared that his son's soul might recognize yours and mistake it for that of his destined true love. Therefore, when he wove the spell to send you back up into the world, he did so on the condition that you be transported back here should his foreboding prove prophetic."

"And it did," Alys whispered, bitter tears of anguish

stinging her eyes. "Oh, Allura! Whatever am I to do? I love Lucian so!"

The fairy shook her head, her expression bleak.

"But there must be a way to make things right . . . a way to save him! There has to be. If Aengus suspected that this might happen, he surely devised a plan to mend the resulting damage. Please, Allura—" A sob escaped her as she desperately latched on to the fairy's arm. "Please, I'm begging you. Tell me what to do. I'll do anything to save him. Anything! No matter the cost to myself. Just give me the chance to make things right."

Allura met her gaze then, and Alys could have sworn that she saw something akin to human compassion in the fairy's normally soulless eyes. "I'm sorry, Alys, truly I am. But it's not in my power to grant you another chance. Only Aengus can do so."

"Then summon Aengus and let me appeal to him myself," she implored, her grip tightening a fraction in her urgency.

The fairy sighed, dropping her gaze as she did so. "I would if I could, but I don't know where he is. Nobody does."

"Then send somebody to find him," she flung back wildly.

"It would do no good. Aengus cannot be found unless he so wishes. You should know that after all your centuries in the otherworld."

"But how can you be so certain that he won't wish to be found? Especially in this instance?" she argued. "Surely he'll want to be informed of his son's peril."

There was an ominous beat of silence, then Allura lifted her gaze back to Alys's. Staring into her eyes in a way that chilled her to her core, she replied, "Why would he wish to be informed when doing so will serve only to cause him torment?"

Alys made an impatient noise. "So he can help save his son," she retorted, wondering when the fairy had become so beef-witted. "Why else?"

The fairy looked at her as if she were the beef-witted one. "The onus of saving Lucian Warre's soul is yours, and only yours. As such, Aengus cannot aid you in any way."

"But why?" She more wailed than asked the question.

Allura sighed. "Didn't you listen to a word I said before I sent you above?"

When Alys merely stared at her, too stricken to even try to remember, she sighed again and elaborated, "I explained then that since it was you who broke Lucan's chain of destiny, that it is you who must mend it. That is why Aengus left as he did. He couldn't bear to stand helplessly by and watch his son die again should you fail in your task. He's to stay away until the dawn of June twenty-fifth, when he'll appear to either reward your success or to punish you for your failure."

"But we can't just let Lucian die," Alys sobbed, tears of despair seeping from her eyes. "We have to at least try and save him."

The fairy studied her solemnly. "And what do you suggest we do? You know what would happen if I were to return you to the mortal world without Aengus's sanction."

Alys's shoulders slumped at that reminder. Oh, she knew all right. Both Allura and Aengus had been careful to warn her on that account. At her first unsanctioned dawn on earth, she'd become as she would presently be had she remained in the mortal world the past five hundred years. That meant that she would turn to bones, long ago moldered to dust.

"That's right. Dust," Allura concurred, as if Alys had verbalized her thoughts. "And reducing yourself to such a disagreeable state would in no way benefit Lucian Warre."

"If it would, I would make the sacrifice in a heartbeat," Alys declared, wiping her tears with the back of her hand. "Oh, Allura! Is there truly no hope for him?"

By the fairy's grim expression, it was clear that she believed Lucian's situation beyond salvage. "Not that I can see. Unless—" Her marble-smooth brow furrowed suddenly and her eyes narrowed as if stuck by inspiration.

"Unless?" Alys's hand tightened on the fairy's arm to such a degree that she'd have probably winced had she been human.

Allura returned her eager gaze thoughtfully for a moment, then finished the sentence, "Unless I can find a solution in the scrolls."

This time it was Alys's brow that creased. "Scrolls?"

"The secrets of our kind are recorded on a hundred scrolls, written by the very first fairies. Though only our kings are allowed to read them, as Aengus's proxy during his absence, it is permissible for me to seek counsel from them."

"And you truly believe that they might contain something to help us?" Alys exclaimed, eagerly seizing upon the proffered morsel of hope.

"Not us," the fairy reminded her. "You. Like Aengus, I cannot aid you with either advice or magic. It will be your responsibility to decide how to use whatever information I give you, and what action to take."

As Alys opened her mouth to assure her that her efforts would not be in vain, Allura added ominously, "I must warn you that even if by some miracle you do save Lucian Warre, your success might not be enough to deliver you from Aengus's wrath. Technically you did fail in your mission, recklessly jeopardizing his son's soul in the process."

"I know, and I'm ready to accept his punishment," she murmured, dropping her hand from the fairy's arm with an air of resignation.

With the regal bearing of a queen granting clemency, Allura inclined her head once and then rose. "So be it."

As she started to move away, Alys reached out and grabbed her arm again, this time to halt her. "Allura, I want you to know that no matter what Aengus chooses to do with me, I shall always be grateful for your kindness."

Looking genuinely regretful, the fairy laid her hand over the one on her arm and gave it a fond squeeze. "And I want you to know, my dear mortal, that I shall do everything in my power to persuade Aengus to be merciful." With that, she stepped away and raised her arms, preparing to spirit her prisoner to the dank fairy dungeon below.

But Alys wasn't yet ready to go. Not until she'd asked the question that lay heavy on her mind. As Allura's hands cut through the air in a broad, arcing motion, she again halted her, this time with an appeal. "Please. Might I beg one small favor before you send me away?"

The fairy froze in mid-motion. "If it's one you're certain I can grant."

Alys bobbed her head to the affirmative.

"Then ask."

"I was wondering, well, could you tell me what Lucian makes of my strange disappearance? Surely he must be shocked by my disappearing as I did?"

"Ah. That." Allura dropped her arms back to her sides. "To his mortal eyes you didn't simply—poof!—disappear. You bolted from his arms, overcome with a sudden fit of virginal terror at his passion." She paused then, gazing intently into the distance. After a moment, her eyes exploded into eerie green flames. It was chilling to see.

Her voice a low, hypnotic drone, she continued, "Right now, he desperately longs to follow you and soothe your fears, but—mmm—I see he possesses much of Lucan's gallantry. He's restraining his impulse so as to allow you time to examine your feelings for him. He—" What was usually her eyes narrowed into fire-licked slits. "He's resolved to seek you out in the morning and propose marriage."

Her lids dropped over her fiery orbs then, and when she lifted them again, her eyes were back to normal. At least as normal as was possible for a fairy. Meeting Alys's gaze once again, she finished, "No doubt he'll search long and hard when he discovers you gone. But of course he shall never find you. For both your sakes, I wish he could."

Charlotte paused on the threshold of Lucian's study, frowning as she viewed her brother. Like yesterday and every other day in the three weeks since Alys's disappearance, he sat hunched over his desk with a glass of port in one hand and a near empty decanter of the same in the other. By the ever-increasing deterioration of both his person and his grooming, she was beginning to suspect that despite Tidswell's claims to the contrary, he'd remained in that position the entire time.

Not that she'd have censured him had he done so.

How could she? He genuinely loved Alys, so it was only natural that he be crushed by her loss. More devastating yet, he blamed himself for driving her away.

As she had often done during the past three weeks, Charlotte said a silent prayer, begging God for Alys's safe return. And as always happened during those heart-voiced communes, Charlotte's eyes glazed with tears.

Over the weeks she'd come to view Alys as the sister she'd always longed for, but never had. Indeed, so great was her fondness that when Lucian had told her of his feelings for the girl on the eve of her disappearance, she'd been unable to contain her joy. That Lucian marry Alys and make them real sisters was her dearest wish . . .

A wish that was becoming less and less likely to be realized with every passing day. For despite the efforts of a dozen Bow Street Runners and the posting of over a thousand handbills offering a king's ransom for her return, they had yet to recover a single clue as to her whereabouts. It was as if she'd simply vanished from the face of the earth. And though Lucian hadn't said so, she sensed that, like herself, he was beginning to fear that Alys had met with foul play.

Staunchly refusing to reflect upon that grim theory, she blinked back her tears and swept into the room. For Lucian's sake, she had to remain strong, optimistic even. How else was she to halt his dangerous downward spiral into despair?

"Luc?" she murmured, coming to a stop before his littered desk.

He didn't spare her so much as a glance of acknowledgment. Not that she'd expected him to. For close to a week now, he'd been withdrawn to the point where it took a deliberate, and often forceful, effort to provoke a response. Determined to do just that, she leaned over the desk and demanded loud enough to rouse a deaf man, "Look at me, Luc. I need to talk to you."

Nothing.

"Lucian? Do you hear me?"

Still nothing.

"Come, come now. The least you can do is look at me so I know you're listening," she scolded, slipping her hand beneath his stubbled chin to force him to comply.

It tipped easily, without the slightest resistance. "Whatever has happened to your Warre tenacity? A real Warre wouldn't give up—" The rest of what was supposed to be an invigorating lecture was strangled by shock as she gaped down at his face.

Dear God! He looked even worse than he had yesterday. His skin, which had been merely pale the day before, had taken on a sickly grayish cast, a hue that made the bruiselike shadows beneath his eyes seem all the more pronounced in contrast. His face, while always lean, had grown thin to the point of gauntness, and as she gently smoothed his unkempt hair from his brow, she noted a sprinkling of silver among the lackluster ebony strands at his temples.

Just when she was beginning to fear that he'd slipped beyond her reach, his dull eyes lit with recognition and his cracked lips silently formed her name. Though she felt anything but cheerful, she forced herself to smile. "Yes. It's me, Lucian."

His mouth worked again, this time managing to croak, "Alys?"

"No news yet. However, I'm certain we shall hear something soon," she reassured him, though even to her ears the words rang hollow. "Until then, you really ought to try and rest. You look exhausted."

"I can't." There was more raw emotion in those two hoarsely uttered words than she'd heard him express in his entire life.

Keenly feeling his ache, yet at a loss as to how to ease it, she feebly countered, "You need to at least try."

"I have, but it does no good." Heaving a weary sigh, he pulled his face from her hand, shakily lifting his glass as he did so. Though his voice was gaining strength with use, it still held a dry, rasping quality as he added, "I'm beginning to think that I shall find rest only in my grave."

"Don't! Don't even think such morbid thoughts," she chided, unnerved by his talk of death. "We shall find Alys and soon. I'm certain of it. In the meantime, you must do everything in your power to remain strong so that you can continue the search. That includes getting rest. If you're having trouble sleeping, we shall send for Dr. Radcliffe and have him give you a sleeping draught."

Lucian paused in raising his glass to his lips long enough to grant her a dark scowl, then drained the entire contents in one swallow. Ignoring her cluck of disapproval, he tossed his empty glass to his desk and lifted the decanter to refill it.

"Please, Luc," she implored, laying her hand over his to stop him. "At the very least let me have Tidswell help you up to bed. You look on the verge of collapse."

"No."

"Lucian—"

"I said no." He slammed the decanter back to the desk with a decisive bang.

She countered with an exasperated grunt. "And I say yes. I will not stand by and watch you destroy yourself for another moment. If you refuse to go to bed willingly, then I shall order the footmen to carry you there. And if you won't drink the surgeon's sleeping draught, I shall pour it down your throat myself." She paused a beat to sweep him with an assessing gaze. "In your present condition, I doubt you'll be able to put up much of a fight."

By the outrage on his face, she expected him to pick up her gauntlet and accept her challenge. She fervently hoped he would. At least then she'd know that his spirit hadn't been completely crushed.

As with her hopes for Alys, her ones for Lucian seemed doomed when in the next instant he uttered a tormented groan and buried his face in his palms. "How I wish it were so simple, that all I need do to find rest is lie in my bed and drink a draught."

"But it is! Dr. Radcliffe gave me a draught just last month that made me sleep like a baby."

He shook his head, his face still pressed into his hands. "His draught might be able to make me sleep, but it cannot bring me rest. How can it when every time I close my eyes I see Alys as she looked that last night? She was so terrified—terrified of me—of my monstrous lust. And she was crying." He shuddered violently. "I made her cry."

"Lucian, don't. Not again," Charlotte pleaded, laying a comforting hand on his shoulder.

But he kept on as if she weren't there. "Dear God! How could I have treated her so . . . groping and slobbering over her like she were some half-crown Covent Garden whore? No wonder she ran away as she did."

He dropped his hands from his face then. "Damn my lust!" he raged, savagely slamming his fist against the desk. "Damn it for driving me to molest her!" *Slam! Slam!* "If I thought it would restore her trust in me, I'd cut off my cursed manhood and offer it to her on a silver platter!" *Slam!*

"I hardly think such extreme measures will be necessary," Charlotte soothed, reaching down to still his fist as he raised it to strike again. "An apology and a marriage proposal should settle matters well enough, especially if you promise to take the physical side of love more slowly in the future."

He yanked his hand from her grip. "You might be correct if it truly was fear that drove her from me."

Charlotte blinked in surprise. "From what you've told me, I cannot imagine what else it could have been."

"Perhaps she was repulsed by my lovemaking. Perhaps she found it so distasteful that she would rather face the dangers of the streets than chance being forced to marry me. I did compromise her, you know."

"Oh, no, Lucian! No!" she exclaimed, hating the self-loathing in his voice. "By the way her face lit up every time she saw you, I'm certain that she found your kisses anything but repulsive. Indeed, I wouldn't be a bit surprised to learn that she liked them too much, and that she fled as much from fear of her own desire as from yours. Don't forget that she spent the last few years at a religious school. No doubt she was taught that she would go straight to hell for feeling the kind of passion she felt for you."

Lucian shook his head. "If that were so, she would have sought some sort of absolution from a member of the clergy, most probably from one of her instructors at Wickington. And I know for a fact that she didn't return there. One of the Runners reported as much yesterday morning."

Charlotte made a helpless little hand gesture. "Well, she might turn up there yet."

His expression grew bleaker, if such a thing were possible. "The Runner said that if she was going to go there, or to any of the other dozens of places we've looked, that she would have done so by now. At this point, he's of the opinion"—he closed his eyes and swallowed hard, forcing out with obvious effort—"that she's fallen into criminal hands."

"No. Oh, no! I refuse to believe such a terrible thing," she protested, shaking her head over and over again. "Alys is a sensible girl. She wouldn't stray off into the dangerous parts of London."

"She's an innocent child, one whom I drove out into the streets," he flung back savagely. "And you know as well as I that a beautiful and virginal girl like Alys doesn't have to stray anywhere to find danger in London. It's always there, lurking, ready to snatch her up the instant she steps outside the door unprotected."

"But if she's been abducted, surely whoever has her would have come forward by now to claim the reward? Lovely though she is, I doubt if even selling her to a brothel would bring the kind of money you're offering for her return."

"True," he agreed grimly. "Which makes me fear that perhaps they cannot return her."

Charlotte stared at him in horror. Though he was merely voicing that which lurked at the edges of her own mind, it was nonetheless shocking to hear. Feeling the tears she'd fought so hard to repress well up in her eyes, she choked, "You don't honestly think that she might be—"

He raised his hand to halt her from uttering the ghastly word. "What else am I to believe?"

"How is Lucian?" Alys exclaimed, bolting from the straw pallet where she'd lain brooding for the past days. Or had it been weeks? She could never be certain for unlike most things in the otherworld, time down here bore no parallel to that of the human world. As erratic as it was, it was even possible that she had lain there mere minutes.

"Hedley, please. Tell me of Lucian," she implored, dropping to her knees before the hob. This was the first time she'd seen him since being transported back to the otherworld, and she was desperate for news of the man she loved.

He regarded her somberly for a moment, then made a gobbling sound and dropped his gaze to his feet, shaking his head as he did so.

"You're not . . . not telling me that . . . ? No! It . . . it can't be over! It can't!" she exclaimed, her voice stumbling on her rising panic. "Oh, please. Please tell me that he's not lost!"

"Nay. Not yet," he muttered, "but he will be tomorrow at midnight."

"Tomorrow? Then today is the twenty-third of June?" she gasped, beset with a terrible sinking sensation. It crashed to the pit of her stomach at his nod. Only one day left, and still no word from Allura. One day. Even if Allura did find something in the scrolls, at this point it was probably too late to put the knowledge to use.

Her heart, sustained these past weeks by hope, seemed to crumble in her chest. "Oh, Hedley," she whispered, tears flooding her eyes. "He's doomed, and it's all my fault. If I'd spent more time matching him to Diana and less time daydreaming about his love, he would be safe now."

"Ye could've tried twice as hard and it wouldn't have done a spit o' good. Seems that Diana Ramsey ain't his true love after all."

Alys frowned, sniffling from her unshed tears as she did so. "What makes you say that?"

"As much time as she's spent with him since he's been back at Thistlewood, they'd be billing and cooing by now if she was." He sighed mournfully. "Nay. She's gone and gotten all moony-eyed over that Lord Horsey-Horse. They're to get buckled at the end of summer."

"Lord Horsey-Horse?" Her frown deepened. "Horsey-Horse? Oh! Do you mean Stephen Randolph, Lord *Marchland*?"

"Lord Marchland. Lord Horsey-Horse." He shrugged. "Don't see how it bloody damn matters."

"But how could such a thing have happened? I

mean"—she gestured her bewilderment—"she and Lucian get on so well, I was certain they were meant to be together."

He shrugged again. "They still get on good. Well, at least they did 'fore he stopped talking. Now she cries all over Horsey-Horse's shirt every time she sees him."

"What? What do you mean he's stopped talking?" she ejected, taken aback by his words.

"Like I said, he don't talk no more. Sometimes he don't even blink. He just lays like a lump o' clay in the west tower, staring up at the ceiling."

Alys gasped, horrified by the dreadful picture he painted. "Are you telling me that he's ill?"

"Course he's ill," he retorted, eyeing her as if she'd just asked the world's stupidest question. "He's dying, ain't he?"

"But how can that be? I mean—" She shook her head as if by denying his words she could render them false. "I've always heard that when a fairy's essence expires that he simply ceases to be, without pain or illness."

"Ye seem to be forgetting that Tight-Arse is made of flesh and blood, and that the fairy part of him is cleaved to a nearly complete mortal soul. That makes him almost all human. And it's human nature to suffer in the wake of death. Don't ye remember how much Lucan suffered in dying?"

Anguish, raw and savage, clawed at her heart at the reminder of Lucan's torment. That Lucian too might be suffering such unspeakable pain was more than she could bear. "Hedley, please," she begged, her banking tears at last spilling from her eyes. "Please, tell me that he's not suffering as terribly as Lucan did."

To Alys's surprise, the hob reached out and laid his tiny gnarled hand on top of hers, as if to comfort her. "His body don't seem to hurt him, not bad like Lucan's did him. It's just getting weak and stopping to work. Everyone's saying that it's because ye broke his heart, and they think they can coax him into getting better."

He made a face showing what he thought of their ignorance. "Course, ye and I know they can coax till they're blue and that it won't do no bloody damn good. Not unless they can find his true love and toss her into bed with him." He gave her a wink that was nothing short of lascivious. "Bet she could coax him back to life quick enough."

Alys sniffled and wiped her wet cheeks with the back of her hand. "If he's as ill as you say, I doubt he's up to the sort of activity you're suggesting."

"A bit of billing and cooing, and he'd be up to it in no time." He cackled at his own double entendre.

She glared her reproach through tear-swollen eyes. "How can you jest at a time like this, especially in such a tasteless manner?"

He looked as wounded as she felt. "Who's jesting? It worked for Esmund and Mertice, ye know."

"Esmund and Mertice?" she echoed blankly.

"Ain't no one told ye that story?"

She thought for a moment, then shook her head.

"Would've thought Aengus or Allura would've told ye about 'em," he grumbled. "Oh, well. Guess I'll tell ye then." Muttering something about having to do everything himself, he hopped up onto her lap. Lounging across her knees as if they were a particularly comfortable sofa, he recounted, "Esmund were a half-fairy fellow that lived, oh, more 'n a thousand years ago. I think"—he frowned—"I think he were the son of Aengus's great-uncle, Rinan, and some Celtic princess." He considered for a beat, then nodded. "Yea. Rinan. Anyhow, this Esmund fellow ended up in the same fix Tight-Arse is in now. Seems he couldn't find his true love either."

"You mean that this has happened before?" Alys exclaimed, hardly daring to believe her ears.

He made a rude noise. "I just said it did, dinna I?"

"And was Esmund saved?"

"I'll tell ye if ye'll shut yer trap long enough to let me finish." When she'd remained silent for several moments, he continued.

"It so happened that his true love, Mertice, were a peasant maid who worked in the manor kitchen. Like Tight-Arse, he were a high-and-mighty muckity-muck who never noticed no one below his station. Mertice, though, noticed him right off and loved him from afar for years. Course she were distressed when he sickened unto death."

"Did he sicken in the same manner as Lucian?" she cut in.

He nodded. " 'Tis said that he lay like a lump o' clay in front of the great hall fire, wasting away. Anyhow, late on the night he were to die, she were sent to the hall to stoke the fire. While she were tossing the fagots onto the hearth, she noticed that Esmund was shivering like he were freezing. Being that she loved him and all, she slipped beneath his blankets to warm him." He paused to cackle. "The muckity-muck didn't have no choice but to notice her then. After that, destiny took over. And when Rinan appeared the next dawn to mourn his dead son, he found him humping Mertice, as hale and hearty as a man could be."

"He recovered so quickly?" Alys murmured in wonder.

"Just said he did, dinna I? Same'd happen to Tight-Arse if his true love was to pop up and give him a tumble."

"Ah! Hedley. Good. You're here. We might need your help."

Alys jumped to her feet at the sound of Allura's voice, ignoring Hedley's squawk of protest as he was tossed to the floor. "What news? Did you find anything in the scrolls?" she cried, rushing across the cell to where the fairy stood.

Allura regarded her gravely for a moment, then slowly inclined her head to the affirmative. "I found something, yes, though I can't promise that it will save Lucian Warre."

"But there is a chance?"

"A slight one, very slight you must understand."

"Even if the odds are"— she gave her hands a dramatic flourish for emphasis—"a million to one against us, we must try."

"You must try," the fairy reminded her. "And you might not be so eager to do so once you hear what is involved."

"I shall do it, no matter what is required," she declared, raising her chin and squaring her shoulders in a show of determination.

"Even if the requirement is that you sacrifice yourself?"

"Even that," she vowed, her gaze unflinching as she met Allura's intense stare. "I truly mean it when I say that I love Lucian. And because I love him so, there is nothing I wouldn't sacrifice to keep him safe. Nothing. Not even myself."

The fairy smiled then, sadly, but with a pride that Alys had never thought to see. "After all these centuries, you've finally learned the meaning of love," she murmured.

The corners of Alys's lips curled faintly in return. "Yes, it seems I have. And I now know the answer Aengus sought when he asked me what my matchmaking experience had taught me of love."

"Gibber-jabber! Bibble-babble! Ye gonna tell us what we're supposed to do to save Tight-Arse?" Hedley interrupted, scampering across the room and hopping up onto the only chair, a rough, rickety affair with one leg shorter than the others.

Allura shook her head, her gaze never wavering from Alys's. "No. I'm going to tell Alys what I found in the scrolls and let her decide what action to take. I can only give her knowledge, I cannot advise her."

"I know that, and I am ready to hear what you've discovered," she replied, ignoring Hedley's less than flattering mutterings about her mental abilities. "Please begin."

The fairy nodded. "The first thing I learned is that all humans have only one destined true love, no matter how many lives they live."

"You mean that mortals don't go straight to heaven or hell when they die?" she gasped, taken aback by the fairy's revelation.

"Oh, no. Most haven't accumulated enough good or bad deeds to qualify for either place after just one lifetime. It usually takes several. That being as it is, true lovers are reborn over and over again, and in most instances are reunited in every life. True love means love for eternity."

Hedley emitted an exaggerated yawn. "That's all fine and jolly, but I don't see what it's got to do with Tight-Arse and his problem."

"If what I suspect is true, it has everything to do with it," Allura countered, her gaze still boring into Alys's. "You see, I have good reason to believe that Lucian Warre has been unable to find his true love because she wasn't reborn with him."

"Not reborn?" Alys frowned. "I don't understand."

"Apparently neither did Aengus. If he had, he might have stopped to consider the possibility that you might be his son's true love before taking you captive."

"Me?" Alys mouthed, pointing to herself in mute surprise.

"Yes, you. It makes perfect sense when you think about it. It would certainly explain why it took Lucan's half soul so long to be reborn."

"It would?" she croaked, still too stunned to see logic in anything.

Allura nodded. "Of course. God was no doubt waiting for Aengus to come to his senses and release you to the earth, so that you might die a human death and be reborn with Lucan. When Aengus failed to do so after all these centuries, He was left with no choice but to return Lucan's half soul to earth, though He knew it was most probably doomed."

"But if Aengus had released me and I were reborn as you say, how would I have known that I was to mend Lucan's chain of destiny?" she asked, growing more bewildered by the second.

"You wouldn't have needed to know. All that is required for you to mend it is to provide him with the true love your selfishness deprived him of in his first life. By loving him in this life as you failed to do in his last, you would have spontaneously done so."

"I do truly love him in this life," Alys whispered, though she knew that it counted for naught under the circumstances.

"I know," Allura commiserated. "And if your mortal state weren't compromised by Aengus's spell, he would no doubt be saved by now."

The sinking sensation Alys had experienced earlier re-

turned with a vengeance. "But it is compromised, and—"
She broke off abruptly, tears of impotent frustration
spilling down her cheeks as she did so. "Oh! What's the
use in even discussing this? The whole situation is
impossible."

"I said there is a chance, didn't I?" Allura calmly
reminded her.

She cast the fairy an incredulous look, sniffling on her
tears as she did so. "Unless you've found a way to break
Aengus's spell and return me to my mortal state, I don't
see that there's any hope of saving him."

"No, unfortunately the scrolls were of no help in regards to the spell. But"—she held up her hand to silence
Alys as she opened her mouth to interrupt—"I did confirm something I have long suspected: if a human is able
to escape the otherworld before he completely loses his
soul, he again becomes mortal. It is true, however, that
without his physical form being restored by his fairy cap-
tor, his body will deteriorate to whatever its present
state would be. You, of course, would turn to dust at
dawn."

Alys's heart seemed to still in her chest as she finally
saw the chance the fairy had hinted at. "If I was to
escape and spend those mortal hours before dawn loving
Lucian, I would save both his life and soul."

"If you really are his destined true love, yes. If I'm
wrong and you're not, well"—she shook her head
gravely—"then you would have sacrificed yourself for
nothing."

"Not for nothing," Alys quietly corrected her. "For
Lucian. And I cannot think of anyone or anything more
worth such a sacrifice. Besides, what am I really losing?
Just centuries of misery in the otherworld."

"You could be forfeiting a chance at being properly
restored to the earth. An excellent one, I might add."

Alys stared at the fairy as if she'd lost her mind. "Aengus isn't going to release me. Not after the dismal way
I failed Lucian. You know that as well as I."

Allura shook her head. "Don't you see? If what I
suspect is true, you didn't fail him, Aengus did. When I
tell him what I've told you, he'll no doubt blame himself
for his son's loss and release you back to the mortal

world. You shall again be Alys Faire, darling of the ton, free to live the rest of your life as you choose."

"But it will be a life without Lucian," she whispered, tormented by the very thought.

"True. It would be too late to save him," the fairy grimly agreed. "Which means you must decide which life to chance saving: his or yours?"

Chapter 19

"I'll be leaving ye now," Hedley muttered, coming to a stop before the moat bridge.

Alys halted as well, gazing wistfully down at the hob as she did so. He stood as she'd seen him stand a hundred times before, with his head bowed and shoulders squared, kicking at the dirt road as if offended by its very presence. Though he tried to hide his feelings behind a mask of indifference, it was clear by the gruffness of his voice that he found this moment every bit as difficult as she did.

And it was difficult, for despite the fact that neither had expressed as much in words, over the weeks they had become friends. Good friends.

Her eyes stinging with the threat of tears, Alys crouched down before him, resolved to confess her feelings before death and destiny parted them forever. Not quite certain what to say, knowing only that she must somehow tell him of her fondness, she reached out and lay her fingertips on his small hunched shoulder.

"Hedley?" she murmured, wishing that he would look at her. He'd barely spared her a glance since leaving the otherworld. By the way he continued to stare at the growing pile of dirt at his feet, it appeared that he wasn't inclined to do so now either.

She sighed inwardly. Ah, well. As long as he listened to her, what did it matter? Swallowing hard to ease the aching tightness of her throat, she said, "No matter where I go, should it be to heaven or hell, or walking the earth as a ghost, I believe that I shall always miss you, Hedley. You've been a good friend to me these past weeks . . . the best! . . . and I want you to know that I love you."

"Ye love me?" He emitted what was no doubt supposed to be a snort, but instead came out sounding suspiciously like a sniffle. "Yer daft, woman! I ain't never done nothing to make ye love me. Well, nothing but help ye escape from the otherworld, and that ain't nothing to get all drippy over."

She smiled faintly at his halfhearted protest. "The love between friends isn't created or demonstrated by grand gestures or deeds. It's built slowly with tolerance, understanding, and acceptance, and proven by small acts of kindness. During the past weeks, you've given me all of that and more. So how can you possibly say that you've done nothing to win my love?"

He kicked at the road so hard that the resulting spray of dirt splattered her white muslin skirt. For a brief instant he stood gaping at the mess as if it were the world's worst tragedy, then darted forward to brush at it, cursing over and over again, "Oh, bloody, stinking damn! Bloody, stinking damn!"

"Shh, Hedley. It's all right. Leave it be," she said, laying two fingers over his hand to still its frantic motion. "These are our last few moments together, and I wish to spend them bidding each other farewell."

He scowled and slapped her restraining fingers away. "Don't wanna say frigging farewell," he growled, the word farewell punctuated by an unmistakable sob.

Had he been of human size, she'd have drawn him into her embrace then and soothed his obvious distress with a hug. Instead she had to satisfy her urge by lightly stroking his hair and back. "Oh, Hedley! Please don't be sad," she begged, stricken to feel his shoulders heaving beneath her touch. "Be happy. I am. My greatest wish is to love Lucian, and I'm going to get to do so for the next few hours."

"Then go!" he snarled, jerking away from her touch. "Go love yer blasted Lord Tight-Arse and leave me be!

I ain't sad, and I don't care if ye turn to dust." He stamped his foot. "Do ye hear me? I don't care!"

"Hedley, please—" she implored, reaching for him again.

Again he slapped her away. "Are ye deaf or just stupid? I said go! I'm sick to death of ye and yer dratted yackety-yammering. Yer nothing but a bloody nuisance and I can't wait to get rid of ye!"

Alys opened her mouth to reason with him, only to close it again in the next instant, softly sighing her defeat. What was the use? Once he was in one of his pets, only time could coax him out of it, and time was the one thing she couldn't give him.

Though she hated leaving him so, she saw no choice but to whisper, "Farewell, my dear friend. I love you, and pray that by some miracle we shall meet again." With that, she rose to her feet, aching at how badly they were parting.

As she turned away, she heard, "Alys." The word was more choked than uttered.

She paused.

"I love you too," he sobbed.

With a sob that echoed his, she spun back around and fell to her knees, holding out her arms as she did so. For several seconds he stood staring at her, tears tracking down his ruddy cheeks, then he practically flew up onto her lap. Burying his face into the folds of her skirt, he wept in earnest, his whole body trembling and jerking with the violence of his grief. Her own cheeks damp with shared sorrow, Alys stroked his back, murmuring mindless words of comfort.

When, at last, the fury of his tears had eased, he clumsily hauled himself to his knees and sat back on his heels, gazing up at her with anguish-filled eyes. "I'll pray for ye," he declared, his voice raw with emotion. "I'll pray hard, I promise, though I doubt God'll bother to hear a fairy's prayers."

She smiled down into his tear-streaked face, touched beyond words by his vow. A fairy pray? Unheard of! He must care for her very deeply indeed to do such a thing. Her heart melting with tenderness, she leaned down and pressed a kiss to the side of his head. "God

hears everyone's prayers, even fairies', if they are uttered with true faith," she assured him.

"For ye, I'll find faith." With that, he planted a kiss on
her cheek. "Godspeed, my friend," he whispered, then
vanished into thin air.

Feeling raw and achy inside, Alys rose again, her gaze
sweeping the night-shrouded castle before her as she did
so. It came to rest on the faintly lit window of the west
tower where first Lucan, and now Lucian lay dying.

Lucian. Her love. Her feet couldn't carry her fast
enough to him. Over the bridge she ran, through the
gatehouse and across the courtyard. By the time she
stood pounding at the front door, she was winded to the
point of collapse.

It was Tidswell who answered her frenzied summons.
When he saw who it was, his normally immobile lower
jaw dropped almost to his chest. "My word! It's Miss
Faire! Wherever have you been?" he ejected, looking
shocked enough to faint.

Staggering from exertion, she stumbled past him, impatiently waving aside his questions as she panted out,
"I'll explain . . . *huff!* . . . later. Right now I need to . . .
puff! . . . . see Lucian."

He was by her side in a flash, bracing his arm beneath
hers to steady her. Dutifully suspending his own curiosity, he half towed, half escorted her through the maze
of halls, grimly informing her of Lucian's declining
health as they went. When they at last reached the foot
of the west tower stairs, he pulled her to an abrupt stop.
Taking both her hands in his, he gravely advised her,
"You must prepare yourself for the sight of his lordship,
my dear. I fear that he is much altered by his illness."

All too aware of Lucian's desperate state, she nodded.

He smiled, a gentle, compassionate smile, and touched
her cheek. To her surprise, his fingers came away glistening with tears. She hadn't even realized that she was
weeping.

"There, there now, miss. I'm certain that everything
will be fine," he murmured, pressing his handkerchief
into her hand. "Indeed, I shan't be a bit surprised if his
lordship makes a miraculous recovery once he sees you
safe and sound."

When she'd dried her tears and he'd coaxed a wan smile to her lips, he grasped her shoulders and turned her toward the spiraling staircase. "Now. Upstairs with you, miss. His lordship needs you."

Impulsively, she spun back around again and gave him a fierce hug. "Thank you, Tidswell . . . for everything," she whispered, though in her heart she said good-bye.

He gave her a fond squeeze in return. "And thank you for coming back to us. I do so hope that I shall have the privilege of serving you as Lady Thistlewood in the future."

"There is nothing I would love more," she honestly replied. Giving him one final hug and a peck on his withered cheek, she turned and dashed up the stairs.

The farther she ascended the faster she ran, her need to hold Lucian growing with every step. Tonight he was hers, all hers. Hers to cuddle and kiss; hers to love and caress. He was hers until dawn . . .

But only if she truly was his destined mate.

She shuddered, chilled by a sudden sense of foreboding. What if, despite Allura's belief to the contrary, it turned out that she wasn't the one? How could she bear to watch him die? True, her sorrow would last only a few short hours, for he would die at midnight, and she at dawn. But for her those black hours would seem like a pain-filled eternity, a punishment far worse than any that might await her behind the murky veil of death.

So entrenched was she in her black thoughts that she didn't notice the small figure huddled before Lucian's door until she stumbled over it. "Ow! Blimey gor!" it yelped, rearing up to reveal itself as Bart.

"Bart?" She blinked twice to make sure she was seeing aright. "Whatever are you doing here at this hour?"

He stared at her wildly for several seconds, then let out a hoarse cry and flung himself against the bedchamber door. Dropping into a defensive crouch, with his fists raised and teeth bared, he growled, "No! Ye canna take 'im! I won't let ye! You'll have ta take me first!"

"Take him?" She advanced a step, frowning at his peculiar behavior. "Bart? Whatever are you talking about?"

He snarled like a cornered wolf. "Ye know bleedin' well wot I'm sayin'. Yer here ta snatch 'is lordship's soul and carry it off to the land o' the dead."

His words took her completely aback. Her, an emissary of death? Wherever had he gotten such a morbid notion? Thinking that perhaps he couldn't see her clearly for the shadows, she moved to stand beneath the blazing wall sconce next to the door. "There now. See?" she said, gracing him with her brightest smile. "It's me. Alys."

"I know who ye are, and ye're dead," he flung back. "Everyone's sayin' so. Yer a ghost, that's wot ye are. A ghost who's come ta take his lordship away."

"Dead?" She gaped at him, utterly flabbergasted by his words. For all of Tidswell's chatter about the events of the past weeks, he'd said nothing about everyone assuming her dead. Shaking her head over and over again in denial of that hideous rumor, she dropped to her knees before him, exclaiming, "No! Oh, no, Bart! I'm alive . . . as alive as you are."

When he merely shrank more protectively against the door, eyeing her as if she were the devil incarnate, she held out her upturned hand to him. "Here. If you won't believe my words, touch me and see for yourself."

"Oh, no. I ain't fallin' fer that trick," he retorted, his voice shrill with bravado. "Everyone knows that if ye touch a ghost, ye'll die on the spot."

She returned his fearful gaze solemnly. "True. Just as everyone knows that it's that particular ghost that must carry you away. Now if I truly am a spirit and you touch me, I shall be forced to take you in Lord Thistlewood's stead, thus sparing his life. If I'm truly flesh and blood, as I claim to be, then you shall be no worse off. Either way, his lordship will be safe."

The boy seemed to consider her argument, his wary gaze darting back and forth between her face and hand as he did so. After several tense moments, he screwed his eyes shut and reached for her.

Touched by his heroic devotion to Lucian, she moved her hand to where he was blindly groping the air, holding stock-still as his palm butted against hers. For a brief instant he prodded it, his face contorted into a mask of dread, then his eyes popped back open again and a broad grin split his face.

"Gor blimey!" he exclaimed, throwing his arms around her. " 'Tis really and truly ye! Yer alive!"

She nodded and folded him into her embrace. "Yes. And I'm here not to take his lordship away, but to help him get well."

His small face darkened again, as abruptly as it had lightened. "Ye can't help 'im. No one can. I 'eard the leech tellin' Lady Lottie so this afternoon. 'E said that 'is lordship is done fer, and that it'll be a miracle if 'e lasts out the night."

"Well, miracles happen every day. And if anyone has the power to bring about one, it's his lordship," she declared, her voice ringing with a conviction she didn't feel.

Bart regarded her dubiously. " 'E does?"

"He made a miraculous change in your life when he rescued you, didn't he?"

He pondered her words for a beat, then nodded.

"And it is the miracle of his love that has brought me back to Thistlewood." She smiled down into his pensive little face. "So you see? His lordship truly is a miracle worker." She was about to add more when the massive door behind them creaked open.

"Bart, I need you to run—" Charlotte broke off with a gasp when she caught sight of Alys. "Dear God! Can it be true? Is it really you, Alys?" she cried, collapsing to her knees in her shock.

Alys gave Bart one last squeeze, then crawled over to where Charlotte sat slumped against the doorjamb, gaping at her in stunned disbelief. Lifting her limp hands to clasp them in her own, she murmured, "Yes, Lottie. It really is me."

Charlotte stared at her, unblinking, for several seconds more, then her face crumpled with tears and she snatched her hands away. "You wicked, thoughtless girl! Wherever have you been?" she sobbed, seizing Alys's arms to give her a furious shake. "Why didn't you send word that you were all right? Didn't it ever occur to you that we might worry?" She gave Alys another shake, this one so hard that her teeth clattered. "And what about Luc? He loves you, you know. Did you ever stop

to think about him . . . about how your foolish prank
might hurt him? Damn it, Alys!" She shook her yet
again. "He was devastated when he discovered you
gone. Do you hear me? Devastated! He refused to eat
or sleep, searching for you day and night until he—
he . . ." A sob splintered her voice then and her hands
fell heavily back to her sides.

"Lottie—" Alys began, her heart aching at the other
woman's anguish.

"He's ill! Oh, Alys. Luc is so terribly ill. The surgeon
says that—that—" Charlotte shook her head, her un-
checked tears dripping from her pale cheeks to her ging-
ham frock as she did so.

"Ssh. Lucian will be fine. He's a strong man, he'll pull
through. I'm certain of it," she crooned, drawing Charlotte into her embrace to comfort her.

The other woman stiffened, and for a moment Alys
thought she would pull away. Then she emitted a hoarse
cry and flung her arms around her in return, crushing
her to her with a violence that left her breathless. Burying her wet face against Alys's shoulder, she choked out,
"You wouldn't say that if you'd seen him. He's in a
wretched state. If I didn't know better, I would think by
looking at him that he was already—"

"No!" Alys practically shouted the word. "No," she
repeated, this time more softly. "Lucian will not die. I
won't let him."

"If he were merely suffering from a broken heart, like
we first suspected, you might be able to help him. But
this—this—" Another sob escaped her, one that sounded
as if it were being ripped from the bottom of her soul.
"The surgeon says that there's something wrong inside
him, something that . . . that's eating away his life. He's
bled him, purged him, dosed him . . . even applied
leeches, but nothing seems to help. Luc just keeps getting weaker and weaker."

Alys glanced at Bart to assure herself that he was out
of earshot, then whispered, "But has he tried magic?"

"Magic?" Charlotte lifted her head to stare at her in
bewilderment.

Alys pulled back a fraction and nodded meaningfully
at her friend's swollen belly. "Yes. Magic."

Charlotte followed her gaze with her own, a look of tenderness passing over her face as she peered down at where her child grew. Laying a loving hand over the slight protuberance, she glanced back up at Alys, her eyes filled with a heartbreaking mixture of hope and wonder. "Oh, Alys. Do you really know a spell that might save him?"

"Perhaps. But before I try it, you must first agree to one condition."

"Anything! Just tell me what to do."

Alys smiled faintly at the eagerness in her voice. "You must leave me alone with Lucian until dawn, and make certain that we're not disturbed before then."

"Done."

Though she hated to do so, Alys felt compelled to caveat, "You must understand that this spell is only a chance. I'll do my best, but I can't promise that it will work."

It was Charlotte's turn to smile. "Spell or no spell, I believe that just having you by his side again will be magic enough to save him. Luc truly does love you, you know."

"I know, and I truly love him in return." With that, she gave Charlotte a fierce hug and kiss. "I love you too, Lottie, as the dearest of sisters," she added, commanding herself not to weep as she uttered that final farewell. Charlotte hugged and kissed her back, then they stood in unison.

Moving over to Bart, who sat a few feet away, sniffling and muttering to himself, Lottie offered him her hand, bidding, "Come along now, Bart. It's time for bed."

"Can't go nowhere," he muttered, wiping his tear-streaked face with his sleeve. "I 'ave to stay and save 'is lordship from the bleedin' ghost o' death."

"*H*ave and *h*is, and you know better than to say bleeding," Charlotte said, gently correcting him.

"*H*ave and *h*is." He gave her a sheepish grin. "Sorry. I keep forgetting me—myself in my worry over *h*is lordship."

She reached down and affectionately ruffled his already tousled hair. "No doubt your forgetfulness is due as much to fatigue as to worry. You've barely slept since his lordship has been ill.''

"Well, somebody has to stay awake and guard him against the ghost,'' he informed her, squinting into the shadows as if he expected his nemesis to emerge at any moment.

"And tonight that somebody shall be Alys,'' she countered in a no-nonsense tone. "Now come along. It's eleven o'clock. Long past both our bedtimes.''

"Eleven?'' Alys echoed in dismay. That meant that she only had an hour to save Lucian.

Both Bart and Charlotte turned to peer at her in query.

She smiled wanly. "I hadn't realized it was so late. Seeing as it is, I shall bid you both a good night.'' With that, she backed into the tower room and closed the door.

Chapter 20

For a long moment Alys stood staring at the ornately carved door, preparing herself for the sight of Lucian. Then she forced herself to turn and gaze into the chamber.

As it had been when Lucan had occupied it, it was elegantly decorated. That, however, was the sum of the similarity between this room and the one that lived so vividly in her memory.

While Lucan had favored his heraldic colors of green and gold, liberally utilizing both in the wall hangings, bedding, and floor tiles, Lucian had selected soothing shades of cream and wine. As dictated by the simplicity of his time, Lucan's chamber had been sparsely furnished, the space dominated by an imposing canopied bed. Lucian's held a half-dozen well-selected pieces, the most prominently displayed being an ivory and gilt harpsichord. His bed, a low, square affair tented in cream, wine, and gold striped damask, was unceremoniously relegated to the far wall.

It was to that bed that her gaze was drawn. Though the side curtains were tied back and the nearby wall sconce lit, the figure within remained obscured by shadows.

"Lucian?" she called out, hurrying across the room.

No response. Not so much as a rustling of sheets.

"It's me, love. Alys. I've—" She broke off with a gasp,

horrified by her first glimpse of the man in the bed. Dear God! Had she arrived too late?

He was pale, terrifyingly so, his face drawn and gleaming with the hideous waxen sheen of a death mask. Though neatly brushed, his once lustrous hair looked dry and lifeless, and when she shoved back the bed curtains to lean in yet farther, the resulting flood of light revealed a threading of silver among the ebony strands at his temples. Most frightening of all, she was unable to detect even the slightest rise and fall of his chest beneath the blankets.

Choking on her panic, she pushed down his high nightshirt collar and laid her fingers against his icy neck, desperately searching for a pulse.

Nothing.

She felt an inch lower. Still nothing—wait! She increased her pressure a fraction. Yes. Yes! It was there. A pulse. It was faint and dangerously slow, but it was there. And as long as a spark of life remained within him, there was a chance that she might save him.

All she had to do to do so was love him.

Her gaze troubled, she stared down at his ashen face, considering what doing so entailed. According to the legend of Esmund and Mertice, she must love him not only with her heart and soul, but with her body as well.

With growing trepidation, she dropped her gaze from his face and skimmed the impressive length of his blanket-draped body. While the heart and soul part of loving him had come to her as naturally as breathing, she was mystified as to how to go about the physical part. For though Lucian had lectured her on the matter that night in the library, his lesson had been a dry dissertation on the mechanics of the act itself with little explanation as to what led up to it. Indeed, all she really knew for certain was that a man must have an erection in order to make love, and for him to get one he must be aroused.

Her bewilderment deepened. How did one arouse a comatose man? She couldn't just lift his nightshirt and fondle him in the intimate manner he'd described when he'd spoken of male release. Why, just the thought of doing so made her face burn with shame. For even if such an act was to produce the desired physical response, it would violate not only his body but his dignity. And the embarrassment that might result on both their parts would more likely than not squash their desire for real lovemaking.

So what was she to do? Frowning, she turned her thoughts from his memorable lesson on the male anatomy to his sequential admonitions against the seductive machinations of rogues.

Seduction? Her eyes narrowed thoughtfully. What was it he'd said on the subject? Hmm. She'd been so . . . um . . . disturbed by his first lesson that she'd barely listened to his second one. After much reflection, she vaguely recalled something about flattery, silver-tongued declarations of love, and stolen kisses.

While she doubted if the first two would have much impact on him in his present state, the idea of kisses held definite promise. For not only were they a physical expression of love, she knew from when they'd kissed in the kitchen that they incited Lucian's passion. Whether they would have the power to penetrate his unconsciousness, she didn't know. All she knew was that she had to try.

Thus resolved, she cupped his cheek in her hand and almost reverently pressed a kiss to his cracked lips.

No response.

Disappointed yet not discouraged, she repeated the kiss, this time slipping her tongue between his lips to stroke the parched inner lining.

Still nothing.

Or was there? She paused, her mouth still molded to his. Yes. There it was again. A definite puff of breath on her cheek. Pulling back a fraction, she stole a glance down at his chest. The covers stirred faintly.

Praying that her eyes didn't deceive her, she pushed the heavy pile of blankets to his waist and laid her palm against his linen-clad breast. Yes. Oh, yes! She had seen aright. His breathing had strengthened, as had his heartbeat.

Charged by renewed hope, she returned her mouth to his, freely surrendering to her centuries-old desire. Over and over again she kissed him; sometimes soft and sweetly; sometimes with savage demand; always she kissed him with love.

With every passionate nip and brush, his lips grew warmer, more supple. And when her tongue boldly invaded the now moist sanctum of his mouth, he let out a breath so explosive that it could easily have passed for a sigh.

Thrilling at his encouraging response, she straddled his blanket-swathed hips and pulled him into her embrace. The instant she did, he began to shiver.

At first it was a slight, almost imperceptible trembling, as if he were possessed by a sudden chill. Then it deepened, growing more and more violent until he shuddered with a fury that terrified her. It was as if he were freezing, though the room was warm to the point of being stifling.

At a loss as to how to ease him, she instinctively crushed her body nearer, blanketing him as best she could with her small form. But it was to no avail. If anything, his shaking grew more intense.

"My poor, poor love. However am I to help you?" she crooned, though, of course, she expected no answer.

To her astonishment, she got one. Well, perhaps not precisely an answer, but the way he molded his body to hers at her query reminded her of how Mertice had eased Esmund's tremors: she'd climbed beneath his blankets and warmed his flesh with hers. According to Hedley, the results had been miraculous.

Alys felt herself flush as she contemplated following suit. In order to do so, she must remove all of their clothing and lie with her bare skin pressed against his. Had she the courage to do something so bold?

Oh, it wasn't that she was afraid of being naked with an equally nude Lucian in her arms. Quite the contrary. There was nothing she desired more. It was just that she was shy about doing so without some sort of invitation from him.

An invitation? She grunted at her own absurdity. In his present state there was as much chance of him issuing an invitation as there was of her surviving the sunrise. That being as it was . . .

With a sigh of resignation, she rose from the bed.

Turning her back modestly if pointlessly to the insentient Lucian, she began to divest herself of her clothes. Piece by piece she undressed, praying as each article fell to the floor for the strength to remove the next. When the last one finally lay at her feet, she sucked her bottom lip between her teeth and turned back to the bed. Now to disrobe Lucian.

Her hands trembling, she began to unbutton his nightshirt. Twice as she worked he rolled over onto his side, his shivering body straining toward hers. Both times she was forced to pause and wrestle him back into a supine position so she could continue.

When, at last, the garment was undone, she reached beneath the blankets at his waist and blindly worked it up over his hips, taking care not to expose his private parts as she did so. To her relief the business of undressing him went far smoother than she'd anticipated. Indeed, the only real difficulty she encountered was extricating his arms from his sleeves. When that battle was won and she'd tossed the nightshirt to the foot of the bed, she took her first real look at his torso.

Like his face, his body was far too thin. Distressingly so. Though his frame was as perfectly formed as she remembered, broad-shouldered with a trim, tapering waist, only the sinewy muscle beneath his almost translucent skin saved it from being skeletal. Seeing a man as strong and vibrant as Lucian reduced to such a pitiful state made her long to weep.

So filled with compassion was she that she quite forgot her maidenly reserve as she slipped beneath the blankets and drew him into her embrace. The instant their flesh touched, he melted against her, a choked sob issuing from his throat as he twined his long body around her small one.

Gently stroking his shuddering back, she crooned, "Everything will be fine now, love. I'm here. I'll take care of you."

He sobbed again and wriggled yet nearer.

For a long while they remained like that; she, whispering words of love and comfort as she desperately sought to ease his soul-deep chill; he, straining against her, instinctively accepting her offering of solace and warmth.

By degrees his shaking abated, and by the time the clock
on the dressing table chimed half past eleven, they had
ceased altogether.

Half past eleven? Panic jolted Alys. That meant that
she only had a half hour to wake him, arouse him, and
make love to him. Dear Lord! However was she to do so
much in so little time? Especially when he didn't appear
anywhere near regaining consciousness?

On the verge of hysteria now, she lifted his face from
where it lay cradled against her throat and covered it
with frantic kisses. "Come on now, Lucian. Open your
eyes and look at me, love. It's me, Alys," she coaxed,
lightly pressing her lips first to one eyelid, then the other.
As she did so, she could have sworn she felt his lashes
flutter.

Her breath catching in her throat, she kissed them
again. Yes. Yes! There was a definite rolling motion beneath his lids. Softly yet insistently, she slapped his
cheeks. "Open your eyes, Lucian. Come on now. Open
your eyes and look at me."

"Alys?" his lips silently formed, though his eyes remained closed.

Her slapping gentled to a caress. "Yes, love. It's me."

His lips moved again. This time he managed to croak,
"Can't be Alys. Alys is . . ." his mouth worked soundlessly for several seconds, then he more moaned than
uttered, "dead."

"Oh, no. No! I'm alive . . . as alive as you are. See?"
She gave him a fierce hug.

"Warm," he murmured hoarsely. "Warm and soft . . .
like Alys." He opened his legs and captured her body
between them, nuzzling his face against her throat as he
did so. "You smell like Alys too . . . sweet . . . like Lily
of the Valley."

"That's because I am Alys."

He shook his head. "You must be an angel. Alys
wouldn't be in my bed, not naked. She's"—a shadow of
pain passed over his face—"afraid of my lust."

"I'm in your bed because you were shivering and
nothing else I did would warm you," she explained in a
logical tone. "As for my being afraid of you, well, if
you'd just look at me, you'd . . . uh . . ." He shifted and

she was disconcerted to feel his male flesh loll against her belly. Even in its flaccid state, its size was impressive. "Uh . . ." What was she saying? Oh, yes. "If you'd look at me, you'd see that I truly am Alys Faire and that I'm not the slightest bit afraid of you." When he hesitated, she kissed the top of his head, cajoling, "Please?"

With visible reluctance, he slowly lifted his head and did as she directed. For a long moment he stared at her, as if he didn't quite believe what he was seeing. Then he groaned and crushed his lips to hers, claiming her mouth with a hunger that was almost painful in its voracity.

"Alys. My poppet. It really is you," he groaned between kisses. "I thought I'd lost you forever."

"Can you ever forgive me for leaving as I did? For hurting you so?" she cried, her heart breaking at the anguish in his voice. "I—"

"You fled because I attacked you like a rutting beast." Sighing, he rested his forehead against hers, closing his eyes as he did so. "Ah, Alys. Don't you see that it is I who must beg your forgiveness? I knew you were innocent, yet I pawed and slavered over you like you were a common trollop. Worse." A grim smile touched his lips. "Never, not even in the eagerness of youth, have I been guilty of mauling a woman the way I did you. My behavior was atrocious. Indefensible. And though I know it doesn't excuse what I did, I—"

"I liked your lust," she interjected shyly.

He drew back a fraction, gazing at her in wonder. "Pardon?"

She felt her cheeks color as she repeated, "I said that I liked your lust."

"You did?" He couldn't have looked more astonished if she'd confessed to being five hundred years old.

She nodded. "Too much. That's why I ran away. I was frightened not of your lust, but of my own." Hedley had told her to say that. What she said next, however, came straight from her heart. "You see, Lucian, I never knew it was possible to feel such passion for a man."

"And I never thought it possible to adore a woman as much as I adore you, my dearest Miss Faire," he countered, crushing her into a possessive embrace. "If you'll have me, miserable, lustful creature that I am, I would like to prove it by marrying you."

Alys gazed into his face, so impossibly handsome with his eyes ablaze with love and his cheeks flushed with joy, and thought how very sweet it would be to wake every morning to see him looking thus.

But, of course, there were no mornings left for her. Wanting to weep at the tragedy of their love, she somehow managed to smile and reply, "There is nothing I desire more than to spend the rest of my life loving you." Speaking of love and life . . .

She peered over his shoulder at the clock on the dressing table, panic welling up inside her again when she saw the time. Only twenty minutes remained.

That called for brazen measures.

Hoping that he wouldn't think her a complete wanton, she added rather timidly, "If you don't mind, I would like to start the loving part now."

Mind making love to her? Lucian gazed into Alys's prettily flushed face, barely able to believe what he was hearing. She must be an angel after all, and this must be heaven. For where but in heaven did all one's dreams come true? And as God knew from his fervent prayers, his most cherished dream was to spend his eternity loving Alys.

And love her he would. Be this heaven or earth, be it for an eternity or just a single hour, he had Alys back in his arms again, and that was all that mattered. Thus resolved, he tipped his head down and eagerly reclaimed her lips with his.

Her mouth was warm and moist, thrilling in its responsiveness. Sometimes she returned his kisses shyly, like the untried maiden she was; sometimes with a boldness that was as surprising as it was stimulating. No matter how she kissed him, the yield was the same: raw, sensual pleasure; pleasure that went beyond any he'd ever experienced before. The impact on his body was swift and violent . . .

. . . so violent and he pulled away abruptly, terrified of losing control and frightening her again.

"Lucian?" she murmured, her eyes slitting open in sultry query.

Mutely he returned her gaze, struck speechless by the provocative picture she made. With her passion-drugged eyes and kiss-swollen lips, she was the very embodiment of the word temptation. The sight of her was more than he could bear. Groaning his torment, he closed his eyes and rolled from her embrace.

"Lucian?" He felt her move on the bed beside him. "Is something wrong?" There was a rustle of linen, then her hand was on his chest, caressing him.

His response was as carnal as if she touched him intimately. "Don't!" he barked, jerking away.

"But why?" Her words were punctuated by bewilderment.

"Because I'm too . . . excited."

There was a beat of silence, then, "I don't understand."

He sighed. "No, of course you don't. How could you? You're a virgin. As such, you have no understanding of the sexual nature of men."

The bed moved again. "No. But I want to understand yours."

"And you shall. I promise. But I must teach it to you slowly."

It was her turn to sigh. "Can't we just follow our desires and let me discover it for myself?"

He smiled faintly at the impatience in her voice. "Unfortunately my desire for you is hard to control. If I give it free rein, I might very well end up mauling you as I did that night in the kitchen. And the last thing I want is for you to grow frightened and flee again."

"Look at me. Do I look frightened to you?" she murmured in husky challenge.

Without thinking, Lucian opened his eyes and glanced at her, an action he instantly regretted. She lounged on her side with her head propped up on her hand, exposing more than a glimpse of her breasts.

Beautiful, flawless breasts, he noted, his stunned gaze riveted on her casually displayed charms. How could he ever have thought her bosom lacking? It was small, true, yet there was something about it that enticed him as his mistresses' more generous ones never had. Indeed, it was all he could do to curtail his urge to gather those dainty globes in his hands and see if they fit as perfectly as he suspected.

"Well?" she purred.

He emitted a strangled groan. "I find that it is I who am frightened . . . frightened at how badly I want you. Dear God, Alys! Do you know how beautiful you are? How very desirable?"

"If you want me, then take me," she whispered, opening her arms to receive him. "Forget your fears as I have mine, and love me."

"Are you certain?" he asked, searching her face for signs of misgiving.

She nodded. "More certain than I've ever been of anything in my life. I know now that it is our destiny to love each other."

One look in her eyes, and he knew she spoke the truth. All his life he'd felt incomplete, as if something inside him were missing. Then he'd met Alys, and through her love had become gloriously whole. It was as if she were an integral part of him and he, her; two hearts bound together by the everlasting chains of fate; each of them created for the sole purpose of loving the other.

Liberated by that knowledge, he dragged her into his embrace and buried his face against her breasts. "Alys. My own true love," he moaned.

She sighed and melted against him. "Yes. And I want to love you as I'm destined to do . . . to give you pleasure. Will you teach me how?"

"There's nothing to teach. Everything about you gives me pleasure. The feel of you . . ." He rubbed his cheek against her silken skin. "The smell of you," he inhaled. "Your laugh. Your smile. The way your eyes light up when you tell your fairy stories." He chuckled and propped his chin up on her breasts to meet her soft azure gaze. "I even adore the way you stammer and stutter when you're flustered."

She shook her head. "I don't mean that kind of pleasure. I mean the—ur—fleshly kind. You know, the sort that—uh"—she turned a particularly stunning shade of peony pink—"will give you an erection. You said a man needs one to make love."

Lucian stared at her in astonishment for a beat, then threw back his head and let out a shout of laughter. "Oh, Alys. My sweet, innocent girl. Just looking at you has given me the strongest erection I've ever had in my life."

"It has?"

He nodded and pressed his hardness against her belly.

Her eyes widened. "Oh, my! You weren't jesting when you said that a man's—ur—sex grows. Uh . . ." Her color deepened from pink to scarlet. "Not that yours was small before—um—not that I looked at it. You rubbed—uh—it against me while I was trying to warm you."

"I see," he murmured gravely, fighting not to smile at her charming confusion.

"Um . . ."

"Yes?"

She bit her lip. "Uh . . . what do we do now?"

This time he did smile, wickedly. "Whatever we please."

"And what would please you?"

He met her guileless gaze for a moment, marveling anew at the miracle of their love, then slowly lowered his lips to her nipple. "This," he whispered, flicking it with his tongue.

She gasped and arched up, thrusting the rosy peak against his lips. Willingly he drew it into his mouth, accepting her impassioned offering. His movements slow yet demanding, he proceeded to tease it, alternately licking and sucking it until it was at its swollen fullest. Then he leisurely kissed his way to its mate.

Oh, such joy! Such undreamed of bliss! Alys stiffened as his lips found her other nipple, startled by the magnitude of her pleasure. Never had she been so aware of her body, never had she imagined it capable of such incredible feelings. With every thrilling lick and pull of his mouth, those feelings deepened, making her tingle in a way that was as electrifying as it was mysterious. Greedy to experience every nuance of the dizzying new sensations, she meshed her fingers in his hair and held his head against her.

Up the underside of her breasts he kissed, down their

upper slopes he nibbled, pausing at every pass to stroke the hardened center crest. Sighing his name, she closed her eyes and let herself be swept away by her whirlwind of passion.

On and on he went, stroking, kissing, fondling, and sucking, until she was emptied of all thought but a maddening sense of want. Exactly what she wanted she didn't know, but it had something to do with the throbbing between her legs, and somehow she knew that only he could give it to her.

And give it to her he would. She had to have it.

Like a woman possessed, and at that moment she was indeed possessed by her need, she wantonly dragged his hand to her intimate triangle, begging, "Lucian . . . please. Oh! please!"

He stilled against her breast, a harsh guttural groan tearing from his throat. After a beat, he combed the curls with his fingers. Again he raked them, then again and again, each time drawing nearer to her aching core. Trembling with anticipation, she splayed her thighs apart, her body taut and expectant as she waited for him to touch the throbbing place between.

For several interminable moments he tauntingly traced around it, massaging her inner thighs and teasing her nether lips, stroking her everywhere but where she desired it most. When she was certain she could bear the torment no longer, he gently parted her and touched the intimate folds within.

She gasped her erotic shock and reflexively thrust against his hand, hot moisture dewing her flesh as she did so. His fingers gentle yet firm, he continued to explore her, separating and spreading her until he found the bedeviling source of her desire. The resulting jolt of sensation was so thrilling, so savagely intense, that her hips writhed in frenzied response and she practically screamed her pleasure.

Over and over again he touched her there, stroke by masterful stroke coaxing her to blissful new plateaus. She arched and moaned, straining to attain yet greater heights of rapture. When at last she thought she'd reached her zenith, he dipped his finger inside her and she touched heaven.

Paralyzed by ecstasy she froze, her legs straining and her back bowed, shuddering as burst after delirious burst of pleasure exploded through her. When the last enthralling salvo had ceased, she collapsed back to the mattress, boneless and spent.

"Oh, Lucian. I never dreamed . . . oh!" she sighed, rolling her head to meet his glowing gaze. "Is fleshly love always so glorious?"

He smiled and drew her back into his embrace. "That, my sweet poppet, was a mere sampling of the delights to come." With that promise he hungrily covered her mouth with his, crushing his arousal against her as he did.

The feel of him, so hard and jutting aggressively against her thigh, drew her from her sensual fog with the reminder that she had yet to satisfy him. Love, after all, be it spiritual, emotional, or physical, was about sharing, and to love him fully she must make certain that he received an equal share of pleasure.

"Lucian?" she whispered, pulling from their kiss.

"Hmm?"

"I want to do to your body what you just did to mine . . . to bring you the same pleasure."

He cracked open his eyes to fix her with a smoldering stare. "Do you indeed?"

She nodded.

"As you wish." He rolled over onto his back and lay perfectly still.

For several bewildering moments, Alys simply gazed at his blanket-draped form, not quite certain what to do.

As if he sensed her confusion, he smiled and reminded her, "I've already told you how much you please me. No matter what you do, you'll please me in this as well. Just follow your instincts."

And her instincts led her to his lips. Feeling shy at first, she lightly brushed and nibbled them, pausing now and again to trace their shape with her tongue. By degrees her reserve melted and she deepened their kiss. Giving herself over to her passion, she hungrily dipped her tongue inside and drank in the sweetness of his mouth, savoring his thrusting response. When she'd thor-

oughly ravished every luscious inch, she drew away and
kissed across his cheek to his ear.

Her mouth gentle yet coaxing she proceeded to tease
it, tickling and titillating it until he quivered and
moaned. Fueled by his heated response, she trailed her
lips down his neck and over his collarbone, shoving the
blankets to his waist to shower his torso with kisses.

While it was true that he was far too thin, he was still
so beautiful that it took her breath away to see him.
Even in his wasted state his musculature was impressive,
the sculpted swells and defining grooves boldly delineated beneath his taut skin.

And his skin . . . oh! She rubbed her cheek over his
chest, captivated by the provocative contrast of flesh and
hair. Never, not even in her most farfetched imaginings,
had she dreamed that a man's skin could be like this: so
smooth and flawless, so very intoxicating in its texture
and scent. Hungry to see if the rest of him was as splendid, she ventured lower.

Down she trailed, down his ribs and over his abdomen, making him alternately tense and writhe as she
blazed the path with kisses and caresses. Guided by the
inky arrow of hair leading from his navel down his belly,
she continued her sensual odyssey until she reached the
edge of his private triangle. Then she paused, lifting her
head to stare at the blanket-draped bulge below. Too
timid to uncover it without consent, she looked to Lucian's face for permission.

He was watching her through slitted eyes, his face so
taut and his expression so strained, that for a moment
she feared he was having a relapse. Alarmed, she cried
out, "Lucian? Love? Are you ill?"

He frowned, clearly perplexed. "Ill?" He shook his
head. "No. I've never felt better in my life. What makes
you ask?"

"It's just that you look so, uh"—what was the word
she was searching for? Oh, yes—"tense."

His frown deepened for a moment, then it cleared and
he chuckled. "I am tense . . . tense with desire. Your
kisses happen to be exceedingly stimulating."

"Oh, then you like what I'm doing to you?"

"Very much."

"Then you won't mind if I pull the covers down farther and touch your . . ." She felt her cheeks burn as she gestured to the mound at his groin.

He grinned. "Please do."

Having been thus authorized, she shifted her attention downward again. Her hands trembling more from anticipation than nervousness, she slipped the blankets lower and exposed him.

Nothing, not his anatomy chart, not his lecture, or her stolen glimpse of the knights in the stream, had prepared her for the sight of him. Oh, she'd known he'd be erect and thus larger than either the gentleman in the chart or the knights. She just hadn't expected him to be so, well, imposing.

Faintly intimidated yet too fascinated to look away, she reached down and touched him. His body jerked and she heard him suck in a ragged breath. Oddly enough, her own respiration altered, growing fast and shallow.

Beguiled by the feel of him, silk-sheathed steel pulsing with life, she circled him with her fingers and lifted him from his nest of curls. Cupping him in her palm, she gently stroked him from tip to root.

Lucian groaned aloud, his whole body tensing at her artless seduction. He'd thought his arousal couldn't worsen, that the throbbing ache couldn't deepen. He'd been wrong. Torturously so. Never, not even beneath the ministrations of his most skilled mistress, had he ever experienced such intense need.

With every inflammatory touch of her hands his urgency grew, wrenching his groin and sensitizing his sex until he was forced to grasp the mattress to keep himself from wrestling her down and plunging himself into her. Manfully gritting his teeth, he commanded himself to lay still.

After several moments of being fondled, his knees started to shake and his toes curled. A few seconds more, and his hips began to thrash. When he could endure the torment no longer, he pulled her hands away and dragged her down on top of him, smothering her startled queries with hungry kisses.

In one fluid motion, he reversed their positions. Still

holding her lips willing captive, he slid his hand up her inner thigh, parting the way for his intimate possession. She moaned and arched against him, crying his name into his mouth.

Inch by tight inch he eased his finger into her, pulling back only to dip in deeper the next time. She dampened even more and he could feel the thundering acceleration of her heart as she arched against him yet again. For several moments he opened and dilated her, preparing her as best he could. When he judged her ready, he gripped her bottom and lifted her to him, whispering, "I'm sorry, love, but this might hurt a bit."

Alys, however, was too desirous to be afraid, too eager to have him inside her to feel anything but joy as the tip of him penetrated her. So impassioned was she that it wasn't until he pushed against the barrier of her innocence that she felt her first real pain. Gasping her discomfort, she tightened her woman's muscles, instinctively trying to push him out.

His hips stilled. "Shh. There now, poppet. I'm sorry. Just try and relax. It won't hurt so much if you relax," he crooned, his hand straying between her legs to stroke her sensitive bud again.

Despite the burning sting deep inside, her tension eased beneath his caresses, her muscles growing slack with her escalating pleasure. When she lay pliant and fully aroused in his arms, he whispered, "I love you," then thrust hard, tearing through the delicate barrier.

She cried out, tears of pain escaping her eyes. As before he stilled, this time to allow her to accustom herself to his size. Again he soothed her by caressing her most secret place. Gradually the pain subsided and when he moved again, she found that she rather liked the resulting sensation.

"Do you want to continue, or are you too sore?" he gallantly inquired, praying that she would reply in favor of the former. As far gone as he was, he'd have to find release somehow, even if it meant skulking off to the privy and doing it himself. Not a prospect he relished.

To his everlasting gratitude, she wrapped her arms around his neck and drew his lips to hers, purring,

"Please continue, my lord. I find that I like the feel of you very much."

She didn't have to ask twice. Groaning his need, he withdrew and buried himself inside her again. She cried out, a soft, amorous sound, and wrapped her legs around his hips, drawing him yet deeper.

Again and again he drove in, his kisses and moans mingled with words of love. She clung to him, her body straining and arching with his, sighing his name with each frenzied thrust.

Never had a woman given herself to him so completely; never had he responded so fully to a woman. The feel of her, hot, wet, and eagerly grasping him, was beyond any pleasure he'd ever known.

When at last he climaxed, he did so in a forceful, liquid stream, writhing in ecstasy as charge after electrifying charge of sensation raced through him. As he silently screamed his rapture, he heard Alys's cries of fulfillment mingled with the clock striking midnight.

As the last chime faded away, he was jolted by another surge of pleasure so fierce, so exquisitely intense, that his brain seemed to explode in his head as did his heart in his chest. Then everything went black.

"That was perfect," Alys sighed, basking in the afterglow of their passion. Apparently Lucian was as swept away as she, for he hadn't moved a muscle since he'd collapsed on top of her several minutes earlier.

Smiling with all the tenderness she felt inside, she ran her hands down the length of his back, her smile broadening into a naughty grin as she cupped his rounded buttocks and gave them a playful squeeze. Choking back her giggles, she waited for him to respond.

He simply lay there, silent and still.

Too still.

Assailed by sudden fear, she breathlessly called his name.

No response.

She called again, this time louder.

Silence.

Growing more panicked by the second, she lifted his heavy head from between her breasts and peered anxiously at his face. His eyes were closed and his features slack.

Unnaturally slack.

Her heart froze.

He looked dead.

With a terrified sob ripping from her throat, she laid her fingers against his parted lips, praying to feel his respiration upon them.

Nothing.

Desperately she felt for the pulse in his neck.

Not so much as a flutter.

For a long moment she lay staring at his lifeless face, too stunned to do more. Then her shock shattered into grief and she wailed her anguish.

Heaven help them both, she wasn't his destined true love after all. She had failed him, and now he was lost forever.

With a strength born of sorrow, she rolled from beneath his limp form and gathered him into her arms. Tearfully keening his name, she rocked him as Aengus had Lucan all those centuries ago.

"My poor, sweet love. I'm sorry, so very sorry," she sobbed, kissing first his forehead, then his cheeks, and finally his pale lips.

The instant their mouths touched his body gave a violent jerk, as if jolted by lightning, and a shuddering breath exploded from his lips. After a beat, his long lashes fluttered on his cheeks.

"Lucian?" she whispered, scarcely daring to believe what she was seeing.

Slowly his eyes opened. "Mmm," he purred, a contented smile playing upon his lips. "That was . . . miraculous."

Alys sagged with relief, a smile curving her own lips as she met his luminous gaze. His eyes were so alive and full of such a wealth of tender emotion that she knew the instant she saw them that he was truly whole at last. Rejoicing in her heart, she softly agreed, "Yes. Miraculous."

His arms came up then and twined around her neck. Pulling her face close to his, he whispered, "Are you ready for another such miracle, my love?"

She replied by claiming his lips with a sweeping kiss.

Thrice more they made love, lounging in each other's arms in the intervals between, laughing and teasing, and whispering the words only lovers dare to speak. Near dawn, Lucian fell into an exhausted sleep.

Her heart breaking at their imminent parting, Alys slipped from his arms and sat by his side, lovingly memorizing his face and body. When every cherished detail was etched into both her heart and mind, she drew the sheet up over his nakedness and pressed a kiss to his lips.

"Please forgive me for leaving again, my dearest," she brokenly whispered. "If I could, I would stay with you forever." Kissing him one last time, she wrapped herself in the coverlet and crept to the window to await the dawn.

Already the night was waning, its stillness broken by the calling of the morning birds. Suddenly more weary than she'd ever been in her life, she rested her forehead against the glass, tears trickling down her cheeks as she watched the first glimmer of light spill over the horizon. Any minute now, her body would crumble to dust.

Vaguely she wondered if it would hurt to die in such a manner, only to dismiss the thought as inconsequential in the next instant. Even if it did hurt, the pain couldn't possibly be worse than the agony she suffered at being torn away from Lucian.

Inch by dooming inch the sun continued to rise, veining the lightened sky with streaks of shimmering pink and gold. When it finally slipped free from the edge of the earth, Alys felt the peculiar tingling pull she always experienced when in the presence of enchantment. Closing her eyes, she uttered a prayer and prepared for the end.

By degrees the sensation intensified, humming through her veins and vibrating in her head. After what felt like an eternity, it gradually faded away.

Am I dead then? she wondered several beats after it had ceased. Hmm. She didn't feel any different. Her eyes still closed, she pinched what should be her arm. It felt solid, the flesh warm and pliant without the slightest hint of desiccation. Frowning her puzzlement, she stole a peek at her surroundings.

She was still in Lucian's chamber, though it was now bathed in the rosy glow of dawn. Not quite certain what to think, she slowly turned from the window to gaze around the room. The scene that met her eyes stole her breath away.

As on the tragic night of Lucan's death, Aengus had appeared and now sat on the edge of the bed, cradling his son in his arms. This time, however, the man in his arms merely slept and the fairy king smiled. Indeed, there was a look of such love, such tender joy on his face, that the beauty of it brought tears to her eyes.

At length he laid Lucian back on the bed, pausing as he did so to stroke his hair. Then he rose and acknowledged her presence. "You've done well, mortal," he said, meeting her gaze from across the room. "His soul is strong and whole."

Alys stared into his aquamarine eyes for several beats, then looked past him to where Lucian lay. Just the sight of him, so handsome and dear, shattered her all over again, and she crumpled to the floor in anguish.

"Oh, Aengus. I love him," she whispered wretchedly, hugging herself in her despair. "He's everything to me. Everything! Promise that you'll look after him when I'm gone . . . that you'll see him safe and happy. Please. Promise me."

In the blink of an eye, Aengus was at her side. Kneeling, he inquired, "Wouldn't you rather stay and see to him yourself?"

"You know I would," she retorted, indignant that he'd ask such a question. "But I can't! You know I can't!"

"Ah. But you can."

"But your spell—"

"Was broken the instant you made the unselfish decision to give your life for his." At her look of bewilderment, he elaborated, "You see, Alys, love . . . true mortal love . . . is stronger than magic. Even mine."

Alys gaped at him speechlessly for a moment, hardly daring to believe his words. "T-then I'm n-not going to turn to d-dust?" she finally managed to stutter, half afraid to ask lest she'd misheard him.

He shook his head and helped her to her feet, pulling the fallen coverlet around her as he did so. "No. You shall marry my son and bear him four extraordinary children."

"Four?" she echoed in delight.

"Three boys and one girl. The girl, like my beloved Rowena, shall be the fairest maid in England."

"Oh, Aengus!" she cried, impulsively flinging her arms around him. "I—oh!—" She shook her head, too thrilled to express her feelings in words.

To her surprise he gave her a fierce hug in return. "You needn't speak," he murmured. "I can feel your happiness with my own heart."

As they stood wrapped in each other's arms, silently sharing their joy, Lucian stirred and called her name in his sleep.

Aengus smiled over at him. " 'Tis time I take my leave. He shall awaken from my enchantment soon, and will want you back in his arms."

"Will I see you again?" she asked, realizing for the first time how very much she loved him.

A shadow passed through his eyes. "I fear not. My thousand years are at an end."

"Aengus, no! You must be mistaken," she cried, staring at him in stunned disbelief. With his flawless skin and flowing mane of fiery curls, he looked to be in the first bloom of youth.

He sighed. " 'Tis no mistake. I feel myself fading even now."

"There must be something we can do, some way to save you," she exclaimed, shaking her head over and over again in denial to the tragic truth. "Perhaps the scrolls—"

"There is nothing to be done." His voice rang with finality.

"Oh, this is awful," she whispered, her eyes flooding with tears.

He smiled gently, clearly touched by her distress. "Ah, please don't cry, little mortal. All might not be lost."

She sniffled. "No?"

He shook his head. "Though it isn't common knowledge, God judges each and every fairy when his time to cease comes. If He finds him worthy, He allows him to be born into the mortal world, thus granting him the chance to earn an immortal soul."

"He does?"

He nodded.

"Then I shall pray for you day and night, begging Him to be merciful," she fervently vowed.

He touched her cheek, an enigmatic smile playing across his lips, then dipped down and kissed her forehead.

"Alys?"

Alys blinked twice, completely disoriented.

"Whatever are you doing over there, love?" Lucian asked, raising to his elbows to view her with drowsy query.

She returned his gaze, her brow furrowing as she tried to recall what had brought her to the window. How very odd. She couldn't even remember rising from the bed. As she opened her mouth to tell him so, she caught a glimpse of the glorious morning sky, and the answer suddenly sprang to mind.

"I was admiring the dawn and thinking what a miracle it is to be alive," she replied, rushing to his waiting arms.

Epilogue

Thistlewood Castle, one year later

"Really, Luc. If you had any consideration at all for your wife, you would send those workmen away so she can get some sleep," Charlotte railed, covering her ears against the racket reverberating up from the courtyard. "In case it's slipped your mind, she was up all night giving you your son."

Lucian glanced up in surprise, frowning as he noticed the noise for the first time. He was so absorbed in admiring his new son that he'd been quite deaf to the sounds of the Thistlewood "goiter" being torn down.

Instantly contrite, he shifted his gaze from his sister to his radiant wife, who lay propped up on a mountain of pillows with their sleeping babe in her arms. "Of course she's right, love. It was inconsiderate of me," he murmured, pressing a kiss to her pink cheek. "I shall go down and send them away immediately."

Alys smiled and shook her head. "Don't bother. The noise has been going on for so many weeks now that I barely notice it anymore. Besides, I'm too happy to sleep. And excited. Oh, Lucian! Just look at our son. Isn't he the most beautiful sight you ever saw?"

Lucian studied the baby for several seconds, touching his smooth cheek and stroking his downy hair. After several moments of doting scrutiny, he shook his head. "Not quite."

"Oh?" Alys and Charlotte uttered in indignant unison, the latter of whom had moved from the threshold to stand by the bed.

He shook his head again. "He's not as beautiful as his mother, though I must admit that he is a close second."

"Well, in any case, he is an extraordinarily handsome babe," Charlotte marveled, leaning over to more closely examine her new nephew. "My Andrew wasn't nearly so pretty when he was first born."

"Andy was a darling from the moment he made his appearance," Alys protested. "And I've heard many in our set say that he's quite the bonniest little fellow in London."

"A title he shall no doubt be sharing with his cousin," Charlotte retorted with a chuckle. "What heartbreakers we've spawned."

Alys smiled proudly at the infant in her arms. "Yes, as is Diana and Stephen's son, Harold. I almost feel sorry for the girls."

"Poor things. They haven't a chance," Charlotte sighed. "Just imagine what a dashing sight our trio shall make: Andy with his fair hair; Harry so dark and handsome; and your son with those stunning red curls."

"I can't imagine where he got those curls," Lucian interjected, lightly smoothing his finger over the fiery spirals in question. "I don't recall anyone on our side of the family having hair this color."

"Nor on mine," Alys countered. "It is an uncommon shade."

"As are his eyes," Charlotte added as the baby made a soft hiccuping sound and awoke.

All three adults paused in reverent silence to admire his bright aquamarine eyes. It was Charlotte who broke their worshipful meditation by musing aloud, "Come to think of it, I do recall reading something about an ancestor with coloring like this. I'll have to consult *The History of Thistlewood Castle* to be certain, but I believe there was a son born to an Elinore de Warre in the fourteenth century with red hair and greenish-blue eyes." She made a dismissive hand gesture. "In any instance, he's beautiful and a credit to the Warre name. Speaking of names, have you decided what you shall call him?"

Lucian nodded at Alys, who smiled and said, "Aengus."

TALES OF THE HEART

WE NEED YOUR HELP
To continue to bring you quality romance
that meets your personal expectations,
we at TOPAZ books want to hear from you.
Help us by filling out this questionnaire, and in exchange
we will give you a **free gift** as a token of our gratitude.

- Is this the first TOPAZ book you've purchased? (circle one)
    YES   NO
  The title and author of this book is: _____

- If this was not the first TOPAZ book you've purchased, how many have
  you bought in the past year?
    a: 0 - 5   b 6 - 10   c: more than 10   d: more than 20

- How many romances in total did you buy in the past year?
    a: 0 - 5   b: 6 - 10   c: more than 10   d: more than 20 ____

- How would you rate your overall satisfaction with this book?
    a: Excellent   b: Good   c: Fair   d: Poor

- What was the main reason you bought this book?
    a: It is a TOPAZ novel, and I know that TOPAZ stands
       for quality romance fiction
    b: I liked the cover
    c: The story-line intrigued me
    d: I love this author
    e: I really liked the setting
    f: I love the cover models
    g: Other: _____

- Where did you buy this TOPAZ novel?
    a: Bookstore   b: Airport   c: Warehouse Club
    d: Department Store   e: Supermarket   f: Drugstore
    g: Other: _____

- Did you pay the full cover price for this TOPAZ novel? (circle one)
    YES   NO
  If you did not, what price did you pay? _____

- Who are your favorite TOPAZ authors? (Please list)

- How did you first hear about TOPAZ books?
    a: I saw the books in a bookstore
    b: I saw the TOPAZ Man on TV or at a signing
    c: A friend told me about TOPAZ
    d: I saw an advertisement in_____magazine
    e: Other: _____

- What type of romance do you generally prefer?
    a: Historical   b: Contemporary
    c: Romantic Suspense   d: Paranormal (time travel,
       futuristic, vampires, ghosts, warlocks, etc.)
    d: Regency   e: Other: _____

- What historical settings do you prefer?
    a: England   b: Regency England   c: Scotland
    e: Ireland   f: America   g: Western Americana
    h: American Indian   i: Other: _____

- What type of story do you prefer?

    a: Very sexy   b: Sweet, less explicit
    c: Light and humorous   d: More emotionally intense
    e: Dealing with darker issues   f: Other

- What kind of covers do you prefer?

    a: Illustrating both hero and heroine   b: Hero alone
    c: No people (art only)   d: Other_____

- What other genres do you like to read (circle all that apply)

    Mystery   Medical Thrillers   Science Fiction
    Suspense   Fantasy   Self-help
    Classics   General Fiction   Legal Thrillers
    Historical Fiction

- Who is your favorite author, and why?_____
  _____

- What magazines do you like to read? (circle all that apply)

    a: *People*   b: *Time/Newsweek*
    c: *Entertainment Weekly*   d: *Romantic Times*
    e: *Star*   f: *National Enquirer*
    g: *Cosmopolitan*   h: *Woman's Day*
    i: *Ladies' Home Journal*   j: *Redbook*
    k: Other:_____

- In which region of the United States do you reside?

    a: Northeast   b: Midatlantic   c: South
    d: Midwest   e: Mountain   f: Southwest
    g: Pacific Coast

- What is your age group/sex?   a: Female   b: Male

    a: under 18   b: 19-25   c: 26-30   d: 31-35   e: 36-40
    f: 41-45   g: 46-50   h: 51-55   i: 56-60   j: Over 60

- What is your marital status?

    a: Married   b: Single   c: No longer married

- What is your current level of education?

    a: High school   b: College Degree
    c: Graduate Degree   d: Other:_____

- Do you receive the TOPAZ *Romantic Liaisons* newsletter, a quarterly
  newsletter with the latest information on Topaz books and authors?

    YES   NO

  If not, would you like to?   YES   NO

  Fill in the address where you would like your free gift to be sent:

  Name: _____

  Address: _____

  City:_____Zip Code:_____

  You should receive your free gift in 6 to 8 weeks.
  Please send the completed survey to:

Penguin USA•Mass Market
Dept. TS
375 Hudson St.
New York, NY 10014